AN AMERICAN STORY

MARK LAGES

authorHOUSE·

AuthorHouse™
1663 Liberty Drive
Bloomington, IN 47403
www.authorhouse.com
Phone: 833-262-8899

Published by AuthorHouse 07/17/2020

ISBN: 978-1-7283-6741-5 (sc)
ISBN: 978-1-7283-6779-8 (e)

Print information available on the last page.

MATTHEW 5:14-16

Make no mistake about it. *You* are now the great pageant of the earth. A country that is built on a hill cannot be hidden. Nor does a wise man burn his candle in a closet, but out in the open so that it gives vision to all who are in the house. Let your great spotlights so burn, that the rest of the world may gaze in awe upon your glorious show of shows and all of your miraculous performers and accomplishments. Break a leg, and make the old man proud!

RIDIN' HIGH IN APRIL

Years ago, Aaron Parks bought his home in Sugar Land, Texas. He lived there with his charming wife and two daughters. It was a great place to live, just a short drive to Houston, where Aaron worked. In Houston, Aaron and his brother owned and operated a busy restaurant they had opened twenty years ago. The name of the restaurant was *Brothers*, named after Aaron and his brother, Jim. Maybe it wasn't the most unique or creative name they could've come up with, and the menu wasn't all that clever. But the place was a great success. They served American food—hand me the salt and pass the ketchup. They cooked up and served all the basics: flame-broiled hamburgers, steaks, chicken pot pies, meatloaf, and baby back ribs. It was a business, not an art. Aaron and Jim were not out to score points with food critics for an exotic cuisine menu. They were in business to give people what they wanted—hearty meals to fill their American stomachs. Full stomachs, good service, soft and comfortable seating, and clean restrooms all combined to make for a thriving restaurant and healthy profits.

Jim was the conservative brother; he looked more like a tax accountant than he did a restauranteur. He invested his share of the profits in blue-chip stocks, mutual funds, government bonds, retirement annuities, and a couple large life insurance policies. There were no delusions or dreams causing turmoil in Jim's rational head, and he didn't yearn for much. He didn't waste time longing for expensive cars, a mansion for his family, trips to the Caribbean, a Rolex watch, or diamond-laden jewelry for his wife. Yes, Jim was boring. If this story were about Jim, I'd tell you to skip it, but this story isn't about Jim. It's about Aaron. He had dreams, and he was, well, interesting.

What is it in life that can make two brothers so utterly different? Jim and Aaron were brought up under the same Texan composition shingle roof, beneath the same Texan sun and moon, by the same pair of Texan parents, in the same Texan community, and around the same time period. Yet they were as different as night and day. By God—and God bless the Lone Star State—Aaron was going places! He was going to make it big! Nothing was going to stand in his way. And how was Aaron going to do this? It was simple. He would seek his fame and fortune through the aggressive accumulation of Texas real estate. He'd seen others do it. He had friends from back in high school who had done it, and he knew about a few neighbors who had done it. He'd watched people on late-night infomercials who were doing it. They all started with next to nothing, and the next thing they realized, after a real estate deal here and a deal there, they were worth millions. They were driving luxury cars, buying jewelry for their sweethearts and wives, and sunning themselves on beaches in Barbados and Martinique. And they were smiling, tan, and happy, and they had loads of free time. And—swear to God—their wives were something else. They all looked just like magazine models, and their beautiful children were getting good grades, staying off drugs, and going to colleges. He'd seen all this success with his own eyes. And if you can't trust your own eyes, what can you trust?

Aaron's first investment property was a modest fixer-upper just outside of Houston that he dressed up and rented. His new tenant was the McGregor family. There was John McGregor, his wife, Eleanor, and their three children. They also had a couple of friendly and well-behaved dogs. Aaron charged an additional security deposit for the dogs, in case they did any damage while living in the house. It wasn't a big deposit, but it should've been enough, according to the real estate broker who had helped him find the tenant. "They seem like a nice little family," the broker said. "I don't think you'll have any kind of trouble with them. The dad has a steady job at a construction company, and their previous landlord had no complaints." Yes, it was exactly what Aaron wanted to hear, and for the first year the McGregors lived in the house, things went without a hitch. Heck, things went perfectly. The McGregors always paid their rent on time, and Aaron drove past the house every now and again to be sure it was still standing. He didn't see anything to cause him alarm.

Aaron was proud of himself. And motivated by his recent success as a property owner, he sold his half of the restaurant to Jim so he could use the money for down payments on more houses. No, he couldn't go wrong. Banks were more than happy to lend him money, and tenants were willing to pay the rent he asked for. And the property values? They were soaring up into the Texas clouds as though there were no tomorrow. This, of course, was right before the Great Recession. After a year, Aaron had bought six houses to rent, and on paper he was now worth close to a million dollars.

You know, there was one thing you could always say about Aaron, and it was a good thing. He was a very generous man. Sure, he spent some of his newly acquired wealth on himself. Who wouldn't? He now drove a Cadillac, and he always dressed in nice clothes. He bought an expensive watch, and he had season tickets to the Rockets' games. They were very good seats, not the cheap, nosebleed seats occupied by the unwashed masses. But Aaron also spent his money on others. His wife, Eleanor, now wore a solid-gold ladies' Rolex watch, and she drove a new Mercedes. And with Aaron's blessing, she shopped at the local mall every other day. She also spent a ton of money on her hair, fingernails, and skin, keeping up. Keeping up with what? Keeping up with her new friends, whose husbands were also raking in the cash. And Aaron spent a ton of money on his daughters. He bought each of them a BMW for her sixteenth birthday, and he gave them their own VISA credit cards and cell phones. They were good kids. They were both admitted to Southern Methodist University, a year apart from each other, and Aaron paid for their room and board, tuition, and all other expenses. It was money well spent. The girls stayed out of trouble and got good grades. They were kind and generous to others, just as their daddy was kind and generous to them.

ALWAYS

"I always felt very secure and very safe with real estate. Real estate always appreciates."

—Ivana Trump

NIGHT SCHOOL

It was eight o'clock in the evening in Norfolk, Nebraska, and as an elderly teacher stood up from his desk, the students stopped talking. It was a community college real estate course titled Ethics Training. The teacher looked out at all the eager faces. He cleared his throat and said, "Welcome to my class. My name is Mr. Glass. I have a question for you. How many of you bright-eyed and bushy-tailed little neophytes and wannabe real estate agents here tonight know what you're going to be selling to the public? Do you know? Are you going to be selling lush front lawns and flower beds crammed with purple-faced pansies and pink impatiens? Are you going to be selling tall, shady trees and white picket fences? Is that what you're going to be selling? Will you be dressed to the nines, chewing on breath mints, hawking spacious kitchens with the most modern appliances? Will you be selling Italian ceramic tile, polished Brazilian granite, top-of-the-line ash cabinets, ornate woodwork galore, sun-fracturing stained-glass windows, and cozy wood-burning fireplaces? What, exactly, will you be selling?

"Can we be honest? Sure, yes, you'll be selling lush front yards, flowers, and fences, but they will all come with a catch, right? They'll come with ants, wasps, fat little fly-eating spiders, crickets, slimy earthworms, snails, potato bugs, burrowing gophers, snakes, lizards, termites, and weeds. Will these new homeowners have even the slightest idea what they're getting themselves into when they do business with you? Will they know that they'll soon be on their knees, slaves to their newly acquired yards, with dirt and filth under their fingernails, calluses on their hands, pesticide in their eyes, and fertilizer on the bottoms of their feet? They'll sweat, curse, sneeze, and bleed, wondering what they were ever thinking when they sat down with you and signed all those papers.

"They were sold a dream, and now the dream is a maintenance nightmare. No, I'm not just talking about yardwork. I'm now talking about the whole ball of wax, the whole nine yards. I'm talking about the never-ending realities of homeownership. I'm talking about what all these unsuspecting clients of yours are really getting for their hard-earned money. I'm talking about roof leaks and plumbing leaks, water dripping from faucets, and running toilets. I'm talking about clogged sewer lines.

"I'm talking about ruptured washing machine hoses. I'm talking about garbage disposals that come to a halt, dishwashers that refuse to cooperate, refrigerators that stop cooling your food, old water heaters that ooze rusty water. There are doors that stick and squeak, windows that won't open no matter how hard you push, mysterious cracks that appear in the walls and ceilings, structural termite damage, screws that magically work loose from hinges, warped cabinet drawers that jam shut, air conditioners that run out of Freon, heaters that reek of gas, screen doors that decay and come completely apart, locks that won't latch, tiles that crack and chip, new hardwood floors that scratch at the slightest touch of a chair leg, and wall-to-wall carpeting that is so full of filth, bobby pins, paperclips, and God-knows-what-else that you're forced to wear shoes in the house just to keep your feet clean. This is what you're really selling, isn't it? All of this is what's in store for the lot of your naive buyers.

"Sure, when they first came to you, they allowed their optimism to run amok, and they pictured wonderful times with their family. They saw themselves on the overstuffed sofa, watching TV, or playing Monopoly and Parcheesi in the game room, or seated in a leather La-Z-Boy chair while reading a good book or magazine, or eating dinner together every night of the week at a big kitchen table, or baking hot chocolate chip cookies or cakes for birthdays, or unwrapping Christmas presents in late December. But what did they really get? What did you sell to them? A dream? A valuable chunk of America? Was it their fair share? Shine, light, shine! Buy, buy, buy.

"It was a once-in-a-lifetime deal. It was you who placed the ad. You wrote, 'This house includes a big, cheerful family room with cable TV and high cathedral ceilings, new hardwood floors throughout the house, and a spacious gourmet kitchen, nestled on a shady and quiet street in a charming and friendly neighborhood in the better part of town—and it's all yours for an amazing price that was lowered just this week. The owner of this property must find a buyer as soon as possible, so no reasonable offer will be refused. Isn't it time you and your family lived the American dream? Call our 800 number! Don't let a great deal like this pass you by!'" The teacher stopped talking for a moment. Then, with a twinkle in his eyes, he said, "Are there any questions? Surely you have some questions." Several students raised their hands, and the teacher looked at one young man and said, "Yes, you in the second row. Yes, you. Speak up so everyone can hear you. What's your name?"

"Bill," the young man said.

"Do you have a last name?"

"Armstrong."

"What's your question, Bill Armstrong?"

Bill paused a moment. He was holding a pencil in his hand. He had been taking notes. He set the pencil down on his notepad and asked out loud, "Are you *crazy?*"

The other students laughed. The man's eyes twinkled again, and he nodded and rubbed his chin. "Maybe I am, Bill. Maybe I am. Maybe I've been at this too long."

SHOT DOWN IN MAY

The Great Recession took a lot of citizens by surprise. Sure, some sort of economic adjustment was inevitable, but few people expected a knockout punch. Their eyes rolled back in their heads, and they hit the canvas with a collective and resounding thump. *Kaboom!* The bottom fell out of the real estate market. The world was suddenly end over end and upside down.

It seemed as if it happened overnight. One day Aaron was on the crest of a wave, and the next thing he knew, he was several million dollars in debt for property that was now lucky to be worth half of what he owed for it. His first property he had purchased and leased to the McGregors was the first to falter. Mr. McGregor was fired from his job at the construction company he worked for, and when the middle of the month came around, Aaron still hadn't received the McGregors' rent check. This was unexpected, since up until that time the McGregors had always paid their rent on time. It was something Aaron had come to expect without even thinking about it. Around the first of the month, the rent check was always in his mailbox. He would always show the check to his wife, waving it in the air as if he were drying the inked signature. "Money in the bank," he would say. "You've got to love those McGregors!"

When the McGregors' rent check was three weeks late, Aaron called Mr. McGregor to see what the problem was. He thought maybe the guy had just forgotten to write the check, or maybe the check had been lost in the mail. Honestly, he wasn't expecting it. He'd never even given the matter much thought.

"I lost my job," Mr. McGregor said.

"I see," Aaron said. The severity of the situation hadn't really hit him yet. It seemed like a temporary problem. And surely the McGregors had some money in a savings account of some kind, or a relative that could help them out until Mr. McGregor found a new job. "I understand your situation," Aaron said, "but you need to pay me your rent on time. I have a mortgage to keep current. So when can I expect your check?"

"As soon as I get a job."

"Do you have something lined up?"

"Not yet."

"But soon?"

"I don't know. No one seems to be hiring."

"No one?"

"My wife is looking. She's a good secretary. She worked before we had the kids."

"Well, I'm sure one of you will find something."

"That's the plan."

"Keep me in the loop."

"What loop is that?"

"Let me know when you or your wife gets a job."

"You'll know because you'll have your rent," Mr. McGregor said. He didn't sound too worried. And if Mr. McGregor wasn't worried, then neither was Aaron.

"Okay, then," Aaron said, and he ended the call. He had faith in the McGregors. He knew one of them would land a job. They were honest and hardworking people.

Aaron didn't start to worry until the next due date came and went without a check from the family. They were now two months behind. Meanwhile, Aaron had to pay the mortgage payment on the house. Now he was growing concerned, and he hadn't received a single call from the McGregors updating him on their situation, giving him something he could chew on. So one week after the second late payment was due, Aaron called Mr. McGregor and asked how things were going.

"Not so good," Mr. McGregor said. "The job market for construction managers is pretty bad."

"How about your wife?"

"She's not finding anything either."

"One of you needs to find a job."

"We're quite aware of that."

"You're two months behind now."

"We're aware of that too. Believe me; if I had the money, I would pay our rent."

Aaron wasn't sure what to say. They did pay on time when they had the money. They were good tenants, and he didn't want to kick them out of the house. No, at this point that seemed too extreme. "I can give you a little more time."

"I appreciate that."

"But this can't go on indefinitely."

"I understand."

"Will you call me in a week—let me know how things are going?"

"I can do that," Mr. McGregor said.

"Hopefully you'll have some good news for me."

"That's the plan."

Aaron then ended the call. Now he was a little worried. Was this recession really as bad as they were saying? What if the McGregors couldn't find work anywhere? What steps would Aaron have to take? Would he have to evict them? This was the last thing he wanted to do.

A week went by, and Aaron received no money from the McGregors; nor did Mr. McGregor call. So Aaron called him, but his phone went straight to voicemail. Aaron left a message. "This is Aaron," he said. "I was looking forward to your call. Please call me as soon as you can. I need an update."

An update? Heck, what he really needed was a check for two months' rent. A full day passed after Aaron left the voicemail message, and still Mr. McGregor did not call him. After two days passed, Aaron decided to visit Mr. McGregor in person. He went to the house in the evening and rang the doorbell, but there was no answer. He rang the bell and knocked several more times, but still no one came to the door. Aaron suddenly had a bad feeling about this, so he turned the doorknob on the front door. It was unlocked, and he pushed the door open. "Jesus," Aaron said softly, seeing that the house was completely empty. The furniture was gone, and there were no pictures on the walls. The McGregors had moved out of the house! And that smell? What the hell was that smell? It was awful. The place smelled like a kennel.

He walked around in the house. There was debris in every room. There were empty boxes, papers, old clothes, dirty paper towels, coat hangers, a filthy old phone, used dog toys, a torn pillow, and a broken chair. The place looked as bad as it smelled. The McGregors hadn't bothered to clean up anything at all when they left. There wasn't even a note. No apology. No explanation. Just an empty house full of trash. And they had seemed like such a nice family.

It was bad, but the McGregors were just the tip of the iceberg. It wasn't long before Aaron was having serious trouble with all of his tenants. Thanks to the recession, people were losing their jobs right and left. He now had only one tenant who was paying rent, and even that tenant was a month late. All the others were two months, then three, then four months behind. Aaron tried to work with them, giving them more time, trying to be understanding, but it quickly became clear he was going to have to evict them. And evict them he did. It was a horrible experience. Aaron didn't derive any pleasure from doing this. It made him feel like a selfish, old skinflint, but he was fighting for his financial life. His mortgage payments and other bills were falling behind because of all the late rent, and creditors were now calling him every other day, demanding their money. It's funny how friendly people can be when you pay your bills on time, and how nasty they can be when you have a little trouble.

For the first time in Aaron's life, he suddenly knew what it was like to panic. Yes, panic. That was the perfect word for it. He tried to keep his composure around his family and his friends, as well as around his business associates, but he was totally overwhelmed with—what? With fear? With embarrassment? With dread? With that horrible, inescapable feeling that things were *not* going to be okay, that the world around him was falling to pieces? And what did this mean? What was going to happen to him? What was the worst case? His credit was already in the toilet, and there was no way to salvage that. It became clear he would have to file bankruptcy. He was going to have to bail. He would seek shelter from the storm and leave it for others to endure. Just like the McGregors, he would make a run for it. Like the McGregors, he would give up. There would be no notes, no explanations, no apologies.

It wasn't as if he hadn't tried. He'd tried to borrow money from his brother and father. He'd tried to borrow money from his friends. "We love you," they said, "but we can't." They all had their reasons, and all their reasons were good ones. He was asking them to jump into the cold, swirling water and drown along with him. If he had been in their place, he would've done the same thing. He would've said no. He would've stayed the heck out of the water. The great light was flickering. Now you see it, and now you don't. Was it a case of faulty wiring or a defective circuit breaker? Or was it a power line? The great light—ha! What good was it now? What a farce. What a low-down, rotten, dishonest lie.

BURIED IN VERMONT

"Nothing in this world can take the place of persistence. Talent will not; for nothing is more common than unsuccessful men with talent. Genius will not; for unrewarded genius is almost a proverb. Education will not; for the world is full of educated derelicts. Persistence and determination alone are omnipotent."

—Calvin Coolidge

BURIED IN THE BRONX

Here's a question for you: What gigantic US retail department store chain fashioned its logo from a tattoo on the forearm of its founder? The answer? It was Macy's. The company's highly respected founder, R. H. Macy, had the red Macy's star copied from a red star tattoo that he got while working as a fifteen-year-old youth on a whaling ship.

What a guy! What an interesting life this man lived, going from a greasy whaling ship to one of the largest and most respected department store chains in history. Did you know that when he was a young man, he tried his hand at prospecting for gold? He failed at this. He opened a dry goods store with his brother, and he failed again. He opened another store, and he failed a third time. He tried again, and you guessed it—he failed for a fourth time. When he opened his first Macy's store in New York, he threw his doors open to the public. His first day's take? The gods were laughing their tails off. He sold just a hair over ten dollars' worth of merchandise. It was a terrible disappointment, to say the least. But he kept at it. Yes, he would've made old Calvin Coolidge proud.

Nowadays, Macy's has hundreds of sprawling stores, and everyone knows who Macy's is. And everyone knows about their parade, about their fourth of July fireworks, about their Christmas Santas, and, of course, about their men's and women's clothing, housewares, and perfumes. Everyone recognizes the red star. The next time you see some kid with a tattoo on his arm, don't laugh. He could be the next R. H. Macy. Don't shake your head or sell the kid short. They say that in America anything is possible. What's that they say? They say that winners never quit, and quitters never win. Winston Churchill said, "Success consists of going from failure to failure without loss of enthusiasm." No, he wasn't an American, but he had the right idea. Winston may have been a cigar-smoking Englishman, but he was an American at heart.

IT COULD GET UGLY

"Do you want me to come with you?" Aaron's wife asked. "I don't mind coming." They were seated at the kitchen table, and Aaron was nursing a scotch and water.

"I should do this alone," Aaron said.

"There's nothing wrong with asking for my support."

"I got us into this mess, and I have to get us out. It's my baby."

"I'll do anything I can to help."

"I want you to stay home."

His wife thought for a moment and then asked, "What do you think is going to happen?"

"I don't know," Aaron said. "I have no idea. It could get ugly."

"Do you think many people are going to show up?"

"They certainly have a right to."

"What do you think they'll do?"

"I don't know."

"Does the judge allow them to speak?"

"Probably." Aaron polished off his drink, poured another scotch and water, and raised the glass to his mouth. He spoke into the drink. "If I were one of them, I would have a lot to say."

"It's not like you caused the recession."

"I may as well have."

"Lots of people made mistakes."

"No one will care."

"Some people probably will. I mean, they may not care, but they'll probably understand."

"A few people, maybe."

"The ones whose opinions matter."

"Whatever that means."

His wife thought again. She then said, "You didn't have a choice, Aaron. You're doing the only thing you can do. There's no choice left for you. They should understand that, if they understand anything."

"They're just going to want their money." Aaron poured another drink and raised the glass.

"You shouldn't drink so much."

"I should drink more."

"It's not going to help."

"It makes me feel better. It does. The more I drink, the less I care. And right now, I really don't want to care."

"That's what I love about you, Aaron. I love that you do care. I love that this hurts you."

"You love that it hurts me?"

"If it didn't hurt you, it would mean you didn't care about others. That's not who I married. I married a man who cares about others."

Aaron laughed. "Right now, babe, I only care about myself. I just want to get through tomorrow alive."

"But you do care."

Aaron took another drink from his glass. "You're right," he said. "Actually, I think I care too much. I've really messed some of these people up. You know, I promised I would pay them. We had a deal. They were depending on me to come through. 'Oh, no,' I told them. 'There's nothing for you to worry about. I'm recession proof. You'll get all your money.' And now? They're getting nothing. Zilch. Nada. I lied to them. That's what I did. I can't pay any of them a dime. Not a fucking dime."

"I'm trying to understand."

"Trying?"

"Listen, sweetheart, no one is perfect."

"Perfect? I'm so far from perfect now that it isn't even funny. I can't imagine what my dad would've thought of all this. 'What the hell, Aaron?' he'd probably say. 'Didn't I teach you anything? Didn't I warn you? Didn't I tell you not to chase those stupid pipe dreams of yours? Why couldn't you be more like your brother. Your brother listened to me, behaved himself, and you don't see him going to bankruptcy court. You don't see him losing his house, cars, and livelihood. You don't see him stiffing people for thousands of dollars, making a damn fool of himself. You don't see him doing any of this, do you?' Oh, my dad would have plenty to say. I can hear him now: 'A deal is a deal,' he'd say. 'A promise is a promise. You're only as good as your word. A damn handshake is all anyone ever needed from me.'"

"I think your dad would've been understanding. He'd know that things don't always work out as planned."

"He would spit on me."

"Your dad would never spit on you."

Aaron stared at his wife. Suddenly he broke down and began to sob. He didn't want to cry, but he was overwhelmed. He bit his lip for a second and then said, "I don't know what we're going to do."

THE HIGHEST LEVELS OF BUSINESS

"What I've done is I've used, brilliantly, the laws of the country. And not personally, just corporate. And if you look at people like myself that are at the highest levels of business, they use -- many of them have done it, many times."

—Donald Trump

DON'T FENCE ME IN

Oh, give me land, lots of land, under smoggy skies above.
Don't fence me in.
Let me drive through the streets of the nation that I love.
Don't fence me in.
Let me gas up my car in the evenin' breeze
And listen to the traffic from all the asphalt streets.
Send me off forever, but I ask you please,
Don't fence me in.
Just set me free.
Let me listen to my station
With the volume turned up high.
I'm hung-a-ree.
Let me wander over yonder
For a burger and some fries.
I'll run the red light where the real estate commences
And gaze at the signs till I lose my senses.
I love pickles on my burgers but can't stand fences.
Don't fence me in.

A LOUSY SANTA

Macy's. I have memories of Macy's. I can recall how the place smelled like a perfume factory. I remember how it sounded, and I remember all the nicely dressed shoppers. I remember trying on clothes in the fitting rooms, wondering why they always booby-trapped the shirts with pins.

I guess it's time for me to introduce myself. My name is Huey Baker. I guess if anyone here in this book could be called a main character, I would be that person. This book is, in its essence, about me. You're going to get to know me very well as we move ahead. Maybe you'll get to know more than you want. Heck, maybe more than *I* want. We're going to cover a lot of ground, but my story begins when I was a boy in Anaheim. I want to begin by telling you one story in particular. I don't know how old I was, exactly. It was near to Christmas, and it was going to be a very exciting Christmas for me. Why? Because I had been promised my first bicycle. This bike was not to be shared with my older brother. No, you can forget about him. He had his own bicycle, and this would be my bicycle. It would be all mine: tires, handlebars, sprockets, fenders, chain, fork, fenders, and seat. No one would be allowed to ride it except for me—unless, of course, I gave my permission, and I wasn't likely to give out my permission to anybody.

I knew exactly what I wanted. I wanted a Schwinn Stingray with gooseneck handlebars and a long banana seat. That's what all the other kids in the neighborhood had, and I wanted to be just like them. When you're a kid, it's important that you fit in with the others. It doesn't seem that important when you're an adult, but when you're a kid, it's critical. It's one of the most important things in your life—not being an oddball, an outcast, or a weirdo. A Schwinn Stingray would secure my place in the society of us boys. I would belong. For all intents and purposes, I would be one of them.

I remember that year well. I remember that a week or so before Christmas day, Mom took me to go shopping with her. I remember the mall. I remember being dragged in and out of all the stupid stores, and I remember Macy's. Santa Claus was there, and there was a long line of runny-nosed children waiting to see him. Most of them were younger than me, and many of them were with their mothers. Such dumb little kids—they hadn't yet learned that Santa wasn't real, that he was just an old fat guy with a fake beard and a hint of liquor on his breath whom the department store paid to act jolly from ten in the morning until seven at night. "Ho, ho, ho," he would say as you sat in his lap, and he'd smile and ask, "So what do you want Santa to bring you for Christmas?" Then, after the kid told him what he wanted, Santa would wink at the parents and say, "We'll see, we'll see. Make sure to be good, now." You know, I don't remember ever sitting on Santa's lap, although I know I did it. I've seen pictures that prove it. My actual memories just don't go that far back, but I do remember the year I was getting my bicycle. Mom asked me that day at the mall if I wanted to see Santa. She was just teasing me, of course. I was much too old for that. But maybe that was my mistake. Maybe I should've said yes.

My dad was now Santa. He was the one who worked five days a week, earning the family's disposable income. He was the one who decided which of us would get what, and he was the one who promised to get me a bike that year. But before I tell you what he did, I should tell you a few things about my dad and what he did for a living. He was an engineer. As a kid, I didn't really care much about what my dad did. So far as I knew, he worked in an office downtown where he did all sorts of complex calculations and drawings for adult-type stuff. It wasn't really interesting to me. Because he was an engineer, or maybe it was more *why* he became an engineer, my dad had his own rational, step-by-step way of seeing the world. He was not a frivolous man. No sir, things had to make sense to him the way they would make sense to a computer. I'll give you an example. Cars were a very big thing when I was a boy. Our next-door neighbor had a Ford Thunderbird, and my friend's mom down the street had a Lincoln. I remember those cars well. They were amazing. I remember that the Thunderbird had a reverb option for its radio and that the Lincoln was big and pink. I remember when it came time for my dad to buy a car and how enthusiastic I was. But what did he get? A Thunderbird? A Lincoln? A Cadillac with fins? A Chevy Bel Air? A Corvette? No, my dad bought an underpowered, boring-as-hell beige Volkswagen bug. Jeez, what the heck was that all about? It was like getting underwear for your birthday. But to my dad it made perfect sense. He had done all the appropriate calculations, and the underpowered beige Volkswagen met his bone-dry criteria.

Anyway, that was my dad. So I shouldn't really have been surprised on Christmas morning. But I was. I was surprised and sorely disappointed. I can't even imagine the look of horror that was probably on my face.

I didn't get the Stingray.

What I got was a five-speed bike. It was bright red, and I had never liked the color red much. It was so big that I nearly needed a stepladder to get onto it. And riding it was like riding a pair of stilts with wheels. It didn't even seem safe. If I had been older and more outspoken, I would've said, "What the fuck is this? Didn't I ask you for a Stingray?" But I was a kid. I knew I was supposed to be appreciative no matter what I got, and I knew my dad thought he had made the best decision for me. "It's so big," I said, and Dad said, "You'll grow into it. Those Stingrays are too small. You'd outgrow a Stingray in a couple years. Those are little kid bikes. This is a bike that will last you for years." Like I cared how long the bike would last.

I felt like a fool that day. I showed the other boys my new bike, and they jumped on their Stingrays and rode circles around me. Such a fool.

Such a dork. That's when I learned that I was never going to belong. Not really. Not in the true sense of the word. And I had my father to thank for that.

It wasn't until I was much older that I realized my dad had maybe done me a favor. I never realized this as a kid or as a young man. But as I grew older, I came to understand something—that I had learned to be an individual and find strength not by belonging to a group but rather by being myself. I think this was a good thing. I think it's important for people to be comfortable with who they are without having to worry about what others are thinking of them. This breeds individuals and not copycats. It breeds men rather than little boys. It makes the world a far more interesting place to live in. It's sort of funny, isn't it? But I still wish I had the Stingray.

I never forgave my dad for buying me that dumb bike. Why my father couldn't have just bought me the bike I asked for was beyond me. Why did he have to name me Sue? Bill or George or anything but Sue!

You know, when dad was dying, and when I was visiting him in the hospital, we talked about old times. When he was awake, he liked to reminisce, and I helped him along. We shared our memories, and we were having a good time doing this. When that five-speed bicycle came up, I told him, "You know, I've never forgiven you for that. It was a rotten thing to do. It was selfish, and it was actually a little mean." I wasn't really all that angry anymore. I was just giving the old guy a hard time.

"I bought you what you needed," Dad said.

"I needed a Stingray."

"Bah," Dad said, and he rolled his eyes.

"How are you feeling?" I asked, changing the subject.

"The same."

"You don't look so good."

"I'm dying, son. What do you expect?"

"Maybe I should get the nurse," I said. And Dad suddenly dozed off. It was like flicking a light switch. One minute he had been talking to me, and the next thing I knew, he was asleep. I remember the nurse came into the room around then, and I told her what had happened.

"Maybe you should just let him sleep," she said.

"Maybe," I said.

"He's a nice man."

"He can be," I said.

"When you're not here, he talks about you all the time."

"He does?"

"You should probably leave him alone for a while," the nurse said. She put her hand on my forearm. This was a nice thing to do. I liked this nurse. She was trying to make things a little easier for me, and I appreciated that. And I remember thinking how difficult a nurse's job must be—watching patients suffer, watching them die.

Dad died that night. I should have told him that I didn't care about the Stingray. It was wrong for me to give him a hard time, even if I was just joking around. Maybe it didn't matter to him, but maybe it did. Who knew? When it came to my dad, I was never quite sure what he was thinking. He wasn't the kind of guy who wore his emotions on his sleeve. But you know what I think? I think he regretted buying me the five-speed. He was a decent and loving father. He really was. It would be wrong for me to tell you otherwise. He was just a lousy Santa. It wasn't his fault. I suppose that some of us make good Santas and some of us don't.

You want to know what else I think? I think the nurse knew he was going to die that night. She just knew. She was being kind to me because she knew. She was a good nurse. I believe that she cared, and how many strangers in your life do you meet that actually care? And she was a stranger. I didn't know any more about her than I did about the hospital's janitor, the women who cleaned the linens, or the gardener who kept up the grounds.

BICYCLE FOR TWO

Clara, Clara, give me your answer, do.
I'm half crazy all for the love of you.
So sad that we'll never be close,
Girl whom I admire most.
But you'd look sweet upon the seat
Of my bicycle built for two.
There is a flower within my heart,
Clara, Clara,

But old time and space keeps us apart,
Beautiful Clara girl.
Whether you'd love me or love me not,
Lost in this crazy world,
I guess I'll never share the lot
Of beautiful Clara girl.
Clara, Clara, give me your answer, do.
I'm half crazy all for the love of you.
So sad that we'll never be close,
Girl whom I admire most,
But you'd look sweet upon the seat
Of my bicycle built for two.
In my dreams we can travel as one,
Clara, Clara,
Peddling away right into the sun,
I and my Clara girl.
And when the road's dark, we can despise,
But I'll always know for sure
There are bright lights in the dazzling eyes
Of beautiful Clara girl.
Clara, Clara, give me your answer, do.
I'm half crazy all for the love of you.
So sad that we'll never be close,
Girl whom I admire most.
But you'd look sweet upon the seat
Of my bicycle built for two.

BURIED IN MASSACHUSETTS

Here's a sad fact. If you were to ask people these days who Kim Kardashian is, they would probably all be able to tell you. At least they would've heard of her. But if you were to ask them who Clara Barton was, I'll bet that 98 percent of them would have no idea whom you were talking about.

Clara was a teacher, a patent office employee, and, perhaps most importantly, a nurse. If you want to get an idea of what this woman accomplished during her lifetime, plenty has been written about the subject. You should just know that she was an amazing American and the founder of the American Red Cross. She devoted her life to helping others. She became known as the Florence Nightingale of America and also the Angel of the Battlefield. In a world that is now dominated by irascible and power-hungry politicians, self-absorbed movie stars, win-hungry athletes, Grammy-seeking musicians, sales-driven artists, greedy businessmen, holier-than-thou preachers, arrogant doctors, and ambulance-chasing attorneys, citizens like Clara Barton are few and far between. She was truly a great national treasure, and everyone should know who she was. She said, "You must never so much think as whether you like it or not, whether it is bearable or not; you must never think of anything except the need, and how to meet it." We could use a Clara Barton today—someone whom our children can look up to. Kim Kardashian? Give me a fucking break. Seriously.

Is it a sign of the times? What does this say about our great country? Did you know that today's "humanitarian-minded" CEO of the American Red Cross is paid over $600,000 a year? Because of what the job entails, they say the Red Cross is getting a bargain. Wow. Clara has to be turning in her grave.

THE TOURNAMENT

Sally lived in Newark, New Jersey. She had lived there for her entire life. Sally knew all about Clara Barton, having learned about the woman during nursing school at Rutgers. For ten long years, Sally was a nurse, and she was a darn good one. She was employed at Saint Michael's until she met her husband, Kaleb. He was a doctor at the hospital, and the two of them fell in love and got married just one year after they met. This was Kaleb's second marriage, and it was Sally's first.

This morning Sally was out of bed at six o'clock, just as she was every morning. She liked to get up early to get a jump on the day. This was especially true today. It was a big day for her. It was a Saturday in April, and the tournament at the North Palisades Tennis Club started in just a few hours. Having been encouraged by Kaleb, Sally had signed up. She'd been playing tennis often at the club for the past several years, but this would be her first tournament.

Today they would hold all the qualifying matches, and the championship game would be held Sunday morning. Sally's first match was at nine. She would be playing against Jessica Atkins, a single girl who had just graduated from college and worked at a local car rental agency. Everyone at the club liked Jessica. She was young and attractive, and she had a great personality. She didn't have a mean bone in her body, and she was respectful of the women at the club who were older than her. The men at the club loved her to death, and they all went out of their way to be nice to her. She showed up Saturday morning with her blonde hair in a ponytail and her racquet in hand. When she showed at nine to play against Sally, she came over and wished Sally luck. It was a nice gesture, because she was a nice girl. Nice, nice, nice. Sally knew that most of the people watching would be rooting for Jessica to win. Kaleb was there. He told Sally not to pay any attention to the crowd. "Kick her butt," he said. "You're not here to be liked. You're not here to be nice. You're here to win."

"Okay," Sally said. Then a thought went through her head. *If only I could win without making Jessica lose. That would be ideal.*

"Kick her butt," Kaleb said again, and he kissed Sally on her cheek.

The match started, and it went well for Sally. Her topspin was working, and her backhand was strong. There wasn't much to Jessica's game, and it seemed as if she wasn't even trying. She could barely hit the ball. It didn't take long for them to reach match point, and Sally served for the win. "You can do it!" Kaleb shouted from the sideline. "Put it in there!" Sally looked over at him, and then she looked across the court toward Jessica. She tossed the ball up high like a pro, swung her racquet, and swatted it. The dumb girl didn't have a chance in hell. She didn't even touch the ball, and the match was over. Sally won, and Kaleb was clapping his hands. "Atta girl!" he shouted several times.

It was funny. Jessica didn't even seem to care that she lost. She came to the net, and the women shook hands. Jessica was all smiles, and when she walked off the court, she was met by several men. They were smiling. In fact, the men almost seemed happy that Jessica had lost the match, because it gave them an opportunity to console her. They went through the motions of caring, and then they all sat down to talk at an outdoor table. Kaleb approached Sally, and he put his arm around her. "You hardly worked up a sweat," he said.

"I played well?"

"You did great."

"I wonder who I play next."

"I think you're up against Madge Harwood."

"Madge," Sally said, biting her lip. "She's a pretty good player."

"You'll beat her," Kaleb said. "Just keep playing like you played against Jessica, and you'll do fine. Don't worry about Madge."

Madge Harwood was a good player. She was a couple years older than Sally, and she was married to a successful attorney. Her husband never came to watch her play. He was always too busy working, defending criminals and trying to keep them out of jail. Sally had met Madge only once, and they didn't have much to say to each other. Madge wasn't exactly the outgoing sort. No one at the club was very close to Madge. She was kind of a loner, and she didn't come to the club to make friends. She came to play tennis, and that was it. But she was good. And she had played in tournaments before, and won first place in a couple of them.

When Sally's match with Madge started, Kaleb was watching from the sidelines, and again he cheered her on. "You can do this!" he shouted. "Show her who's the boss!" It made Sally feel kind of bad that no one was cheering for Madge.

It was a close match. Sally did better than she expected. Kaleb kept shouting, and so did a couple of his friends. Still, no one was cheering for Madge. About halfway through the match, Sally began to feel sorry for the woman. She was playing a tennis match for whom? For herself? What if she won the match? Who would congratulate her? Who would pat her on the back? And if she lost, would she just go home alone, take a shower, and make lunch? "Get tough!" Kaleb shouted to her. "Stay away from her forehand! Hit the balls to her backhand! And whatever you do, don't let her come up to the net!" Sally did her best, despite her empathy for Madge, and finally it was match point. Madge was to serve. She threw up the ball on the second serve and hit it with all her might. But the ball flew out of bounds, and the match was over, just like that. It was another win for Sally. Madge came to the net to shake Sally's hand. "Good match," she said, and Sally thanked her. And that was the end of it. Madge was now out of the picture. She collected her things and walked away alone. "You did it!" Kaleb exclaimed. Again, he had his enthusiastic arm around his wife. "One more match and you're in the finals!"

Sally's final match for the day was against a woman named Andrea Pollard. Andrea was a friend of Sally's—well, not a close friend, but someone at the club whom Sally got along with. They'd had drinks together several times in the lounge with some of the other women. Andrea was Sally's age. Unlike Sally, the nurse, Andrea had never worked a day in her life. She'd married a man named Ernest Pollard, who worked for his father's local car dealerships. His father owned several of them, and the guy was rolling in money—or at least it appeared that way. The dad was grooming Ernest to take over the business, while Andrea was in charge of looking after their three children and maintaining the household. Tennis was important to Andrea in that it kept her in good physical shape, but winning and losing? It was as if she didn't care either way, and she had entered the tournament only because Ernest had wanted her to. He wanted to see her being more competitive. Ernest had come to the club to watch her play, and like Kaleb, he shouted from the sidelines. "You can do this!" he shouted. "Remember what we talked about! Stick to the game plan!"

The match was close for a while, and Sally began to wonder whether she'd be able to win. Andrea's husband kept shouting, and so did Kaleb. It was very annoying, listening to the men shouting. It got worse as the match went on. Then Sally began to get an edge. She was winning, and she could sense that Andrea was losing interest. Andrea's serves were landing out, and she was missing some easy shots. Her husband kept shouting at her. Sally really wished the men would keep quiet, but they didn't. When the match point came, Sally was serving for the win. She smacked the ball to Andrea's backhand, and Andrea swung. The ball hit the frame of her racquet and flew about fifty feet up in the air as though it had been shot out of a cannon. Her husband shouted, "Jesus Christ, Andrea! What the hell was that?" Andrea stepped up to the net to shake Sally's hand.

"Good match," she said.

"You're a good player," Sally said.

"Not good enough."

"Are you going to be okay?" Sally's nurse's instinct had kicked in, causing her to ask this question.

Andrea gave Sally a weird look, confused by her concern. "I'll be fine," she said. "Good luck tomorrow."

"Thanks," Sally said.

"I hope you win."

"Me too," Sally said.

As Sally walked off the court, Kaleb met her. He was grinning from ear to ear, and again he put his arm around his wife. "That was a tough one," he said. "But I knew you'd come through."

"I guess I'll be playing tomorrow."

"Sure as hell."

"Do you know who I'll be playing?"

"I do," Kaleb said. "You're up against Gail Andrews."

"The *Beast*," Sally said.

"The Beast?"

"That's what the other women call her."

"Beauty versus the Beast," Kaleb said, and he laughed at this.

"She's going to take me apart."

"She doesn't stand a chance."

"You've obviously never seen her play."

"I don't need to see her play. I've seen you play. You've got what it takes to win this thing."

IRON MIKE

I want to rip his heart out and feed it to him. I want to kill people. I want to rip their stomachs out and eat their children.

— Mike Tyson

THE BEAST

Sally woke up Sunday morning at four. She tried to fall back asleep, but she couldn't do it. She was wide awake. Besides, more sleep wouldn't help. She would just dream about playing tennis as she had been doing all night, swinging her racquet and mishitting balls, and missing balls completely. Tennis balls were coming from every angle and flying off her racquet and out of the court. *Jesus!* It was a nightmare, literally, complete with tossing and turning. Now it was probably too early to be up, but it was a relief to no longer be dreaming.

Sally climbed out of bed, causing Kaleb to open his eyes and look at her. "What are you doing up so early?" he asked.

"I can't sleep."

"Are you worried about the tournament?"

"Not really worried."

"What then?"

"I can't get it out of my mind. Maybe I am worried. Maybe that's it."

"You're going to do fine."

"You keep saying that."

"I know what I'm talking about. You're going to play great. You've got nothing to worry about."

"I'm going to make some coffee."

"I'm going back to sleep," Kaleb said. He groaned and rolled over.

Sally kissed her husband on the forehead. Then she left the bedroom and walked downstairs to the kitchen. She brewed a pot of coffee and made some toast. She put butter and marmalade on the toast and took a bite. It was just what she needed! It helped to settle her stomach, which was still doing flip-flops as she thought about her match. The Beast! She would have to play the dreaded woman. In her mind's eye, she pictured Gail: her muscular body, her frightening face, her steel-wool hair, and her angry, penetrating eyes. Surely Gail ate women like Sally for breakfast. She would tear Sally up into a mass of marmalade and spread her on toast. She would open her jaws and eat Sally like a Tyrannosaurus Rex devouring one of its own, two hundred pounds in a single bite. *Chomp, chomp, chomp.* Bones, brains, and jewelry.

When Sally and Kaleb arrived in their car at the club later that morning, Sally's hands were shaking. The adrenaline was already pumping. She wasn't even on the court, and her body was trembling with energy. "You can do this," Kaleb said. "Just keep your wits about you, and don't get nervous. Play just like you're playing any other match. Don't let this woman intimidate you. It's all in your head."

"Okay," Sally said.

"Do it one serve at a time."

"One serve."

"And don't be afraid to go to the net. I asked around, and Gail doesn't do well with volleys."

"Okay," Sally said.

"I'll be there all the way."

"I know you will."

When it was time to play, Sally and Gail Andrews took their places on the court. It was still morning, but it was already very warm. Sally was up to serve first. Gail was crouched and swaying back and forth, ready to receive. She was dressed in a solid black tennis outfit, and her hair was tied back into a ponytail. Her hair was pulled back so tightly that it appeared to be stretching the skin of her forehead and raising her eyebrows. And those eyes! They were staring, waiting for Sally to serve the ball. "Let's have it," Gail said. That was all she said. She wasn't known around the club for being very talkative. She came to win tennis matches, not to make friends. *Here goes nothing*, Sally thought, and she served the ball. It was a decent serve, hard and—Sally hoped—difficult to return. But Gail whacked the ball with no problem, sending it over the net to Sally's backhand. Unfortunately, Sally hit the ball right into the net. It was not a good way to start the match. They got ready again. "Love fifteen," Sally said quietly, and she hit her second serve. This one was out by a mile. Kaleb groaned.

Soon Sally was down by three games. "Hang in there!" Kaleb shouted. "You've still got plenty of time!"

Then, by some miracle, Sally won the fourth game, and then the fifth. Finally she began to feel confident. Maybe she did have a chance to beat this woman. So did she? Well, yes, it turned out that she did. She couldn't believe it. She served the match point, and Gail couldn't even get her racquet on the ball. Kaleb ran out to the court to hug her before she even had a chance to shake Gail's hand. There were a few nice people who applauded. It was pleasant to hear the applause.

"Jesus Christ, you actually beat her!" Kaleb exclaimed. He hugged Sally again. As Sally looked over his shoulder, she saw Gail stuffing her racquet into her bag. Gail looked terribly unhappy. She wasn't angry; she was just unhappy, looking as if she was going to cry. *The Beast? About to cry?* Sally had brought the woman to her knees, and everyone at the club would know. "How does it feel?" Kaleb asked.

Sally smiled and looked at Kaleb and said, "Yes, I'm happy. If it makes you so happy, then it makes me happy."

SEAT 113

Were any of you watching the seat 113 game? Do you know what game I'm talking about? It was at Wrigley Field, and the Chicago Cubs were playing against the Florida Marlins on October 14, 2003. They were playing for a place in the World Series, and it was the eighth inning of game 6. The Cubs had already won three games, and they were ahead 3-0. The Cubs were about to seize their first National League pennant since 1945 when all hell broke loose.

The Cubs were just two outs from ending the eighth inning with their three-run lead, when Luis Castillo of the Marlins hit a fly ball into foul territory of left field. The ball sailed into that precarious area of the ballpark where the stands meet the playing field. The fans raised their hands up to catch the ball, as they always do. As the ball came down, Cubs outfielder Moises Alou reached to catch the ball, but the ball bounced out of his reach, off the hands of a fan named Steve Bartman. Alou threw a fit and showed his frustration with Bartman by slamming down his glove and yelling. He thought he could've caught the ball. Instead of going into his mitt, the ball bounced from Bartman's hands and dropped into the lap of another nearby fan. What happened after that? The Cubs wound up losing by a score of 8-3. Then they lost the next game, and the Marlins went on to the World Series instead of the Cubs.

The fan reaction to Bartman's action was ugly. I mean it was *really* ugly. They all began chanting, "Asshole, asshole, asshole," and they threw drinks and debris at Bartman. He had to be escorted out of the stadium by security guards, and soon after the game, his name and personal information were all over the internet. His phone started ringing, and he received all kinds of threats from angry Cubs fans. The police came to his house to protect him. There were as many as six police cars there. This went on and on, and he finally had to change his phone number. It was unbelievable. The hate and scapegoating were relentless, and it went on for months. The governor, Rod Blagojevich, suggested that Bartman join a witness protection program, while Florida governor Jeb Bush called Bartman on the phone and offered asylum. It was no joke. The poor guy feared for his life.

You may already be familiar with this story, but here are a few things you may not know. Did you know that they changed the seat Bartman had occupied from section 4, row 8, seat 113 to section 2, row 8, seat 108? They said this had nothing to do with the Bartman incident. Yeah, right.

Here's something else you may not know. The fan who wound up with the ball put the ball up for auction in December of 2003, hoping to use the profits for his kid's college education. And who do you think bought it? It was crazy! The ball was purchased by none other than Harry Caray's restaurant, for $113,824. In February of 2004, at the restaurant on West Kinzie Street, Oscar-winning special-effects artist Michael Lantieri drilled a hole into the ball, injected explosives, and blew it up. Emcee Tim Walkoe told the crowd and a national TV audience, "You're now all looking at $113,000 worth of string." This string was put on display in a glass case at the Chicago Sports Museum in Water Tower Place. Then, in 2005, the remains were used by the restaurant to make a pasta dish. While no part of the ball was in the meal, the string was boiled and the steam was captured, distilled, and added to the sauce. Mind you, these things were done by adults.

It took a while, but Bartman was finally forgiven. The team reached out, wanting to make amends on behalf of the fans. They asked if he would toss out the ball when they finally went to the World Series, but he declined. Then, when the Cubs won the Series, Bartman received his own championship ring as a special gift on July 31, 2017. The Cubs said, "We hope this provides closure on an unfortunate chapter of the story that has perpetuated throughout our quest to win a long-awaited World Series. While no gesture can fully lift the public burden he has endured for more than a decade, we felt it was important Steve knows he has been and continues to be fully embraced by this organization. After all he has sacrificed, we are proud to recognize Steve Bartman with this gift today." Too little, too late? I don't know what to think. Maybe you can tell me.

WORLD PEACE

He said, "I always had anger issues because that's all I grew up around—anger. I also had love, and that's why people see two sides from me. I saw my parents happy and mad. I grew up with friends who were happy one moment, and the next moment guns were firing. As a kid it was unbalanced and confusing. There was never a chance to relax. It was just get up and see what's going to happen today. I might have a good day. I might wake up on the other side of the bed. I was suspended in nursery school, kindergarten, and the first through twelfth grades every year for fighting. In college I got in trouble, and in the NBA I was in trouble for something or another every year except my last year."

So said Ron Artest, aka Metta World Peace. In my opinion, he is a great guy and a terrific athlete. No kidding. He is not exactly someone you might choose to call a hero, but a hero he was and is.

Where to start? Let's begin with the day he was brought into this world. He was born November 13, 1979, and raised in the Queensbridge projects in Long Island City, Queens, New York. It was a tough place to grow up. As a youth, for example, Ron witnessed the grisly murder of a fellow young player during a game in Niagara Falls. He tells us about that game: "It was so competitive, they broke a leg from a table and they threw it. It went right through his heart and he died right on the court. So, I'm accustomed to playing basketball really rough." The player who died was nineteen-year-old Lloyd Newton. He was indeed killed, as Ron said, in the YMCA-sanctioned basketball tournament. What were you doing when you were nineteen? Were you watching kids being murdered? I was drinking Coors beer and peacefully watching reruns of *Star Trek* with my friends in our college dormitory. Or maybe I was reading a book for my English class. Or maybe I was working out calculus problems. I don't remember any bloodshed.

I'm going to call him Ron Artest for now. He hadn't gone through the process of changing his name, and we will get to the name change later. Ron was very good at basketball. As a young man, he was a standout, and he soon went on to play in the NBA, making a name for himself as a scrappy ballplayer. All said and done, he played for six different NBA teams. He played his tail off and developed a reputation for playing aggressively and edgily. While playing for the Bulls, he was named to the NBA All-Rookie Second Team in the 1999–2000 season. During his 2003–2004 season with the Pacers, he averaged 18.3 points, 5.7 rebounds, and 3.7 assists per game, making the 2004 NBA All-Star Game as a reserve. He was also named Defensive Player of the Year. But despite his success as a ballplayer, he also had problems. In 2003, Ron got into a verbal altercation with Miami coach Pat Riley, and he flashed an obscene gesture at the crowd. He was suspended for four games. Then, on November 19, 2004, Ron was at the center of a fight between players and fans during a game against the Detroit Pistons. It was a brawl that resulted in the game being stopped with less than a minute to go. Several players were suspended right after the game. A day later, the NBA suspended Ron for the rest of the season. Ron missed a total of eighty-six games. It was the longest suspension for a fight in NBA history.

So what was the big deal? The incident was like nothing the NBA or general public had seen. It was weird. It was out of control, and they showed it on TV over and over. The brawl began with 45.9 seconds remaining in the game, and Indiana was leading 97–82. The Pistons' Ben Wallace was fouled from behind by Ron, who slapped him across the back of the head during a layup attempt. Wallace later said that Ron had warned him he was going to be hit. An irate Wallace shoved Ron in the face, causing the players from both teams to come out and try to keep Wallace and Ron apart. Pistons coach Larry Brown was not yet alarmed, because fights in the NBA rarely last for more than several seconds. But during the scuffle, Ron walked away and lay down on the scorer's table to calm down. Indiana Pacers president Donnie Walsh later said that by lying down, Ron was following advice he'd received on how to control his temper. But it didn't work. And it rubbed fans the wrong way.

While Ron was still lying on the scorer's table, Wallace threw a towel at him. A fan then threw a cup of beer at Ron, hitting him in the chest. Ron jumped up from the table and ran into the stands, grabbing a man he mistakenly thought was responsible for throwing the beer. A broadcaster stood up to try to hold back Ron but was trampled hard in the effort and suffered five fractured vertebrae and a gouge on his head. Then fellow Pacer Stephen Jackson followed Ron into the stands and punched a fan in the face in retaliation for the man throwing another drink. Other Pacers players went into the stands to break up the fighting. Ron was punched twice in the head, and more fans began throwing drinks and other objects.

As Ron left the stands, he was confronted by two more fans. Fists started swinging, and the security staff struggled to enforce some order. While the police had plans to handle disorders and had three officers there in the arena, they were unprepared for what took place. Coach Rick Carlisle said, "I felt like I was fighting for my life out there." One reporter recalled that a player "went through me like I was butter," and the NBA's David Stern, watching the game on TV, recalled that he just exclaimed, "Holy shit!" Pacers assistant coach Chuck Person compared the altercation to being "trapped in a gladiator-type scene where the fans were the lions and we were just trying to escape with our lives. That's how it felt. There was no exit, and that you had to fight your way out."

The referees finally ended the game with 45.9 seconds left and gave the Pacers the win. Fans booed the Indiana players as they were escorted from the court by security, and they continued to throw drinks, popcorn, and other objects, including a folding chair that nearly hit one of the players. Larry Brown tried to talk to the fans over the loudspeaker in an attempt to calm them down, but he threw the microphone in disgust after he realized that no one was listening. The Pistons' public address announcer, John Mason, then implored the crowd to leave because the game was over, and the police officers were finally able to gain control of the arena, threatening to arrest those who would not leave as asked. All said and done, nine fans were injured, and two were taken to the local hospital. The powers that be decided that it was all Ron's fault, so they suspended him for the rest of the season.

After playing for the Pacers, Ron went on to play for the Kings, Rockets, and Lakers. Officials watched him like a hawk because of his bad boy reputation. The last thing they wanted was a rerun of the Pacers–Pistons fiasco. Subsequently, there were several ejections and suspensions, but Ron had no intention of changing his playing style to appease anyone. He said, "I'm still ghetto. That's not going to change. I'm never going to change my culture." And what exactly was his culture? He was a street fighter raised in a tough neighborhood, and he played as though his life was on the line. Not only did players dislike playing against him; some didn't even like playing with him. And now it wasn't just his basketball game that was getting noticed; it was his private life. On March 5, 2007, Ron was placed under arrest for domestic violence and excused from the Kings indefinitely. On March 10, the Kings announced that Ron would return to the team while his case was being reviewed by the district attorney. Then, on May 3, he was sentenced to twenty days in jail. While he spent only ten days in the jail, the league suspended Ron for seven games because of his legal problems. Everyone agreed that the guy was a problem.

He was finally ordered to get professional help as one of the court-ordered conditions of his domestic violence case. He was sent to a doctor for diagnosis and treatment. Ron has seen this doctor regularly ever since. He said, "I was the best two-way player in the league at twenty-four. I was also spiraling downward emotionally. My emotions were eating away at my skills, like a parasite eating away at your body. It was eating away at my skills and my work habits and my mental focus and my discipline." He also said, "Before I got into the big brawl, I wanted to retire. I requested papers to file to the NBA. I knew something was terribly wrong and nobody really knew. The league called and asked if I really wanted to do this. I needed time away because I couldn't get a hold of myself. There were so many things bothering me, so many things I couldn't handle. I was going crazy."

So what happened? Well, thanks to his doctor, this great man completely turned his life around. Still a tough ballplayer on the court, he was able to get his life under control. Then he legally changed his name, and everyone laughed. He wanted to be called Metta World Peace. He no longer wanted to be known as Ron Artest. He said, "Changing my name was meant to inspire and bring youth together all around the world." He said he chose Metta because it is a Buddhist word that means "loving kindness and friendliness toward all." Now World Peace was active in projects outside of basketball. And he spoke out every chance he had. He talked to the press and anyone else who would listen about the importance of dealing with mental health issues. He made people feel less ashamed and more willing to seek help. He became a spokesman and an inspiration. He became a role model. He donated large sums of cash from his salary to mental health charities, and he auctioned off his championship ring and gave the proceeds to various mental health causes. Do you think he was crazy to do this? I don't think he was crazy at all. I think Metta World

Peace is a real hero. I, too, laughed when I heard about his unusual name change, but I'm not laughing now—smiling, maybe, but not laughing.

THE ESSENCE

"Battle is the most magnificent competition in which a human being can indulge. It brings out all that is best; it removes all that is base. All men are afraid in battle. The coward is the one who lets his fear overcome his sense of duty. Duty is the essence of manhood."

—George S Patton

MY COUSIN TIM

God, how I looked up to my cousin Tim. I loved the guy as if he were my brother. I had a brother, Bob, but I think I loved Tim a lot more. My brother treated me like a dope and a pain in the neck, and for all intents and purposes, he would never give me the time of day. I embarrassed him. When we were kids, he didn't like having a little brother around at all.

But Tim was different. He was six years older than me, and three years older than Bob. Tim liked me. He was an only child who lived with my aunt and uncle just several blocks from our little house in Anaheim. He would let me hang out with him and his friends after school, and I liked it. I became a kind of mascot. They teased me a lot, but it wasn't mean spirited. They just gave me a hard time, as you would expect older boys to give a younger kid who was hanging out with them. I remember when Tim got his driver's license and I was in the fifth grade, Tim asked me if I wanted to come to the drive-in with him and his friends on a Saturday night, and I asked my parents if I could go. They trusted Tim, and they allowed me to tag along. I'd been to the movies before, but never without my parents. It was exciting to be with the older boys. I remember the movie that was playing: *Dr. Goldfoot and the Bikini Machine*. It had Vincent Price, Dwayne Hickman, and Frankie Avalon. Of course, everyone knew who Vincent Price was, and I'd heard of Frankie Avalon. I knew who

Dwayne Hickman was; he was Dobie Gillis. We all piled into my uncle's station wagon, and Tim drove us to the drive-in. I sat up front, between Tim and Ernie. Ernie was one of Tim's friends. The other boys sat in the back.

I don't know why, but this movie had a huge effect on me. I remember it in detail to this day. Maybe it was the girls in their golden bikinis that caught my attention. I'd never seen so many beautiful girls in a single movie, walking around and wearing so little. It drove me a little crazy, being a boy who was just discovering girls. The plot was simple. Vincent Price played a mad scientist named Dr. Goldfoot, poking fun at the *Goldfinger* and *Dr. No* James Bond movies that were popular at the time. He had a stupid assistant named Igor, and a science fiction factory that manufactured beautiful female robots in golden bikinis. The whole point of the operation was to send the girl robots off into the real world to seduce and entrap unsuspecting rich men and steal their fortunes. I was young, so I probably took the plot more seriously than I was supposed to. In fact, I'm sure of this.

There are several things I remember about this movie with great clarity. The first is the trench coats. Each girl sent out by Dr. Goldfoot would wear a trench coat over her bikini. It was silly, but it seemed to make sense to me. As I said, I was just a kid. I remember one scene in which one of the robot girls wearing a trench coat came upon a bank robbery in progress. One of the robbers shot her full of bullets, but the bullets didn't hurt her. There was no blood at all. Then, later, in a cafe, she drank a glass of milk, and the liquid squirted out of the bullet holes as though she were a fountain. It was funny. I also remember one of the girls getting hit by a car while crossing a street. She wasn't even fazed, but it made a wreck of the car. It was the same girl who had gotten shot and turned into a fountain. She was going after Dwayne Hickman, who played a young rich kid who fell in love with the robot girl. He was kind of an idiot, and I remember it was weird seeing Dobie Gillis in color. I'd always seen him in black-and-white on our little TV set in the family room. But here he was at the drive-in, larger than life.

I loved those years, and I loved being a kid. I loved that Tim liked me and brought me along with his older friends. The world was so much different back then. We didn't have violent video games or cell phones.

Back then, there was no such thing as the internet, and there was no cable TV. Our TV was hooked up to a big antenna on the roof of our house, and the idea of paying for TV was unthinkable. The world barged into our house through the RCA set in our family room. There were sports, all with slow motion and instant replay. There was the news with Walter Cronkite. There was *Gilligan's Island*, *Get Smart*, and *The Addams Family*. There was Jack LaLanne in the mornings, cartoons on Saturdays, and old Laurel and Hardy movies late at night.

A MISTAKE

"I covered the Vietnam War. I remember the lies that were told, the lives that were lost - and the shock when, twenty years after the war ended, former Defense Secretary Robert S. McNamara admitted he knew it was a mistake all along."

—Walter Cronkite

THE CHANGE

I have Tim to thank for introducing me to the wonders of alcohol consumption: not beer, and not hard liquor, but wine—as in that Gallo-made swill they sold in those big-bellied 1.5-liter green glass bottles with the twist-off tops. There was a picture of a Spanish sailing vessel on each label, and they sold it cold at the local market.

I remember the first time I drank Spanada. I was with Tim and one of his friends, a boy named Joey Parker. It was early on a Friday night, and we had told our parents that we were going to the high school football game. My dad thought it would be a good idea for me to go to the game. He'd always wanted me to become interested in sports, especially football. I think my lack of interest up until that time concerned him. And why did it concern him? I'll tell you why, and you might find it hard to believe. But those were different times. People looked at the world differently. My dad was concerned that I was a queer, because according to conventional wisdom, only queers weren't interested in football. You didn't have to play football. It was okay to be a spectator. But you had to love the sport, or you were probably a queer.

So it was easy to get permission to go out with Tim that night. In fact, Dad was thrilled. It was the proof he needed that his eleven-year-old son was normal after all. And who knew? Maybe I'd even want to play. Maybe I would try out for the team when I was in high school. I can't think of anything that would have made my dad happier.

Joey was driving that night. He owned his own car. He had a job after school at a gas station, and he had saved up enough money to buy his own ride. It wasn't much of a car. In fact, it was a pile of crap. It was a '53 Chevy with half its chrome missing and the other half rusted. The rear fender was dented badly, and a headlight was missing. And the upholstery inside was a mess, worn and torn. The inside of the car smelled like a dead skunk, and the engine was amazingly loud because there was a large hole in the muffler. But it was transportation, and it would get us around that night. One good thing about the car was that the radio worked, and Joey wasted no time turning on our favorite AM station.

"You know, we're not going to the football game," Tim said to me.

"We're not?" I asked. This was news to me. I had fallen for the lie like my father.

"We're going to Vietnam."

"Vietnam?"

"That's what we call the place."

"It's cool," Joey said.

"But first we're going to the market."

"The market?"

"To get some wine," Tim said.

"Oh," I said. I was half worried and half excited. But I would never let Tim think I was worried. I wanted him to think I was cool.

"We just need someone to buy it."

"Who's going to do that?" I asked.

"Someone will."

"Someone always does," Joey said.

"I don't get it," I said.

"You will, soon."

"Okay," I said. I was trying so hard to act cool. Tim had been nice enough to bring me along, and I didn't want him to regret it. Joey drove us to the market, and he parked his jalopy off to the side.

"You guys wait here," he said. "This shouldn't take long."

"What's he doing?" I asked Tim.

"He's going to get us a bottle of Spanada."

"Does he have a fake ID?"

"No, nothing like that," Tim said. "He's going to get someone to buy it for us."

"I still don't get it," I said.

Then Joey stood outside of the market, interrupting the customers who were on their way inside. "Can you buy us some wine?" he would ask. "We have the money, but we need someone to buy it for us." Joey had no problem doing this. I mean, he asked everyone. He was fearless. He even asked old people who were obviously going to say no. It took about forty minutes before Joey finally found someone who would make our purchase. He was a younger guy, probably barely of age to drink himself. I remember he had long hair, like a hippie, and he was barefoot.

"Sure, man," I heard the guy say.

"We need a bottle of Spanada."

"Cool, man."

"Here's the money," Joey said, and he handed the guy our cash. Bingo! Forty minutes of asking wasn't bad. I learned later that it could sometimes take a lot longer. In no time, the guy came out of the store with his beer in one bag and our wine in another. He handed Joey the bag.

"Stay out of trouble," he said.

"We will."

"Far out."

"Thanks a lot."

"Peace," the guy said, and he walked away.

Joey climbed into his car with us and handed the bag to Tim. "We're in business," he said.

"I don't know why we buy this stuff," Tim said. He had pulled out the bottle and was looking at it.

"Why?" I asked.

"It tastes like shit."

"But it does the trick," Joey said. Then Joey looked at me. "Have you ever even drank before?"

"No," I said.

"You don't have to if you don't want to," Tim said.

"I want to," I said.

"The kid is game."

"You'll like it," Tim said. "You won't like drinking it, but you'll like the way it makes you feel. It makes everything in the world seem great. It's like magic."

"Abracadabra," Joey said.

Joey drove us to the high school. We went past the lot where all the cars were parked for the football game and down a service road that took us to the lower fields. There was an area to park, and ours was the only car. Joey parked, and we climbed out into the night air.

"Vietnam," Tim said.

"What's Vietnam?" I asked.

"This is."

"It's what we call it."

They were referring to the undeveloped land at the edge of the field. The area was overgrown with trees and vegetation. It was a strange little place, unusual for Southern California. It wasn't really a jungle, but it was kind of like one if you used your imagination.

There was a dirt path that wound into our jungle, and we walked on the path and entered a thicket of trees. The path led to a rocky area, which was perfect for sitting down. We all sat on the large rocks, and Tim pulled the Spanada out of its bag. In the meantime, Joey removed a pack of cigarettes from his jacket pocket, and he looked over at me. "Want one?" he asked.

"He doesn't smoke, retard," Tim said.

"Just offering."

"He's too young to smoke."

"But old enough to drink wine?"

"I'm old enough for both," I said.

"Wine is different," Tim said.

"How's it different?"

"Wine won't give you cancer."

Joey lit a cigarette and blew the smoke from his mouth. "You got me there," he said.

Tim unscrewed the top of the bottle and took a big swig of the wine. He then passed the bottle to Joey, who took an even bigger swig. Joey then handed the bottle to me. "Drink up," Tim said. He and Joey were laughing.

I raised the bottle to my lips and proceeded to drink. I didn't drink a lot. But Jesus! The stuff tasted like rotten fruit and gasoline. It was awful, and I must have made a face, because Joey and Tim were now laughing again.

"This stuff tastes really bad," I said.

"It is pretty bad," Tim agreed.

"Take another swig," Joey said. "You hardly drank enough to give an ant a buzz."

Tim reached and took the bottle from me before I could take a drink. "I don't want him getting too drunk," he said. "I've got to take him home to his parents." Tim then took his second big swig, and he handed the bottle to Joey.

"This place is pretty cool, right?" Joey said to me.

"It is," I said.

"No one ever comes here."

"Except to drink or smoke," Tim said.

"Vietnam," Joey said thoughtfully, nodding his head. He looked around. "I love this place."

About halfway through the bottle, the alcohol hit me. I have to say, it was like nothing I'd ever experienced. It was nothing short of amazing. How would I describe it? It was as though I was suddenly lucid, as if I could see and understand everything around me. I mean, it all made sense. And Vietnam? It was all Vietnam: all the trees, bushes, and scraggly grass. And colors seemed brilliant, as if everything had all been plugged into a wall socket. And I was, well, happy! Yes, that's what I was. I was happy. Tim and Joey were my best friends, and the Spanada no longer tasted so bad. And the more I drank, the more I was talking. I could hear myself. I have no idea what I was going on about, but I was talking up a storm. Tim and Joey were now laughing at me. "Jeez," Joey said. "Your cousin sure talks a lot."

"Let's go to the game," Tim said.

"Is there any more wine?" Joey asked.

Tim turned the bottle upside down, and nothing came out. "All gone," he said.

"Then let's go," Joey said.

"We're going to the game?"

"That's what we told your dad, right?" Tim said. "You don't want to lie to your dad, do you?"

"I guess not," I said.

"It'll be fun," Joey said.

"Who are we playing?" Tim asked.

"Who cares?"

Tim threw the empty bottle into the bushes, and we all stood up from the rocks. We then walked along the path to Joey's car. We didn't give a second thought to Joey driving while drunk. In those days, it just wasn't an issue. Besides, he wasn't really drunk. He was just high. People drove high all the time.

Joey drove us to the main parking lot and found a place for his car. We piled out and walked to the football game. The bleachers were filled with cheering people, most of them adults—most of them parents. "Look at all these idiots," Joey said, grinning from ear to ear.

"Rah, rah, rah," Tim said.

"Do you think we'll get in trouble?" I asked.

"Trouble?"

"You know, for drinking."

"No one's going to know," Tim said. Then he pointed toward the bleachers. "There's an empty spot in the stands. We can sit there."

So we climbed up to the spot and sat in our seats to watch the game. Honestly, I had no idea what was even going on. I was a lot drunker than I thought, and none of the game made any sense. There were just a lot of stupid kids dressed in football uniforms running around, shoving, tripping, and falling. And there were a lot of people in the stands yelling things at them. Joey stood up suddenly and yelled, "Tear their heads off! Show them who's boss! Rip their guts out!" A few adults looked at Joey, annoyed, and then he sat down. Then a minute later, he stood up again. "Gouge their eyes out!" he yelled. "Chew up their hearts! Bite their necks and suck the blood out of their veins!" I saw a woman whisper something into her husband's ear about Joey, but I couldn't tell what she said. But I thought Joey was maybe going too far.

Then it happened. I didn't feel too good. My head began to spin, and my stomach was churning. "I feel sick," I said to Tim.

"It'll go away," Tim said.

But it didn't. Actually, it got worse. I tried to ignore the nausea, but it was no use. And that's when I finally did it. Jesus! I lunged forward and vomited all over the back of the woman sitting in front of me. It was not just a little, but a lot. It was disgusting. The puke splashed all over her nice sweater, and some of it was in her hair. "What the hell?" her husband said.

"Good God!" the woman exclaimed.

Everyone was staring. Tim and Joey started laughing, which certainly didn't help matters.

"You think this is funny?" the husband asked.

"No, of course not," Tim said. Now he was trying not to laugh.

"What is wrong with you boys?" the man asked.

"He's my cousin," Tim said. "I guess he's sick."

"Let's get out of here," Joey said. He was still laughing. The three of us stood up and left. We couldn't seem to get out of there fast enough. And the woman? Who knew? I have no idea what she did. She probably had to go home. It was an awful lot of vomit. And it stunk like hell.

We decided to leave the football game, and we went back to Joey's car. "So now what do we do?" Tim asked.

"We need to do something with your cousin."

"We can't take him home like this."

"Maybe if we get some food and coffee in him," Joey said.

"Good idea," Tim said. "I could go for something to eat. I'm hungry. I could eat a mule."

So we wound up at a Denny's. By the time we got there, I was feeling much better. But I was still a little drunk, and my stomach felt weird and empty. We took a seat at the counter, and the waitress gave us some menus. "What do you feel like?" Tim asked me.

"Bacon and eggs," I said.

"That sounds good to me."

"Same here," Joey said, closing his menu. "That's an excellent choice, sir."

The waitress returned and we gave her our orders. She then brought out our coffee. It was fun. I was now feeling a lot better.

"Fucking football," Joey said.

"The game should be over," Tim said.

"I wonder who won?" I asked.

"Who gives a shit."

"My dad's going to ask me."

"Tell him you left early."

"He won't like that."

"Tell him you left with a girl. Tell him you met a girl there."

"He won't fault you for that," Tim said.

"He'll be proud of you," Joey said.

"Maybe he will."

"Of course he will."

Well, it worked like a charm. When Tim and Joey brought me home, it was the first thing Dad asked me. "So, Huey, who won the game?" he asked. I told him I didn't know because I met Susan Brickman there, and the two of us left the game early.

"A girl, eh?"

"Yeah," I said. "We, you know, messed around a little until the game was over."

My dad smiled. "That's my boy," he said. If he knew I'd been drinking Spanada and that I barfed all over that woman's back, he would've killed me, to be sure.

Good times.

I always had a good time with Tim. As I said, I wasn't that close to my brother, but Tim liked me. Then a year or so went by, and Tim was drafted into the army. They wanted him to fight in Vietnam. It was the real Vietnam, not that dumb place near the high school. There were real bombs and bullets. There would be real blood. I say that now, but back then it didn't seem like such a big deal. I knew Tim wanted to go, and that he wanted to be brave, and that he wanted to be a patriot. Sure, there were kids who were burning their draft cards and refusing to go. There were kids who were moving to Canada. But not Tim. "They're all pussies," Tim told me, and I believed him. They were *all* pussies.

So off Tim went to war. In the meantime, I was doing the things that kids do. I was going to school, trying to meet girls, getting in trouble now and again, and generally enjoying the heck out of life. I missed Tim, but I knew he'd be okay. There are some things in life that you just know. Don't ask me how; you just know them. And I was right about Tim.

After his tour, Tim returned home to my aunt and uncle's, not even wounded. There wasn't a scratch on his body. Then my parents asked my aunt and uncle to bring Tim over for dinner to eat, drink, and celebrate his safe return. They agreed to come, and I remember that dinner. It was nothing like I thought it would be. Tim came home from the war in one piece, but he was so different. He had changed. I guess the best way to put it was that he was no longer a kid. The fun was gone. The joy was gone. All the things that made him so much fun to be around had been lost in the war. He was now an adult. He talked like an adult, and he acted like an adult. He was one of them. Honestly, one could only imagine what the war was like, so I really couldn't figure it. It was not until I got older that I realized what had happened. Back then, I was just being selfish. I wanted my cousin back, and he wasn't there. God knows what he saw. God knows what he experienced in those bloody jungles. And you know what? We never talked about the war, ever. Not even when we were much older.

CUSTER'S LAST STAND

The RV was rolling merrily along. The scenery was passing, and the air conditioner was humming. Meet the Freeman family, all four of them. There was Roger Freeman, the dad. He was behind the wheel of the rolling behemoth, listening to the radio and keeping an eye on traffic. There was Joanne Freeman, wife and mother, sitting at the table and playing cards with the kids. There were the two kids, Jason and Emily. Jason was eight, and Emily was eleven. They were getting along for the time being, which was a nice change of pace. Usually they were at each other's throats.

Roger was thirsty, and he asked Joanne to bring him a Coke. There were a couple six-packs in the refrigerator that they had picked up from a convenience store that morning. Joanne stood up from the table to get Roger's drink.

"How much farther?" she asked.

"Not far," Roger said.

"Where are we going?" Jason asked.

"I told you this morning."

"I forgot."

"Already?" Roger asked.

"I can't help it."

"He can't help it if he's stupid," Emily said.

"I'm not stupid," Jason said. "I just don't have a good memory."

"We're going to a battleground."

"A battleground?" This caught Jason's attention. War was always interesting. Wars were cool.

"We're going to see Custer's Last Stand," Emily said.

"Who was Custer, anyway?" Jason asked.

"Don't they teach you anything in school?"

"I don't remember anything about a Custer."

"When I was a kid, we learned about Custer in the first grade, for crying out loud," Roger said.

"Schools are different now," Joanne said. She handed Roger his Coke.

"What the hell *do* they teach to you kids?"

"They teach us a lot," Emily said.

"But not about Custer?"

"Never heard of him," Jason said. "So who was he? You said we're going to a battlefield. Was he a soldier?"

"He was a great general. A very famous man. He went to West Point. Did you know he graduated at the bottom of his class?"

"So there's hope for you," Emily said to Jason.

"Bite me," Jason said.

"It just goes to show you that you can be a success in this country, even if you are the underdog," Roger said, ignoring the kids. "Who'd think Custer would become one of the Civil War's great leaders? Bottom of his class, hell. But he was quite a guy regardless. He was a great man."

"So what is Custer's Last Stand?" Jason asked.

"It's where the great man died."

"Fighting the Civil War?"

"No, fighting Indians."

"I thought you said he fought in the Civil War."

"He did, but then when the war was over, they sent him west to fight the Indians."

"The Indians were a problem," Joanne said.

"Because they wouldn't let us live here?"

"They were savages, and they thought they owned the whole country free and clear. They wanted it all to themselves. They didn't want to share."

"So we killed them?"

"It was either kill or be killed."

"Our teacher says we're not supposed to call them Indians," Emily said. "We're supposed to call them Native Americans."

Roger shook his head and opened his Coke.

"What does 'native' even mean?" Jason asked.

"It means they were here first."

"Here first maybe," Roger said. "But they were in the way of destiny."

"Destiny?"

"Let me put it this way. Would you jump in front of a train and expect it to stop for you?"

"I guess not."

"The idiots didn't stand a chance."

"But they killed Custer?"

"Indeed, they did."

"So why do we want to go there?"

"It was a wake-up call for America. It was time to bring these savages to their knees once and for all. It was time to pull out all the stops. You know, it was like Pearl Harbor."

"So we beat the Indians?"

"Beat the living daylights out of them."

"Do you want anything else before I sit down?" Joanne asked Roger.

"Some potato chips sound good."

"I think we have a bag already opened."

"I like the kind with ridges. Not the plain ones. I think the kids opened the plain ones, but I like the ridges. They're in the cabinet, above the Oreos."

THE STREETS OF LAREDO

As I walked out on the streets of Laredo,
As I walked out in Laredo one day,
I spied an old cowboy wrapped in Old Glory,
Wrapped in Old Glory as cold as the clay.
"I can see by your smile that you are a kind man."
These words he did say as I slowly walked by.
"Come an' sit down beside me an' hear my sad story.
I've lived by my gun and never will die."
"First were the redcoats who came from the ocean,
In from their island to force the King's way.
I shot them all down with balls from my musket.
They said to give up, and I said no way.
"Then Johnny Reb wouldn't get with the program.
He said his ways were forever to be.
I shot him stone dead and burned down his cities.
I called forth his slaves and set them all free.
"Then the Injuns got nasty and scalped our good settlers,
Made off with women, and murdered the men.
I shot them all dead and named my towns after them.
We should not be hearing from them again.
"Then Europe got ugly and asked for my bullets.
I've always believed in helping a friend.
I fired my gun like there were no tomorrows.
I drank champagne when it came to an end.
"Then Hiro and Adolph tried to rule the planet.
They tried to carry the world away.
I blew them to pieces and bombed them senseless.
They lowered their flags and called it a day.
"Then the Commies got busy with their plans to rule.
They wanted to color all of me red.
By the heat of my gun, I've maintained my freedom.
'Better dead than red,' is what I have said.
"Now the Arabs all hate me and plan their attacks.
They can't tolerate my good Christian ways.

But their primitive weapons are no match for mine,
My pearl-handled gun keeps them at bay.
"So beat the drum slowly and play the fife lowly,
Play the death march as I bury the dead.
Down in the green valley, I lay the sod o'er them.
Such the wages of freedom," the old cowboy said.

LINCOLN

Have you seen *Lincoln*? It's a Steven Spielberg movie. It gives us a great view into the life of one of our greatest presidents. He was such an interesting man, and Daniel Day-Lewis really did a terrific job. The movie itself was about the final months of Lincoln's life. It covered the passage of the Thirteenth Amendment, the end of the Confederacy, and the assassination. I originally saw this movie in the theater when it first came out. I'm going to tell you a true story. Sitting next to me was a bald man and his red-headed wife. There were some battlefield scenes at the opening of the movie, and the bald man was wide awake during the scenes. But he slept through the rest of the movie. I could hear him snoring. It was pretty annoying, and I tried to ignore it. He woke up when his red-headed wife shook his shoulder and told him the movie was over. On the way out of the theater, I overheard the couple talking. "It was a pretty good movie," the bald man said. "But it could have used more war, and a lot less talk. Man, could Lincoln talk. It's no wonder it took him so long to win the war."

MR. KERRIGAN'S FLAG

I was supposed to be at the public library, studying. This was during the pre-internet stone age when we kids did our schoolwork at public libraries. It was a Tuesday night. I was supposed to be working on a history paper about famous American inventions, but I wasn't at the library at all. I had met up with two friends in Vietnam, that same place where I first drank wine with my cousin. I was now with Ted and Marty, high school buddies. Ted had scored a lid earlier in the week from a kid named Chris Perkins. Chris was our go-to guy for marijuana, but we had to keep an eye on him.

He would sell us a bag of oregano if he thought he could get away with it. "I went through it with a fine-toothed comb before I gave him any money," Ted said to us. "There are no stems or seeds at all."

Marty looked into the plastic bag. "Looks good to me," he said.

"Did you bring papers?" I asked.

"Got them right here," Marty said. He reached into his coat pocket and removed a white pack of Zig Zags.

"Cool," Ted said.

"How about matches?" I asked.

"I forgot matches," Marty said, patting his pockets.

"I have some," Ted said. "I always have matches. One should always be prepared."

"Who wants to roll?" Ted said. "I can't roll a decent joint to save my life."

"I'll do it," Marty said. Ted handed him the lid, and Marty went to work, rolling us a joint. He was good at it. He was much better than I was, and surely better than Ted. His joints were always smooth and tight.

"Light it up," I said.

Ted lit the end of the joint and took a deep drag, holding the smoke in his lungs. He then passed the joint to Marty, and Marty took a drag before passing it to me.

"Your hair is getting long," Marty said, looking at me.

"It's getting longer."

"Doesn't your dad give you any grief?"

"He used to, but I think he's given up. He no longer bugs me about it."

"My dad is on my ass all the time," Marty said. "He makes me go to the barber every two weeks. 'There'll be no hippies in our house,' he says to me."

"My hair is getting longer," Ted said.

"Huey's hair is longer than yours."

"My hair grows pretty fast," I said.

"You're lucky."

We were quiet for a moment, taking turns passing around the joint. Then to Marty I said, "I heard your brother got drafted."

"He leaves next week," Marty said.

"That sucks," Ted said.

"He says he's looking forward to going."

"Your brother must have a screw loose," I said.

"I think he just wants to impress our father," Marty said. "Dad says he's proud of him. My brother is into that shit. He isn't like me."

"Do you think your brother is scared?" Ted asked.

"I think he's scared out of his mind."

"That sucks."

"Man, Vietnam is the last place I want to be," I said.

"They say the war will be over soon."

"They've been saying that for years," Ted said.

"They want peace with honor," Marty said, blowing out smoke and talking at the same time.

"Whatever that means."

"Seriously, they should just pull out. No one likes the war. Who cares about that country anyway? Let them all be communists. Who the heck cares?"

"I've heard we already dropped three times as many bombs on Vietnam than we dropped in all of World War II," I said.

"Seriously?" Marty said.

"Yet those freaks keep on fighting," Ted said. "They're fucking crazy."

"I sure as hell don't plan on going over there," I said. "You couldn't get me to go for anything."

"What if you're drafted?"

"Then it's Canada for me."

"That's kind of drastic, isn't it?"

"It's better than jail. And it sure as heck is better than getting your ass shot off by a bunch of angry gooks."

"Roll another joint," Ted said to Marty. "This one is about done."

"Will do," Marty said.

"Our government is bullshit," I said.

"Agreed," Ted said.

"Who do you have for civics?" Marty asked me.

"Kerrigan," I said. "Second period."

"Same here, except I have his fifth-period class."

"I'm in Marty's class," Ted said.

"That dude is an ass," Marty said.

Ah, Mr. Kerrigan. He was the school's only civics teacher. I suppose other teachers could've taught the subject to us, but Mr. Kerrigan had carved out his niche. The man loved government and politics, and he loved teaching civics. He began each of his classes with a couple days talking about how our country was founded, and why the structure of its government was so special and important. "We are living in the greatest country man has ever established," he would say. "Never in the history of the world has a country like ours been in operation. I hope by the end of this civics class you kids will appreciate it—not just appreciate it, but love it. I hope you will love it for what it is, and for what it always will be—a government for the people and by the people. Our country. A government that belongs to you and me."

The guy was such a dick. What did he think we were all going to do? Jump up and salute? I remember thinking, *If our government truly belongs to you, then it can't possibly belong to me. For you and me are as different as tabby house cat and a giraffe.*

Why did I think that? It was because Mr. Kerrigan was so different from me. For one thing, there was his appearance. I don't mean things that he couldn't help; I mean things that were directly under his control, such as his hair. Jesus, who wore hair like that nowadays? He looked like a freaking drill instructor for the army. Do you know what I mean? Remember that little freak who was always yelling at Gomer Pyle? That's who he looked like, except that he was taller. Mr. Kerrigan was over six feet. When he put his hands on his hips and stood in front of the blackboard to lecture, he seemed even taller. It was an authority thing. People who have authority always seem taller than they actually are.

Mr. Kerrigan wasn't shy about expressing his opinions, and he had an opinion on everything. It was his opinion on the war in Vietnam that really rubbed me the wrong way. In fact, all adults who were for the war rubbed me the wrong way. It was an age thing. None of these idiots had to go there. They were all fine and comfortable here in the United States, living out their American lives in the land of the free. Yet for some odd reason they felt compelled to send their children overseas to fight in that humid hellhole, and for what? For democracy? What did I care whether Vietnam was democratic or communist? The truth was that I couldn't have cared less, and I didn't get why we were killing off hundreds of thousands of human beings, including our own boys, when there were so many things that we could've been improving and doing here at home. You may disagree, but that's how I felt at the time.

So how did other kids at our high school feel? A lot of them agreed with Mr. Kerrigan. They were high school students. They weren't yet thinking much for themselves. And it bugged the crap out of me, listening to this fool go on and on about how great America was when I knew that, despite the patriotic sales pitch, the logic was deeply flawed. It bugged me that no one argued with him during class. It bugged me even more that I didn't raise my hand and let him know exactly how I felt. So what did that make me? Was I just a coward for not speaking up? Maybe I was.

Anyway, back to the story. In Mr. Kerrigan's classroom, there was a large American flag draped up high across the back wall. As Ted, Marty, and I were talking about Mr. Kerrigan's class, the topic of the flag came up, and it was Marty who first voiced the idea. "Let's steal the flag," he said.

Ted and I stared at Marty. Then Ted said, "Steal his flag? Are you kidding?"

"I'm not kidding."

"Jesus," I said. I was thinking about this. It was a crazy idea. A good idea, but crazy.

"The guy would freak."

"What the hell," Marty said. "He'd literally go through the ceiling!"

"Ha, he would," Ted agreed.

"Can you imagine it?"

We all stared at each other, and then I said, "I think we ought to do it."

"I'm all for it," Marty said.

"I guess I'm in," Ted said. "But we have to make sure we don't get caught."

"We won't get caught."

"I can't afford to be in any more trouble. The principal already told me I was on thin ice."

"I promise we won't get caught."

"How are we going to get into his room?"

"We'll try the door. If it's locked, we can get in through one of the side windows."

"What if the windows are locked?"

"We'll break the glass," Marty said. "Nothing to it."

"That's illegal, isn't it?"

"Only if you get caught," Marty said. "And I told you, we won't get caught."

"We need to smoke another joint first," Ted said.

"That's fine with me," Marty said.

"Roll a fat one," I said. "I need to be good and high before we do this."

Marty rolled the joint, and by the time we were done with it, it was around ten o'clock. We walked up to the school from the lower fields, and went to the main building. Mr. Kerrigan's classroom was on the first floor. We tried to open the door in the hallway, but it was locked. So we went outside to the windows. The windows were all latched shut, so we looked for something to break the glass. Marty found a rock about the size of a softball, and he walked up to the window. "Do you guys see anyone around?"

We all looked. "I don't see anyone," I said.

"Me either," Ted said.

"Then here goes nothing," Marty said, and he hit the glass with the rock. The glass cracked, but there was no hole. He needed to hit it harder. So he smacked it a second time, and this time the rock broke a wide hole in the glass. The hole was large enough to reach a hand through, so Marty stuck in his hand and reached for the latch. He undid the window and then pushed it open. "Nothing to it," he said.

We all looked around again. It was dark, but no one seemed to be watching. "The coast is clear," Ted said.

"I'll go in first," Marty said, and he climbed in through the open window. Then Ted and I came into the room, following Marty.

So we were in! And now we were laughing our heads off, looking at the flag. We were then standing atop the rickety chairs to reach it. We undid the flag from the wall hooks, and continued to laugh. "Dude, Kerrigan is going to have a heart attack."

"Hurry up. We need to get out of here."

"What I wouldn't give to see the look on his face when he first comes to class Monday morning."

"No kidding," Marty said.

"What do you think he'll do?"

"He'll probably call the cops."

We all laughed. Then we climbed out of the room and took off. I was holding the flag; it was folded and under my arm. "You ought to stuff that thing under your jacket," Ted said. "Just in case."

"Good idea," I said. I crammed the flag into my coat. I then made sure none of it was showing. It made me look sort of fat, but it was hidden.

"So where are we going?" Marty asked.

"I'm hungry," Ted said.

"I'm starving," I said.

"Anyone have any money?"

Ted and I shook our heads. We didn't have a dime. All we had was an American flag and a plastic baggie full of weed. And matches and cigarette papers.

"My parents went out to a party tonight, and they won't be home until late," Ted said. "They probably won't be home until after midnight. We can go to my house. My sister will probably be home, but she's cool. She won't bother us, and there's plenty to eat in the kitchen."

MARCHING HOME

When Johnny comes marching home again,
Hurrah! Hurrah!
There won't be much of a welcome then,
Hurrah! Hurrah!
The men will jeer and the boys will boo.
The girls will make them feel like fools.
And we'll turn our backs
When Johnny comes marching home.
The old church bell will toll in pain,
Hurrah! Hurrah!
The storm clouds will gather and rain,
Hurrah! Hurrah!
Should be cheering, but all we've won
Is blood on the hands of our sons.
And we'll turn our backs
When Johnny comes marching home.

53

Bombing enough for World War III,
Hurrah! Hurrah!
Napalm afire in the trees,
Hurrah! Hurrah!
The thorny wreath is ready now.
Place it on their murdering brows.
And we'll turn our backs
When Johnny comes marching home.
Let love and friendship bite the dust,
Hurrah, hurrah!
We acted as we thought we must,
Hurrah, hurrah!
And now it's clear that we were wrong.
Let's sing loud this pitiful song.
Yes we turned our backs
When Johnny came marching home.

OFFICER OBIE

We were getting close to Ted's street when the police car pulled up to the curb with his lights whirling. The cop stopped and rolled down his window, telling us to stop. Turning off the lights, he threw open his door and stepped out of the car. He walked up to the three of us, and my heart was beating up into my mouth. I was sure we were busted. For the flag. For the weed. For everything!

"Evening, boys," the cop said.

"Good evening, officer," we all replied in unison.

"Where you boys headed?"

"We're going to Ted's house," I said.

"Who's Ted?"

"I am," Ted said.

"Staying out of trouble tonight?"

"Yes sir," Ted said.

"Where are you boys coming from?"

"We were just walking around," I said. "We weren't going anywhere in particular. Now we're on our way to Ted's house."

"Yes, you told me that."

"Yes sir."

"Do you know what time it is?"

"No sir," Ted said.

"It's ten-thirty."

"If you say so, sir."

"Do you know what time curfew is in this town? It's ten o'clock. How old are you boys?"

"We're sixteen."

"Do you parents know where you are?"

"Yes, they do."

The cop rubbed his chin, and then he finally smiled. "How about if I give you kids a ride home?"

"That would be good," I said.

"Climb in," the officer said as he walked back to the patrol car. "You boys shouldn't be out this late. Nothing good ever happens late at night."

So the friendly cop took us to Ted's driveway, and we all climbed out of his car and said thanks. "My pleasure," he said. He then drove off into the night, and we walked into the house. Like Ted said, his parents were gone. His sister wasn't home either. We had the house to ourselves.

"I thought we were sunk," Marty said.

"I thought we were toast," I said.

"He was a pretty nice guy for a cop," Ted said. "Cops are usually such jerks."

"Did you know there was a ten o'clock curfew?"

"Never heard of it," I said.

"What's to eat?" Marty asked.

"Yeah," I said. "I'm starving my butt off."

We then proceeded to eat everything we could get our hands on. When I got home from Ted's house, it was midnight. My mom and dad were both asleep, and so was my brother. I went to my room and took off my coat, dumping the wadded-up flag on my bed. I wasn't sure what I was going to do with the thing. What do you do with a stolen American flag?

I decided to stuff the flag under my bed. Then I took off my clothes and climbed into my covers, and within minutes I was sound asleep.

Well, the next morning, Mr. Kerrigan threw a fit. He was out of his mind, and he wanted his flag back. And by God, he was going to get it back. He didn't waste any time. He got a list of all the students' parents, and he sent out a form letter to each of them that described the theft and asked each parent to be on the lookout for the flag. He was positive that one of us kids was responsible, and he was hopeful that the flag would turn up. My parents got one of these letters, and they asked me if I had any idea who the thief was. Of course, I said no. "If you should hear anything, let us know," my dad said. "Such a shame, such a shame."

I never did do anything with the flag. It remained hidden under my bed for weeks. It was safe and sound until the fateful afternoon that Mom decided to clean my room. My room was always a mess, and she was cleaning it as a favor for me while I was at school. She wanted to surprise me. Well, the woman surprised me all right! That was when she found the flag, and when I came home from school, she had the darn thing spread on our dining room table like a tablecloth. She wanted me to explain myself. "What is this?" she asked. "Is this Mr. Kerrigan's flag? Is that what this is? Tell me the truth."

"It is a flag," I said.

"What was it doing under your bed?"

"Why were you looking under my bed?" I asked.

"I was cleaning your room. I was trying to be nice. I was going to surprise you."

"Oh," I said.

"So is this the flag?"

Now I had to decide what to do. Would I make up a story to explain the flag under my bed, or would I tell the truth? Would I tell Mom that I was the thief? Would I tell her about Marty and Ted? What could I say? I was screwed! I didn't think anyone would ever find the flag, so I had no prepared lie to tell.

"It's the flag," I said quietly. I didn't see any way out of this mess without fessing up.

"You're the thief?"

"I am," I said.

"Good God, Huey."

"I'm sorry."

Then Mom asked me what all parents ask their kids at times like these. "What were you thinking?" she said.

"I guess I wasn't."

"We'll have to tell you father about this," Mom said in a stern voice. "He'll know what to do. And we'll have to return the flag to Mr. Kerrigan."

When Mom told Dad about the flag, the old man was furious. I thought he was going to hit me, but he didn't. Instead he calmed down and tried to come up with a plan. As far as anyone knew, I had taken the flag myself. I didn't get Marty or Ted involved. Dad finally decided that I would return the flag to Mr. Kerrigan. He said I could do it after school so as not to interrupt the class. "And you better explain to him how sorry you are," he said. "No telling what the guy is going to do about it. You could be suspended or expelled. He might even turn you in to the police. There's no telling. You're going to be at his mercy. You'd better have one hell of a good apology in your pocket."

Jesus, I was in trouble. Who knew what Mr. Kerrigan would do? I was in for it!

The next day, I brought the flag to school in a paper bag, and I put it in my locker. When my last class was over, I got the bag out of the locker and took it to Mr. Kerrigan's class. He was at his desk, talking to a couple students. I waited for them to be done with their conversation, and when the students left, I walked up and handed Mr. Kerrigan the bag.

"What's this?" he asked. He looked inside the bag, and he exclaimed, "My flag! You've found my flag."

"Yes sir," I said.

"Where did you find it?"

"Actually, my mother found it."

"Where did she find it?"

"Under my bed, sir."

"Under your bed?"

"I'm the one who took it," I said meekly. I felt like such an idiot, and Mr. Kerrigan was no longer smiling.

"You?" he said.

"I'm sorry."

"You're sorry?"

"Yes sir. Very sorry."

"Why?" Mr. Kerrigan asked. "I don't get it. Why would you do such a thing?"

"I don't know."

"Did I do something to upset you?"

"It wasn't that."

"Then what?" Mr. Kerrigan asked.

"I don't know," I said.

We stared at each other for a moment, and then Mr. Kerrigan took the flag out of the bag. He looked it over to be sure it wasn't damaged. Then he looked at me again. He didn't seem very angry, which surprised me. "I'm trying to understand," he said.

"Sir?"

"I must have done something to upset you."

"Not really."

"Listen," he said to me, and he leaned back in his chair. He clasped his hands behind his crewcut head. "I know I can seem like kind of slave driver in class. But I'm really not as bad as I pretend to be. I'm a teacher, son. I became a teacher for a reason. I care a great deal about the kids in my classes. I would never have become a teacher if I didn't care about you kids. Am I making any sense to you?"

"Yes," I said, although I didn't really understand where he was going with this.

"You're one of my students."

"Yes sir."

"You're important to me. I really want to understand why you took the flag. I want to understand why. You had to know that it would upset me. You knew that, right?"

"I suppose I did."

"So you wanted to upset me?"

"Maybe I did," I said.

"But why?"

Now this was weird. I really hadn't expected Mr. Kerrigan to behave like this at all. I thought the guy would be furious and grab my ear, dragging me to see the principal. I thought he was going to throw the book at me, but instead he just wanted to understand. It was a side of Mr. Kerrigan that I hadn't even known existed. He actually seemed to like me, and he really did want to know why I stole his flag. Then the words spilled from my lips, almost involuntarily. "I don't want to go to the war," I said.

"You what?"

"I don't want to go to Vietnam."

"No one *wants* to go."

"I mean, the war seems wrong. In class, you always make the war seem right. I don't agree with you. I feel like you don't respect those of us who disagree with you."

"Ah," Mr. Kerrigan said.

"Aren't you mad at me?"

"I'm not mad at you," Mr. Kerrigan said thoughtfully. He was still leaning back with his hands clasped behind his head. Then he unclasped his hands and leaned forward. "Listen," he said. "I feel bad about this."

"Sir?" I said.

"If I explain myself, will you listen to me?"

"Of course," I said.

Mr. Kerrigan stared at me for a moment. Then he asked, "What does America mean to you?"

"I'm not sure."

"It means freedom, right? Freedom to live our lives as we please. Freedom to practice our own religions. Freedom to have our own opinions. Isn't that right?"

"Yes," I said.

"We hold our freedoms dear?"

"Yes," I said again.

Then Mr. Kerrigan talked more. I mean, he spoke to me for well over an hour. The man was speaking right from his heart. He spoke of history and facts. It became clear that I knew next to nothing and that this man knew *a lot*. He wasn't just some dipshit high school teacher there to make our lives miserable. The man cared about what he was saying, and he'd put a lot of thought into his opinions. He wasn't condescending. He didn't make me feel small or stupid. Instead he made me feel honored to have the opportunity to listen to all he was saying. And it made so much sense at the time. Yes, we lived in the greatest country on the planet. We were lucky as hell. And we had an undeniable obligation to be more than just lucky inhabitants. We were all obligated to believe in the system, for it was this system that, despite all its flaws, made our freedom possible. And if the elected powers that be decided it made sense for us to go out in harm's way to protect our way of life, then by God, that's what we owed each other. Sure, it was okay to voice your opinion, but you owed your friends, neighbors, and countrymen your ultimate loyalty. For we were all in this game together. We were, no matter how different, all as one. And the world had to know we were united. They had to be aware of the fact that we were not relinquishing our freedoms under any circumstances. And we would put our lives on the line to keep them. "We are you, and you are us," Mr. Kerrigan said. "It is this love and respect that keeps us together. It is our undying love of our freedom and respect for each other that makes us unbeatable. It is this gift from God that makes us all Americans."

Well, I have to be honest. The man froze me in my tracks, and I was not intellectually equipped to argue with any of his words. Now I suddenly felt like getting a haircut. I felt like clicking my heels and saluting Mr. Kerrigan's flag and reciting the Pledge of Allegiance. It was amazing. The man was a true inspiration.

It wasn't until several days after I met with Mr. Kerrigan that I came to my senses. It was nice of the guy to let me off the hook for stealing his flag. I appreciated that. But he was wrong about Vietnam. The war *was* bullshit, and blind patriotism was foolishness.

Did I ever go to Vietnam? The answer is no. I graduated from high school in 1973. The war ended one year before I came of age. Would I really have moved to Canada? I guess we'll never know.

DO IT

So how old are you? Do you know who Jerry Rubin was? In his temper tantrum 1970 book *Do It*, he states, "The history books will see us – the freaks and not the straights – as the heroes of the 1970's. We know that because we are going to write the history books."

I never did read this crazy book when it first came out. I was aware of it, but I didn't read it. In 1970 I was fifteen years old, and I was more concerned with saving money to buy a car than I was with tearing apart an entire country. True, I was against the war. And I was growing my hair long, smoking marijuana, and listening to rock 'n' roll. But no, Jerry, the freaks did not write the history books. You were wrong about that. You were wrong about a lot of things.

As I read this book now, I have the benefit of seeing how things turned out. So it isn't altogether fair for me to harp on how far off Jerry's predictions were. However, it is fair to be critical. Do you want to know what this book reminded me of? The whole time I read it, I pictured a three-year-old child, out of control and throwing a temper tantrum. The child is saying, "I'm not getting my way, so I'm going to throw a fit and break everything in sight, and then hold my breath until I turn blue." I was cognizant during the 1970s, so don't tell me that I just don't understand— that I had to be there. I *was* there. And the childish lunacy called for in this book is just that. It is a temper tantrum. The truth is that there were a lot of good people in the sixties with a lot of great ideas, and they did influence this country for the better. But after reading this book now, I can say that Jerry Rubin wasn't one of them.

Don't get me wrong. The guy did have a plan. A few of his written objectives state explicitly that "police stations will blow up. There will be no more jails, courts, or police. There will be no such crime as stealing, because everything will be free. The Pentagon will be replaced by an LSD experimental farm." Okay, I know it's hard to know when the guy was being serious or when he was just trying to make us laugh. But if he was just trying to make us laugh, why didn't he tell us so? I think he really believed his crap, the same way the Ku Klux Klan believed they were good for America, fighting the righteous fight. When I read this book, I think that Jerry did more harm to the sixties movement than he did to help it make the changes that this country needed.

One thing this book has which I found interesting are all of its drawings and pictures. They are amusing, and they brought back some memories. I laughed when I saw all the people without clothes. I'm curious. Did Simon and Schuster make them sign releases? All the nude photos of people in the book also made me realize something I already knew—that human beings look a lot better when they're wearing clothing than they do when they're naked. I mean, animals look fine sans clothing, but us people? I don't think so. Not for the most part. Seriously, keep your clothes on Becky, or Sally, or Fred, or whatever your name is. I know you think that everyone is beautiful, but in reality, some stuff is best covered up. Most of us without our clothes haven't got much to brag about.

Am I glad I read this book now all these years after it was published? In a way I am, but in another way, it is kind of a letdown. I think my temper tantrum analogy is totally fitting, and do you know what became of Jerry once the tantrum was over? He became a multimillionaire stockbroker. He lived like a king in a penthouse on Wilshire Boulevard in Los Angeles. So much for all the materialistic pigs! So much for the hippies taking over! Jerry Rubin died when he was crossing the street. He was hit by a car and died a week or so later. Tom Hayden said, "He was a great life force, full of spunk, courage and wit." So I guess that's one way of putting it. But if you want the truth, read *Do It* and decide for yourself.

BURIED IN DETROIT

"The man who will use his skill and constructive imagination to see how much he can give for a dollar, instead of how little he can give for a dollar, is bound to succeed."

—Henry Ford

MILTON'S EMPIRE

They had no real nutritional value to speak of. They were bad for your teeth. They were cheap. In the scope of things, they were completely unnecessary, yet they were ubiquitous. It was as easy as pie to ask for one. They had a name that was easy to pronounce, and their wrappers were iconic. Archie Anderson was an employee at the factory where they were made. He had a wife and three children, and they lived in town along with all the other factory workers. The name of the town? It was Hershey, Pennsylvania. The year was 1937, and the month was April. All hell was about to break loose.

They wanted Archie to join them. They tried to wear him down, but he wouldn't commit to their dubious cause. And why should he? Life was good in Hershey. He had lots of work to keep him busy and fed during the Great Depression, which was more than one could say for the rest of the country. True, it wasn't easy work, and the hours were long. At times, it could reach over a hundred degrees in the factory, and many of the bosses could be assholes. But it beat the heck out of living in a tent, wearing rags, and standing in bread lines. Who cared if Milton lived like a king in conspicuous splendor and affluence on the top of the hill? The man deserved it, didn't he? Sure, he could be overbearing. Was he a pain in the rear? Was he arrogant? Was he opinionated to the point of stupidity? Yes, maybe he was all those things, but he provided jobs and a fine place to live. Quality of life. Why throw the baby out with the bathwater?

Harold came by early that morning. Harold Fox was Archie's good friend. Archie was up, eating breakfast with his wife. He had been reading the paper, digesting all the news that was fit to print, so Archie knew what was going on in the rest of the country. Citizens were still recovering from that awful Ohio River flood. Nearly four hundred people had died, and a million others were homeless. It was tragic and hard to imagine, but it made Archie's bad working conditions at the Hershey factory seem insignificant by comparison. And those poor people in Texas! A natural gas explosion at the New London School had killed three hundred students and teachers. The paper said it happened just like that, in one blast. All those lives lost! And now here was Harold, who had let himself in through the front door. He was complaining out loud again that the temperature inside the factory was too high, that the hours they were working were too long, that the pay was too low, and that Milton was too much a part of their lives. Harold was a fool, or so Archie thought. A good friend, but a fool. They were all fools, really. Didn't these idiots ever read the paper? Didn't they know how good they had it?

"Are you one of us?" Harold asked. He grabbed a strip of bacon from the table and munched on it.

"I'm me," Archie said.

"We're going to get our way."

"Maybe you will, and maybe you won't."

"Oh, we will."

"But at what cost?"

"Cost?"

"You're just trading one form of oppression for another."

"I'd hardly call a union oppressive."

Archie thought for a moment. Then he said, "I don't like being told what to do."

"Milton has been telling you what to do for years, hasn't he? Don't you mind that?"

"I can quit any time."

"And find a job in another factory?"

Archie stared at his friend for a moment. Then he said, "That is precisely my point, my friend."

"You're not making any sense."

"I'm making sense for me."

Harold stared at his friend and said, "Well, come join us if you change your mind."

"I'll never change my mind."

"Never say never."

Harold grabbed another strip of bacon and poked it into his mouth. He patted Archie on the back, and Archie smiled at him. "I know your heart is in the right place," Archie said. "It's just not for me. So good luck."

"I love you, pal."

"I know you do," Archie said. "I love you too. We're just going to have to agree to disagree."

Then Harold went off to the factory, and Archie stayed home with his wife. Archie resumed reading the paper and eating, and a couple hours after he was done, he was paid a visit by Zeke Allen and two of Zeke's friends. Zeke was holding a hammer in his hand, and his friends were holding baseball bats. This was not a good sign, but Harold let them into his house. The men wanted to talk to him. They wanted him to join them. "Grab whatever you can," Zeke said. "We're going to chase those bastards out of our factory once and for all."

"And if they refuse to leave?" Archie asked.

"Then we'll make them leave," Zeke said, and he pounded his hammer into the palm of his hand to show that he and his friends meant business. "We'll work them over good."

"Jesus," Archie said.

"Enough is enough."

"We want to work," one of Zeke's friends said.

"I want to work too," Archie said. "But waging war on your own friends?"

"Friends? Listen, Archie, you're either with us or you're against us," Zeke said.

"This is crazy."

"Is it? Do you want to work or not?"

"Yes, I want to work."

"They don't have a chance," Zeke said.

"We've got the dairy farmers with us," Zeke's friend said. "They're ready to fight."

"The farmers?"

"This afternoon," Zeke said. Again he was pounding his hammer into the palm of his hand. "Fur is going to fly. We're going to bust those fuckers up good." Zeke and his friends then turned and walked out of Archie's house. They didn't bother to say good-bye.

Now Archie was worried. He understood both sides of the issue, but he still couldn't take either side. But what could he do? He could help Harold. He could get Harold out of the factory before he got hurt. Archie knew that, adding in all the dairy farmers, the strikers at the factory would be completely outnumbered. They wouldn't stand a chance. And their eviction from the factory would be violent and ugly, and Harold could be seriously injured. True, Harold was asking for it. But Archie didn't think his good friend Harold really believed it would all come down to this. Baseball bats and hammers, and God knew what other weapons were now in the hands of angry and frustrated men. Archie needed to warn Harold. He needed to get Harold out of the factory. He needed to bring his friend home to his wife and children where he belonged.

So Archie went to the factory that morning. There were men carrying signs and chanting union slogans. He made his way through the picket lines and into the building. He searched for his friend, and he finally found him sitting on the floor with a group of other striking employees. They were playing cards. He made eye contact with Harold, and Harold stood up. "Excuse me gents," he said. Then he walked to Archie, smiling. "So you decided to join us?"

"No," Archie said. "I've come to take you home."

"Take me home?"

"You've got to get out of here."

"We've been over this," Harold said.

"I mean, seriously. This whole thing is about to get ugly."

"Ugly?"

"Come with me, please."

"Fat chance of that," Harold said. He was smiling again. He was glad that his friend cared about him, but there was no way he would leave. "Come on and sit down with us," he said to Archie. "Play a few hands. Meet my new friends."

"I'm not kidding," Archie said.

"Neither am I," Harold said.

Then there was a loud ruckus outside. A man shouted the final ultimatum: "Either the factory opens and we all go back to work, or you all get the living shit kicked out of you."

The strike leader replied, "We're not going anywhere until Milton meets our demands. The ball is in Milton's court. He knows what he has to do."

Then Archie heard the man shout to the others, "Get 'em!" There was a lot of yelling. It sounded awful. Then the factory doors were opened wide, and the angry men came pouring in. They were carrying all kinds of crazy weapons to beat the strikers with. And suddenly it was mayhem. Weapons were flailing, and clenched fists were swinging. Men were groaning and shouting, some of them crying out in pain. It was so ugly. It was even uglier than Archie had imagined. Then a rake came down on top of Harold's head, and he fell to the floor. Blood was gushing from the wound in Harold's scalp, but Archie couldn't look at him for long. He was now defending himself. Men were getting hit, and there was shouting. Blood was everywhere. Some men fell to the floor like Harold, and others stomped and kicked them while they were down. Then Archie was hit in the mouth with a baseball bat, and he could feel the result. His teeth were broken to bits. Then something whacked him on the back of the head, and he fell to the floor, unconscious. When he came to, the fight was finally over. Archie had three broken ribs, a fractured wrist, a broken nose, broken teeth, and a cut on his lip that would require twelve stitches. And for what? For the price of a few chocolate bars?

The next day, in Tulsa, Oklahoma, a housewife was buying a cart of groceries. A pimply-faced kid was bagging her goods, and as the cashier punched in the price of the last item, the woman grabbed a Hershey bar and handed it to him. "Add this to the total," she said. He rang the price of the Hershey bar up, and handed it back to her.

There was no nutritional value. It was bad for the teeth. Totally unnecessary. But as far as this shopper in Tulsa was concerned, it was worth a few extra cents and every drop of blood that had been spilled to make it so. Or maybe she didn't know about the blood. I suppose that's possible.

Alfalfa for the Rabbits

"Advertising is the art of convincing people to spend money they don't have on something they don't need."

—Will Rogers

"Advertising is the very essence of democracy."

—Anton Chekhov

"It is the advertiser who provides the paper for the subscriber. It is not to be disputed, that the publisher of a newspaper in this country, without a very exhaustive advertising support, would receive less reward for his labor than the humblest mechanic."

—Alexander Hamilton

Where the Ads Take Aim

The year was 1954. It was not exactly an earth-shattering year, but it was an interesting year nonetheless. Eisenhower was our president then, and Dick Nixon was his sidekick. This was the year that "under God" was added to the Pledge of Allegiance. It was also this during this year that Eisenhower warned against US involvement in Vietnam. It was a bad idea, he said. We should have listened to him. It was also this year when that raving idiot Joseph McCarthy was finally being put in his place. He had picked on the military. This was a bad idea. This was also the year that the TV dinner was introduced to the public, and the year that the first Burger King opened. Yum! Bon appetit, America! Lots of crappy food for you and me! And the wedding bells were ringing in 1954. Marilyn Monroe tied the knot with good old Joe DiMaggio. Of course, they divorced nine months later, so it wasn't much of a marriage. This was also the year before I was born. I was born in 1955, the year that Marilyn was off and running with Arthur Miller. They would marry the following year, in '56.

Welcome to the advertising agency of Haskell, Jones, and Able. You could say that 1954 was a good year for them. They were one of the top agencies on Madison Avenue, and clients were rushing to their front doors in droves. There was a meeting going on. In charge of this brainstorming session was top adman and senior partner Andrew Jones. Also present were eight of his top young soldiers. They were dressed in suits and ties, puffing away on Chesterfields and Lucky Strikes. Sandra Flowers was in the room with them, taking notes in shorthand. Andrew called the meeting to order, and Sandra stood and closed the conference room door. "Is everyone present?" Andrew asked, and Sandra took a count of noses, nodding her head.

"We're all here," she said.

"Good, good, let's get the show on the road. Who wants to start? I'm ready. I'm all ears. Who wants the ball?"

"I'll start," Jeffrey Atkins said.

"Good, good, that's what I like—someone who isn't afraid to jump into the game. Have at it, kid. Let's hear what you've got."

Everyone watched Jeffrey as he began to talk. He cleared his throat and said, "The way I see this campaign is that we're going to have to generate lots of sex appeal. I'm not talking about making the actual product sexy; I'm talking about making the people who buy the product sexy. Buy this product and guess what? You're Marilyn Monroe. You're Paul Newman. You're the sexiest son of a gun in town. You look terrific, and you smell like heaven. Everyone wants to be close to you, and everyone wants your autograph. You're irresistible. You're truly one of a kind. You make Cleopatra, the darling of the Nile, look like a worn-out babushka. You make Charles Atlas look like a ninety-eight-pound weakling. You make the opposite sex tremble with desire. On odd days, you drive a red Corvette; and on even days, you drive your silver Porsche Speedster. On Sundays you get your hair trimmed. When you strike a match and light a smoke, your fans all swoon. When you bend over to tie your shoes, the clouds in the heavens part and the blazing ball of sun ignites everything in sight. Girls write poetry about you, and all the boys daydream about kissing you. Your breath smells like sweet red roses, and your hair flows like liquid gold. Everyone says you should be in the movies. Yes, your footprints belong at the Chinese Theater. And artists want to paint your portrait, and the songwriters want to sing about you. You appeal to everyone on the planet Earth. Even Albert Einstein thinks you're out of this world."

Jeffrey stopped talking, and the group was still looking at him. It was obvious that he knew what he was doing. "Good, good," Andrew said. He clapped his hands to applaud, and then he moved on to Edward Jasper, who was seated to the right of Jeffrey. "Now it's your turn, Edward," Andrew said. "Let's hear what you've got. Wow us, man."

Edward wasn't one to mince any words. He started off with a profane bang. "You're the most powerful fucker the world has ever seen," he said. "You can chop down fucking mountains. You can twist the arms of millionaire fucks. Your US Senator drops everything when you call him on the phone. People do what you say because they're afraid of you, and you do tell them what to do. You're not afraid to throw your weight around. You never have to say anything twice, because people listen to everything you have to say. You demand attention. Everyone you deal with knows you have the power to make their lives either astounding or miserable, and they choose wisely. You're happy to know that you can help people out, but you don't do it very often. You don't want others to have the wrong idea—that your power is to be readily shared. It's yours to dole out to them as you see fit, and you're rightfully stingy. Everyone wishes they were your best friend."

"Good, good, yes!" Andrew exclaimed. "I love what you've done here. So now we have sexy and powerful. How about you, Terry?" Terry Blackstone was seated next to Edward, and it was now his turn to talk.

"I say you're going to get rich," Terry said. "Rich beyond your wildest dreams. Howard Hughes rich. Getty rich. Diamond-studded gold Rolls Royce rich. Yes, you live in Malibu, and you have your own private beach that you sometimes share with your movie star friends. You have a different luxury car for *each* day of the week, and you have closets full of clothes that are bigger than most people's houses. You have a private jet and full-time pilot, and if you want to go shopping in London, or have dinner in Paris, or swim in Tahiti, you simply climb aboard your jet—no problem. You collect art: not art by second-rate artists, but the sort of art you find described in art history books. Your living room is like the Louvre, and your circular staircase is like the Guggenheim. You own real estate all over the world, and you have a full-time staff devoted to keeping the properties up. You have a full-time cooking staff, a butler, and a team of maids. You have a stable filled with million-dollar race horses, and in your spare time, with your spare change, you go after the Triple Crown. You invite the world's most famous characters to your house, and they stay in guest cottages, swim in your Olympic-sized pool, and play chess with your solid gold chess pieces. All the planet's most talented and renowned musicians of all time come to perform at your home, providing background music for your cocktail parties. When they're done playing, they mingle with your famous friends and talk about the stock market."

"Ah, yes!" Andrew exclaimed. "Rich is very good. Rich is perfect. Good, good; yes, that's very good." Then Andrew moved on to Arnie Weathers. Arnie was sitting next to Terry. "How about you, Arnie? What wonderful magic trick do you have up your sleeve?"

"I say you're going to be an athlete," Arnie said. "But not just any old athlete. You'll be the real deal. You'll be a gold-medal athlete. A champion! Today's Jim Thorpe. There's no sport you can't master. Basketball, baseball, tennis, and football—you name it. Everyone wants you on their team, and you'll be breaking records right and left. Your picture will be on cereal boxes. You'll make a fortune doing TV commercials, and your name will become a household word. Fans will go crazy every time you hit a homer, score a touchdown, serve up an ace, or win another race. Parents will raise their children to be just like you. Kids will copy your hairstyle and talk like you, walk like you, eat like you, and drink the exact same sodas as you.

You will be a modern Heracles—brilliant, able, strong, and invincible. No one can beat you."

"Good, good, I love it," Andrew said, clapping his hands. He really seemed to like this one. But then he moved on. It was time to call on Fred. "Your turn, Fred," he said. "What do you see?"

"I see raw intelligence," Fred said. "I see someone who is extraordinarily smart—as in Mensa smart. Top 2 percent of the population, and as smart as a whip. Not necessarily a genius, nor an eccentric, but smarter than everyone else. You're smart enough to be a successful doctor or a lawyer, or a scientist. Not in a weird way, but you're looked up to by all your friends and associates. They know you have the answers. They know you can figure things out. You make good decisions. You are a whiz at solving even the most difficult sorts of problems. You can put a complicated jigsaw puzzle together in no time. Child's play. In fact, most of the problems that come your way are so easy to solve that it sometimes surprises even you. And you like being bright. You like it when people come to you with their problems, asking for advice, picking your brain. It's a compliment of the highest order. You are important. You are invaluable. You are needed."

"Smart, yes; it's good to be smart. Good, good, I like it. Not genius-weird smart. Just smart. Now let's move on." He looked at Frank, who was next. "Your turn to swing the bat, Frank. What do you have for us?

"Good looks," Frank said. "If you are a man, you will be made handsome, and if you are a woman, you will be made beautiful. Simple as that. Nothing complicated about it. Never mind sexy or powerful or rich or athletic or smart. All you need in this world are some simple, old-fashioned, all-American good looks. And you shall have them, instantaneously. And just look at you! Your face will be thumbtacked on boys' and girls' bedroom walls. You'll be on glossy magazine covers and illuminated billboards. There won't be a person in this country who doesn't recognize your amazing smiling face, and corporations will name colognes and perfumes after you. You might even have your own clothing line. Or maybe you'll become a spokesperson. For what? For automobiles, for department stores, for cosmetics, for the latest medications, and for restaurants. I say that the sky is the limit for the beautiful person, and everyone will want to stand next to you. I do mean everyone. At your side, they'll all want to associate."

"Hallelujah!" Andrew exclaimed. "Yes, you have something there. Who doesn't want to be beautiful? Who doesn't want to be on a billboard?" He was really getting excited now, and he moved on to the next young man. His name was Delbert O'Toole. "It's your turn Delbert. What great dish are you bringing to the table for us to devour?"

"Youth," Delbert said. "Nothing more, and nothing less. You will be young. Who in America doesn't want to be young? Heck, even the young want to be young. Everyone wants to be young. Forget all those aches and pains. No wrinkles or age spots. No arthritis, dementia, or annoying forgetfulness. A sparkling fountain of youth is what I'm talking about. Just think of it! Your bright eyes will be clear and full of life, and your thoughts will be fresh and lucid. The world will seem new, wondrous, and exciting. You won't have the heavy regrets of a lifetime weighing you down. You'll be as light as a feather, and the wind will carry you into the clouds among castles and kings. You'll believe in old fairy tales and new urban legends. You'll be as naive, happy, and free-spirited as a bird in flight. The world will seem as large as a universe, and the universe will be a total mystery. You'll believe in God, Santa Claus, and the Easter Bunny, and you'll look forward to getting your adult teeth. A convertible Mustang will be the greatest and most amazing thing on earth, and your driver's license will be the ticket to the rest of your life. Oh, to be young. To be young now and forever!"

"Jesus, yes!" Andrew exclaimed. "Good, good, you've hit the nail right on the head." He then looked at Paul, who was next. "How about you, Paul. What do you see?"

Paul adjusted his weight in his chair, and then he spoke. He said, "All of these things are fine, but what does every man and woman long for, really? Looks? Wealth? Youth? I don't think so. I believe that what we all long for is family. But not just any family. A good family. A loving family, and a healthy family. We long for the perfect mom, dad, children, dog, and cat, in the perfect house, in the perfect neighborhood, in the perfect city, with sunny days and starlit nights. Charming little houses with clean cars in the driveways, green front lawns, and friendly neighbors. You have a handsome husband who is kind, considerate and hardworking, and a wife who is always loving and supportive. Maybe the wife works too. Why not? So long as everyone is happy and the bills are being paid. So long as the children are all behaving themselves. You'll be proud of your spouse and kids. Especially the kids. They'll get good grades. They'll be accepted to Ivy League colleges, and they'll graduate with highest honors. They'll meet nice boys and girls, fall in love, get good jobs, have a litter of children, and then you'll be the happiest grandparent on earth."

"Yes," Andrew said. "Who doesn't want a happy family? We all want that. And our product will give it to them, along with everything else we've been discussing here this morning. It'll be the perfect campaign. Who wouldn't want to buy our product? But I do have a question. What is our client selling? That's sort of weird, isn't it? I forgot what the product is. Ha, it's on the tip of my tongue. It's a—damn, what the hell is it?"

"A car?" Frank asked.

"No, no," Andrew said.

"Is it a soap?"

"I thought it was a lipstick."

"No, no, it's clothing."

"Clothing?"

"No, it isn't clothing either."

The group all sat there, staring at each other for a minute and thinking. No one could remember. Then they suddenly broke out laughing.

DISCOVERIES

Maybe you're wondering what I did in high school besides smoking weed, worrying about the war, and stealing a flag from a civics teacher. In fact, I was quite the artist. I spent most of my free time drawing and painting, and I was pretty good at what I was doing. I wasn't great, but I was pretty good. Of course, I thought I was better than I actually was. I soon had dreams of becoming a great and famous artist like my heroes, Salvador Dali and M. C. Escher. I adored those two men and was crazy about their work. I spent hours in my bedroom trying to measure up to them. I felt as if we were close pals and comrades, although obviously neither of these men had the slightest idea who I was. It was the heady stuff of pimply-faced adolescence—big dreams, and bigger plans! When it came time for me to go to college, I went to UC Berkeley with the intention of studying art and learning how to be great. I would be a great artist! That's what I was going to be.

The business world? It didn't even cross my mind. It was about as far away from me as the little once-was-a-planet Pluto. Business majors were a joke, and advertising was their language: lies, lies, and more lies, all told with one goal in mind. And what was the goal? To get rich as soon as possible and buy all the junk of the quote-unquote successful American idiot: fancy cars, golf club memberships, vacations to the Caribbean, diamond and gold jewelry, big ostentatious homes, and artwork to hang on their walls. Who cared what the art represented, so long as it appreciated in value like stock in a company. No, none of these things mattered to me when I was a freshman in college. Yes, I was going to be an artist, not a businessman. People were going to write about me and my work and say I was amazing. They were going to say I was deep, talented, intelligent, insightful, and creative. And I could do it. I knew I could. I was young, and anything was possible.

My first year in college was amazing. I was suddenly deep into subjects I didn't even know existed, and I learned that I was smart. I held my own and got good grades. And my art? It was, in my humble opinion, the best of the lot.

It was sometime during my second semester that I came upon Berkeley's architecture school. I remember that one day I wound up in Wurster Hall and saw all the projects the kids were working on. There were models of buildings and cities. There were the most amazing drawings, and they all spoke to me. They said, "This is what you need to be doing! This is the direction you must take!" This was art, but it was art made real, art one could live in, feel, and experience. Real art. Not just a lot of two-dimensional pictures to be hung on some rich guy's walls. It was art as life, living and breathing, rooted to the soil and reaching up for the sun. I immediately met with a counselor and changed my art major to architecture. The door had been thrown open wide, and I marched in.

I immersed myself in it. I read every book on architecture I could get my hands on. Architecture was all I thought about, morning, noon, and night. I learned all about classic Greek and Roman architecture. I learned about Persian Islamic, Byzantine, Gothic, Renaissance, neoclassical, Bauhaus, postmodern, Beaux-Arts, and art deco architecture. Greek and

Roman buildings were my favorites, with postmodern works coming in a close second. I then studied columns, beams, arches, trusses, vectors, moments of inertia, tensile and compressive strengths, and deflections. I buried myself in materials. I learned about bricks, concrete blocks, lumber, glass, steel, wood shingles, aluminum veneers, plastics, and good old portland cement. I became familiar with the works of Frank Lloyd Wright, Le Corbusier, Gaudi, Mies Van der Rohe, Eero Saarinen, Louis Kahn, and Buckminster Fuller. I knew that one day I would join their ranks. One day I would be great! I was sure of this. It was in the cards.

It was during my sophomore year at Berkeley that I met my wife, Rhonda. We are still married to this day. We were the same age when we met, and we married when we were both twenty-two. She was a fellow student in my classical literature class, and as fate would have it, she was seated next to me. I really liked that class a lot, and not just because Rhonda sat beside me. I enjoyed classical books, and I liked writing about them. Rhonda was the most beautiful girl I'd ever seen. Seriously, I think it was love at first sight. Every single feature on her face was perfection, especially her eyes. She had the sort of peepers that drew you into her warm soul and made you feel at home—amazing eyes! When the class was about to conclude, I got up the nerve to ask her out on a date. She said yes, and we went to a movie. I don't remember which movie we saw. All I could think of the entire night was Rhonda and whether I'd have the intestinal fortitude to kiss her when I dropped her off at her dorm.

I had no idea back then of the big change in my life that was about to come. It would be a big change—yes, a very big change. I look back now, and I regret it a little. I regret it, and yet I don't. Sometimes I wonder what my life would now be like if I'd stuck to my guns. Would I be happy, miserable, or proud? Or would I just be leading a depressing Thoreauvian life of quiet desperation?

So what is the change I'm talking about? I'll tell you what happened. I got my first job after graduating from college. It was shortly after I had married Rhonda, and maybe that was part of the cause. Marriage can change a man. I'll describe my first job to you. You might find my job interesting in light of the very high regard I had for myself. I was going to take the world by storm. I was going to be famous, admired, and revered. My first job was at an architectural firm owned by a man named Richard

Smiley. The name of the small but busy firm was Smiley & Associates. Richard had a small office in downtown Santa Ana. I remember I came to work wearing slacks and a tie. I wanted to look my best. I was assigned to a drafting table in a room with three other draftsmen. Our job was to draw up plans and details. We were coffee-drinking drawing machines—nothing more, and nothing less. I was now a drone.

THE POETS

"The scientist has marched in and taken the place of the poet. But one day somebody will find the solution to the problems of the world and remember, it will be a poet, not a scientist."

—Frank Lloyd Wright

BEIJO

Tall and tan and young and lovely,
The Muse who I imagined came walking.
And when she saw me,
Each time she saw me,
She smiled.
Now she walks and I'm reminded
Of summer days when I knew freedom.
It saddens me,
But when she passes,
I smile.
Oh, as I watch her pass by me,
How can I tell her I miss her?
Gone are the days when she loved me.
Now each day as she walks to the sea,
She looks straight ahead, not at me.
Tall and tan and young and lovely,
The Muse who I imagined comes walking,

And when she passes, I smile, but she
Doesn't see. No longer sees me.
No longer sees me.

THE EIGHTIES

My current psychiatrist's name is Janet Williams. We don't spend a lot of time talking about my past. I told her when I first came to see her that I didn't want to dig up old memories, that I wanted to stay in the present. I'm a firm believer in leaving the past in the past, but during my most recent visit with her, we got to talking about the eighties. I don't recall how we got on the subject, but I found myself reminiscing, and I told her about my life back then. I wasn't seeking any resolutions to past dilemmas. I was just rambling on, and the doctor seemed to find the subject interesting. "That was when I made the change," I said. "Everything changed. I made a total U-turn."

"How did things change?" the doctor asked. "I mean, if you don't mind me asking."

"No, I don't mind. That's when I decided I didn't want to be an architect. I didn't want to be an artist. I decided to become a building contractor, a guy who just puts all the parts together in real time—a businessman."

"You didn't like architecture?"

"My priorities changed."

"In what way?"

"I looked at my boss, Richard. I looked at his life. Do you know what kind of car he drove? He drove a little eight-year-old piece of crap Toyota. I mean, seriously, it was a pile of junk. The paint was faded. The upholstery was worn out, and the glove box wouldn't shut. The rear end was dented from an old accident, and a taillight was broken. He never did repair the taillight. It was probably because he couldn't afford it. I felt embarrassed for him, driving around in such a pathetic excuse for a car. Seriously, I don't know how he drove to work each day without just slitting his wrists."

"Maybe cars weren't important to him."

"But it wasn't just his car. It was his clothes. It was like he hadn't purchased any new clothes for years. His shirts were sometimes missing buttons, his pants drooped on him like they had no life left in their fabric. And his shoes? Jesus, his shoes were disgusting. He wore old athletic shoes, and they looked like he'd robbed a homeless man for them. They were worn and terribly filthy. They were the color of shit."

"Oh, my," the doctor said.

"Well, maybe not shit. But you get the idea."

"Yes, I understand."

"And you should've seen this guy's house. Good God, he was an architect, right? You'd expect him to live in a nice house that he'd designed and built, but he lived in a tract house that he seemed to deliberately ignore. By 'ignore' I mean it looked like no one was maintaining the place. The paint was peeling, and the yard was overgrown with weeds. Shingles were missing, and the windows were filthy. He invited everyone in the office over to the place for a Christmas party the first year I worked for him. That's when I saw the house. I just couldn't get over it. It didn't sit right with me. Was this my future? Was this what was in store for me?"

"So you became a contractor?"

"Yes, I did. Often contractors would come to the office to pick up drawings or get clarifications on the projects they were building. That's when I met these guys. What an eye-opener. They were nicely dressed, and they drove expensive new trucks with all the bells and whistles. I was surprised, to say the least. Before I had this job with Richard, I'd always pictured contractors as boorish slobs who cussed a lot and drove around in crappy, dirty trucks. True, there were some guys like that, but most of them were well-groomed and classy men who had what? What did they all have that Richard didn't have? They had money. It was the big secret they kept from me when I was at Berkeley. Architects are poor. Architects are slaves with fancy college degrees. Maybe Richard just wasn't a good example, but he was all I had to go by. So I wanted out. I wanted to be like the contractors I saw. I wanted to be one of them, out in the fresh air, making things happen, putting things together and getting paid a ton of money."

"Sounds like your mind was made up."

"It was. I immediately looked for another job. I found a position working for a developer who built all his own houses. He hired me to do some drawings and to oversee his construction projects. I quit my job with Richard and went to work for this guy. I worked for him for two years, and I learned the ins and outs of the construction business. Then I took my state test, and I got my contractor's license. Once I had the license, I quit working for the developer and went into business. It was good-bye architecture and hello money. I was so sure of myself. I was going to make a fortune."

"And how did it go?"

"At first it went great. I loved what I was doing, and I was making a lot of money. It's funny; I didn't think twice about it. Remember when I wanted to be an artist? Art was my primary passion. I wanted to create, and I wanted to be patted on the back for my creations. Seriously, this meant everything to me. Never did I have any plans to become a businessman, and now here I was, writing and signing contracts, scheduling work, putting out fires, dealing with customers, and shuffling money around, all so I could afford a nice car, nice clothes, and a nice house. I had turned into exactly what I once despised, and I had no idea how it happened. In fact, I didn't even question it. I was too busy. God, was I busy! I was working around the clock."

"How did your wife feel?"

"I bought her a BMW."

"That's all she wanted out of life?"

"Of course not. She's not that shallow. But it was a hell of a good start."

"So when did the drinking become a problem?"

"Ah, the drinking. It took me completely by surprise. In fact, I think it took everyone by surprise. It came out of left field. I don't think I even knew what was happening when it happened."

A GOOD HOSTESS

"No party is complete without cocktails! My friends all have different tastes when it comes to their drink of choice, so I like to maintain a well-stocked bar with different kinds of alcohol to keep everyone happy."

—Khloe Kardashian

My Choice

What could be more American than Alcoholics Anonymous? And who has been more of a true-blue American than its founder and most senior member, Bill W.? Bill is no longer with us, but in 1999, *Time* magazine listed him as one of the most important people of the twentieth century. Bill is considered to be a great human being. His well-known group started up when Bill took a shot at helping out one fellow alcoholic. It was just two men in a room (sort of like Steve Jobs and Steve Wozniak working out of their garage). Today there are over a hundred thousand AA groups and over two million active members. Its manual, a book written by Bill and referred to as the Big Book, is one of the best-selling books of all time, having sold over thirty million copies. Its teachings have become ingrained in our American culture. Today Bill's eight-acre estate in New York is open to the public. It was designated as a national historic landmark in 2012. You'd think the guy cured cancer.

Over the course of my eventful life, I have attended close to a thousand AA meetings. When it comes to AA, I think I know what I'm talking about. If you want the rest of your life to be defined by an affliction, then have at it. But it's not for me. There is much more to life than following twelve steps until the day you die. There is *much* more. I am not a robot, and I have no desire to be programmed as one. As well-intentioned as the Big Book was, I think that's what has become of it. You either follow the twelve holy steps to the letter, or else. Or else what? Or else you drink to excess again. Or else your rotten life becomes miserable and unmanageable. Or else you hurt the people you love. Or else you betray your God, if you even have one. We live in a big, wonderful world full of options, ideals, decisions, and choices. No, I wasn't going to allow one lousy affliction to define me.

I will tell you what I did do. It was very simple, but it worked for me. It wasn't easy. But since when are good things easy?

You're Fat

The early eighties. Wow. It's a wonder I can remember anything at all from those years. But I remember a lot. I remember that Ronald Reagan was our president, of course. I remember how the hostages were set free by Iran right after Reagan was sworn in. I remember John DeLorean and his goofy stainless-steel sports cars—how they were fun to look at, but how no one wanted to buy them. I remember Mario and Donkey Kong. I remember the Major League Baseball strike, and the Commodore computer. Vic Morrow and two children died while filming *The Twilight Zone*, and John DeLorean was arrested by the FBI for selling cocaine. Meanwhile, I was drinking, and I was drinking a lot.

It's funny how it creeps up on you. I mean, I had always liked to drink, and I guess I drank a lot. But I always kept my drinking limited to evenings and weekends and had never even considered drinking during working hours. The idea of drinking while I worked didn't even cross my mind. When I first started up my construction business, I quickly signed up a lot of work. I discovered that I was an excellent salesman. People seemed to like me, and they wanted me to build their projects. I had a trustworthy face and a reassuring demeanor. Business was good.

Rhonda and I moved into a penthouse apartment in Newport Beach that looked out over the bay and ocean. We went out and bought all new furniture, and we filled our place with all those crazy gadgets we found in the Sharper Image catalog. We bought our coffee beans at an exclusive coffee place in Lido Island, and we did our grocery shopping at the upscale Gelson's. Rhonda had her BMW, and I bought a brand-new GMC truck with leather seats and a wood-grain dashboard. The car payments were ridiculously high, but we were making them on time. And that was when I began to drink more and more. Why? It was because I was an alcoholic. That's what alcoholics do.

It was amazing just how fast things began to go downhill.

It was incremental, but it was very fast. And things began to go wrong. I wasn't paying attention to my projects, and there were problems. And I didn't pay attention to the problems. I was too busy being a big shot. Ha, ha, another round. Ha, ha, make them all doubles! Then the phone began to ring, and customers were getting angry. Subcontractors were not getting paid on time, and they, too, were getting fed up. And suddenly, as if it happened overnight, the whole thing became a living nightmare. I don't know how it happened so fast, but it did. My entire business was upside down, and every project I had was in a state of chaos. I was no longer answering the phone. What would be the use? It would just be another furious customer or unpaid worker or subcontractor demanding that I step up to the plate. But with what? I was out of money. I was deep in the hole, and I couldn't even pay our rent on time. We were evicted from our penthouse apartment, and we moved into a dreary little apartment in Irvine. I remember that place. And I remember that Rhonda had to get a job to bring in some income.

Rhonda got a job at her father's advertising firm, and her dad paid her a decent salary. But it wasn't near what we needed for me to dig myself out from under the mountain of debt I had created. And while Rhonda was at work, I hid out and drank. I remember those days clearly. She would go off to work, and I would then drive to the liquor store. I would spend the rest of the day in the apartment, on the floor, drinking and watching TV. I would order pizzas to be delivered. I would make grilled cheese sandwiches. I would eat and drink, and drink and eat, watching TV. Sometimes I would answer the phone, but often I wouldn't. I remember once looking at my face in the bathroom mirror. The whites of my eyes were turning yellow, and my face was bloated and slimy with sweat. And my body! I must have gained forty pounds from all the alcohol, pizza, and grilled cheese sandwiches. I looked like a pig. But I didn't do anything about it. I just went to the living room and poured myself another drink, calling in another pizza order. And I watched *The People's Court* on TV. I liked watching Judge Wapner. He made me laugh when nothing else was funny.

I was in my own personal hell. I don't know where others in my life were. I don't know what Rhonda was thinking back then. I don't know what her parents were thinking. And my parents? I don't know anything about them either. I was in a disconnected world, lost and spiraling downward, deeper and deeper into the chilling loneliness of my alcoholism. Deeper and deeper each day. I remember that one night while Rhonda was sleeping, I ran out of booze. I had to make a run to the liquor store, which was about a mile from our place. I grabbed my keys and sneaked out the front door, being careful not to wake up Rhonda. I then went to my car, and I drove. I was terribly drunk, and it was tough to make sense of the roads. In my rearview mirror I saw the whirling police car lights, and I heard the siren. I was being pulled over.

I pulled to the curb, and the patrol car stopped behind me. The officer got out and stepped to my window. I tried to act sober. I really did my best, but when I couldn't find my car registration, the cop asked me to get out of my car. "I'm going to give you a sobriety test," he said.

"I've been drinking a little," I said. "But not that much. A couple drinks, maybe."

"Please get out of the car."

I did as I was told, and the cop performed the test. It was awful. I couldn't do a single thing right. I couldn't even recite my ABCs correctly. I knew I was screwed. The cop then asked me to put my hands behind my back, and he cuffed me. He then instructed me to get into the back of his car. "What about my car?" I asked.

"It'll be towed."

"To my house?"

"To an impound lot."

"Where are you taking me?"

"To Santa Ana. Just relax."

"Can I call my wife?"

"You can call from the jail. They'll give you a phone call after you've been booked."

The cop then got on his radio, and he learned that I had five warrants out for my arrest. "They must be mistaken," I said. I knew nothing about this.

"Bench warrants," he said.

"For what?"

"For bad checks. Have you been writing bad checks?"

I had, but I didn't realize there was a law against it. "I may have written a few by mistake," I said.

"You'll need to clear them up."

The tow truck came and took away my car, and the cop drove me to Orange County Jail in Santa Ana. I was booked six times, once for the drunk driving and once for each of the bad checks. It was a nightmare, being moved from one filthy steel cage to the other, having to empty my pockets, then being allowed my phone call. I would have to call Rhonda. I knew she was going to shit bricks when I told her where I was. She would not be a happy camper. What a mess this was. I was told to shower and was then given an orange jumpsuit and sneakers. The jumpsuit was too small, and the sneakers were too large. I wound up in a jail cell with four other inmates. There were no bunks left, so I sat on the floor. It took Rhonda all the next day to arrange for my bail and get them to let me out. My dad had to put his house up as collateral for the bond.

When I came out of the jail, Rhonda drove me home in her car. She only said one thing to me. She said, "This has got to end." I didn't reply, but I knew she was right.

It's terrible to lose control of your life. But that's what had happened. I was off the rails, and I had no way to climb back up without what? Without admitting I was a total failure and accepting help.

Here's something I noticed during the next several weeks. People began talking about me in front of me but as if I wasn't there. It was soon decided for me that three things were going to have to happen. One, Rhonda and I would have to file for bankruptcy as soon as possible. Two, we would have to move somewhere to hide. And three, we needed to hire an attorney to help clean up all the criminal charges and the drunk driving mess. No one asked me for my opinion. The plan just went into action, and you know what I was thinking? I was trying to figure out how I could get my hands on a bottle of tequila. *Seriously, do whatever you want with me. Just don't take away my booze!*

As it turned out, it was going to require thousands of dollars to get me out of the jam I was in and move us into a new apartment. My dad said he could contribute some of it, but my dad didn't have a lot of money. Rhonda's dad agreed to provide the rest, but with a provision. He said I had to agree to quit drinking and go to AA meetings—one AA meeting per day for one full year. He had heard somewhere that this was what alcoholics had to do in order to kick their habit. I'm not sure where he heard this, but apparently he had been asking around. My dad said this sounded like a good idea, and he agreed to attach the same strings to the money he was providing. So did I have a choice? No, I really didn't. So I had to go to the meetings. What was the big deal? How bad could they be? I knew nothing about them.

The months that followed were awful. I could no longer drink. I had no work to keep me busy. I had the bankruptcy hearing looming over my head. Who would show up? What would they have to say? I was sure I'd made a lot of people very, very angry. "Just don't drink," Rhonda said. She was scared to death I'd start drinking again. She had to go to work during the day, but she'd call me every couple of hours to check on me, to be sure I wasn't doing anything stupid. I felt bad for what I'd done to her. I had turned her into a nervous wreck. I had turned her world upside down, and there was now nothing I could do to help but stay sober and make all my court dates. What a worthless, troublesome, lying, irresponsible, loathsome piece of crap I had become. Now more than ever, I just wanted to get high. One pint of tequila would wipe away the pain. I wouldn't have to get drunk. No, just a pint. That was all I needed, and as the bankruptcy hearing date approached, the urge to drink grew stronger, and it was three days before the hearing that I finally succumbed to it. Rhonda left for work at eight in the morning, and by eight-thirty, I was at the liquor store, buying my pint.

I brought it home and drank it. And it worked. I felt great for about fifteen minutes. I felt lucid and relieved and as light as a feather. Bankruptcy hearing? Who cared? An hour or so and I would be out of the courtroom, debt free. Fuck all those people anyway. They were driving me crazy. Then it occurred to me that if one pint made me feel good, another ought to make me feel even better. Better yet, I would buy a quart just in case. I had the whole day to kill before Rhonda would be home. So yes, I went back to the liquor store and bought a quart. I don't remember much after that. I went into a blackout, and when I came to, I was on the floor of our kitchen with my wrists slashed and a crowd of EMTs around me. Blood was everywhere. It was all over the countertops and puddled on the floor. It was really quite a mess, and one of the EMTs kept telling me to hold still. Rhonda was in the living room, and I could hear her sobbing. A female EMT was comforting her. There were also a couple of cops there. They were having a private conversation in the hallway.

I was drunk. I mean I was *really* drunk. The EMT beside me told me that if I didn't hold still, they were going to have to restrain me. I didn't know what that meant, but I assumed I wouldn't like it, so I calmed down. Then it was off to the hospital in an ambulance, where a very cranky doctor proceeded to sew up my wounds. I got the impression that he either didn't like his work or he just didn't like suicide attempts. When he was done, he handed me a sheet of paper that said they were taking me to another hospital for observation. "That's fine with me," I said. I was still drunk. And what did I care what they did with me? I didn't even care if I lived or died. "Take me wherever the hell you want."

I was released from the mental hospital two days later. It took me that long to sober up and convince the resident shrink into believing that I wasn't going to slash my wrists again when I got home. When it was finally time for me to go, Rhonda was in an important meeting at work with her dad. They called my mom and asked her to pick me up. Ah, dear old mom. She showed right up, and she quietly led me out of the building and to her car. She didn't say a word. It was very strange, and I had the impression that she was angry with me. As we drove toward the apartment, she turned and looked at me. Finally she spoke. All she said was "You're fat."

It seemed like such a strange thing to say. I don't think I realized just how sick of me everyone was. Even my own dear mother. I didn't respond to her comment, and we were quiet the rest of the way home.

BORN ON THE FOURTH OF JULY

His name was Jonathan Farnsworth, and he taught economics at the University of South Carolina. His wife's name was Samantha, and she worked in administration. They lived in a quaint old home in Columbia that they had prepared for a new occupant—their newborn baby, who was due to be delivered any day. They knew the baby's sex. It was going to be a baby boy, and this was good. Jonathan told everyone he and Samantha had always wanted a son. Of course, if the baby was a girl, they would've said they'd always wanted a girl. The truth was that they didn't care one way or the other; they just wanted the child to be healthy and born without any complications.

Since they knew the sex of the child ahead of time, they prepared the nursery in their home for a boy. They painted the walls and ceiling of the room pale blue and plastered half of the walls with a sports wallpaper. There were footballs, basketballs, and baseballs everywhere. There was also a framed and autographed photo of Freddie Freeman of the Atlanta Braves on the nightstand, and there was a poster of Cam Newton on the wall above the crib. Jonathan loved sports, and so would the kid, who would be named Miles, after the famous musician. Jonathan loved jazz music almost as much as he loved sports. Miles Davis was his all-time favorite.

It was the Fourth of July, and Jonathan and Samantha were getting ready to go see the fireworks show. Jonathan had put a couple lawn chairs in the trunk of their car, and Samantha put some snacks in a basket. It had been hot and humid that day, and both of them were wearing shorts and short-sleeved shirts. Samantha had her blonde hair tied in a ponytail to keep it from sticking to the sides of her face. They were just about to hop into the car to leave when Samantha suddenly put her hand on the car door handle and bent over. "Oh," she said. "That one hurt."

"Are you okay?" Jonathan asked. He was on the other side of the car.

"I don't know."

"Are you having contractions?"

"I think I am, Jonathan. Oh, maybe it's time."

"Seriously?"

"Yes, I think it's time."

"Get in the car."

"Is the bag packed?"

"It's in the trunk."

"Yes, I think we'd better go."

"Do you need anything from the house?"

"No, no, just take me to the hospital."

"I'm on it," Jonathan said.

They drove to the hospital. The traffic was light, and it didn't take long to get there. They parked, and Jonathan grabbed the bag and held Samantha's arm to keep her steady as the two of them walked to the hospital doors.

Well, as far as deliveries go, this one went smoothly. It was painful and scary, but it actually went pretty well. It was not nearly as bad as Jonathan and Samantha had expected. They'd heard so many horror stories. When Samantha was wheeled into her recovery room, the nurse brought the baby to her. The child was clean and wrapped in a light blue blanket, and Samantha held him in her arms. "My sweet, little Fourth of July baby," she said.

"A patriot," Jonathan said.

"Miles."

"Yes, Miles Farnsworth. You know, he looks like a football player. Doesn't he look like a football player?"

"He's so precious."

"The nurse said he's perfectly healthy."

"Of course he is."

"Ready to face the world."

"All ready," Samantha said.

"Look how he clenches his little fists. You know what he is? He's a natural born fighter. Born on the Fourth of July. Home of the brave, and land of the free. Liberty and justice for all. He isn't going to take any crap from anyone."

"I think he has your nose," Samantha said.

"You think so?"

"And he has my father's ears."

"I can't tell, honestly."

"I can tell."

The couple was quiet for a moment, both looking at Miles. The baby was sleeping. "He's so comfortable in your arms," Jonathan said.

"You want to hold him?"

"I do," Jonathan said, and Samantha handed him the baby. Jonathan smiled. He was surprisingly warm.

"Be sure to cradle his head."

"I know."

"He has no neck muscles."

"I know, I know."

"What do you think?" Samantha asked, smiling. It was such a joy, seeing her husband with their newborn son.

"I think Miles is lucky."

"Lucky?"

"The luckiest little man on earth."

"Why do you say that?"

"Because he has us as parents."

"We'll be good parents, won't we?"

"Of course we will," Jonathan said.

"We'll do and say all the right things?"

"Always."

"And he'll always feel safe and loved."

"Yes," Jonathan said. He was now looking at Samantha. Her eyes were welling with salty tears. But she wasn't smiling, and the big tears in her eyes didn't seem to be tears of joy. She looked a little frightened, and Jonathan asked, "What's the matter?"

"He's so perfect right now."

"Perfect."

"Do you really think we'll be good parents?"

"That's the plan."

"But don't you suppose everyone says that?"

"Says what?"

"That they'll be good parents."

Jonathan smiled. He was now looking at the baby, and he said, "But we actually will be."

But fast-forward twenty some years. If Samantha is called to pick Miles up one day from a mental hospital, and if Miles's recently sutured wrists are wrapped up with medical gauze and tape, what will she say then? And what the heck will Jonathan say? This is a fair question to ask, isn't it? Was it their fault? Or is this just the way the cookie crumbles with men, women, and countries?

BURIED IN NEW JERSEY

"Nearly every man who develops an idea works it up to the point where it looks impossible, and then he gets discouraged. That's not the place to become discouraged."

—Thomas Edison

THE FIRST DRINK

When people learn that I'm an alcoholic, 90 percent of them say, "Oh," and then change the subject. But some of them ask me how I stopped drinking. So how did I stop drinking? For me it was very simple. I followed the advice of a long-time sober fellow whom I met at an AA meeting. He was a pretty nice guy, and not a book-thumping AA fanatic. He told me, "Just don't take the first drink." If you are not an alcoholic, this advice may seem sort of silly to you. But it was profound—maybe the most profound advice I ever received.

So what does it mean? It means this. Once an alcoholic starts to drink, he loses control. He is no longer a rational human being. The alcohol is doing his thinking for him, and it is telling him to drink more, and the more he drinks, the more he's told to keep drinking. It's the alcohol, and not his sober consciousness, that is moving him forward toward his eventual destructive drunkenness. So what? So is there anything he can do to stop this? It turns out that there is, absolutely, and the solution is simple and obvious, once you see it. There is one time during this cycle when the alcoholic is sober and in charge of his thinking. It's when he's deciding whether to take that first drink. At that time, and during no other time, he is sober and *he knows better.* At that time, the alcohol is not in his bloodstream, telling him how to behave, telling him what to do. So if you're an alcoholic, you don't take the first drink. Not ever. Not under any circumstances. You have control, and you are in charge, and at that point in time, you are capable of preventing the chaos.

So that's what I decided to do. Now I never take the first drink. My sobriety wins out, and my alcoholism never has a chance to take over my life. Is it easy? No, not always. But it's a heck of a lot easier than drinking and suffering the dire consequences.

It was in November of 1983 that our bankruptcy was over and final. I have to tell you that it was a huge relief. And I'd been able to stop drinking for about six months when I sat down and asked myself, "So now what?" What was I going to do? I was still young. I could do about anything. There was no law that said I had to be a building contractor, or even an architect. I could go back to school and learn a completely new trade. I was still only in my twenties. I could take an entry-level job, but doing what? Who knew. I had thousands of different roads ahead of me, and so for a week or so I considered them. Well, some of them. And then, totally sober, I came to my decision.

John Henry and Friends

When John Henry was about three days old,
Sittin' on his papa's knee,
He picked up a hammer and a little piece of wood,
Said, "Building's gonna be the death of me, Lord, Lord.
Building's gonna be the death of me."

When Todd Taylor was about four days old,
Sittin' on his papa's knee,
He picked up a pencil and a clean sheet of paper,
Said, "Pushing pencils gonna be the death of me, Lord, Lord.
Pushing pencils gonna be the death of me."

When Abe Picard was about five days old,
Sittin' on his papa's knee,
He picked up a syringe and a cotton wad,
Said, "Doctoring's gonna be the death of me, Lord, Lord
Doctoring's gonna be the death of me."

When Bill Cahill was about six days old,
Sittin' on his papa's knee,
He picked up a contract and signed his name,
Said, "Signin' contracts gonna be the death of me, Lord, Lord.
Signing contracts gonna be the death of me."

When Joe Epstein was about seven years old,
Sittin' on his papa's knee,
He picked up a vase and some long-stemmed flowers,
Said, "Makin' bouquets gonna be the death of me, Lord, Lord.
Makin' bouquets gonna be the death of me."

When Harry Smith was about eight years old,
Sittin' on his papa's knee,
He picked up some burger and a steel spatula,
Said, "Flippin' burgers gonna be the death of me, Lord, Lord.
Flippin' burgers gonna be the death of me."

When Jeff Andrews was about nine years old,
Sittin' on his papa's knee,
He picked up a trumpet and blew out a tune,
Said, "Blowin' tunes gonna be the death of me, Lord, Lord.
Blowin' tunes gonna be the death of me."

When Fred Toomey was about ten years old,
Sittin' on his papa's knee,
He picked up a paintbrush and opened a can,
Said, "Paintin' houses gonna be the death of me, Lord, Lord.
Paintin' houses gonna be the death of me."

Uncle Sam smiled wide at these children,
He was so glad to see them all coming around.
He did a wild dance and waved his American flag,
Said, "Keep your young feet on the ground, Lord, Lord.
Keep your feet on the ground."

The children grew up to have more kids.
You could hold them in the palm of your hand.
They all sang at the top of their tiny lungs,

   Sang, "God bless the nail hammerin', pencil pushin', doctorin', contract
signin', flower bouquet arrangin', hamburger flippin', tune blowin', house
paintin' man, Lord, Lord.
   God bless them and shake their hands."

WE ARE CONCRETE

I'm going to tell you now about a shopping center project that I built in
1987. Times were good in '87, and I had a lot of work under contract.
This particular shopping center was located in Fontana, and I had just
been awarded the contract to build it. The developer was a man named
Clarence O'Neil, and I had built several projects for him before. I had to
submit a bid for the work. Although he liked me a lot, there was no way
Clarence would ever award the contract to me without making sure my

price was competitive. He gave me two months to prepare my bid, and he gave two other contractors the same amount of time. All said and done, my price came in at the middle. The lowest price was not that much lower than mine, so I agreed to match it in order to get the job. Clarence liked me, but he was a businessman, always looking to keep his costs down. The price I agreed to was a good price, and I could make decent money building the project. I would have to drop my profit margin by a couple points. It was no big deal.

In case you don't know how the construction bidding process works, I'll explain it quickly. There is a list of line items that must be priced. There is the foundation, framing, roofing, siding, drywall, painting, and so forth. Some of these items I could price on my own, using my experience. Some of the items I would need to have priced by subcontractors, to be sure the numbers I was using were accurate. I always got subcontractors to price my foundations. They are often designed differently. It's not something you can just price with a ruler and a pencil and your past experience. I had three concrete subcontractors give me prices for the foundation when I put in my bid for Clarence's project. The prices were all about the same. I used the lowest price to prepare my bid.

It was about a week after Clarence told me I would be the contractor that I received a call from a young man named Sam Barlow. Sam said he wanted to put in a bid on the foundations, and he said he thought he could give me a good price. I figured what the hell, why not? There was nothing wrong with getting another price for the work, so I had a set of plans delivered to Sam so he could calculate his bid.

It took Sam only a couple days to get back to me. I liked that he didn't drag his feet, but I liked his low price even more. He was almost $20,000 below my lowest other price. It was easy money in my pocket. It told Sam I'd never heard of his company. The name of his outfit was We Are Concrete. It was kind of an odd name, but so what? If he was going to save me that much money, I didn't care what he called himself. It turned out that We Are Concrete was a partnership. Sam was the guy who worked in the office, and a fellow named Terrance Hill worked in the field. "I'll need some references," I said to Sam. "Your price is reasonable, but I've never heard of you. I need to talk to some of the people you've worked for. If your references check out, you have a good chance of working for me."

Obviously, I didn't tell Sam how low his price was. That just wasn't how things were done.

Sam gave me three references. All of them were for home remodel projects done over the past year. I was hoping for some commercial references, but it turned out that these were the only projects Sam and Terrance had completed. "Please talk to our references," Sam said. "I'm sure you'll be happy with what you hear. We'll do anything to make our customers happy." At first I hesitated, but then I decided to call his references. I figured, what the hell. Sam seemed competent, why shouldn't I give his company a chance?

When I called his people, I heard nothing but good things. Sam and Terrance were hardworking and honest, and their prices were great. There were no problems, and the jobs had gone smoothly. This was good, right? This was exactly what I wanted to hear. I thought about it one more day, and then I decided to call Sam and award him the contract. "You won't be sorry," he said. He sounded very excited. "Come over to our office, and I'll have your signed contract there for you to pick up, and I'll introduce you to the boys." I laughed at this. No contractor I know of ever gives a shit about meeting "the boys," but I figured, why not? I liked Sam, and I wanted to see what he had going on.

The next day, I visited Sam's office. It was a much nicer office than I expected. He must have been paying a pretty penny for rent. And his trucks? He had three brand-new Chevys in the parking lot with the name of his company on the door panels and tailgates. The trucks were loaded up with brand-new lumber racks and shiny new tool boxes. As I walked into the office, I stepped into a nicely furnished waiting room and was greeted by a young receptionist who had been reading a novel before I got there. She asked me whom I was there to see, and I said either Sam or Terrance would do. Then she asked for my name, and I told it to her. "Oh, yes," she said. "They're both expecting you. Follow me." She walked down a hallway, and I followed. We passed several offices, a conference room, a men's and women's bathroom, and a lunchroom before we got to a back door. Then she pushed the door open, revealing a garage that could've held nine or more trucks.

Inside the garage, Sam and Terrance and their workers were seated on some fold-up chairs, and they were in the middle of a talk about job safety.

Sam heard me enter with the receptionist, and he turned around and spoke to me. "Mr. Baker!" he exclaimed.

"Please call me Huey," I said.

"I want you to meet everyone. You just met our secretary, Karen. We just hired her."

"Yes, we met."

"And you know Terrance, of course."

"Good to see you again, Terrance," I said, smiling at him. He stood up from his chair to shake my hand, and then he sat back down.

"These are the boys," Sam said. "This is Hank, Chris, Ed, and George. They'll all be working on your project. We were just going over some jobsite safety procedures."

"Nice to meet you guys," I said, and they all smiled and nodded.

"We're looking forward to working on your project, Mr. Baker," Ed said.

"That's good, but please call me Huey."

"We were going over the plans this morning."

"That's good."

"There's a lot of concrete."

"Yes," I said. "The soil is pretty bad."

"That explains the six-inch slabs.

"It does," I said. I wanted to laugh, but I didn't. I felt as if I were at a Cub Scout meeting. "Do you have the signed contract?"

"I do," Sam said. "It's in my office."

We left Terrance with the boys, and I walked with Sam to his office. The secretary returned to her desk to read her novel. "Nice digs," I said to Sam. The office was very nicely furnished.

On Sam's desk was our contract, signed in blood and ready for me. He picked it up and handed it to me. "You're going to be glad you picked us for this project," he said.

"I hope so."

"We want to do all of your concrete work."

"Let's see how this one goes first."

"Of course," Sam said.

"My superintendent will be calling you next week. His name is Rich."

"Rich, yes. I'll look forward to his call."

Two weeks later, We Are Concrete started their work on my job. The civil engineer had staked the building corners, and the new Chevy trucks were all there. The boys were all there. A pile of steel rebar and some lumber had been delivered. A backhoe was digging the trenches, and everything appeared to be in order. I asked Rich what he thought, and he said it seemed they knew what they were doing. I had a ton of office work, so I didn't return to the job for several weeks. When I did return, I asked Rich how Sam and Terrance had done, and he said everything had worked out fine. Then I got a call from Sam, and he said we had to meet as soon as possible. He sounded out of breath, which I thought was strange, but I agreed to meet him that afternoon in my office.

When Sam showed up, he tried to smile, but he wasn't doing a very good job at it. I told him to sit down, and he sat in front of my desk. He had some papers with him, and he placed them in front of me so I could look them over as he spoke. So what were the papers? Well, he had brought a complete breakdown of every single dime he had spent installing my foundations. All his labor, materials, and the rental of the backhoe were spelled out. It was all there, written down in black and white. What he was trying to show me was how much money he had lost on the project. "I guess I underestimated the scope of the work," he said. "My contract price should've been twenty thousand dollars higher."

"And you're expecting me to do what?" I asked.

"I'm hoping you can help me out."

"Help how?"

"Can you pay me the twenty thousand? You're happy with our work, right?"

"You want me to pay another twenty thousand?"

"If you can."

I stared at Sam for a moment. Then I said, "I'm sorry, but that isn't going to happen. It can't be done."

"Why not?"

"Because my agreement with the owner was based on your original price."

"Was it?"

Well, it wasn't. But I insisted that it was. "You can't just ask for more money. The business doesn't work that way. You should know that."

"But this job is going to bury me," Sam said. Now he sounded like he was going to cry.

"I'm sorry," I said.

"It's going to put me out of business."

"Don't you have other jobs?"

"We have one other."

"Isn't that one making money for you?"

"It's a problem as well."

"Jesus," I said. "I don't know what to say."

"Can you talk to the owner? Maybe he'll understand. Maybe he'll listen to you."

"He won't," I assured Sam.

We looked at each other for a moment, and then Sam gathered his papers from my desk. He had a look on his face as if his wife had just died. I watched him walk out of my office. When he was gone, I stepped to my bookkeeper's office and asked her if we'd paid Sam's company in full for the job. She said we still owed him his final 10 percent, and I told her to be sure all his suppliers were paid off before she released any funds. She said she would call the suppliers. "Get final lien releases from all of them," I said. "And make sure Sam gives you final lien releases from his laborers. The guy just told me he is having money problems, and we have to be careful."

Two weeks later, I got a call from Rich. He said he had called We Are Concrete to clean up some of the debris they had left behind, but their phone had been disconnected. I hung up and tried to call myself. Sure enough, Rich was right. Then I drove to their offices to see what was happening. The front door was locked, and there was a For Lease sign taped to the window. I looked inside, and all the new furniture and office equipment were gone. Their company was no longer.

Had I put him out of business? I told myself no. That was not the way to look at it. He had put himself out of business. He had tried to play the construction game with the rest of us, and he had lost. Too bad, right? He was a nice guy, but if I made a habit of paying for every stupid mistake a subcontractor made, I would be out of business myself, with a For Lease sign on my office window. Everyone knew this. And Sam should've known this.

So what about the $20,000 I saved on this deal? It was a terrific little windfall. I used the money to buy Rhonda a new gold Rolex ladies' watch, and the rest of it I put into savings for our upcoming summer vacation. Rhonda and I went to Barbados later that year and had the time of our lives. We stayed at a place called Sam Lord's Castle, a resort that was centered around a Georgian mansion that was built in 1820 by the notorious buccaneer Samuel Hall Lord. Legend has it that he acquired his wealth by plundering ships he lured onto the reefs off the coast by hanging lanterns in the island's coconut trees. Clever, right? Unsuspecting captains of passing ships mistook the lanterns for the lights of Bridgetown and wrecked their ships on the reefs. Then Sam and his buccaneers would take everything they could get their hands on.

LOTS OF BABIES

Over four million babies are born in the United States every year. That's a heck of a lot of disposable diapers and baby powder. July, August, and September are the most popular months for childbirths. The most popular day is Tuesday, but I have no idea why that is. Thanks to social shifts, greater literacy and the availability and acceptance of contraception, childbirth in the United States is on the decline. Utah has the highest birth rate of all the states in America, and Vermont has the lowest total number of births. And just so you know the truth, all newborn babies are not born with blue eyes. The little blue-eyed fish is a myth.

ONE FISH TWO FISH

One fish two fish red fish blue fish.
Black kid brown kid yellow kid red kid.
Some will smile and some will cry.
Some can swim, but none can fly.
Some are sad, and some are glad.
And some are very, very bad.
Does anything make them get mad?
I don't know. Go ask your dad.

Some are thin, and some are fat.
The fat one has a yellow hat.
From there to here, from here to there.
They're too young for underwear.
Hope you have a pile of dough.
They cost a lot, lot, of it, so
Oh me! Oh my!
Oh me! Oh my!
What a lot of funny things to buy:
Diapers, rattles, and teddy bears,
Fine brushes for their baby hairs.
Where do they come from?
I can't say.
But the storks drop them off on their birthdays.
We see them poop.
We see them eat.
Some are fast
On little feet.
Some eat mush
And some drink milk.
Not one of them is like the other.
Don't ask us why.
Go ask your mother.

WHO'S YOUR DADDY?

On the TV was a host. In my opinion, he was a sleazebucket, but people looked up to him. They liked him. They took his word for things. He was nicely dressed, and he had a calm and friendly way about him. I watched.

Enter Cynthia.

The storyline went like this: Cynthia was the main guest of the show. She was a big girl, in her mid-thirties, and she looked like someone who did all her clothes shopping at the Salvation Army Thrift Store. Her blouse and pants were too small, making her appear heavier than she probably was. She also had long red fingernails, and there was a tattoo of a tiny rose on the fleshy calf of her very formidable leg. She talked to the host. They were on a first-name basis. She was explaining her situation, and it had to do with finding out who her baby's father was. On the wall behind them, there was a projected photograph of the baby, a cute little girl with yellow ribbons in her hair. Mom was not married, but she said she'd had sex with a guy named Dave, who she was sure was the father. They then projected a photo of Dave on the wall, and she pointed out confidently that Dave and her baby had the same nose. This was silly, of course. A man's nose on a baby would look ridiculous. Nevertheless, that was what the woman said. It turned out that Dave was a bartender. Cynthia said she met him at his place of work. She said that Dave drove her to his place, and that they had sex nine months before the little girl was born.

Enter Dave.

"You're crazy," Dave said. "You and I never had sex."

"Oh, no?"

"Hell no."

"Then how do you explain Lucy?" Lucy was the name of the baby girl.

"How should I know how you got pregnant."

"You know good and well."

"I don't know anything."

"So you're saying the two of you never had sex," the host said to Dave.

"Never!"

"Oh, right," Cynthia said, rolling her eyes. "Look at the picture. She has your nose."

"If you're looking for the father, bring in her boyfriend. Did she tell you she had a boyfriend at the time?"

"I wasn't even seeing him then. We broke up the month before."

"You're referring to Frank?" the host asked.

"Yeah, Frank," Dave said.

"Let's bring in Frank," the host said.

Enter Frank.

"You're not going to pin this thing on me," Frank said. "That baby doesn't look anything like me."

"She has your forehead," Dave said.

"My forehead?"

"No, she has your nose," Cynthia said.

"Are you telling us you weren't with Cynthia during the time in question?" the host asked.

"Nowhere near her."

"I saw the two of you drinking together," Dave said.

"We may have had a couple of drinks. But that was all we did."

"He doesn't even like me," Cynthia said.

"If you really want to know who the father is, why isn't Chuck in here?"

"Who's Chuck?" the host asked.

"He's Cynthia's other boyfriend. I saw them together at the bar too. Several times."

"Chuck and I had nothing going on."

"Then what were you doing with him?"

"We're just friends."

"Just friends?"

"I didn't know you were still seeing Chuck," Dave said.

"I wasn't seeing him."

Enter Chuck.

"Don't blame me for any of this. Cynthia and I never even had sex."

"No one believes that," Dave said. "And the girl has your chin."

"My chin?"

"Did you have sex with Chuck?" the host asked.

"Not so as he would've got me pregnant."

"You can say that again."

"Then what were you doing together?" Dave asked.

"We were just talking," Chuck said.

"You two were doing more than talking."

"How would you know?"

"I just know. I heard things."

"From who?"

"From Judy Anne."

"Judy Anne. She's a liar!"

"She has no reason to lie."

"We just happen to have her here. Send in Judy Anne. Let's hear what she has to say."

Enter Judy Anne.

"What do you know about all of this?" the host asked.

"I know plenty." Judy Anne spoke forcefully, as if she knew it all.

"She's a liar. I don't even need to hear what she has to say, and I know she's a liar."

"If you want to know who the father is, you're all barking up the wrong tree," Judy Anne said. "Bob is the one you need to be talking to."

"Bob?"

"Liar," Cynthia said.

"You know I'm telling the truth."

"Who the hell is Bob?" Dave asked.

"He's her cousin. The girl has his ears. Look at her ears."

"Jesus."

"I have to ask," the host said, "did you have sex with your cousin?"

"Judy Anne is a liar. Lucy's ears don't look anything like Bob's. She just wants Dave to herself. Forget the ears. It's the nose. She's just jealous. She's always had a thing for Dave."

"That's news to me," Dave said.

"Don't listen to her."

"At least I'm not a liar," Cynthia said.

"You know she has Bob's ears. It was you and Bob. I'm sure of it."

All the guests were glaring at each other, and the camera moved to the host's face. He smiled and said, "We now have to cut to a commercial break. But when we come back, we'll get to the bottom of this. The DNA test results are in."

"You'll be sorry," Cynthia said to Dave.

"Not as sorry as you."

Cut to the commercial.

They were selling superabsorbent paper towels, and then some laundry detergent. Then they were selling a new kind of eyeliner. Seriously, you can't make this stuff up. As I got up to get a Coke, I opened the refrigerator and thought to myself. I wondered if the child with the yellow ribbons in her hair would ever get a copy of the videotape of this show. No doubt she would. And what would she think? Does it go through anyone's mind? And why do we all think this is okay? Are we really that callous? Sure, it's only daytime TV, but it says a lot about America. It amazes me who and what we're willing to sacrifice for a little afternoon entertainment. I got my Coke and sat down. The commercials were over, and it turned out that

Chuck was the daddy. He turned around and said to the cameras, "I'll do everything I can to be a good father." Sure, buddy, whatever you say. The host patted Chuck on the back because he was such a good sport, and the audience displayed its approval by applauding.

USEFUL ADVICE

"It's disgusting, but my father taught me when your mouth gets dry, just suck the sweat out of your own jersey. There's no bravado to any of it; it's just a disgusting little trick."

—Kobe Bryant

KID STUFF

Rhonda and I had only one child, a boy we named Thomas William Baker. There are so many things I could tell you about this wonderful little boy, but most of what I would tell would be of interest only to me. I've noticed that when you have your own child, stories about that kid's formative years fascinate you a lot more than they do others.

At the risk of boring your pants off, I'm going to tell a few stories about our boy from when he was between the ages of zero and five. First there is the story about the white couches. Just prior to our decision to bring Thomas into the world, we decided to go out and buy new furniture for our place. We'd been living with old hand-me-downs, none of it what we really wanted, and all of it having seen better days. It was a lot of fun going to the big department stores with our credit cards in hand, choosing our new furniture. We decided on a pair of solid white sofas for our living room. With some colorful pillows, an end table, a coffee table, a couple of lamps, and a handful of reasonably priced objects d'art, it looked like a little family room right out of the pages of *Architectural Digest*. But the solid white couches are what made the room so nice. They really did look great.

It was around then that Thomas learned to write his name. We taught him to write T-O-M. He would write it over and over, and he was so proud of himself. Then he got a hold of a permanent black marker, and while we weren't watching him, he proceeded to write his name twenty or thirty times on the fabric of the white sofas. "Tom, Tom, Tom"—he was so proud of himself! Jesus, I think Rhonda nearly had a fucking heart attack. No, we couldn't bring ourselves to yell at him or spank him. We calmly told him not to do it again. I don't remember what we did with the ruined sofas. I think we covered them up with big blankets. Anyway, here's some advice for new parents: Don't furnish your home with solid white sofas if you have a child on the way, and be sure to keep your black felt pens someplace where your little name-writing child won't be able to reach them. Kids do like to write their names.

There is also the story about Seymore. When Thomas was young, he had lots of stuffed animals, and Seymore was one of his favorites. Seymore was a stuffed monkey dressed in denim overalls, and one of the shoulder straps of the overalls was torn and always dangling loose. It was no big deal. I mean, Thomas loved the little animal anyway. One afternoon Rhonda took Thomas to our local grocery store, and as they stood in line to check out, Thomas became interested in the two men who were in front of them. One of the men was an African American who was wearing a pair of denim overalls, and as luck would have it, one of his shoulder straps was unbuttoned and dangling loose. Thomas was delighted to see the loose strap. He pointed at the black man and said, "Look, Mommy; that man looks exactly like my monkey!" Wow, talk about embarrassing. The man pretended not to hear Thomas, and so did Rhonda. I can't even imagine what the poor guy was thinking.

I'll tell you something interesting about children. They like their world just as it is. They don't need any help with it. What do I mean by that? Thomas, for example, used to love making trains. He made them all the time. He'd get his stuffed animals, videotape cassettes, books, toys, and anything else he could get his hands on, and he'd line them up on the floor like a long train. His trains would start in his bedroom and go into the hallway. Then they'd go through the bathroom door and into the bathroom, and they'd come back out and down the hallway again, toward the next room. It was amazing how long Thomas's trains could get, and he never grew bored with them.

So in all our parental wisdom, what did Rhonda and I decide to do? We went out and bought him an actual toy train set. We thought he'd love this. It would be a *real* train, a train with an engine, cars, caboose, and snap-together tracks. The truth is that Thomas couldn't have cared less about it. It didn't interest him at all, and it sat in its unopened box on a shelf in his closet, like, forever. And do you want to know why he didn't play with this train set? It was because it wasn't *his* train. His train was made of stuffed animals, videotapes, books, and toys, and to his way of thinking, that was a real train.

There are so many other stories I could tell. There was the time Thomas flicked a spoonful of vanilla milkshake across the room at a restaurant where we were eating. The ice cream landed on the side of a man's head and ran down into his ear. He had no sense of humor at all, and we couldn't keep ourselves from laughing. The more we laughed, the angrier he got. Then there was the time Thomas ate his first strawberry. The look on his face was priceless. He may as well have been chewing on a lemon. There was also the time we went to an Italian restaurant in Laguna Beach and Thomas ordered a pizza from the kids' menu. They served the pizza with sprigs of green herbs embedded in the cheese, and Thomas started crying. Rhonda asked what was wrong, and he said, "They put *weeds* in my pizza!" He thought the chef was playing a mean trick on him. And I'll never forget Thomas's first T-ball game. He smacked the ball, and we all told him to run. He ran out to the pitcher's mound, around the pitcher, and back home. He had no concept of running around the bases. I also remember Thomas's first Halloween. At the first house we came to, a man opened his door. The nice man dropped a handful of candy into Thomas's bag, and hoping Thomas would thank the man, Rhonda said, "What do you say, Thomas?" Thomas looked at the man, dead serious, and he said, "Close your door!"

I wish I'd kept a journal those years. I'm sure Thomas did and said many fun and amusing things that I've forgotten. For all intents and purposes, many of those memories are as good as gone. They've turned brown and fallen to the ground like dead leaves from a tree.

BURIED IN LOS ANGELES

"You can't be a real country unless you have a beer and an airline. It helps if you have some kind of football team, or some nuclear weapons, but at the very least you need a beer."

—Frank Zappa

THE PARTY

Do you remember Tipper Gore and the PMRC? They wanted to slap warning labels on popular music albums. Tipper's interest in labeling these albums resulted from the day her eleven-year-old daughter brought Prince's *Purple Rain* home and played one of its songs on the family stereo, "Darling Nikki," a song about masturbation. Tipper was outraged. She said she didn't want her young daughter singing along with this, and I can't say I blame her. This was back in the eighties. Of course, Prince is nowhere near as provocative as some of the artists kids listen to now.

They held Senate hearings, which included some interesting testimony from Frank Zappa and others. PMRC advocate Susan Baker, said there were many causes for the ills in America but that it was her belief that messages aimed at children promoting and glorifying suicide, rape, sadomasochism, and so on, were a big part of the problem. She called for the record companies to place warning labels on their products that were inappropriate for younger children. Hence, we now have the labels.

And what was the result of this labelling? The truth is that kids these days are much more likely to buy the albums with the warning labels than they are to buy the dull, goody-two-shoes albums without the labels. So who won the PMRC battle? It was the music industry. The music industry didn't have to clean up their act at all. In fact, the music they produce today is more violent and profane than any music sold in the history of this country. Thomas Jefferson wrote that "The tree of liberty must be refreshed from time to time with the blood of patriots and tyrants." He was right about this, but just to be more current and accurate, we should add that the tree demands the blood of our children. See Dick and Jane bleed, and smell the stench of the manure we feed to them. And see the rock star's sprawling estate high upon the hill. We are paying for his guitar-shaped swimming pool and the Rolls Royce parked in his driveway. Open your eyes! See all of his famous guests mingling and drinking champagne. What are you doing here? Were *you* invited to the party?

DON'T FROWN

About 41 percent of first marriages in the United States end in divorce. The average length of a marriage that ends in divorce is just under eight years. Also, people who frown in photographs are five times more likely to get divorced, and people who have children are more likely to stay married. Did you know that you're more likely to divorce than get hit by a car? There are a hundred or so divorces every hour in the United States, and your chances of getting hit by a car are way less than that.

WHO KNEW?

Who knew? I certainly had no idea. I didn't have a clue. They had put on such a good act, my mom and dad. Everything seemed to be fine and dandy until I got the call from my mom. She was crying and cussing like nothing I'd ever heard from her. "What do you want me to do?" I asked.

She said, "I want you to come over here and kill your fuckhead of a father." I laughed, but it wasn't very funny. I laughed because I didn't know how else to react. It all just seemed so absurd to me. My mom and dad giving up on their marriage? Throwing in the towel after forty-two years? No way, Jack. It wasn't possible.

Marriages can get complicated, especially after forty-two years. Lots of things happen. There are lots of good times, and many not-so-good times. There are all kinds of betrayals, successes, lies, disappointments, and celebrations. There are usually all kinds of everything. Forty-two years covers a lot of ground. Now, I'm not going to let you in on the details of my parents' behavior, because quite frankly, it isn't any of your business. The divorce is a public statement, but the many reasons behind it should remain private. I will say this, and I'm not saying anything that both of my parents haven't already told the world. My dad, God bless his treacherous and self-absorbed heart, decided to have an affair with another woman, and he refused to end the affair when my mom found out about it. And as if that wasn't bad enough, he married his mistress six months after the divorce. Clearly, he had no intention of staying married to my mom. He desired a life with this other woman, plain and simple. For him the divorce was exactly what he wanted. For my mom, not so much. She did not get what she had bargained for when she agreed to her vows and said, "I do." Oh, Mom wanted the damn divorce, all said and done, but it wasn't the outcome she'd been hoping for. What she really wanted was for my dad to come to his senses.

Listen, I lived with my parents for eighteen years, and I have a pretty good idea of what a lot of their issues were. And I have my opinions as to who wronged whom, and who was generally the bad guy, and who was the good guy. But the truth is that what went on between Mom and Dad really isn't my business, just as it isn't your business. I did take sides in the breakup. I took my mom's side, and I'll tell you why. She had always been loyal to my father. She never cheated on him or had any kind of an affair with another man, emotional or physical. It just wasn't in her to do something like that. She took the wedding vows she agreed to seriously, and had planned to stay with my father through thick and thin, doing no matter what it took in order to keep them together. But my dad? Throw a younger girl his way and tempt him (as we are all tempted), and he didn't have even a morsel of personal integrity. I couldn't live with this. I *had* to take my mom's side. There was no other option. I had to stand at Mom's side 100 percent. She needed me, and I was there for her. Was she perfect? No, of course not.

I don't know. Looking back now, maybe it was the wrong thing to do, but I dropped an axe on my relationship with my father, just like that. I told him never to call me, saying that I didn't want to talk to him, ever. Given the same set of circumstances, I would probably do the same thing again. I told him, "Don't call me, ever, and don't expect me to call you."

Following the breakup, my mom was a mess. Everything she had believed in turned out to be a lie, and she was lonely and hurt. Slowly but surely, I helped put her life back together. We spent hours and hours talking, planning, and setting a few new goals for her. I gave her a job at my construction company, even though I didn't really need her. She worked long hours, trying to keep her mind off the divorce. She got an apartment close to my office, and she bought a new car. The car was a Mustang. This was funny. Before the divorce my dad had kept her in little, economical compact sedans. Boring cars. Cars with no life. "You're single now," I said. "Get a new car that *says* you're single and proud to be single. Get a Mustang." And I'll be damned if she didn't go out and buy herself a bright red-and-white Mustang.

Meanwhile, my brother, Bob, stayed in touch with Dad. He decided not to take sides. He had always liked Dad a lot more than I did, so this made sense to me. Bob could also relate to my father. Bob was married for three years before he had an affair, got divorced, and married his mistress. Two peas in a pod, Dad and my brother. They were cut from the same cloth, so it was no wonder the two of them stayed in touch after Mom and Dad divorced. I don't think Bob saw anything wrong with what our dad did. He probably figured it was unrealistic to expect two people to stay in love forever. "You know, things happen, and people drift apart," he said to me. Ah, but the question I have is that if this is what Dad and Bob believed, then why did they marry again? I knew my brother and his new bride were already having problems. I just think the way a lot of people in this country look at marriage is weird. I think Dad and my brother were weird. Until death do us part? Not realistic? So why agree to it?

Was I mad at my father? I guess I was. I guess the truth is that I was furious. And why shouldn't I have been? My dad didn't have to pick up the pieces of his infidelity. He didn't have to clean up any of the mess. I'm the one who was there with the dustpan and broom. He just moved on and married his cute little girlfriend.

RID OF YOU, BABE

They say I'm smart and I should see
The writing on the wall that you and me
Have reached a point where we are through.
Thank the Lord that I'm now done with you.
Babe,
Rid of you, babe.

Rid of you, babe.
You said until death do us part,
And then you said you had a change of heart.
Oh, what a sucker I have been.
You're not even a mediocre friend.
Babe,
Rid of you, babe.
Rid of you, babe.
You gave her flowers in the spring.
Held her hand despite your ring.
When she cried, you wiped her tears.
Don't want to see you for a million years.
And please don't feel sorry for me,
'Cuz I'm so glad that we're no longer we.
Each day goes by, I love you less,
And I never could stand the smell of your breath.
Babe,
Rid of you, babe.
Rid of you, babe.
Rid of you forever now,
Rid of your crap, oh and how,
Rid of you, happy to be
Rid of you, now it's just me.
Rid of you picking your toes,
Rid of you blowing your nose.
Rid of you, your bag is packed.
Rid of you, never come back.
Rid of you, babe.
Rid of you, babe.
Rid of you, babe.

DR. ALEX

Only a few people know that just a few months after my parents were divorced, I went to see a psychologist. I wasn't going crazy; it was nothing like that. But I did feel a need to talk to someone who could help me deal with the weird feelings I was experiencing. You might ask why I didn't just talk about them with Rhonda, but I did. And Rhonda truly was helpful, yet it was Rhonda who suggested I talk to a professional. Rhonda got the name of a psychologist who had been recommended to her by a friend. I gave this guy a call, and we met on a rainy evening in November of 1991.

I remember 1991 well. It was the year of the Gulf War and Operation Desert Storm. It was the year of Scud missiles, Geraldo Rivera on the front lines, and General Schwarzkopf on the TV. It was also the year that a handful of LAPD police officers were indicted for beating the living daylights out of Rodney King, and the year that that the evil Dr. Kevorkian was arrested for murder in Michigan. Jeffrey Dahmer was arrested for his multiple murders in 1991, and Mike Tyson was arrested for the rape of a beauty pageant contestant. Yes, I remember 1991.

The psychologist I went to see was a man by the name of Dr. Aristotle Alexandropoulos. He liked to be called Dr. Alex, his last name being what it was. Dr. Alex had a nice way about him. He was empathetic without being effeminate. I have to say that I liked the guy right off the bat, and I took a seat in a chair in front of his desk. Dr. Alex didn't waste any time with small talk. He asked, "So what brings you to see me? What makes you think you need to talk to a psychologist?"

"I guess I'm here because of my parents," I said.

"Your parents?"

"They just got divorced."

"Ah, of course."

"I'm surprised it has bothered me so much, but I can't stop thinking about it."

"Are you having unpleasant thoughts?"

"You could say that."

"Such as?"

"Such as, what does it mean for me? As in, will my wife and I also get divorced? Will our marriage fall apart? Am I doomed to be unhappy? Are we all doomed to be unhappy?"

The doctor leaned back in his chair and looked at me with one eye open. "Do you get along with your wife?" he asked.

"Quite well," I said.

"Do you two fight often?"

"No, not really."

"Do either of you threaten divorce when you do have an argument?"

"No, not ever."

"That's very good. I always worry about couples who bring up divorce whenever they argue. I guess I don't understand why you're worried. It sounds like you two are happy and getting along fine."

"It's because my parents also seemed to get along quite well. They were always a team. They seemed like they were on each other's side and on the same page. They seemed so happy together."

"And then they got divorced."

"Exactly," I said.

"Out of the blue."

"Something like that. Yes, you're right; I really didn't see it coming."

"Were there others involved?"

"Others?"

"As in lovers. Were they cheating on each other?"

"My dad had a girlfriend."

"How about your mom?"

"She was loyal to my father until the end."

Again the doctor looked at me with one eye open, and he asked, "Do you have a girlfriend?"

"No," I said, and I laughed. "That's about the furthest thing from my mind."

"Does your wife have a lover?"

"No, I'm sure she doesn't."

"Then why are you worried?"

"Shouldn't I be? I mean, who's to say I won't have a love affair in the future? Who's to say my wife won't do the same? I don't think anyone plans for these things to happen, but they do happen. My parents were married forty-two years. I would never have guessed that they would get divorced. But it happens all the time, doesn't it? I've seen it happen. I saw it happen to my parents. I've seen it happen to people I know. I even saw it happen to my brother."

"Your brother had an affair?"

"Yes, he did."

"And he got divorced?"

"Yes," I said. "Then he remarried. He said he'd finally met the love of his life. But now he's miserable. He told me so."

The doctor thought for a moment. Then he smiled at me. He said, "I think I can help you."

"That would be good."

"But are you willing to change?"

"Change?"

"You are an American, are you not?"

"I am, obviously."

The doctor picked up a pen from his desk, and he started to play with it. "I assume you're familiar with the Declaration of Independence?"

"Of course," I said. Was this guy a nut? What could the Declaration of Independence possibly have to do with my mom and dad divorcing?

"It is full of some powerful words?"

"Yes, it is."

"You know, Thomas Jefferson had it all wrong. He made a mess of things. He really screwed things up. I'm sure his intentions were good, but he got all of us off on the wrong foot. It was like telling a man to run the fifty-yard dash after tying his shoelaces together."

I stared at the doctor for a moment, and then I said, "No offense, but I have no idea what you're talking about."

The doctor set down the pen he was playing with, and he said, "Life, liberty, and the pursuit of happiness."

"I don't understand."

"It's all wrong. Jefferson had the whole thing wrong. It was his vision for independence. The famous words were supposed to inspire us to pick up arms and fight the British. But now, a couple hundred years later, we're all running around the country with these silly words echoing between our ears like they were spoken by God himself. Now we're making total disasters of our lives. Most of us haven't got a single clue what's wrong with us. Life, liberty, and the pursuit of happiness. Let's start with life. What does life mean to you? Do you believe life is an unalienable right given to us by our creator, a right that our government is obligated to protect?"

"Why wouldn't I believe that?" I still had no idea what this discussion of the Declaration of Independence had to do with my parents getting divorced, but I played along.

"What about war? Doesn't the government expect young men in this country to risk their very lives defending the American way?"

"I suppose so."

"And what about health care? Shouldn't all health care in this country be free? Life is, after all, an inalienable right. Don't we all have the right to stay alive?"

"Free health care might be hard to swing."

"But impossible?"

"Probably not."

"And what about bad drivers?"

"Bad drivers?"

"Don't they put our lives at risk? Sure, we have traffic laws, but are they really sufficient? Is the government going far enough? Aren't bad drivers all traitors, risking our lives—our inalienable right to be alive? Aren't we supposed to put all traitors to death? Do you know how many people die in this country each year due to car accidents that are caused by bad drivers?"

"A lot."

"Yes, a lot. And what about cigarette companies? Aren't they also traitors? Shouldn't all people involved with making and selling deadly cigarettes be hanged by their necks or fried in electric chairs or given lethal injections—and I mean every single one of them, including the executives, all of the workers, and all of the minimum-wage cashiers who sell them to you at the gas station and the local convenience store?"

"That's kind of ridiculous."

"Is it? Isn't life an unalienable right? Isn't treason a capital offence?"

I thought about this, and then I said, "What does any of this have to do with my parents?"

"You haven't thought about it, have you?" the doctor asked, ignoring my question.

"Not really."

"Here's another one for you. What about all the people who die from alcoholism? Shouldn't the government be going out of its way to protect them? Why is alcohol even on the market when it's responsible for so many deaths?"

"They have tried to outlaw alcohol, and it didn't work," I said.

"Precisely."

"Precisely what?"

"That's the whole point. Life *isn't* an unalienable right. Life is a gift from God, and it's *your* job to protect it. It's not your neighbor's job. It's not anyone else's job, and it is certainly not the government's job. Jefferson meant well but had it all wrong. He made a promise that could never be kept. Life is not an inalienable right."

"If I agree, will you tell me what this has to do with my parents getting divorced?"

"I'm getting to that. We're only partway there."

"There's more?"

"How about liberty? Isn't this another one of Jefferson's rights? Life, *liberty*, and the pursuit of happiness?"

"Yes, liberty is a part of the equation."

"Do you think that people should be at liberty to do what they want?"

"Well, I think Jefferson meant within reason. Within the laws."

"Did your dad break a law?"

"I guess not."

"Wasn't he just exercising his liberty?"

"I suppose you could say that," I said.

"Then how can you object to what he did?"

"He hurt my mother."

"Ah, yes he hurt her. But don't we all hurt others when we're free to do what we wish?"

"Do we?"

"We hurt others all the time."

"I'm not sure that's true."

"We have freedom of speech, right? Don't our words often hurt others? We have freedom to choose, but don't our choices hurt those we do not choose? We are at liberty to form our own opinions, but where does that leave those who disagree with us? And then you have to also sit down and ask yourself, Are we really even free? Are you free to live wherever you want? Are you really free to earn what you think you deserve? Are you free to go to the mall and buy any damn thing your heart desires, or free to travel to any country you wish whenever the urge strikes you? Are you free to fly first class? Is that one of your inalienable rights? No, of course not. I can think of a thousand things that you're not free to do. This whole idea of freedom is absurd on its face. We say we cherish our liberty, yet we don't even know what the word means. We live our lives out shackled by a million rules, laws, dues, prices, conditions, fares, taboos, codes, obligations, and limitations. This whole idea of liberty is childish at best, and it has no bearing on the real world. Is any of this making sense? Are you following me?"

"I guess."

"Then let's have a look at part three."

"Part three?"

"The pursuit of happiness."

"Okay," I said.

THE BUTTERFLY

"Happiness is like a butterfly; the more you chase it, the more it will elude you, but if you turn your attention to other things, it will come and sit softly on your shoulder."

—Henry David Thoreau

WAKE UP!

A week or so after I met with Dr. Alex, I woke up in bed with Rhonda. I looked at the clock on the nightstand, and it was a little after nine. This was a problem. It wasn't a problem for me, because I didn't have anything scheduled that morning until eleven. But Rhonda? It was a big problem for her. She had an important meeting with a client scheduled for ten, and it would take her at least thirty minutes just to drive to the office. I shook Rhonda's shoulder to wake her, and I said, "Get up! You need to wake up. You're going to be late for your ten o'clock meeting."

"Meeting?" Rhonda asked sleepily. She was still half in a dream.

"Your meeting," I said.

"Oh, shit!" Rhonda suddenly exclaimed. She looked over at the clock and then jumped out of bed.

That was how her day started. It would not be a good day for Rhonda. By skipping breakfast, she was able to get ready and leave the house on time. But I knew Rhonda. She always said breakfast was the most important meal of the day, and now she had left for work on an empty stomach. But at least she was on time, right? Well, not exactly. She would've been on time if there had been no traffic, but as luck would have it, there had been a car accident on the freeway. The traffic was backed up something awful. By the time she got to the office, she was a half hour late, and the client she was supposed to meet had been waiting and waiting. The client was not happy about this, and he told Rhonda she should've left home earlier in case there was traffic. He was right, of course. Rhonda apologized, and they got on with their meeting.

The meeting did not go well. Rhonda was supposed to present her ideas for an ad that would be in *Los Angeles* magazine, but the client hated all her ideas. "This is a mess," he said. I thought you people were supposed to know what you were doing." So much for her ten o'clock meeting. It was all a bust, and she went back to the drawing board.

Rhonda also had a one o'clock meeting that same day. This meeting went a little better than the first meeting—that is, until Rhonda was interrupted by her secretary and told that she had an important phone call. Rhonda apologized to the client and took the call in the other room. It was our son Thomas's day care center, calling to let Rhonda know that Thomas had punched another kid in the face. Apparently it was the kid's first day, and his mother was dropping him off. Thomas had walked up to the kid and punched him in his nose. The nose bled. The mother threw a fit, and now they were calling and asking Rhonda to take Thomas home. "We need you to pick up your son," the woman said. Rhonda tried to get a hold of me, but as she paged me, I didn't call back. I was in the middle of my own important meeting, and I couldn't be interrupted. So Rhonda had to close her meeting with her client abruptly to go and pick up Thomas. Needless to say, Rhonda's client was not happy. It was just what she needed—another angry client.

By the time I learned what had happened, it was after four in the afternoon, so I wouldn't be able to help out. Rhonda's afternoon was shot. She tried to do some work at home but was unable to proceed without the project files, which were at the office. So she decided to go grocery shopping instead. This made sense. She drove to the market with Thomas and filled her shopping cart. We were low on a lot of things, so the shopping cart was stuffed. The good news was that Thomas was behaving himself. The bad news was that when the cashier rang up all the groceries, Rhonda went through her purse but was unable to find her wallet. "I must've left my wallet in my other purse," she said to the cashier, which is precisely what she had done. She had taken the other purse to work that day, and forgot to grab her wallet before going to the store.

"Oh, God, I just wanted to crawl into a hole," Rhonda told me while we were having dinner that night. "We were all bagged and ready to go. Everyone was staring at us." Then Rhonda set her fork down gently on the side of her plate and looked at me, thinking.

"Are you happy?" I asked.

"Am I happy?"

"Yes," I said.

She said, "Yes, I am. I'm very happy."

"Okay," I said.

"Why do you ask?"

"I guess because you look like you're going to cry."

"You asked me if I was happy," she said. "You didn't ask me how my day went."

She was right.

And you know what? It occurred to me that she understood. She was a smart girl—smarter than I would ever be. Smarter and a lot prettier.

The Log Cabin

What is more iconic than the humble log cabin? America: apple pies, moms, and log cabins—right?

A lot of people think log cabins were invented in America, but they would be wrong. Log cabins were brought to America by Swedish immigrants. Apparently log cabins had been a big thing in Scandinavia for many, many years prior to the discovery of the New World.

But nothing says America like a nice little log cabin with a stone fireplace to keep its occupants warm in the winter months. Think Log Cabin syrup. Think Abe Lincoln as a child. Think *Little House on the*

Prairie. Well, maybe the little house on the prairie wasn't a true log cabin, but it should've been. Then think the presidential election of 1840. Talk of log cabins resulted in an election where William Henry Harrison beat the incumbent, Martin Van Buren. Van Buren supporters tried to paint Harrison as a backward yokel who would be content to sit in a log cabin and drink hard cider for the rest of his life. America loved it. America loved log cabins, and Harrison won by a landslide. Lesson learned? Don't mess with the icon. Who cares where they came from? Log cabins are as American as a Model T Ford, as American as a Fourth of July parade, as American as Archie and Edith Bunker singing "Those Were the Days."

And nowadays? We are still building log cabins. Now they are much more than just a place for some furniture, a fireplace, and an old feather bed. Now they are America on steroids. Now they are mansions and works of art. The greatest log cabin ever built was put together by a man named Louis G. Kaufman, a banker, a financier, and one of the founders of General Motors. He was hoping to compete with the great summer estates being built by the well-known Vanderbilts, Guggenheims, and Rockefellers. He built his log cabin on the shores of Lake Superior in Michigan on eight square miles of land. The twenty-six-thousand-square-foot log cabin cost him $5 million back then, $70 million if built today. Kaufman employed twenty-two architects and God knows how many workers. I'm not sure if Kaufman drank hard cider or ever planned to run for president.

Trabuco Canyon

It was time. It was 1992, and it was time for us to build our own log cabin. Okay, maybe not a log cabin. But we were ready to move out of the duplex and into a place we could call our own. Rhonda and I were both thirty-seven, and Thomas was nearly five. We didn't want to buy just any old house that was up for sale. We wanted to design the house ourselves and build it. This limited us to where we could live. The real estate market in Southern California wasn't exactly flooded with vacant lots suitable for custom single-family homes, and most of the lots available were out of our price range. We wound up looking in the community of Trabuco Canyon, which was in Orange County and had some good possibilities for us. There were some very nice homes there, and some very run-down shacks. It was kind of a hodgepodge of residential real estate. We looked and looked, and finally we found a one-acre vacant lot that we felt would be perfect. It was off a quiet road, nestled in a small ravine of tall weeds and live oak trees. It was a great location, and the price was right. And our timing couldn't have been better. The real estate agent told us that the owner had to sell the lot fast. We worked out a good deal with him, and the next thing we knew, we were the new owners.

I remember the day escrow closed; we went to the lot and celebrated. We brought some soft drinks, cheese, a big loaf of sourdough bread, some sliced meats, paper plates, and a blanket. We spread out the blanket and sat among the weeds and trees to eat, drink, and enjoy our acquisition. "It will take about a year and a half," I said. "Soon the three of us will be living in bliss right here in our brand-new home, right here, where we are all sitting now."

Immanuel Kant once said that there are three basic rules for happiness. You have to have something to do, someone you can love, and something to look forward to. At that point in time, Rhonda, Thomas, and I had all three. We had it all! I was truly happy.

I decided that I would design the house myself. There was no need to go out and hire an architect. We would save a bundle of money right off the bat with me doing all the design work and drawings. I bought a drafting table and equipment and had all the stuff delivered to my office. I then went to work, laying out rooms and picking materials and locating the house on our little piece of land. It was fun. And it was the perfect time for the project. The economy was in the crapper, and there wasn't much construction work, which meant I had some free time. Yes, I had plenty of time. In fact, it was the perfect chance for us to build a house. The plan was to stay out of the sickly business world for a year or two and concentrate on our project. I figured that once I was done building our house, the country's economy would be back on its feet.

I picked three of my favorite workers and laid off everyone else. The four of us would build the house. Once I was done with the drawings, I submitted them to the county to get the necessary permits. I also went to several banks to find one that would lend me the money I needed. I finally found a banker I liked who seemed eager to fund my project. His name was Harry Patterson, and he liked to listen to classical music, eat French food, and shoot guns. And best of all, he liked contractors. Most lenders are wary of contractors because of all the things they try to get away with, but Harry liked me right off the bat. He told me so. He said, "Huey, I like you—even if you are a contractor."

So I had my loan. And I had my drawings and permits. We started the project by having a friend of mine remove several of the oak trees and grade the pad for the foundations. This good friend was a fellow named Danny Abrams, and he'd worked for me for years on my other projects. I totally trusted him. He'd done some very difficult jobs for me, and he knew what he was doing. Not only would I have him grade the pad; I would also have him dig the trenches for the house's foundations with his backhoe.

A MAN NAMED GUTZON

One can only imagine how the man felt. There were all the years of careful planning, and years of trying to explain his vision to the public and the powers that be. He had the hot fire burning in him—the sort of fire that was making America great. It was the fire to tame, build, create, and transform America's virgin landscape. And he was a patriot's patriot. How could one argue with a patriot? Yes, he represented everything that was great about our country. He had a vision. He had hands of steel and a strong work ethic. He had a never-say-die attitude mixed in with a little good old-fashioned red-white-and-blue lunacy. No one knows his name these days, but nearly everyone recognizes his work. His name? It was Gutzon Borglum.

He didn't name the mountain. At one time, the mountain had no name. It was located just north of Custer State Park in South Dakota's Black Hills National Forest. It was named for a lawyer who had traveled to the Black Hills in 1884 to inspect mining claims. When the lawyer asked a local man the name of the mountain, the man replied that it didn't have a name, but from now on would be known by the lawyer's last name. The last name of the lawyer was Rushmore. Now known as the "Shrine of Democracy," the well-known Mount Rushmore welcomes two million visitors every year, and it is one of America's most popular tourist attractions.

A mountain of granite, it was the perfect location for Gutzon. Indians complained about the defacing of the mountain, and politicians complained about the cost, but somehow Gutzon sold his idea to Calvin Coolidge. Work commenced in 1927 and went on until late 1941. Over four hundred workers were employed on the project, and over four hundred fifty thousand tons of rock were removed with pneumatic hammers and dynamite. The work was arduous and dangerous, but not one man lost his life. Have you ever been to Mount Rushmore? I like to think of Gutzon and myself as kindred spirits. You laugh? Well, okay, but the way I see it, we are important. Long live Gutzon, and long live people like us—people who aren't afraid to leave their mark on the landscape, and people who aren't afraid to stir up the soil and blast the rock and cut down the trees. This country likes to despise us, but they need us like the cherry tree needs the honey bee, like silence needs music, like an empty canvas longs for paint.

A KID NAMED DALLAS

I told you that I kept three of my best employees to work on my house. Their names were John, Dewey, and Carlos. When we were working on the foundations, Carlos got a call from Mexico. His mother was ill and hospitalized, and his family wanted him to come see her. The doctors said her condition was terminal, so obviously I didn't object to Carlos leaving. Then Dewey got the flu. His wife called me and said he was as sick as a dog. This left John and me to finish tying off the rebar and pouring the concrete. It was a three-man job, so I asked John if he knew anyone who could come help. John said that a kid had stopped by earlier in the week looking for work. He had left John his phone number. I told John to give the kid a call and see if he was available for a few days. The kid's name was Dallas, like the city, and he said that he very much wanted to work for us. I asked John if Dallas understood that it was only for a few days, and he said the kid knew.

I met Dallas the next day at the jobsite. I talked to him for a while before hiring him. I wanted to be sure he was our kind of guy. I had a specific question I always asked people who wanted to work for me. This question was meant to see if they were reasonably intelligent. I hate to say this, but in the construction business, you get a lot of idiots looking for work, and I didn't want some dope on my payroll who would cause more problems than he helped to solve. So I asked Dallas the question. I said, "A guy named Dave comes up to you and says his father had three sons. He named the first son Snap, and the second son Crackle. What did he name the third son?"

I asked this question, and then I watched Dallas's face. He thought for a moment, and then his eyes opened wide. He said, "The third son was named Pop."

The first thing I said was, "Shit." The kid asked me what was wrong, and I told him, "Listen, we're really stuck here. We have to pour the foundations Wednesday, and you're all I seem to have. Put on some gloves, and John will show you what to do."

Yes, he got the answer to the question wrong, but I didn't have time to look for someone else. Besides, he seemed like a nice kid. It was Monday, and the concrete was scheduled for Wednesday. We had a lot of rebar to tie off in the meantime, and we also had some wood forms to install. John showed Dallas what needed to be done, and then the two of us drove off to the lumberyard to get some more materials. We were gone for about two hours, and when we returned, we found Dallas hiding out in the job shed. He was sitting with his head down on the drawing table, sound asleep. On the drawing table were several sheets of paper filled with signatures. "Wake up!" John shouted into Dallas's ear, and he sat up. "What the hell are you doing in here?"

"I had a question," Dallas said, rubbing his eyes.

"You couldn't keep working?"

"I needed to know the answer."

"What the hell are these?" John asked, referring to the pieces of paper.

"I was practicing my signature."

"What for?"

"You know, for when I'm famous."

I looked at John, and he looked at me. Without saying a word, we said to each other, "What the fuck?"

Well, that was Monday. I should have fired the kid right then and there, but like I said, we were in a bind. Tuesday went much better than Monday, which was encouraging. I thought we were through the worst of it, but I was wrong. On Wednesday the concrete trucks and the pump showed up, and it was time to pour. It was very hectic. There was still some rebar work that needed to be done in one of the deeper foundation footings, and John sent Dallas to do the work. In the meantime, we began pouring the concrete in the other footings. It was going well, and we were making good time. But when we came around the corner to the footing Dallas was supposed to be finishing, we discovered that instead of the work being done, Dallas was on his back at the bottom of the trench, sound asleep. The wet concrete was gushing through the trenches and coming around the corner where Dallas lay. Before we knew it, Dallas was covered with concrete from head to toe. "Jesus!" John exclaimed. "Turn off the pump!" The guy in charge of the pump shut it down, and John and I yelled at Dallas, trying to wake him up.

We reached down and grabbed Dallas, pulling him up and out of the trench. You should've seen the kid's face. And he was a mess. He was covered with wet concrete, and John took him over to the front of the house to hose him down. "What the hell were you even thinking?" John asked.

"I fell asleep," Dallas said.

"No kidding."

"You should've checked the footing before you began pouring concrete," Dallas complained.

"Why were you asleep?"

"I was tired."

"He's an idiot," I said.

"I think that means you're fired," John said to Dallas, shaking his head.

"Go home and clean up," I said. "Come back tonight and I'll pay you what you're owed."

Dallas climbed in his truck and drove off. Honestly, I thought that was the last we would see of him. I didn't think he'd have the nerve to come back and ask for money. John and I finished pouring the foundations by ourselves that day, and when five o'clock rolled around, Dallas returned. He climbed out of his truck in clean clothes and handed me a paper with his hours for the three days written down. For Wednesday he charged me a full eight hours. "What the heck is this?" I asked. "You mean you're charging me eight hours for today?"

"I am," Dallas said.

"How do you figure I owe you for eight hours?"

"I worked two hours this morning. Then thanks to you guys, I spent the entire morning cleaning myself off, then cleaning my shower, then washing my clothes, and then wiping concrete from the inside of my truck. There was concrete everywhere. Then, as I was getting dressed, I noticed a bad cut on my leg. I must've cut it on the rebar wire when you yanked me out of the trench. I had to go to the doctor to get it treated. I also had to get a tetanus shot. Then I had to drive all the way back here to get paid."

"All because you were sleeping on the job."

"I was tired."

"I'll pay you two hours for today."

"But that isn't fair."

"It's more than fair," I said. I got out my checkbook and paid the kid with a check. After I handed him the check, he looked at it for a moment. Then he just stormed away and got back into his truck.

"Where do they come from?" I said to John.

"Who knows?" John said.

Well, that wasn't the end of Dallas. The next day, an OSHA inspector showed up at the house, and he said they'd received a complaint from an employee that my jobsite was unsafe. It was Dallas, of course, getting even for not paying him the hours he thought he deserved. The inspector brought up the incident with Dallas and the concrete, and I tried to explain what happened in a calm and rational way. But the inspector had no desire to hear my side of the story, and he couldn't understand why we didn't know that Dallas was in the trench working while we were pouring concrete. Then the inspector asked to see my first aid kit. Well, I didn't have one to show him. "Are you aware your employee required several stitches to treat a laceration on his leg?" he asked. "What did you do to treat the wound?"

"I didn't even know he was cut," I said.

"Probably because he was covered with concrete."

"Probably."

"You are required by law to have a first aid kit on site at all times."

"Okay," I said.

"I'll be back tomorrow, and if you can't show me a legal first aid kit, I'm going to shut your project down and hit you with a fine."

"Very well," I said, but I didn't say it nicely, because it was dumb. In my opinion, first aid kits are a joke. Listen, I do care about my workers, and I take care of them. I carry full workers' compensation insurance to pay the doctor and hospital bills, and if someone gets seriously injured on one of my jobs, I take them promptly to the nearest clinic or emergency room. That's where they belong. They don't need to be messed around with by some amateur with a silly first aid kit. Have you ever checked out one of these kits? They hold Band-Aids, ointment, tape, gauze, aspirin, scissors, latex gloves, tweezers, and an assortment of other such ridiculous things—none of which are helpful when someone is really injured. I say let the doctors do their job. And I say that if you have some little cut or bruise, you should suck it up and keep working. It's a construction site, not a nursery school.

Anyway, for a couple hundred dollars, I had a first aid kit delivered to satisfy the OSHA inspector. It was a lot cheaper than being fined and having my job shut down.

But that was not the last of Dallas. He also went downtown and filed a complaint with the labor board, telling them I had refused to pay him wages that were due. An idiot from the labor board called me to schedule a hearing. He sounded like a real tiger over the phone. A hearing? Jesus, it was exactly what I didn't need—more time away from the house. And to do what? To defend myself from a complaint filed by a kid who fell asleep on my job not just once, but twice. I talked to John about it, and he said I should just pay Dallas the money he was asking for. It wasn't that much, and it was certainly cheaper than my time messing around at a labor board hearing.

So I paid him.

I guess that in the scope of things, the cost of the first aid kit and the money I paid Dallas didn't amount to very much. It probably shouldn't have bothered me as much as it did. It was like a drop in the bucket. But you know what they say; they say to keep your eye on all the dimes, nickels, pennies, and quarters, and the dollars will fall into place. I'm not sure that I believe in this, but it's what I've been told.

Speaking of money, building this house turned out to be one of the smartest things I ever did financially. The equity did wonders for our net worth. The lot cost me $153,000. It cost me about $257,000 to build the house. I recently had the house appraised, and the appraiser said the property was worth well over a million dollars. It's so funny to think that when Rhonda and I were newlyweds, the two of us were so in love that we weren't even thinking about things like appraisals, equity, and net worth.

OUR HOUSE

I'll mow the lawn, while you vacuum the floors
And clean all those dirty windows.
Watching the TV for hours and hours,
I'll sit and listen to you list my chores
All day long for me; it never ends.
Come to me now, and close your mouth for just five minutes.
Don't you fret, 'cause
I built this house, and it has appreciated
By far more than we anticipated.
Lots of cash for you and for me.
Our house is a very, very, very fine house
With lots of equity.
Honey, don't you see.
Now everything is easy 'cause of me.
La la la ...
Our house is a very, very, very fine house
With lots of equity.
Honey, don't you see.
Now everything is easy 'cause of me.
Mowing the lawn and vacuuming the floors,
Who could ask for anything more?

Honey from the Comb

"Do you know the only value life has is what life puts upon itself? And it is of course over-estimated since it is of necessity prejudiced in its own favor. Take that man I had aloft. He held on as if he were a precious thing, a treasure beyond diamonds or rubies. To you? No. To me? Not at all. To himself? Yes. But I do not accept his estimate. He sadly overrates himself. There is plenty more life demanding to be born. Had he fallen and dripped his brains upon the deck like honey from the comb, there would have been no loss to the world. He was worth nothing to the world. The supply is too large. To himself only was he of value, and to show how fictitious even this value was, being dead he is unconscious that he has lost himself. He alone rated himself beyond diamonds and rubies. Diamonds and rubies are gone, spread out on the deck to be washed away by a bucket of seawater, and he does not even know that the diamonds and rubies are gone."

—Jack London

Buried in Portland

Meet Blair White. Blair graduated from the business school at Stanford University and was then offered a job in Portland, Oregon, as a junior executive for Chatsworth Industries. In a matter of sixteen years, Blair worked his way up to being the president and CEO of the company. The only man who was more rich or powerful than Blair was old man Chatsworth himself, who kept an eye on Blair but who, for all intents and purposes, had removed himself from the day-to-day concerns of the company so he could play a lot of golf and read.

Blair was a big man. He was big in several ways. First, he was six feet four inches tall—not thin and lanky, but thick like a professional wrestler. He also had a big personality. He was loud and self-confident, and when he was in a room, others knew he was there. There was no ignoring or missing Blair. He was also big financially; Chatsworth Industries paid the man a fortune in the form of a huge salary, plus bonuses and stock options. He was the sort of man you would meet for the first time, and after a mere handshake, you'd immediately know you'd just met someone important. He was just the kind of guy you'd love to have in charge during a crisis. He was that kind of guy—big, rich, important, and capable.

Blair married a woman who was twelve years younger. They met when Blair was thirty-eight and she was twenty-six. Her name was Suzie Boothe, and she was a cheerleader for the Portland Trailblazers. Blair went to the games religiously. He was a big fan of basketball, and he met Suzie at a party for coaches, players, and a handful of wealthy fans such as himself. Suzie told everyone that it was love at first sight, but for Blair it was more of a purchase. You might say he drove her off the showroom floor like a blonde and blue-eyed Lamborghini from an exotic car dealership. Vroom! He would put the pedal to the metal and turn this cheerleader into a loving wife.

During the first several years of their marriage, Suzie was the perfect mate. She strived to make her husband happy. She did things for him, cooked for him, helped him to pick out his clothes, and made sure there were always fresh flowers in the house. And she looked good. No, she looked terrific. What man in his right mind wouldn't want a lovely young wife such as Suzie hanging off his arm? She knew what to say at parties, and all of Blair's friends loved her. It was during their fourth year of marriage that Suzie became more aware of herself. Yes, Blair was a powerful man, but she, too, had power. She had power over the powerful man. She never hit Blair over the head with it, but she began to use it to her advantage to get the things she wanted.

It was then that Suzie began to have an interest in art. She took several art history classes at Portland Community College, and she bought books on art, artists, and museums. She never became an artist herself, but she was a student and an ardent admirer. She encouraged Blair to invest in fine art for their home, but Blair resisted. He didn't understand art, and he had no desire to own it. He was perfectly content with what they had. Suzie called it sofa art. But Blair also wanted his wife to be happy. Happy wife, happy life, right? And he did still love her. Well, he loved her as far as he knew what the word meant. It was during their fourth year of marriage that Blair decided to do something really special for Suzie. He had Bertram Kamps come into his office, and they set Blair's plan into motion.

Bertram was the vice president of marketing at Chatsworth Industries, and like Suzie, he was a lover of fine art. Blair knew about this. He made it his business to know about all of his subordinate employees because it made it easier for him to manage them. It made it much easier to know which strings to pull when he wanted something out of them. Blair asked Bertram to do him a favor that day. It was a personal favor, and it had to do with Suzie. Bertram was more than happy to oblige when he heard all the details. The favor was to accompany Blair to an art auction and help him pick out something special for Suzie. Since Blair didn't know anything about art, he wanted Bertram to come along. He wanted Bertram to help him pick out the article and be sure he wasn't overpaying.

The day of the auction came, and Blair and Bertram sat down in the audience. "We're only here to buy one piece," Blair said to Bertram. "One piece, and then we get the hell out of here."

"Got it," Bertram said.

"Hopefully we won't be here all damn day."

"Yes sir," Bertram said.

The first piece came up for bidding and sold, and then the second came up, and then the third. Blair kept looking over at Bertram, but these were not what Blair needed. They were nice things, but Bertram shook his head each time, telling Blair to sit tight. "I can't believe what all these fools are willing to pay for this crap," Blair finally whispered to Bertram.

"Yes sir," Bertram whispered.

"I wouldn't display half of this stuff over the toilet in my bathroom."

"No sir."

"I wouldn't even want it in my attic."

Bertram chuckled.

Then came the piece Bertram had been waiting for. It was a small painting in a gilded frame. The auctioneer put the framed painting on display and then stepped to the podium to start the bidding. "This is the one," Bertram whispered to Blair.

"It is?" Blair whispered. "What the hell is it?"

"A painting," Blair said.

"I know that. I mean, what's it supposed to be?"

"It's a Kadinsky."

"Oh?" Blair said.

"He was a Russian painter."

"A Russian? You mean a communist?"

"I don't think he was political. At least I'm not sure. He was an artist."

"His stuff is worth money?"

"Oh, yes."

"He's in museums?"

"Yes, of course. Suzie will know who he is."

"Good, good," Blair whispered.

"Go ahead and bid on it. But don't act too eager. You don't want to get the others all fired up."

"Fired up?"

"Bidding against you. As far as anyone here knows, you can take it or leave it. Just act like you're slightly amused, but also act like you don't really like it."

"That will be easy."

So the bidding started, and there seemed to be four of the audience members who were interested in the Kadinsky. The price went up and up, until there were only three. Then it was Blair versus one man with a beard and a corduroy coat. The man who was bidding clearly wanted the painting, and he countered every one of Blair's bids. "Who is this jackass?" Blair whispered to Bertram.

"I don't know."

"How long is this going to go on?"

"Until one of you stops."

"Well, fuck this," Blair said. He stood up and announced a price that no one in their right mind would match. The audience gasped. The bearded man did not counter, and the painting now belonged to Blair.

"You paid too much," Bertram whispered. "It isn't worth that much."

"This crap appreciates, right?"

"Yes, it should."

"Then someday it will probably be worth more than I'm paying. I'm just buying it ahead of time. Think of it that way."

"If you say so, sir."

"I say so. Now let's get the hell out of here before you have me buying more."

"Yes sir."

The two men arranged for payment and delivery, and then they drove to a little restaurant for lunch. "Suzie's going to crap a brick," Blair said.

"Yes sir."

"She won't believe it."

"No sir, she probably won't."

"What was that guy's name again?"

"The painter?"

"Yes, the painter."

"Kadinsky."

"Russian, eh?"

"Yes sir."

"I guess this Kadinsky now makes me an art collector. How about that, Bertram? Who would've thought? I don't even know what the hell I was buying, and I paid a fortune for it. Really pissed off the guy in the corduroy coat. He didn't know who he was dealing with."

"No sir."

"You know, wasting money makes me hungry."

"What are you going to order?"

"I'm going to ask for a big Rueben sandwich and a bowl of minestrone soup. I also want a side of onion rings and a side of coleslaw. Maybe something for dessert."

"That sounds good."

"The sandwiches here are huge. Have you ever been here before?"

"No, I haven't."

"They have great sandwiches. And they use quality meats. You can't argue with their meats."

It was one year later that Blair had his heart attack. He was at his office, about to go home. It had been a long and trying day, but the attack was a total surprise. Everyone who knew Blair figured he was as strong as an ox. Three hours after the heart attack, his heart failed, and he died in Providence Medical Center. Lots of people came to the funeral. Everyone was dressed in black. A lot of people cried.

Several months after they buried Blair, Suzie called up an interior decorator, and she had the woman come out to the house. Suzie realized how nice it was to have the house to herself, but the place needed a serious face lift. There was just too much of Blair in the house, and it made her sad. She did not want to live in the past. As she strolled through the house with the interior decorator, she spouted out ideas. "All of this stuff has got to go," she said, but when they came upon the Kadinsky, she said she wanted the painting to stay. "We'll need to find a place for it," she said.

"What is it?" the decorator asked.

"It's a Kadinsky."

"Is he a local artist?"

"He's a dead Russian."

"Oh, I see."

"It isn't going to go with anything we're doing. Maybe it can go in one of the bathrooms. Like above one of the toilets. Blair was always so sweet. He was always thinking of me. God only knows how much he paid for this thing. Now tell me, what do you have in mind for the furniture in the living room? I've been thinking of the new sofas. I picture something floral and colorful. You know, something cheerful. I'd like to see some fabric swatches."

THE GREEN STUFF

"Money has never made man happy, nor will it. There is nothing in its nature to produce happiness. The more of it one has, the more one wants."

—Benjamin Franklin

JACK THE DRIPPER

This is the story of Jackson Pollock. Let us begin with the ending first. I'm going to tell you how this idiot died. I call him an idiot because I have earned the right to call him this. Like me, he was an alcoholic. Like me, he drove his car while drunk; but unlike me, he wasn't so lucky. He was forty-four and had two women with him in his car. He plowed into a tree less than a mile from his house and was thrown fifty feet into the air, and into a tree. He died instantly. Another woman in the car also died. MADD would have a heyday railing about this guy today, and he'd be scorned endlessly for the irresponsible jerk that he was. But things were different in 1956. Four months following the accident, Pollock was given a memorial retrospective exhibition at the Museum of Modern Art in New York City. Poor guy. What a shame. Pour me another glass of champagne.

Surely you're familiar with his work, especially all the crazy paintings he produced during his "drip" years. It was the kind of work that made laypeople laugh while experts called it genius. Drip, splash, drip! *Time* magazine called him "Jack the Dripper." Yet in 1949, French artist Georges Mathieu stated he considered Pollock the "greatest living American painter." Me? Honestly? I've definitely seen stuff done by preschool kids and kindergarteners that was equally interesting. My son, Thomas, for example, did some very sophisticated finger paintings which I framed and hung in my office. I'm proud of Thomas, but that's because he's my son. I'm not expecting the Museum of Modern Art in New York to exhibit his work, ever.

Most renowned painters are not all that successful in their lifetimes, and most of them live in poverty. Hence, we refer to them empathetically as "starving artists." Was Jackson Pollock successful in his lifetime? I suppose he was, but he never was rich. He was always short on cash and wasn't exactly being driven around in a limousine. Now his works sell for a fortune. Just ask a man named Kenneth Griffin. In 2016 he bought one of Pollock's drip paintings for $200 million. Money in America—it can sure be strange.

I could give you lots of information about where Pollock was born, where he was raised, where he studied, who he married, who his mistress was, where his works were shown, who treated his alcoholism, and more of what others said about him. But all of this information is about as interesting as his paintings. $200 million? Wow. If you are a Pollock fan, I hope you will accept my apologies. Personally, I like Norman Rockwell. Now *there* was a true American treasure. And Norman didn't even call himself an artist. He referred to himself as an illustrator.

THE ESSAY

When Thomas was in the fifth grade, his teacher asked the class to write essays. The essays were supposed to be about America. The student could pick the subject, so long as it was about what the kid liked or didn't like about living in our country. This was my son's first essay. The subject Thomas picked was money and capitalism. I saved the essay. I'm not sure why. I loved Thomas, but I wasn't in the habit of saving his schoolwork. But this particular essay intrigued me. It was written as a single paragraph. It had many punctuation and spelling errors, which I have corrected. Word for word, it went as follows:

> My name is Thomas Baker, and this is my essay about money in America. This is my first essay. I'm going to stick to our teacher's definition of an essay. According to my teacher, an essay is simply a short piece of writing about a subject. So, while an entire book could be written about this subject, I'm going to keep this short and sweet. I'm going to talk about my day last Saturday. I'm going to begin when I woke up. It was about nine in the morning. I woke up in bed—a bed my parents purchased from a mattress store. I climbed out of the covers, which my parents purchased at Bed Bath & Beyond. I put on my clothes. We bought my jeans, belt, boxers, and socks at Target, and we bought my T-shirt from Tilly's. My shoes were purchased last week at Van's. I walked across the floor to my bathroom, where I brushed my teeth with a toothbrush and toothpaste we bought at CVS. I brushed my hair, but I'm not sure where we bought the brush. I had a baseball game that morning, and Dad was waiting for me downstairs. Mom fed me breakfast with food she purchased at the grocery store, on dishes she bought from Macy's. I also had a cup of coffee. My parents like to buy their coffee from a little place downtown that specializes in fresh coffee beans. I then left the house with my dad—a house that cost my parents a fortune. They had to get a loan to buy it. Dad told me that getting the loan was a real pain. The way I understand it, if Dad doesn't make his payments as promised, the bank can take the house away from us. My baseball gear was in the trunk of dad's

car. Dad also had to take out a loan for the car, and just like the house, the bank can take it back if his payments aren't made on time. My baseball gear was all brand-new. We bought the gear at a sporting goods store. Dad said we had to stop and get gas, so we drove to the gas station, where Dad used a credit card to buy his gas. The price of the gas was posted on the pump, and the pump calculated the total due. While Dad pumped gas, I went into the convenience store. Everything inside had a price tag. I bought a bag of Doritos. I paid the clerk, who was getting paid by the hour to process my sale. When we finally arrived at the park, all the other kids and their parents were there. All of them had paid the league so their kids could play on the teams. It was a nice park. The county paid their gardeners to keep the place up. They kept the grass watered and fertilized, but I have no idea how much this cost. Joey Perkins was there. He got injured last weekend when a ball hit him in the nose. They had to take him to the doctor. I've been to a doctor before. They charge lots of money. My dad says they charge too much. Dad thinks doctors are a rip-off. He says to never trust a man who offers to help you and then drives home from his office in a brand-new Mercedes. My dad told me he'd like a Mercedes. My dad told me this, but he still drives a truck. I think there are a lot of things my dad would like to buy. A nicer house is one of them. Sometimes, on Sundays, Mom and Dad will go look at houses for sale. I'm not sure why they do this, since they had to borrow money to buy the house we're living in. After the ballgame, Dad and I drove home on the streets paved with tax funds, under the phone lines paid for with utility bills, rolling on the rubber tires dad purchased from the Goodyear tire company. We listened to the radio as we drove. The newscasters were talking excitedly about *Titanic*. The movie was setting all-time records at the box office. Money, money, money. "That movie *ought* to be good," Dad said. "Think of all the cash they have paid to those actors. Those freaking people are all making a fortune." Then the newscasters talked about sports and about how much money Tiger Woods was making. Then there were commercials, and Dad asked me, "What do you think Drew Carey got paid to do that Nokia ad during the Superbowl?" I looked at my dad, and it occurred to me that this is what America is about. Everything has a price tag, and everything has a value. Everything is for sale. We are living in one humongous department store. On the first floor they have men's and women's clothing; on the second floor they have housewares and furnishings. On the third floor are the appliances, and on the fourth floor and up there is the rest of the world. The woman at the cash register says, "Apply for a store credit card and we'll give you ten percent off your first purchase. If you can't pay the credit card bill, no problem. We'll just charge you eighteen percent interest. It's only money, right? So sign up now. It takes only two minutes to complete an application. Are you new here? Welcome to America!"

At the top of the essay in red ink was Thomas's grade, along with a comment from his teacher. She had given him a B. Then she had written, "You have eloquently and creatively written about something you perceive to be a problem, but you have offered us no solution." I'm not sure what the teacher expected. Seriously, the kid was only ten years old.

I was forty-three when I first read this essay. When I was done reading it, I realized just how old I actually was. I had become a part of the status quo. And I remembered back to when I was Thomas's age. For just a moment, I felt as free as a bird. I remembered what it was like to be so creative and idealistic. The sky was my home, and the treetops were my best friends. And things *could* be better.

THE CONSUMERS

The year was now 2000, and I was forty-five. When I was a kid, I used to wonder if I'd make it to the year 2000. Now here I was, alive and well. I was still busy building my construction projects, and business was good. Between Rhonda's steady salary from her dad's advertising agency and my rapidly rising income, we were making a lot of money.

It was the very last year of the twentieth century. It was also the year that computers were supposed to go haywire. The computer concern turned out to be nothing of significance. So what was significant? The final original *Peanuts* comic strip was published following the death of the amazing Charles Schulz. Not much else of interest happened in 2000. Pope John Paul II apologized for the misbehavior of the Roman Catholic Church down through the ages—a so-what. The Yankees beat the Mets in the World Series—a double so-what. The billionth baby was born in India—a triple so-what. Aside from being the last year of the twentieth century, there wasn't much to be excited about during this year. But as I said, Rhonda and I were making a lot of money. So it was a good year. You know, you can deride money all you want, and it may not buy happiness, but it sure is fun when you have plenty of it.

So what did we do with our money? Did we put it into a savings account? Did we buy an annuity? Did we save up for Thomas's college or our retirement? Heck no, we were Americans. We looked for ways to spend it.

I bought myself a Rolex watch. I decided to be thrifty about it, so I went on eBay and looked for a used one to get a better deal. I found an eighteen-carat gold-and-stainless-steel Submariner that was only a couple years old. Then I bought a new gold wedding band. I had lost the old one years ago and never got around to replacing it. Then we went out and bought Rhonda a new wedding ring. Her old one was literally wearing out, and the diamond was embarrassingly small. The new ring we bought for her was expensive but worth every penny. We found the new ring at an exclusive jewelry store in Newport Beach that catered to rich people. The diamond in this new ring was two carats, and it was a VVS-2. Just knowing it was a VVS-2 made it seem as if our marriage would last forever.

Then there were the cars. We traded Rhonda's BMW 320i in for a 735il. It was a big car, but Rhonda deserved it. There were two models of the car available, so we bought the longer model. It was built four inches longer than the standard model for an additional four thousand dollars. It was a thousand dollars per inch, so the salesman told us, and we laughed at that. It seemed to be worth it. I mean, it's hard to put a price on legroom for your passengers. Then I traded in my old truck for a new Chevy Tahoe with soft leather seats and a burl wood-grain dashboard. It was real wood, mind you, and not that fake stuff. And I got the special chrome wheels. Seriously, it was a Chevy Tahoe, but it looked like a Cadillac.

Then along came our annual vacation. Up until that year, we had been taking our vacations at the least expensive resorts available, but now we were ready to take *real* vacations. "Where do the wealthy people go?" Rhonda asked our travel agent, and the agent recommended that we go to the Four Seasons in Costa Rica. We were sold. We booked two weeks. We hopped aboard a plane at LAX, and off we went, the three of us. It was Rhonda, Thomas, and me, with our new suitcases stuffed full of paperback novels, clothing, and toiletries. The bags were loaded by the airport workers into the belly of the plane while the three of us located our seats.

We didn't like Costa Rica. We *loved* it! The Four Seasons was first class all the way. There were the tropical drinks and monkeys in the trees. There were delicious meals, morning, noon, and night. The grounds were picture perfect, and I'll bet we took over a hundred photos.

Bad Credit, No Problem!

Visi-AI-Y765-38 49" 4K Ultra HD LED TV: Brilliant clarity and contemporary styling are yours with this state-of-the-art TV. It comes to you from one of the top names in TV technology. It delivers lifelike image quality that jumps right out of the screen. Whether you're watching the news, a crime drama, a sitcom, or an old movie, a modern ultra HD LED panel provides you with an astonishingly unparalleled viewing experience. And the eighty-two-inch screen option is perfect for your oversize rooms and home theaters. This unit comes with voice-controlled remote control and modern streaming. Visit our showroom and see this TV for yourself. Bad credit? It's no problem! We guarantee financing for everyone.

THE THINK-A-TRON

Oh, man, did he ever want one in the worst way. Who was he, and what did he want? His name was Bobby O'Dell, and he was a nine-year-old freckle-faced red-headed boy who lived with his parents, older sister, and cocker spaniel dog in a modest three-bedroom home at 348 Cactus View Lane in Phoenix, Arizona. And what did he want so badly? I'll get to that shortly. First let me tell you about Bobby's dad, Sean.

"One hell of a nice guy," everyone said when his name came up in conversation. That was Sean. He'd moved to Arizona from New York fifteen years earlier. It was no secret that he never graduated from high school. Instead of going to school with the other kids his age, he worked. And he was proud of it. He put in twelve hours a day and six days every week at his father's junkyard. He worked like a dog for his dad until he moved west to Phoenix with his fiancée, Adelle Carson. Why Phoenix? "Why the hell not?" Sean would say. There was no snow, no bitterly cold winters, no real traffic to speak of, and lots of friendly people. Sean and Adelle were married in 1949, and they brought Bobby into the world in 1951. They moved into the Cactus View house in 1954 when Bobby was three years old. Sean had a steady job with the city's sanitation department. It was a good job, and he got plenty of exercise and fresh Arizona air. In other words, he was a garbage man.

Sean was not an unhappy man, but he hoped for a better life for Bobby. He and Adelle decided to live in a nice house in an upper-middle-class neighborhood. There Bobby would be able to make the right kinds of friends and be influenced by the right kinds of people, and he would go to good schools. Yes, school. Bobby would do well in school. He would study hard, and he'd get good grades. He would fit in with the other kids, and maybe he would play a few sports. Who knew? Maybe he would be class president, and maybe he would date a cheerleader or the school valedictorian. Maybe a reputable college in Arizona would offer Bobby a scholarship. Or maybe a college in another state? The world would be Bobby's oyster; thus the house on Cactus View Lane. No, there weren't many garbage men living there; in fact, Sean was the only one. It took every dime Sean had just to pay the rent, and that was working overtime. And that was also with Adelle doing some seamstress work on the side, which didn't pay a lot, but every little bit helped.

The neighbors were polite to Sean and his family. They all knew what he was. He was a garbage man. They didn't treat him like one of their own, but they weren't rude to him. And they were polite to his wife and son. It was a strange politeness, as though they felt sorry for his family. Sean figured that it helped them feel good about themselves to allow the O'Dells into their social circles, to invite them to their parties, and to let their children play with Bobby. And Bobby did make friends. For example, there were the Richards brothers next door. There was Lewis across the street, and there was also Ricky just a few houses down. These were the four boys Bobby spent the most time with, especially Lewis. Bobby loved going across the street to Lewis's house. He was always welcome, and the blonde, blue-eyed Lewis had just about everything a kid could have. There wasn't a toy on the market his parents didn't buy for him. To Bobby's way of thinking, the family was rich. Lewis's dad was a manager at an electronics company, and he seemed to make more money than the family could spend.

It was on a pleasant fall day in 1960 that Lewis's dad came home with the amazing toy. Bobby was there to see the thing, and he was immediately obsessed. He had never seen a toy like it in all his life. It was complicated, modern, and made of shiny plastic, and it had all sorts of little flashing lights and knobs. It was a computer! It was a computer for kids! Lewis's dad removed the toy from its box, and he put in the batteries. Bobby looked at the box while Lewis and his dad tried to figure out how to operate the machine. "THINK-A-TRON," it said. "The machine that thinks like a man! Made by Hasbro. It thinks! It answers! It remembers! Feed it the questions into here, and it answers them in lights." Holy sweet Mary and Jesus! Bobby had never seen anything like this, ever.

TRASH MAN

One, two, three, four,
One, two—one, two, three, four!

Let me tell you how it will be.
You put it in a can for me,
'Cause I'm the trash man.
Yeah, I'm the trash man; yeah, I'm the trash man.
Hot summer, spring, winter and fall.
Be thankful that I take it all.
Cause I'm the trash man.
Yeah, I'm the trash man; yeah, I'm the trash man.
Got your rotten eggs,
I'll take the goo.
Got your spoiled meat,
I'll take it too.
Got your smelly fish,
It's good as gone.
Got your old tin cans,
Just say so long.
Trash man!
Cause I'm the trash man.
Yeah, I'm the trash man; yeah, I'm the trash man.
Don't ask me what I want it for.
(Ha, ha, Mr. Wilson).
Imagine if I lived next door.
(Ha, ha, Mr. Heath).
Cause I'm the trash man.
Yeah, I'm the trash man; yeah, I'm the trash man.
Now my advice to all of you:
(Trash man!)
Be nice to me, don't treat me rude.
(Trash man!)
All of you need me.
Yeah, I'm your trash man. Yeah, I'm your trash man,
And I ain't hauling your trash for free.

A Garbage Man's Son

The first thing Bobby did that night was ask his dad for his own Think-A-Tron. "Please, please, please," he begged. "I'll do a hundred extra chores. I'll do anything. I'll earn it." Sean laughed and then agreed to consider his son's request. In fact, that Saturday, Sean took Bobby to the toy store to look over the toy. "It's a very popular item," the owner of the store said to Sean. "The darn things are selling like hotcakes. Can't keep them on the shelves." Sean was smiling at the friendly man, and Bobby was too. Then Sean asked how much the thing cost. When the man told Sean the price, Sean's smile vanished. "I see," Sean said.

"It's educational," the man said.

"Educational?"

"The kids learn."

"What do they learn?" Sean asked. Now he was just making small talk. It was obvious he had no intention of buying the toy.

"The questions all come from the *Book of Knowledge*. You know, the children's encyclopedia."

"Ah," Sean said.

"They learn a lot."

"Why not just buy the encyclopedia?"

"Because the Think-A-Tron is fun," Bobby said.

"Who said learning was supposed to be fun?" Sean said with a frown.

"The kids really get a kick out of it."

"Yeah, well. I guess we'll have to think about it." But Sean wasn't going to think about anything. It was way too much money to spend on a toy. Even if Bobby worked extra chores, it wouldn't make the toy any more affordable. Ultimately, the cash would come out of Sean's pocket, and he and Adelle were barely able to pay the house rent. "I know you're disappointed, son," he said to Bobby on their way home. "Your birthday is coming up soon. Maybe Mom and I can get you something else— something reasonable."

My dad is a garbage man, Bobby thought. *My dad is a dirt-poor garbage man.*

That night, Bobby made a decision. He was going to get a Think-A-Tron for himself, by hook or by crook. And by hook or by crook meant doing whatever it took.

The following weekend, Lewis and his parents left to visit Lewis's aunt and uncle up in Flagstaff. They were going to stay overnight, and that's when Bobby came up with his plan. Why should Lewis have a Think-A-Tron? He didn't even seem to like it that much. He seldom wanted to play with it. It just sat on the floor in his bedroom, unappreciated. Yes, Bobby decided to sneak into Lewis's room late Saturday night. He would steal the toy and bring it home. He would keep it hidden under his bed, and it would be all his. He could play with it late at night while his mom and dad were sleeping. This was a crazy scheme. Bobby knew it was a little crazy, but thinking about the Think-A-Tron was making him even crazier. He couldn't stop thinking about it. He had to have it, and he deserved it. He knew he was clever, and he wouldn't get caught. No way. No one would ever know anything.

So, while Lewis's family was out of town, and while Bobby's parents were sleeping, Bobby climbed out of bed and got dressed. He wore all black. He would be a shadow in the night. He made his way out of his room and to the front door. Carefully, he opened the door and stepped outside, not making a sound. Then he walked across the street and to Lewis's house. He went around the side yard, where the window to Lewis's bedroom was located. Lewis always kept his window open a crack to let in fresh air, and sure enough, the window was open a couple inches, unlatched. Bobby removed the screen, slid the window open, and hoisted himself up and through the opening. It was easy. Bobby turned on the light. The Think-A-Tron was on the floor in the corner of the room. He picked the toy up and turned off the light. He then made his way out the window opening, and once outside, he closed the window and replaced the screen. It was the perfect crime!

Bobby looked both ways before crossing the street. It was dark and quiet, and no one was in sight. He made his way back to his house and, finally, to his room. His heart was beating a million beats per second. He took off his black clothes and put them away. Then he looked at his toy and softly whispered, "I got you!" He had his Think-A-Tron! Now he needed to go back to sleep. He slid the plastic toy under his bed after wrapping it with an old T-shirt.

It was the next day that Lewis's family returned from Flagstaff. At first nothing happened. Well, nothing as far as Bobby was concerned. Then, around dinnertime, Lewis's father came to the front door. Sean answered, and the two men said hi. At first there was some talk about their trip, and then Lewis's dad was talking in a low voice. Bobby was in the front room watching TV, but he couldn't make out what was being said from where he was sitting. His heartbeat began to speed up. He did hear one word, if you can call it a word. He heard Lewis's dad say, "Think-A-Tron." Yes, he was sure that he heard this! They had discovered that the toy was missing, and they had come to Bobby's house. But why? Was it because they suspected Bobby? How would they even know? A clue, maybe? Did Bobby leave a clue? This was *not* good. Then Bobby heard his father say, "I'll talk to him. I'll find out." Then the two men were done talking. Sean closed the door, and Bobby's mom said it was time for dinner.

The three of them sat down for dinner. They ate quietly until Sean finally spoke. Bobby was staring at his plate, but the food was no longer appetizing. And now there was a knot in his stomach the size of a basketball. He could feel his cheeks and forehead burning.

"I have a question for you, son," Sean said.

"Yes sir?"

"I think you know what it is."

"I do?"

"Don't you?"

"I'm not exactly sure."

"What's going on?" Bobby's mom asked.

"Bobby knows," Sean said.

"What's your father talking about?" Bobby's mom asked.

"I don't know."

"Son, it's in your best interest not to lie to us," Sean said.

"About what?"

"What on earth are you two talking about?" Bobby's mom asked.

"Lewis," Sean said firmly.

Bobby stared at his dad. He wasn't sure what to do. Did his dad know, or was he just guessing? What exactly had Lewis's dad said to him? He knew he was only making things worse by this game with his dad. He was only going to get himself into more trouble. But he was a kid, so he acted like one.

"I want to hear it from you," Sean said.

"From me?"

"I want you to be honest with me. Are you sure there isn't something you want to tell us?"

"Okay," Bobby said. "Okay, okay." There was no point in pretending to be innocent any longer.

"Okay what?" Bobby's mom asked.

"I took it."

"Took what?"

"I took the Think-A-Tron."

"That's what I thought," Sean said, shaking his head in feigned disbelief.

"That's the toy you wanted your father to buy for you?"

"Yes," Bobby said.

"You stole it?"

"That's exactly what he did."

"Oh my," Bobby's mom said.

"We're going to try to make this right. Do you understand what I'm saying?"

"Yes sir," Bobby said.

It was decided. Well, in fairness to Bobby, it was decided by his father. They would take the Think-A-Tron to Lewis's house as soon as they were done eating dinner. The toy would be given back to Lewis, and Bobby would apologize to their family. He would apologize for breaking into the home, and he would say he was sorry to Lewis for stealing his toy. Bobby would offer no excuses. He would be a man about it. He would be a nine-year-old man.

So that's exactly what they did. Bobby was terrified. He was afraid of what Lewis's father would say. He'd never seen the man angry before. And Lewis? What would Lewis think? Would he be angry too, or would he just think it was amusing? Would he be laughing at the fact that Bobby had been caught and was now in trouble? It was horrible. It was as bad as Bobby imagined it to be. He barely got the words out of his mouth. His knees were weak, and his armpits were sweating. "Anytime you want to come over and play with the toy, you're welcome to visit Lewis," the dad said.

"That's very nice of you," Sean said.

"Thanks, sir," Bobby said.

"I hope you've learned a lesson."

"Oh, yes sir."

"It's a lesson he won't forget," Sean said. "His mom and I will see to that."

That night Bobby was told to go to his room and think about what he'd done. There would be no TV, no after-dinner dessert. It was just Bobby alone in his room, thinking and thinking. He knew what he was; He was a kid, and he wanted a Think-A-Tron. He was even willing to steal for it. He would've done anything. Anything at all. But it hadn't worked out. It would never work out. He thought, *I'm not Lewis, and Lewis's dad is not my dad. I'm just Bobby O'Dell, a poor garbage man's son. The son of a garbage man.* Then he lay down on his bed and slept. When he woke up in the morning, he would climb out of bed and put on his clothes. He would pee in the toilet and brush his hair. Then he would go downstairs, and his mom would serve him breakfast in the kitchen. It would be a fresh new day, but he would still be a garbage man's son.

WHAT'S THAT SMELL?

"Human society sustains itself by transforming nature into garbage."

—Mason Cooley

GARBAGE STEW

This is a tried and true all-American stew recipe passed down from our early settlers and augmented over the decades to keep it current with modern trends. Ingredients can be adjusted to taste. This is one of my all-time favorite dishes. Allow one hour for preparation. Don't be surprised if your guests demand second helpings!

Serves 330 million.

Ingredients:

A hefty heap of bullshit

One cup of hatred

One quart of fear

Two tablespoons of paranoia

Three quarts of idiocy

Six handguns (two semiautomatic rifles will do)

Three corrupt citizens or public officials

Two gallons of overt sexuality

Two cups of gratuitous violence

Six outright lies or ten half-truths

A so-called expert

One cup of diced hysteria

Three cups of indignant outrage

One half teaspoon of minced political bias

Step One

Shovel all the bullshit into a very large ceramic bowl. Stir in the hatred, fear, and paranoia until thoroughly mixed to a pasty consistency. There should be no lumps. If it's lumpy, continue to stir. Set mixing bowl aside.

Step Two

Heat some oil in a large skillet on high until nearly smoking. Then, one by one, add all the handguns or semiautomatic rifles and the corrupt citizens or public officials. Stir until brown, and then sprinkle with the violence and sexuality. Don't worry about the awful odor. The smell will go away when you add the idiocy. Turn off the burner and set the skillet aside.

Step Three

In a second ceramic bowl, combine your experts with the lies and half-truths. This will also smell pretty awful. You should not worry about this. The idiocy will take care of it. Mix well with a large spoon, and then set aside.

Step Four

Into the first mixing bowl, add the diced hysteria, outrage, and minced political bias. Stir gently. Be careful not to over-stir. Now add the contents of the skillet and continue to stir. Once the ingredients have been thoroughly combined, pour all the contents of this first mixing bowl into the second mixing bowl. Stir for just a few seconds. The stew should have a nice marbled appearance.

Step Five

Now place your large mixing bowl into your oven, and heat up the stew for two minutes. Once it is hot, you'll be ready to serve your guests. Pour the stew carefully from the large mixing bowl into individual soup dishes one at a time. You have only one thing left to do.

Step Six

Pour the idiocy all over each serving of stew in generous, even amounts. The idiocy should be warmed before adding. Remember: it is a topping. You should have plenty of idiocy to work with. Then, voilà! You are done! Your guests will devour this swill as though it's going out of style. But be warned; they will surely want more. You'll probably be cooking the same recipe the next day, and the next. Once you whet your guests' appetites with a taste of this delicious dinner, it's all they're going to want to eat.

Step Seven

Wash your hands thoroughly. We can't stress the importance of this step enough.

Step Eight

Run to your nearest Catholic confessional and begin by saying, "Forgive me father, for I have sinned." Don't be surprised if you have to stand in a long line. Tell the father what you have done. He will probably have you say a couple quick Hail Marys. As the church is accustomed to serving the public with its own versions of this dish, it's usually not a big deal. It's just another day in the kitchen.

THE UMBRELLA

Several weeks ago, I drove to the local post office. It had been raining off and on all day, but I needed a few rolls of stamps. It was not raining when I arrived, but I brought my umbrella just in case. Then I stood in a short line with the rest of the postal customers as the clerks tended to the people ahead of me. I like our post office. I mean, the atmosphere is awful, but the clerks are friendly and the lines are usually not too long. Once in a while, there will be an irate customer yelling at one of the clerks, but this doesn't happen often. Usually people behave themselves. The stereotype of the postal employee shooting everyone in sight is a myth. Once in a while I'll see someone I know in line, and we'll chat for a minute or so. I once saw a famous tennis star, but for the life of me, I can't remember his name. But I'm sure it was him.

Anyway, after I purchased my stamps, I stepped out of the building. It was pouring. It was really coming down in buckets. It wasn't raining when I entered the post office, but as I said, I brought my umbrella just in case. As I opened my umbrella, I noticed an elderly woman standing at the curb. I'm guessing she was in her eighties. She was being protected from the rain by the awning, but she had no umbrella. It was obvious she was waiting for the rain to let up before walking back to her car. After my umbrella was opened up, I tapped her on the shoulder. "Ma'am?" I said.

"Yes?" she replied.

"Are you waiting for the rain to let up?"

"I am. I guess it took me by surprise."

I smiled and said, "I'll share my umbrella with you if you want to walk to your car."

"Would you do that for me?"

"I'd be happy to."

"Oh, my, that'd be wonderful. I need to leave. I'm going to be late for my doctor's appointment. I've been running way behind this morning. And now all this rain. I didn't think it would be raining like this."

"Which car is yours?" I asked, and I held the umbrella so it was over her.

"Right over there," she said, pointing to a gray sedan.

"Well then, let's go," I said.

We walked through the heavy rain to her car. I held the umbrella over her while she searched for her keys in her purse. Finally she unlocked and opened her door. After she climbed in, she looked up and smiled. And I'll tell you what. You'll never see a story like this on the evening news. You'll never read about it in a newspaper or magazine. It won't be mentioned on the radio. Now, if I'd removed a handgun from my pocket and shot the woman in the heart, everyone in the world would know my name. Especially if she'd been a black woman. Go figure. It's shameful, but it's true.

SOME PERSPECTIVE

In the United States of America, the odds that you will die by your own hand in a suicide effort are significantly greater than the slim odds you will die as the result of some nutty stranger shooting you with a gun.

EVERY COIN

I have to tell you the truth. When 2001 rolled around, I was a little disappointed. When I was a kid, I thought by 2001 we'd be deep in space, living on whirling, state-of-the-art Ferris wheel space stations à la Arthur C. Clarke. I thought we'd be in touch with the obelisk-and-light-show meaning of the universe. Never in my wildest imagination did I anticipate our primitive commercial jetliners being flown into the sides of buildings by a handful of bearded religious fanatical terrorists. The whole thing caught me completely by surprise. And like so many other people in this country, I was shocked and incensed. And while heartbreak and horror were the first things to consume my mind, the second feeling that overwhelmed me was a desire for revenge. I think these feelings were only natural, and I don't think you had to be an American to feel this way. You simply had to be a human being. And I had this feeling in common with a lot of people. There's nothing quite like a common evil enemy to pull citizens closer together, and we now had a veritable, evil, and very real villain at hand, who went by the dreaded Arab name of Osama bin Laden.

My feelings about September 11 have changed over the years. Don't get me wrong; I still think terrorists are our enemies, and I think we should do everything humanly possible to destroy them and turn their lives to shit. But we should be honest with ourselves. What do I mean by that? I'm going to explain it by telling you the story of two friends of mine, Robbie and Cynthia Regan. I first met them in college. They divorced six years ago.

It was a brutal and ugly divorce, and to hear them talk about each other, it made me wonder how the two of them ever fell in love and got married in the first place. I remember that when I first heard about their breakup, I got a call from Robbie. It was late at night, and Robbie had been drinking. I knew he'd been drinking because he kept telling me over and over that I was the best friend he'd ever had. He always got emotional and nostalgic about our friendship like this when he drank. "Do you remember back in college?" he asked. "Do you remember when I first met Cynthia? She was so sweet, wasn't she? Didn't you think she was sweet?"

"She was," I said.

"Do you remember how she looked up to me?"

"She seemed to do that."

"I don't know what happened."

"What do you mean, exactly?"

"She doesn't look up to me now at all. She changed, Huey. I don't know why, but she changed. I annoy her. She doesn't like listening to me talk. Whenever I voice an opinion, she rolls her eyes. Whenever I tell her how I feel, she acts as if she's disgusted with every square inch of me. It's awful. Do you know what it's like to live with someone who doesn't like you? Forget about love; she doesn't even *like* me."

"Have you talked to her about this?"

"Talk, shit. Talking does nothing."

I felt for Robbie. I really did. But I had a feeling that Robbie was misinterpreting Cynthia. It was hard to believe that Cynthia actually felt this way. I thought there was a chance that Robbie was overreacting to something Cynthia had said to him. I knew Cynthia loved him. She did use to look up to him, and it was hard for me to believe that she had done an about-face for no good reason. So what did I do? I called Cynthia to talk to her. I thought that maybe I could help the couple communicate better. That's what I thought the problem was.

"Did you know that Robbie feels you don't love him?" I asked her. "I think he still loves you. I think he just feels sad and hurt. Maybe you inadvertently said something to hurt him?"

"It figures he would say something like that," Cynthia said.

"Why do you say that?" I asked.

"Do you know what he called me?"

"No," I said.

"Called me, yes. He called me 'the human icebox.'"

"Because you were cold?"

"It was hurtful. If I said anything hurtful back to him, I was only reacting to what he called me. No wife wants to be called a human icebox.

So maybe I didn't want to have sex with him every hour of the day, but I didn't deserve that."

"Did you bring it up to him?"

"Of course I did."

"Do you mind if I talk to him about it?"

"Be my guest."

So I did talk to Robbie about the human icebox crack. I felt as if I was getting somewhere—as if there was a chance that I could help my two friends mend their relationship and get back together. I probably should've minded my own business, but I didn't. I called Robbie, and I told him what Cynthia said. He just laughed and said, "She's still harping on that? Listen; she deserved it. The woman was as cold as a bucket of dry ice. No warmth at all. Making love to her was like making love to a cadaver."

"That's hard to believe," I said.

"Well, believe it. It started on our honeymoon night, and it just got worse every year we were married."

"But you loved each other?"

"I suppose we did."

"So?"

"So what?" Robbie said.

I talked to Cynthia again. I said I hoped she didn't mind me getting involved but that I cared about her and Robbie and hated seeing them break up. Before I could get a word out, she said, "Did you know Robbie spent our money on prostitutes? Did you know that?"

"No, I didn't," I said.

"I put up with it for years."

"Did you talk to him about it?"

"What would I say?"

"I don't know," I said.

"He called me a human icebox, and then he'd go out and have sex with women who didn't care if he was dead or alive. What the hell was that all about? Can't you see why that kind of behavior would bother me?"

"I guess I can."

"You want to get to the bottom of this? Ask Robbie about his whores."

And that was exactly what I did. I called Robbie and said, "Cynthia told me that you were sleeping with prostitutes. Is any of that true?"

"It is," Robbie said.

"Don't you see how that would upset her?"

"I wanted to upset her."

"You wanted to?"

"Did she tell you about Jack Tillman?"

"Who is Jack Tillman?"

"Her old boyfriend from high school. Did she tell you that she had an affair with him?"

"An affair?"

"It didn't last long. It didn't last because I found out about it. So what did Jack Tillman have that I didn't have? She married me, right? Didn't she marry me? Didn't she promise to be faithful?"

"She did," I said.

"So ask her about Jack Tillman."

"I will," I said.

Now, I realized this was getting to be a little ludicrous, going back and forth between my friends. But honestly, I still thought I could help them repair their marriage, and now I felt as though I was finally getting somewhere. I called up Cynthia and asked, "Did you have an affair with Jack Tillman?"

"Oh, Jack," Cynthia said, laughing. "Is he bringing up Jack again? Why don't you ask him about Clarissa Sanchez? I bet he didn't tell you anything about Clarissa."

"He didn't," I said. "Who is she?"

"A girl he knew in college."

"Did he have an affair with her?"

"Ask him."

"But I'm asking you."

"Ask him why he spent hours on the phone with her at night when he thought I was sleeping. I heard those phone calls. I listened to all of them. I was there. I heard every word. It was disgusting."

"Did he have sex with her?"

"Who knows, and who cares?"

"Did you talk to him about her?"

"I asked him about her, but he played dumb. He was such a liar. He'd lie right to my face."

"I don't remember Robbie ever lying to me."

"That's because you weren't married to him. He was a liar. A compulsive liar."

"Did he lie about anything else?"

"He lied all the time."

"For example?"

"When we bought our house, he lied on the loan application. I signed my name to it, but he lied on it. I trusted him, not knowing about the lies. I didn't read the application he filled out, so I didn't know what he did. He listed my annual income as double what it actually was. And I signed the goddamn thing because I trusted him. I was furious when I found out. I also caught him lying on a loan application for my car. That was when he told me about the house. 'You're expected to lie,' he said. Well, not as far as I knew. I signed my name to a pack of lies. What if something had happened? What if the bank ever found out about the lies? My signature was at the bottom of the page. It was *my* signature. What the heck, Huey? What the heck was that all about?"

"I don't know," I said.

"A liar."

"Maybe so."

"And who knows how long Robbie had been cheating on me with his whores. All I know is what I know. He could be lying about that. Maybe he was seeing his disgusting prostitutes before we were even married. Do you see what I mean?"

"I guess I do."

And now I began to realize something. If I went to Robbie and asked him about Cynthia's complaints, he would probably have more complaints of his own. I was not getting anywhere. I was looking for the wrong things. I was only finding out something I should already have known—that every coin has two sides. So now you're probably asking, "Fine, your friends were a mess, but what in the world does any of this have to do with the terrorist attacks on September 11?"

I'll tell you. You may find it hard to digest, but I'm going to tell you exactly how I feel.

I was horrified when I first watched the attacks on our TV, and then the horror morphed into anger. And then I saw a bigger picture. I saw the truth! It shouldn't have surprised me, but it did.

I'll tell you something personal about myself. The Vietnam War still secures a powerful spot in my psyche. It was a very big deal when I was a kid, and I think that it is when we are kids that our strongest feelings about the world are formed. I was scared to death that I would be drafted. The war ended just as I came of age, thank God. But would I have gone? I honestly don't know. I will tell you this: The war was wrong. In fact, it wasn't just wrong. It was obscene. It was *horrible!* Do you know that we killed a million of their people? And why? Because we didn't want them to choose the form of government they desired. We wanted them to have *our* government—the government of this little country on the other side of the planet. It was insane, bloody, destructive, and immoral, and honestly, it all made the violent loss of life and destruction of property on September 11 look like a pitiful little firecracker tossed into a crowd by comparison.

No, America isn't, by any rational definition, perfect. Far from it. And we are hardly innocent. We are *not* an innately good people, no matter what we believe. Our country has been built on the gravesites and burned villages of tens of millions of innocent Native Americans. Think smallpox and bullets. And many of our forefathers were slave owners. Look it up. You'll see that I'm right. And most of our present-day politicians are a bunch of liars and thieves. And our businessmen are selfish and greedy. And we throw our weight around in the world like a bully in a schoolyard. We have no clue what the CIA, NSA, and DOD are up to. Like so many sheep, we just assume that they're patriots and good people. I'm just saying that when we blow the brains out of the world's terrorists, we ought to do it with our eyes wide open. That's all I'm saying.

JOHN 8:7

When they kept on annoying him with their stupidity, he stood up straight, pointed his finger, and said to them, "Let any of you jackasses who is without sin be the first to throw a stone at her."

It's a Jungle Out There

Some people love to throw stones. Some people make a living by throwing stones. Some people make a living by teaching kids about people who have made a living by throwing stones.

When I was in junior high, we were required to read a book that our teacher said changed America for the better. I still remember reading this novel. I remember staying up late every night and consuming it page by page. It was shocking. It was revolting. It was hard to believe. The name of the book? It was *The Jungle*, and it was written by Upton Sinclair. The man was palmed off to us as one of America's great writers.

I read it again just recently, and again it had an effect on me. There is a point to the book, and it is true, isn't it? Left to their own devices, businesses are all businesses, and corporations are corporations. Left to their own devices, who knows what businessmen won't do to turn a healthy profit for their shareholders? It wasn't so much that the people of the time were evil. It was the system that was flawed. If you don't recall this book from your childhood, or if you've never read it, it is a sickening account of the meatpacking industry in America. I recommend it. It will turn you into a vegetarian. Of course, things are a lot different today than they were when the book was first written. Our government now oversees and inspects the bloody and disagreeable business of slaughtering and butchering animals. They say this is all thanks to this popular novel. At least this is what I was taught in school back in the sixties. But what I wasn't taught was that this government intervention was not what Upton Sinclair wanted. He really hoped for socialism to take hold in America. He wanted to end capitalism once and for all. Disappointed with public's reaction to his book, he said, "I aimed at the public's heart, and by accident I hit it in the stomach."

Now, fifty years later, reading this novel for the second time, I can see what Mr. Sinclair was actually driving at. He felt that immigrant workers in this country were being wrongly exploited and that socialism was the answer. Oddly enough, as I've read more about Mr. Sinclair in recent months, I have not found a lot of articles saying, "Wow, what Sinclair did for the United States was terrific! What a great mind! Where on earth would we be without men like Upton Sinclair?" Instead I found a lot of articles criticizing Upton's socialism. Many people viewed him (and still view him) as an anticapitalist muckraker who was primarily concerned with shocking the public with lies and exaggerations so that he could turn them into socialists. Could this really be? Was my teacher wrong? Had she lied to us? I was twelve years old when I first read *The Jungle*, and when I was a kid, I didn't question my teachers. If a teacher told me black was white, I probably would've believed her. All this time, I had thought of Sinclair as a red, white, and blue hero.

Here's something our teacher never told us when we read *The Jungle* in her class. Teddy Roosevelt described Mr. Sinclair as a "crackpot." He wrote, "I have an utter contempt for him. He is hysterical, unbalanced, and untruthful. Three-fourths of the things he said in *The Jungle* were absolute falsehoods. For some of the remainder there was only a basis of truth." So what was Upton exactly? Was he just a crackpot? Was he a liar? And why didn't these comments from a revered president make it into our classroom discussions?

Here's something else we weren't taught in class about Mr. Sinclair. He was a staunch supporter of prohibition—a lost cause. It never had a prayer. And in a way, it shows how totally out of touch he was with America's patriotic beer- and whiskey-drinking workforce. Nowadays the American worker would tell Mr. Sinclair to go crap in his hat.

You might be interested to know that he ran for governor of California in 1926 as the candidate for the Socialist Party of America. He lost that election. He ran again in 1934, but this time as a Democrat, maintaining that capitalism had hit a brick wall. His plan to win this time included a proposal for a cooperative system for America's unemployed, "producing everything which they themselves consume and exchanging those goods among themselves by a method of barter, using warehouse receipts or labour certificates." He lost this election. His campaign also split the Democratic Party and the Socialist Party of America, and many of his colleagues were furious. Sinclair's own son, David, accused him of "insane opportunism." Apparently he was a far better writer than he was a politician. Or maybe he *was* just a crackpot. Maybe he wrote some good books but had some dumb ideas and some questionable means of seeing them become a reality.

I will give the guy credit for sticking to his guns and putting his money where his mouth was. By the middle of 1906, he had earned a great deal of money from sales of his book, and rather than waste it on capitalist luxuries, he bought a place called Helicon Hall, a former boys' school in New Jersey. He turned it into a utopian socialist colony for artists, writers, and social reformers. At its peak, the Helicon Hall colony had several dozen members. Unfortunately, it burned to the ground in 1907, and Upton moved on.

Anyway, no matter what you think of Upton and his ideas, *The Jungle* is well worth reading. Is it a pack of lies? Is it a brilliant piece of writing? Is it no more than a blatant piece of socialist propaganda? I guess you can take your pick, but it *is* worth reading. It is, without any question, a historically significant book, and it did help to make this country a little more humane and a less revolting place for you to work, live, and eat.

Me? I'll take the inch-thick porterhouse, lightly salted. I'll have it medium rare with a baked potato and some coleslaw on the side. I've never been to a slaughterhouse, and I have no desire to visit one. The whole idea of slaughtering millions of fellow living and breathing mammals to fill our dinner plates drives me a little crazy. I have never been wild about killing animals to eat. I never have been, and probably never will be. I would just like to eat my beef in peace, like any other red-blooded American. Some steak sauce would also be appreciated. A-1 if you have it.

STEAK FOR DINNER

"I can remember 1987 when I had my first amateur fight in Michigan, weighing sixty-four pounds. I was ten years old. I was the youngest and smallest guy on my team. I can remember what I ate. There was this restaurant called Ponderosa, and my dad made me eat a steak. I was happy. It was a first-round knockout. I slept with my trophy for two weeks."

—Floyd Mayweather Jr.

MERRY CHRISTMAS

It was Christmas day of 2004, and Rhonda was in the kitchen with my sister-in-law, preparing dinner. My sister-in-law's name was Margaret. My brother Bob and I were in the backyard, sitting on the outdoor lawn chairs. I haven't told you a lot about Bob. Margaret was his third wife. He divorced his first wife, Sue, to take up with a younger woman named Veronica, and he divorced Veronica when he met Margaret. Bob and Margaret seemed to be getting along well. I think Bob had finally found someone he could stay married to for longer than a few years. I liked Margaret. I liked her a lot more than I liked Sue or Veronica. Sue was as mean and contentious as an alley cat, and Veronica was as dumb as a doorknob.

While Bob and I sat outside, we mostly talked about work. Bob owned seven local pizza restaurants. According to Bob, the restaurants were doing well, and he was telling me about his grand plan to open an eighth restaurant in Simi Valley. I was happy for Bob. Life seemed to be going well for him. I was especially pleased to hear how well his daughters were doing. They were both from his first marriage, and they did not take the divorces well. Nor did they like Bob's second wife. But they both seemed to like Margaret. During the two divorces, the girls were misbehaving and getting into a lot of trouble, and they weren't doing well in school. But now they were enrolled in college, one of them studying to become a nurse and the other to become a dental hygienist.

While we talked in the backyard, Bob brought up one of my workers, Mateo Gonzales. Bob knew Mateo. When Bob was building his sixth restaurant, I had sent Mateo over to help Bob with the painting. Bob had a painter who was supposed to be doing the work, but the guy was a flake and was way behind schedule. Bob bought Mateo the paint, brushes, and rollers he would need and showed him what needed to be done. Mateo went to work and knocked the project out in just two days, and Bob was thrilled. "He's a trooper," Bob told me. "No fuss at all. He just worked his tail off. He didn't even take off for lunch." I told Bob to pay Mateo cash because Mateo didn't have a bank account or the proper ID to cash a check. This was because he was a Mexican. I don't mean that as an insult; I just mean to say that he was a Mexican who had come the United States illegally to find work. I liked Mateo a lot. He could knuckle down and outwork any white kid on the block, and he demanded only about half the hourly rate. Of all the illegal immigrants I've hired over the years, Mateo was by far the best—until he messed up, that is. What did he do wrong? A couple things, actually, and I'll get to them. But first let me tell you more about our Christmas dinner.

Like I said, Rhonda and Margaret were cooking our dinner in the kitchen while Bob and I were outside. Just as I was about to tell Bob about Mateo, Rhonda called us in to eat. There were a lot of us at the table. My mom was there. She had been watching TV in the family room. Mom watched a lot of TV these days. This afternoon she was watching a show about remodeling houses. Bob, Margaret, and their two daughters were also at the table. Rhonda and I were there, and so was Thomas. I guess the only person missing was my father, whom I was still not speaking to and who was therefore not invited. Margaret had us all hold hands as she said grace. Then we dug into our salads. "How'd the prime rib come out?" I asked.

"It looks perfect," Margaret said.

"I can smell it," Thomas said.

"I look forward to this meal every year," Bob said.

"Same here," I replied.

"We used a different recipe for the creamed corn this year," Rhonda said.

"It's my mother's recipe," Margaret said.

"How's your mother doing?" I asked.

"She's doing well."

"Where is she today?"

"She's having Christmas dinner with my sister's family in Austin. Everyone in my family still lives in Texas. I'm the only one who moved out here to California."

"You must miss them."

"I do. But as you know, we visit them at Thanksgiving. I get my fill of them then."

"Is you sister still married to that mobile home guy?" I asked.

"She is."

"Dapper Dan, your tradin' man," Bob said with a feigned Texan accent.

"That's him," Margaret said, laughing.

"Who's Dapper Dan?" I asked.

"That's what my brother-in-law calls himself on the TV and radio ads. He says Dapper Dan will trade for anything. They take all kinds of junk in on trade for the mobile homes. They have a whole warehouse full of stuff they've taken in. You wouldn't believe all the crap they've collected."

"What are they going to do with it?" I asked.

"I don't honestly know. Most of it's worthless. They've got old furniture, radios, TVs, videocassettes, clothing, old toys, sports equipment—you name it. It's just a gimmick to get people to come in and buy their mobile homes. The buyers think they're getting one-of-a-kind deals because of the trades, but the truth is that the eventual price of any home they buy from my brother-in-law would be the same with or without the junk they bring him."

I laughed at this.

"You didn't get to tell me how Mateo is doing," Bob said to me. "I kind of miss the little guy."

"I'm not sure how he's doing," I said.

"Not sure?"

"I fired him."

"I thought you hired him back," Rhonda said.

"I fired him two months ago, and then I hired him back. Then I fired him again, three days ago."

"Right before Christmas?"

"He messed up."

"I thought you liked him," Bob said.

"I did."

"I can't believe you fired him right before Christmas."

"I had to put my foot down."

"What'd he do wrong?" Bob asked.

"Is everyone done with their salads?" Rhonda asked. "I think it's time for the meat."

"I'm done with mine," I said.

"Looks like we're all done," Margaret said, looking around at all the empty salad bowls.

"Bring on the beef," Bob said.

Rhonda and Margaret then went to the kitchen to bring out the rest of the food. While they were gone, Bob pressed me on Mateo. "Why did you fire him?" he asked.

"First it was the streetlight. That was two months ago."

"The streetlight?"

"I was finishing up our shopping center project. The one in Mission Viejo. The landscaper was supposed to be grading the planters. He had dropped off his tractor, but no one showed up to do the grading. I was under a lot of pressure. The owner of the project was driving me crazy. He told me the bank required him to be done with the project by a certain date, but I don't know if that was true or if he was just making the deadline up. But he was all over me. Then Mateo told us he knew how to operate a tractor, and we figured, why not? I told Mateo to start up the tractor and to start grading the planters. I would charge the landscaper for Mateo's time. I had a good relationship with the landscaper, so I knew this wouldn't be a problem. Mateo went to work. I watched him for a little while, and he seemed to know what he was doing. Then I got called to the building by the plumber, who was having a problem installing one of the sinks. The next thing I knew, I heard a loud crash outside. I ran out to see what it was, and it was Mateo."

"Mateo?"

"He had backed the tractor into a city streetlight in the planter, and he knocked the entire thing over. It had fallen into the street, and it was in pieces. I ran out to Mateo and asked him what happened, and he told me he hadn't seen the light, that it was an accident. An accident? Can you believe that? Do you know what those streetlights cost? They cost several thousand dollars apiece. This job had been difficult from day one, and I was barely making a profit as it was. And now I would have to pay through the nose for a new streetlight? And all because Mateo didn't watch where he was going? Okay, so maybe I lost my temper. But I had a right to. And I had to set an example for the other workers. They had to know that I expected them to be careful. So, yes, I fired Mateo. Right there on the spot. I told him to grab his tools and go home. I told him to come back and pick up his final check the next day. I was done with him. Jesus, I was pissed. I felt like slapping the snot out of him."

"But you did hire him back?"

"I guess I calmed down."

"No one is perfect," one of Bob's daughters said.

"No," I said, agreeing with her.

"But you fired him again?" Bob asked.

"Three days ago."

"What did he do this time?"

"Dinner is served," Rhonda said, interrupting. She stood there before us, holding the large platter filled with prime rib cuts, and Martha was right behind her with the creamed corn and green beans.

"Oh, wow," Bob said.

"It looks terrific," I said.

"It smells even better," Thomas said.

"They're kind of bloody," Rhonda said, looking them over as she prepared to serve them.

"They look perfect," Bob said.

"They do," I agreed.

Rhonda then walked around the table, serving the prime rib. When she was done, she took the bloody, empty platter back into the kitchen. Then she sat down next to me.

"So what did he do?" Bob asked me, with his mouth full of meat.

"What did who do?" Rhonda asked.

"Mateo," Bob said.

"Are we still talking about Mateo?"

"We are," I said.

"Did you tell him about the streetlight?" Rhonda asked me.

"I did," I said.

"He was going to tell me what Mateo did three days ago."

"Oh, yes," Rhonda said. "What did he do?" Rhonda cut off a piece of meat and stuffed it into her mouth.

"Huey fired him again."

"Yes, I heard," Rhonda said with her mouth full.

"He messed up again," I said. "Do you recall the shopping center I built in Riverside last year?"

"Of course," Rhonda said.

"Well, we had a roof leak in one of the suites. I called the roofer, but he was swamped. It had been raining a lot, and roofers are always busy when it rains. He couldn't get to my job for a week, and according to the weather report, a big rain was forecast for that night. It wasn't a horrible leak, but the tenant was freaking out about it. It had been dripping over his expensive copy machine. I went to look at it and discovered it was leaking because the sign installer had put a couple screws in the roof membrane to attach the guy-wires for his sign. It wasn't a big deal. Someone simply needed to mastic around the screws. Since the roofer was too busy to come out right away, I sent Mateo over there, and I told him what to do. It wasn't a permanent solution, but it should've stopped the leak for the time being. So fine, Mateo went to the job, and it took him an hour or so. I figured we were in good shape."

"But?" Bob asked.

"But late that night, it rained like crazy, and the leak was a hundred times worse. The water was literally pouring in. It was splashing all over the tenant's expensive copy machine. It ruined the machine, and the floors in the copy room were an inch deep in water. It was a mess, and the tenant called me in the morning, fit to be tied."

"Why did it leak so bad?" Thomas asked.

"On the roof over the copy machine area was a roof drainage well. All the roof water drained into this recessed well and down the drainage pipes, which discharged into the parking lot. It was a big roof, so there was a lot of water—I mean a *lot* of water. Anyway, while Mateo was working on the mastic for the guy-wire screws, he must have stepped on the roof well and cracked the drainage pipe. The crack left a gaping hole, so all the roof water poured out of the crack, down from the tenant's ceiling, and all over the top of his darn copy machine. Seriously, they may as well have thrown the machine into a swimming pool. It was soaked. I sent two other men out there to put buckets under the leak to collect the water, but it was too late. The copy machine was ruined, and not only would I have to buy the tenant a new machine, but I would also have to clean up the mess, and I would also have to send a plumber out to fix the cracked roof drain pipe."

"Jesus," Bob said.

"It sounds horrible," Margaret said.

"It's literally going to cost me thousands."

"I'm sure Mateo feels awful about it," Rhonda said. "Of course, that isn't much help to you."

"No," I said.

"Damn," Bob said.

"It's so hard to find good employees," Rhonda said, shaking her head.

"That's a fact," I said.

"What an idiot," Thomas said.

"I guess I would've fired him too," Bob said.

Then it happened.

Everyone at the table was oddly quiet. I figured they were thinking about Mateo. They were all chewing their prime rib when the strangest feeling came over me. I sat and watched my family, and all I could see was a sea of mouths, chewing on the meat like mad. All I could see was the tender cooked flesh in their gnashing teeth, the fat and the blood. And I saw Mateo coming home to his family and telling them he had lost his job. *God, what are we?* I thought to myself. *What the hell is this? What kind of people have we become?* And now I could even hear the eerie chewing, louder and louder, like some crazy Hollywood sound effect for a movie. "Jesus Christ," I said. "Excuse me a minute."

I set down my fork and knife, and I stood up.

"Where are you going?" Rhonda asked.

"To make a call."

"In the middle of dinner?"

"I'm going to call Mateo," I said.

"Why?" Rhonda asked.

"I'm going to tell him he isn't fired. I'm going to give him his job back."

Everyone at the table was staring at me.

"Tell him I said hi," Bob said. "Tell him I said Merry Christmas."

"Sure," I said. "I'll tell him that."

MOVIE MAGIC

It is one of my all-time favorite movies. I first watched it six years ago. I had heard of it before then, but just never got around to seeing it. One of the top stars of this film is Warren Beatty, and I'm not a big Warren Beatty fan. He's always seemed to me like more of a men's clothing model than a serious actor, but maybe that's just me. It was probably my low opinion of Warren's acting abilities that kept me from turning the movie on. Or maybe it was because the film was a love story, and I've never been a big fan of love stories. A love story starring Warren Beatty? It sounded awful. Further, I didn't like the name of it—*Splendor in the Grass*. The title was lifted from a line in a William Wordsworth poem. He was a romantic, and I've always been more of a nuts-and-bolts type of guy. Thank you very much Hollywood, but no thanks. I've always preferred Clint Eastwood and John Wayne. Then, six years ago, I was up late at night watching TV, and I figured, "What the hell, I'm going to watch it." Well, from early on in the movie, I was mesmerized. As I said, it is now one of my all-time favorite films. Natalie Wood stars in the movie, and she is amazing. She nearly walked away with an Oscar for best actress, losing to Sophia Loren for *Two Women*, but just between you and me, I think Natalie should've gotten the trophy.

The storyline? I won't go into a lot of detail on this. Let's just say a wealthy and vacuous boy meets a sweet girl and it doesn't work out. The boy goes his way, and the heartbroken girl goes into a mental hospital. Finally, the girl is released, and she gets her life together. She marries a doctor, and at the end of the movie she goes to visit the boy she loved. His life is, well, ultimately less than stellar, and it turns out that she was better off without him after all. It turns out that Warren Beatty was not all he was cracked up to be.

This movie has a lot to say about sexual repression, money, peer pressure, and social status in America—blah, blah, blah. But ultimately, the movie is a love story. And like I said, Natalie Wood is amazing. I rarely fall for movie actresses, but I fell head over heels for her. I wanted her. I wanted to meet her, and I wanted to get to know her, and at times I even *was* her. I don't think a teenager in love has ever been portrayed better. The high school hall scene and the bathtub scene are magical. These scenes will live with me forever.

So why did this movie have such a powerful effect on me? I've thought about it a lot, and I think I know the reason. It was because I, like Natalie Wood, fell head over heels in love in high school. It was a love that seemed to have a chance but was ultimately yanked out of my life mercilessly. The girl I loved was named Rosie Nichols, and for me it was nothing less than a case of love at first sight. Rosie moved into our town during the summer of 1971, and as luck would have it, she was in my second-period English class. She sat two rows over from me, and I had a clear and unobstructed view of her. I just couldn't believe my eyes. She had to be the loveliest creature God had ever planted in a high school. She had a personality to go with her looks. She was outgoing, friendly, and loaded with life. She amazed and intrigued me. She was new to our school, yet she had no problem making new friends. And I yearned to be one of them. I had to get to know her, but as things stood, she didn't even know I existed.

I would sit in that English class, and I would daydream. We would be laughing together, and we would take walks together. We would tell silly jokes and complain about our parents and siblings. Who knew? Maybe we would even hug, hold hands, or kiss.

THE ROSIE SONG

I don't want a pickle;
I just wanna be with my Rosie Nichols.
And I don't want a tickle;
I'd rather be with my Rosie Nichols.
And I don't wanna die;
I just wanna be with my Rosie Ni … chols.
It was late last night, the other day,
Was feeling blue all the way.
Longing for Rosie to stay,
There was only one thing I could say was I …
I don't want a pickle;
I just wanna be with my Rosie Nichols.
And I don't want a tickle;
I'd rather be with my Rosie Nichols.
And I don't wanna die;
Just wanna be with my Rosie Ni … chols.
Late last week I was on the couch;
I admit that I was a slouch.
My back hurt, and I said ouch;
Then I stood up from the couch and cried …
I don't want a pickle;
I just wanna be with my Rosie Nichols.
Yeah, and I don't want a tickle;

'Cuz I'd rather be with my Rosie Nichols.
And I don't wanna die;
Just wanna be with my Rosie Ni ... chols.

THE VOID

After four weeks of daydreaming about Rosie, I finally decided to make my move. I had to do something. I decided I would introduce myself to her after class and ask her out. I would ask her to see a movie. Everyone liked the movies. I checked to see which movies were playing nearby, and I decided on *The Last Picture Show*. I knew it was an adult-themed movie, and I thought she would be impressed with my mature choice. I tried to get her attention several times after class to ask her, but she was always busy talking to other kids. I was standing right there, nearly beside her, and she didn't even notice me. Then, finally, I got lucky. I caught her alone in the hallway while no one was pestering her. "Excuse me," I said softly. She looked at me.

"Yes?" she said.

"My name is Huey Baker."

"Okay."

"I, uh, wanted to know something."

"To know something?" she laughed, and I felt ridiculous. But there was now no turning back. I was committed. I had to say something.

"I was curious if you'd like to go to a movie with me."

"A movie?"

"Yes," I said. I could feel my armpits getting wet, and my cheeks were heating up. I was very uncomfortable.

"What was your name again?"

"Huey," I said.

"I don't even know you, Huey."

"You're in my English class."

"We're in the same class?"

"Yes," I said.

"Are you asking me out on a date?"

"No, nothing like that," I said, lying. "Just a movie."

"Wouldn't a movie be a date?"

"I suppose you could call it that."

"Do you have a car?"

"I can borrow my dad's car. I have a license."

"Ah, a license."

"But if you don't want to, I'll understand," I said. I was already giving up. I was making a fool of myself, and now I just wanted to make an exit as quickly as I could. But she reached and grasped my hand.

"No, no, don't give up."

"No?" I said.

"I'd like to go to a movie with you. But I need to know you first."

"Know me?"

"We need to be friends. You can't just appear out of thin air and ask a girl to go on a date. You have to get to know her first."

"Oh," I said.

"Can you meet me for lunch today?"

"For lunch?"

"You do eat lunch, don't you?"

"Yes, of course."

"Meet me at the front lawn. I'll be sitting near the flagpole. We can eat lunch together."

"Okay," I said.

"Then after we've had a chance to talk, you will know me. And then you can ask me out to a movie."

"Okay," I said.

And that was that. I couldn't believe it. I had actually asked Rosie out on a date, and she hadn't said no. I felt so accomplished. And she seemed to like me, didn't she? I mean, I wasn't repulsive to her, and I didn't scare her off. I didn't even seem to bother her.

That day at noon, I met Rosie for lunch on the front lawn, and we talked and ate. We got to know each other, and I liked her. She was everything I thought she would be. She was kind, and she had a good sense of humor. And she was smart. And she wasn't at all conceited. And best of all, she was the prettiest thing I'd ever seen—and she was talking to *me*!

That Friday I took her out to see *The Last Picture Show*, and then we went to Bob's Big Boy for hot fudge sundaes and coffee. She asked me if I thought Cybill Shepherd was pretty, and I said yes. Rosie said she thought

Cybill was the prettiest actress she'd ever seen. I didn't say it, but I thought Rosie was a lot prettier. Of course, I was biased.

During the weeks that followed, we saw each other more. I went over to her house and met her parents and older brother. Then I began going over to her house often. She would cook tacos for me, and we'd watch *Dark Shadows* on the little TV set on the kitchen counter. It wasn't my kind of show, but Rosie liked it. We'd also sit on the porch swing in the backyard and talk. I recall that she had a big calico cat named Chester, and Chester would sometimes jump up and sit in my lap. When Rosie's brother was out of the house, we'd go in his bedroom and listen to his rock 'n' roll music collection on his record player. He would've killed us both if he'd known we were playing around with his records. God, I still cherish those times. Rosie got prettier with each day that passed. She had such bright eyes and such a clear complexion. I remember her mouth and all those perfect teeth. I loved her soft blonde hair, and I loved the way she smelled. She never wore perfume. She kind of smelled like warm oatmeal: healthy, perfect, with just the right amount of milk and sugar.

Then it was like a horrible storm blew in without warning from the horizon. I didn't even see it coming. I had no idea. I was a stupid, clueless kid who thought the times I was having with Rosie would last forever. I remember the awful day. It was a Saturday, and I had called Rosie to see if I could come over. I could tell right away that something had changed. It was in the tone of her voice. She wasn't rude or unfriendly. She pitied me. She told me she had another boy at her house and that I probably wouldn't want to come over. A boy? I guess I was shocked. I mean, we weren't boyfriend and girlfriend, but I hadn't seen this coming. The boy's name was Eric House, and I knew who he was. He was a year older than us, and he played on the varsity football team. He was a jock. Jesus, a *jock*! The first thing I thought of was this guy's hands all over my Rosie, his mouth on hers, and who knew what else. It was horrifying and heartbreaking. I hung up the phone and went to my room to cry. I can't even describe the pain I felt that day. It was as if someone had kicked me in the stomach and plunged a rusty sword into my chest. I had lost the girl of my dreams to a musclebound jock moron who probably had an IQ comparable to that of a chicken. Cluck, cluck, cluck—Rosie was gone!

That was when I learned about the void. That's what I call it. The void is that empty, bottomless abyss you fall into when God deals you a crap hand. You can hear him laughing out loud. "Sucker," he says cruelly. "What cards did you *think* you were going to get? A full house? A royal flush? Give me a fucking break!" This was the void—black and as cold as ice. Lifeless and without mercy. Poor, pitiful me. God, how I felt sorry for myself, and how I suddenly hated life. How I suddenly wanted to die. I wanted to cut my wrists, swallow a bottle of pills, jump out an open window. I could see my lifeless body, contorted and cold. I would play my demise over and over in my head, killing myself a hundred different times. Then a hundred and one, and then a hundred and two. And then more.

It was not healthy. A normal high school student would've picked himself up off the ground and moved on. A normal kid wouldn't fantasize about suicide. But what did I know? No, I didn't know any better, and I learned nothing. No one knew my pain. No one could give me advice, because I acted like I was okay. Just like dear Natalie Wood in *Splendor in the Grass*, I should've been awarded an Oscar for my performance. As I said earlier, it's a great film. If you get a chance to see it on TV, don't miss it. It's a terrific story. Natalie is superb, and the ending is priceless.

AMERICAN INGENUITY

They say necessity is the mother of invention. Do you believe this? If it's true, then there must have been an awful lot of necessity in the United States. Inventors and inventions have always been a big thing in this country. And I think Americans admire inventors almost as much as they do movie stars and pop musicians. There is something especially American about a man or woman figuring out how do to something a better way. "Design a better mousetrap," they say. "Patent it, put it up for sale, and you're financially set for life."

What are some of America's greatest inventions? I remember learning about Eli Whitney's cotton gin when I was in junior high school. I remember learning about Fulton's steamboat, and Henry Ford's assembly line, and Edison's lightbulb, phonograph, and kinetoscope. But here are some American inventions you may be taking for granted. First, there is Scotch tape. How often has each of us used this product without knowing who invented it? In fact, the pressure-sensitive tape was invented in the 1920s by a man named Richard Drew. Why is it called Scotch tape instead of Drew tape? Legend has it that the first tapes sold to the public didn't stick so well, and so someone told Drew to take the tape back to the Scotch (cheapskate) manufacturer and tell them to add more adhesive. What else has been invented in America? There is the wire coat hanger, invented by Albert Parkhouse of Jackson, Michigan; the Band-Aid, invented by Earle Dickson of New Brunswick, New Jersey; the flyswatter, invented by Frank Rose of Weir, Kansas; the clothespin, invented by David Smith of Springfield, Vermont; and the handy can opener, invented by Ezra Warner of Waterbury, Connecticut. Before Warner invented his can opener, cans had to be hammered open. The can opener was patented in 1858 and adopted by the Union Army during the Civil War. There was also Coca-Cola, invented in 1886 by an Atlanta pharmacist named John Pemberton, who was trying to concoct a medicine. There was Earl Tupper of Berlin, New Hampshire, and his Tupperware, and Ruth Handler of Denver, Colorado, and her Barbie Doll. Jesus, I could keep going forever.

THE CRASH

Is it really any surprise that Americans were the inventors of that magic, marvelous, remarkable, and turn-your-life-around medication that we call Prozac? I'm not sure when exactly I began taking the drug. I remember going to see a psychiatrist and asking for a prescription. I told him I didn't want to be drilled about my childhood, my relationships, my work life, or anything else. I just wanted something to keep me from feeling down. All my life, I had wrestled with periods of melancholy and sadness, and I was tired of struggling to work my way out of them. Looking back now, my best guess is that I saw the psychiatrist around 2002. Prozac was at the apex of its popularity then; I heard they wrote over thirty million prescriptions that year alone. The doctor agreed to help me, and the next thing I knew, I was taking Prozac daily. And it seemed to help me. In fact, it helped a lot. I was productive, happy, and enjoying my life. There were times I felt so good that I felt like a superman—like a god. I felt as if I could do anything at all, as if I could conquer the world, and as if I would live forever. Then, in 2005, it was all over. Everything came crashing down around me.

Of course, looking back now, this collapse now makes sense to me. But back then it was bewildering. It was a terrifying mess of fear, unhappiness, and doom. It's difficult to put my finger on the beginning of it, since it didn't just take place overnight. I wasn't working, and perhaps that was part of the problem. I was in between projects, and I had a lot of time on my hands. There wasn't an issue at first, because I had a lot of things I needed to do: things to keep me busy—things that I'd been putting off while I was working. And I remember making a list of what I had to get done. I put the highest-priority tasks first, and then tackled them one by one. It was while I worked on this list that my mind began to play tricks on me—tricks that had nothing to do with the list but that had to do with Rhonda. It was mystifying, but I was being convinced that she no longer loved me.

I didn't suspect Rhonda of having an affair with another man. It was nothing like that. What I thought was simply that she didn't love me anymore, that she didn't like what I did for a living, that she didn't care about me, that I annoyed her to no end, and that the very idea of having sex with me was repulsive to her. I guess it started with the sex. Every time I made advances, it seemed to bother her. Now I know this was in my mind, but back then it seemed so confoundedly real. It always seemed as though I was imposing on her. Honestly, I don't know how to put these feeling into words. They were, after all, just my feelings. I don't recall anything specific that Rhonda did to make me feel the way I did. And now that I look back, I think it *was* in my mind. But it seemed so real at the time. I was sure that my wife was about as interested in having sex with me as she was in reading an algebra book or going to the DMV to get her driver's license renewed. What was it about me? What made me so repulsive? It got to the point where I left her alone in bed. I would just lie there beside Rhonda, not angry but hurt. And I couldn't fall asleep. I'd just lie there with my head on the pillow and my eyes wide open, wanting to cry.

Then these feelings crept into the daylight hours. Slowly but surely, I began to misinterpret things. Rhonda would say something to me, and I'd be convinced that her words were just further proof that she no longer loved me. It got to the point that no matter what she said, I could twist her words and use them against her. It was awful. Honestly, I believed what I was thinking. I felt I had insight. I felt I was being true and rational. But when I spoke up, Rhonda would tell me I was being silly or ridiculous. But I knew! I knew she no longer loved me, even if she didn't see it herself. Then my hurt began to morph into anger. Rhonda's disdain for me began to make me mad, and I wanted to hurt *her*. So how could I do this? How could I break her heart? How could I make her feel as bad as she was making me feel?

I wasn't depressed. I knew what it was like to stand on the edge and look down into the that awful darkness. I knew what depression felt like. No, this wasn't the void. This was something entirely different. There was an energy about it, a mania. And it was *real!*

Around the time I was having these feelings, Thomas was a senior in high school. I was so caught up in my own nonsense that I wasn't paying any attention to Thomas at all. I assumed he was doing okay in school, and I assumed he'd applied to a few colleges. Rhonda was probably helping him out with this. Did he have a girlfriend when he was a senior? I didn't know. And what were his dreams? I didn't know that either. All I knew was that my wife didn't love me. I do remember going to Thomas's high school baseball games. Thomas played shortstop. He was a good player, and like a good dad, I went to all of his games to cheer him on. So at least I wasn't missing those. But why was I going to these games? Honestly, I remember very little about them. What I do remember is Carol Carson. I remember sitting next to her. I remember her kids, and I remember talking to her on the phone. God, we talked for hours.

Carol's son was on Thomas's baseball team, and that was how we met. I don't remember first meeting her. I just remember that we became close friends. We sat next to each other during every game. Rhonda didn't come to the games, because she didn't care much for sports, so she had no idea about Carol. Somehow I got in the habit of calling Carol, and our conversations would go on for hours. It was crazy. We never talked about love or cheating. And we never did cheat. Well, not as in having sex, but maybe what we did was worse. We talked and talked, and the more we talked, the closer we became, and the closer we became, the more we liked each other, and the more we liked each other, the more we talked. It was so strange how this all happened. It was as though I had a second wife. It was like having a wife who liked me.

Then it got even worse. By "worse" I mean I became obsessed with Carol. I couldn't get her lovely face out of my mind. She was all I thought about, and I began pay close attention to what she was wearing when I saw her, how she smelled, and how she wore her hair. I wanted to know everything about her, and I wanted to show her how much I loved and respected her. I wanted to bring her bouquets of flowers, and I wanted to write poems about her. Seriously, I was composing one silly poem after the other in my mind. Then I remember catching myself and thinking, *What the heck is wrong with me? What are you doing? What are you even thinking?* There was no way in hell that this woman was ever going to be mine. I knew that. She had a nice husband and three kids, and she was happily married. Honestly, did I even want a new wife? It was all a crazy, foolish, sick-in-the-head fantasy!

Meanwhile, my fears about Rhonda were growing worse. Now I was convinced that she wanted a divorce. I was growing worried that she'd cheat on me the moment the right sort of guy crossed her path. She would have an affair, and the affair would surely blossom into something serious. Rhonda and her new lover would decide it was time for her to ditch me so the two of them could get married so that Rhonda could, once and for all, be happy and content. "I don't even know what I was thinking when I married Huey," she'd say to her new lover. "It was such a dumb thing to do. I must have had a screw loose." I heard her saying these words over and over in my mind. And I could hear Rhonda laughing. It was a real laugh. It wasn't a forced laugh. It was real, brought on by genuine joy, love, and fulfillment. This new man made her happy. She was holding her lover's hand and laughing her head off.

Like I said, this was not the dark and depressing void I talked about earlier. This was entirely different. My mind was racing a million miles a minute. My heart was beating as though I had just run a couple laps around the block, and I was sweating like a pig. God, half the time I was soaked! Then, I remember, I finally had enough, and one afternoon I looked for my car keys. I wanted to leave. I debated whether I should leave Rhonda a note. *Fuck it*, I thought. I would be leaving no note and no explanation. I would just be gone, and gone for good. I was doing her a favor, right? What did she care about how or why? I would be out of her life forever, and she could get on with her life.

I walked out the front door that day, climbed into my car, and started the engine. Then I backed out of the driveway and sped away. Where was I going? To the first liquor store I could find. Sixteen years of sobriety down the toilet. What a joke. For sixteen years I hadn't touched a drop of alcohol, and now I was going to get good and plastered. It was a done deal, and nothing was going to stop me. I'd stop at a liquor store, and then I would go to the bank.

I went to the liquor store about a mile from our house, and I walked inside. I swear to God I could hear the bottles talking to me. "Pick me," they said. "Pick me, Huey, and I'll take you where you want to go. To nothingness. Far, far away from this rotten world, once and for all!" So I grabbed a bottle of Jose Cuervo, a bottle of Jack Daniel's, and a bottle of Crown Royal. I also grabbed a small bag of Doritos and a couple of Hershey bars. The clerk was a seventy-something-year-old man with a bulbous nose and purple spider veins on his cheeks. His eyes were too small for his face, and they seemed to have lost their color from years of drinking. Maybe they were once blue, but now they were gray, rheumy, and dull. "Having a little party?" he asked stupidly.

"You could say that," I said.

"If you buy two bags of Doritos, you get a discount."

"I only want one bag."

"Maybe you'll want a second bag later?"

"I only want one fucking bag," I said.

"Fine, fine," the man said. "No need to bite my head off."

"You don't understand."

"Maybe I do, and maybe I don't."

"What time is it?" I asked. I had left my watch at home.

"It's four-thirty."

"Hurry up. I need to make it to the bank before five. I think they close at five."

The old man proceeded to ring my booze and snacks up on his cash register. He had stopped his yapping, which I appreciated. *What a pathetic old shit*, I thought to myself. Then he opened his mouth again. He asked, "Do you need any cigarettes?"

"I don't smoke."

"We have good deals on cigarettes. A lot of people just come here to buy cigarettes."

"Good for them. What do I owe you?"

The man told me the total, and I pulled my wallet out from my back pocket. I handed him a credit card. He completed the transaction, and I signed for it. He then pushed my bags toward me, and I grabbed them. "Have a good one," he said.

"Yeah, right," I replied. I don't know why exactly, but I really disliked this guy. I grabbed the bags and walked back to my car. I had twenty minutes to reach the bank. It shouldn't have been a problem, and I made it there with five minutes to spare. There weren't any lines, and I walked right up to the teller, an obese woman with thick black hair. She was wearing a Navajo squash necklace, and she reminded me of an Indian woman. Maybe she was an Indian, and maybe not. But who cared? I just wanted my cash.

"I need to withdraw ten thousand from my checking account," I said.

"Do you have the account number?"

"I don't," I said.

"What's your name?"

"Huey Baker."

"Do you have two forms of ID?"

I pulled my wallet out and gave her the IDs. She did some typing to find my account. She then proceeded to write a withdrawal slip for me, and she asked me to sign it. She did some more typing and then called the manager over. "There should be plenty of money," I said.

"I just need to get an approval," she said.

"Okay," I said.

The manager came over and did some more typing. Then she smiled at me and said, "Thank you for waiting."

"No problem," I said. These two women were nearly as dumb as the guy at the liquor store. Day after day they went through the motions of living, and for what? A few bucks above minimum wage? Who knew? I had no idea how much these people got paid to piss away their lives.

I got back in my car and left. I looked forward to driving on the interstate, speeding through endless gray vistas of flat desert and purple crumpled-paper mountains. Nothing was going to stop me, and it would be the end of the line for Huey Baker. Soon I would be in Vegas. Late tomorrow morning they would find my body, cold and lifeless, my bloodstream teeming with whiskey and tequila, an empty Dorito bag on my pillow. There would be a couple Hershey Bar wrappers on the nightstand. The hotel drapes would be pulled shut, blocking the silvery glare of the morning sun. Gone, gone, gone.

EVERYTHING

"I love Las Vegas. I like that Las Vegas has everything. Everything and anything you want to do, you can do in Las Vegas."

—Drew Carey

THE NOISE

Obviously, I did not kill myself in Vegas. So what did I do? I arrived at the Venetian and went to the first bar I could find. I ordered a double VO and water, and I talked to the young women there. There were several prostitutes at the bar, and I talked up a storm with them. I don't recall any of our exact words, but we talked a lot. I think they figured me for a potential paying customer for a blow job or a tumble in a hotel bed, and I viewed each of them as an empathetic person I could talk to. I viewed them as saviors. What a joke! I was putting my life in the hands of women who feigned love and affection for money. It was insane, but I was insane. Then I was no longer so sure I wanted to die. Or was I? Well, maybe yes, and maybe no. Maybe tomorrow, and just not today? It was confusing. I ordered another drink, and then another. I asked one of the women if she would come up to my room with me and stay by my side until I fell asleep. I didn't want any sex. I just wanted someone to keep me company and make sure I didn't kill myself. After talking to three gals who thought the idea was too weird for them, I finally came upon one who was willing. It cost me a fortune, but she agreed to my plan. We went to my room, and she lay down with me and let me caress her phony wig hair until I passed out. I probably talked to her, but I don't remember what I said. I probably told her all about Rhonda. I probably told her a lot more than she wanted to know.

It turned out that I would stay four nights in Vegas. I was drunk the entire time, and I don't remember much of what I did. Finally I drove home. I wanted to sleep in my own bed, and I wanted to sober up. When I arrived home in the afternoon, Rhonda was at work and Thomas was in school. I climbed into our bed and fell sound asleep. When I woke up, Rhonda was beating on me with her fists and cursing me. She was sobbing. She was out of her mind. I don't think I had ever seen her so hurt and angry. "You bastard!" she cried. "Where have you been? We've been looking all over for you! We called the police! We called hospitals! We hired a private investigator. We had no idea where you were, or if you were even alive."

I opened my eyes and said, "Gee, this is some fine welcome home I get."

"I don't know if you're even welcome."

"Not welcome?"

"Where have you been?"

"Las Vegas."

"Las Vegas? What the hell were you doing in Vegas?"

"Drinking," I said.

"I know that. I saw the booze bottles in your car. Who have you been with?"

"I'm not sure."

"You bastard!" Rhonda cried. She was beating on me with her fists again.

"I came home."

Rhonda burst into tears again and said, "I just don't understand you, Huey."

"I guess I'm sorry."

Rhonda did finally calm down, but she was still furious. Then we talked. I didn't feel much like talking, but Rhonda insisted. Jesus, we wound up talking about everything under the sun. We talked until about eight that night, when Rhonda made some dinner. It was good. She grilled some steaks and boiled some baby potatoes. Jesus, I was starving, and I wondered if I had eaten anything at all while I was away, or if I just drank the whole time I was there. "This can't happen again," Rhonda said while we ate. "Not ever."

"I understand," I said.

"I'll leave you."

"I get it."

"I won't go under with you."

"Go under?" I asked.

"I won't let you pull me down with you."

"I won't do that to you."

"And there's Thomas to consider."

"Yes," I said.

"He needs a father."

"He'll have one," I said. So now she was talking about Thomas needing a father? It was apparent to me that while we had just talked for several intense hours, Rhonda really didn't understand a word of what I'd said to her. And then the noise came back: that awful noise in my head—that deafening self-pity! I could hear my inner voice trying to be heard over the din, saying, "No one loves you, Huey. Everyone in your life is out for themselves, and no one cares. The world is a horrible place to live. Nothing is ever going to change."

The next eight months were a blur. I told you earlier that the year was 2005. Thomas was a senior in high school, but I remember nothing about him. It was as if he were a ghost. And I remember little about Rhonda. I also remember next to nothing about Carol Carson or her son, or Thomas's high school baseball games. I don't even know whether I was still going to them or just letting Thomas drive himself. I don't recall my parents at all, nor my brother, nor Rhonda's parents. But I do remember many strangers. I recall all those people that came into my life by way of my drinking. It was such a strange, strange time. Lots of strangers! I had lost control of it all, and I was spinning recklessly into a bad dream, a nightmare, an eight-month-long black-and-white episode of *The Twilight Zone*.

For example, just three weeks after I had returned from Las Vegas, I did it again. I made another run for it—not with the intention of killing myself, but of escaping. Those voices were urging me on. I was being fueled by the alcohol and *the noise*. This time I drove to Tijuana. I found a group of younger kids in a bar who were up for a good time. Looking back, I think they were simply attracted to my American money. What did we do? Honestly, I remember very little. I remember a few motels, beaches, naked dancers, restaurants, and lots of booze. There were a lot of people speaking Spanish. There were some kids playing volleyball in a street lined with trash. I remember having sex with a young girl, and I remember vomiting into a trashcan. Then I remember coming out of a blackout while driving the wrong way down a one-way street. That's when I decided that enough was enough, and I found my way back to the US border. I drove home, and again Rhonda was furious, but she didn't leave me or kick me out of the house. I remember cleaning a dozen or so empty beer cans from the floorboards of my truck while Thomas watched me. Jesus, was Thomas really a witness to all this? I remember so little of him.

I was completely out of control. My escapades were almost weekly events. I remember one night when I found myself in Los Angeles with a prostitute named Mimi. We drove all over the city in my car and wound up at the Beverly Wilshire. When I woke up the next morning, the bedsheets were soaked in blood, and there was a nasty gash on my hand. I had no idea where it came from. Mimi was gone, and I was alone and bloody. I was alone. I don't think I've ever been that lonely my entire life. I thought back, and I could remember standing outside of a club, sobbing. A man was trying to calm me down. You know, I recall only bits and pieces from those awful months. I was in a club in Huntington Beach. I was in a park in Corona del Mar. I was in Mexico again, looking for my friends, and then I was on a plane to Las Vegas. I remember the plane, and vomiting in the little restroom, then ordering a cocktail from the stewardess. Then there was the alley. I passed out beside a trash bin. I think it was in Beverly Hills. What was I doing there? There were other places, and some other bizarre memories.

Finally I agreed to go into rehab. Again Rhonda was threatening to leave me. She said it was either rehab or she would be packing her bags. So I went. Then I went to a second rehab. This time I walked out of the complex at night and went to a liquor store to buy a quart of vodka. A couple hours later, I was pounding on the door of the resident manager with my wrists slashed and blood splattering everywhere. I was taken by ambulance to the local emergency room, where they sewed up my wounds and sent me to a mental hospital. Then it was back to rehab. Then I went into the office of the doctor who owned the rehab center. He wasn't kidding around. He was serious. He said they were going to give me just one more chance. I had to promise to see Doctor Wilcox, a psychiatrist. "She's had some success with some of our most difficult patients," the doctor said. "But you're going to have to do what she says. No more horsing around." I didn't laugh, but I thought it was funny that he would refer to a suicide attempt as "horsing around."

I went to see Doctor Wilcox. My wrists were bandaged, and my ego was beaten senseless. I was ready to obey. I did my best to listen to everything this doctor had to say. She was nice, which I liked. I'd expected her to be a lot tougher than she was. We talked for three hours, and do you know what we talked most about? It wasn't Rhonda. It wasn't me. It was Thomas. Honestly, it was like being shot in the heart with an arrow.

SAYS THE BRIT

"Fatherhood made everything more straightforward. I was relieved that no longer did I have to agonize over what meaning I had in my life."

—Bill Bailey

THIRTY DAYS AT A TIME

They called it Stormy Monday,
But Tuesday was just as bad.
They called it Stormy Monday,
But Tuesday was just as bad.
Lord, Wednesday was worse,
And Thursday was also sad.
I saw the doc on Friday;
Saturday, went out to play.
I saw the doc on Friday;
Saturday, went out to play.
Four bottles of pills—

Gonna last me thirty days.
Hello, Sunday.
Lord have mercy on me.
Hello, Sunday.
Lord have mercy on me.
Was looking for a smile;
Doc brought the smile to me.

THE LETTER

On June 2, 2006, I wrote a letter to Thomas. My life was back together, and I was thinking clearly again. My father wrote a similar letter to me right after I graduated from high school. Thomas would be leaving for college soon, and there were things I wanted to say to him. I had had been given eighteen years with my kid to teach him, to impart my wisdom to him, and to love him. But where the heck did the time go? It seems like you blink your eyes, and the next thing you know, your child is an adult. It's funny. You look back to the time you had with your son and think of all the opportunities squandered. Don't get me wrong; I think that for the most part, I was a very good dad. It's just that there were several things I never said that I should've said that should now *be* said. I don't think I ever told my dad how much his letter meant to me. I should've told him, but I didn't. I now had a hunch that Thomas would also not tell me how he felt about my letter to him. That would be okay, so long as he read it. Word for word, here is what I wrote to my boy:

Dear Thomas,

Where does the time go? It seems like only yesterday we were at the park, working on your baseball skills. I'd hit ground balls to you. Do you remember when we bought your first mitt? You were so proud and excited. Do you remember your first Little League game? I remember it. You hit a double when the bases were loaded. You guys won that game by a run. And do you remember Sarah Jenkins? She was your first girlfriend. She used to come watch you play, and she'd jump up and down and scream every time you hit the ball. She was a nice girl. It was too bad her family moved away. I remember all of your friends, not just Sarah. You knew some nice kids. Except for Martin Crabtree. I never could stand that kid, but let's forget that. Who knows; maybe he was just going through a phase. I did like his parents. I played golf with his dad several times. Do you remember when you boys discovered pop music? All of you were looney about Alanis Morissette. You used to play *Jagged Little Pill* over and over, and you kids knew all the song lyrics by heart. Do you remember how we'd go to Angels games, and you kids would all sing in my truck? I remember that I'd go broke buying you boys hot dogs. You kids loved those hot dogs.

Now you're going to college. You're no longer a kid. You're a young man. Wow, you're old enough to vote and old enough to fight in a war. How do you feel about this, son? Do you feel like a man? Do you feel like an adult? Do you feel prepared for what lies ahead? Are you prepared to be responsible for yourself? I remember that when I was your age, I felt like I had the world by the tail, and I believed I knew what was going on. I was in the driver's seat, and I was in charge. But do you know what I soon discovered? It turned out the world was actually a lot different than I expected. It was like a spiderweb. The more I kicked and struggled to get free, the worse I was caught tangled up in its sticky and deadly threads. I learned also that there are some tricks of the trade. There are ways to avoid the venomous fangs of the spider.

First, you must separate your friends from your foes. By "friends" I mean those people in your life who are on your side no matter what. It's easy to find foes and cowards and turncoats and outright enemies. It is especially easy to find fair-weather friends. Beware of them. They are a dime a dozen. But *true* friends are especially hard to find, and to be honest, you won't know who they are until you put them to the test. Times will come in your life, as they come in every man's life, when you will find out who your friends are. No one goes through life without facing tough circumstances, and when those times come along, take count. Take inventory of the people who are on your side, even at the risk of hurting their reputations, costing them money, offending their friends, or insulting their superiors. You will find that true friends are worth their weight in gold. A fool makes friends with everyone who he meets, while a wise man cherishes his *real* friends. And he extends the same love and loyalty to them as they would to him.

Then there's family. You have a good family, Thomas. You have a family who loves you and who would do anything for you. Your mom and I would walk barefoot on hot coals for you, and don't ever forget that. So you should never be shy about asking us for help. I know what it's like to be your age, to yearn for independence. I know what it's like to want to tackle life on your own, no longer as a child, but as a man. But I tell you, there is nothing at all wrong with even the strongest and most independent man reaching out to his family in times of need. That's what family is for—not just to be there when you're young, but to be by your side forever. There won't be a time in your life when your mom and I would shun you. Someday you will likely have kids of your own, and you will understand the longevity of parenting. No, we don't just *allow* you to count on us. We look truly forward to it; don't ever forget this.

But back to the purpose of this letter. You are about to go off to college, and now is the time you need to be asking yourself what kind of man you want to be. I am going to make some suggestions. First, always be a man of your word. Do you know what I mean by this? I mean if you make a promise to someone, keep it. This will be very important. There is nothing worse than a man who does not keep his word. There is nothing more disappointing. You will learn as you go through life that people will depend on your promises, and the more often you keep your word, the more people will appreciate you. This may seem trivial and obvious now, but trust me; it is not. You will surely find yourself in situations where keeping your word is not as easy as it seemed when you gave your word. Don't be a weakling. Don't be a coward. Be strong and come through. Not only will others respect you, but more importantly, you will respect yourself.

You should also be true to yourself. A lot of people don't know what this means. You'll find that a lot of men lie to themselves constantly. At times, it may seem like a national pastime, even more popular than baseball. But you will not do this. You will be honest about each challenge that you face, and each situation you're in, and you will assess your God-given talents, skills, desires, needs, and obligations honestly. Don't be afraid to do this. I think a lot of people think that if they're self-honest, they will be disappointed in themselves, so they lie and gloss over the truth. But believe me when I say that lies and reality do not mix well. So be courageous, son. Yes, it takes courage to be honest with yourself, but being a man is all about being courageous. It is, in part, how a man defines himself. Will you be afraid? Yes, you'll probably be scared. But courage is not a lack of fear. Courage is the way a man stands and faces his fears.

You have so much to learn. I am fifty-one years old, and I am still learning. You will be learning at my age too. Don't be afraid to learn. Don't ever think you know it all—ever. One thing I have discovered is that life on this planet is vast. Does this make any sense to you? The older I get, the more I realize how little I knew when I was younger. When I was your age, I thought that I knew it all. My advice to you? Never be afraid to learn more than you knew the day before. Always keep your eyes wide open. And what's most interesting is that you'll discover you can often learn from the most unexpected events, from the least likely people, and from the most badly written books and magazine articles. Be a student of the world, and keep an open mind to it all. Never lock up your doors or close your windows. Be open to all new ideas. One day you may see things one way, and the next day you may see things the opposite. But that's okay. It shouldn't frustrate you or make you feel dumb or vulnerable. Revel in it. All that it means is that you're making progress, and learning more and more each day of your life can only make you a smarter and wiser human being.

One of the things I have learned over the years is the importance of a sense of humor. I think that when I was your age, I tended to take some things a little too seriously. And yes, some things are serious. But you're going to find that having a sense of humor is indispensable. It's the grease that keeps the machinery from wearing itself out. You might even say it's the essence of life. I can think of nothing worse than taking advice from someone who had no sense of humor. God gave us the ability to laugh for good reason. You can tackle serious matters and laugh at the same time. Don't let the friction and stress build up inside of you until you lose your joy. Do you know what the greatest joke of all is? It's the fact that we're all going to die. We strive, work, labor, sweat, scheme, and expend all our energy trying to make the world a better place to live. And for what? So that we can ultimately have a sheet pulled up over our head? Take some time to think about it. One day the sun will turn to ice, and everything we worked so hard to improve will be gone and forgotten. Death, Thomas, is the biggest and funniest joke of all jokes. Have a sense of humor. Learn to laugh, son, and you won't regret it.

Another thing you will notice as you get older is that people are not perfect. This may sound obvious, but you'd be surprised at how many people expect perfection from each other and from themselves. As you go through life, you're going to learn that people do and say a lot of really dumb things. Don't judge them too harshly, because it is likely someday the same will be said of you. Perfection is just an ideal. It is something in your head that has little to do with reality, and if you truly want to be happy, you'll need to pay more attention to the real world than you do to your fantasies. Love yourself and all your imperfections, and learn to love others with the same tolerance. Love, and not perfection, is the energy that makes the world go around. Learn to love the chinks in the armor as much as you love the armor itself, and you will realize the glory of being alive.

Of course, knowing that you're less than perfect does not mean you should give up the fight to be better. You should always give every venture in your life your best and most intense effort. Succeeding is not necessarily getting what you want. Succeeding is simply putting forth a best effort. People in America have a difficult time getting this. We are so often blue ribbon and championship trophy crazed, but try not to fall into this trap. It is nice to come in first place now and again, but it is your effort that will ultimately count the most. There are some people who are simply blessed with talent, and some people who are lucky. But you are never going to talk me into believing that every second-, third-, fourth-, fifth-, sixth-, and seventh-place contestant in an Olympic event is, in fact, a loser. People in our country don't like to hear this, but we are all winners so long as we did our best with what we had, and so long as we had the guts to compete. There are a lot of real winners in the world. Winning is trying your very hardest and does not always involve breaking through the iconic tape at the finish line.

Now I'm going to tell you something you may laugh at. And that's fine. Go ahead and laugh. But do you want to know what one of the best-kept secrets to happiness is? Never mind achieving great things or making tons of money. The real key to happiness is keeping busy. My advice to you? Do something with your life. Keep yourself busy. I don't care what you decide to do; just keep from becoming idle. They say idle hands are the devil's workshop. Let's take it a step further. Idle hands are *misery's* workshop. If you really want to be unhappy, be lazy. Lazy people are the unhappiest and most miserable people in the world. And you know what the sad thing is? Most of them don't even realize how unhappy they are. They have nothing to compare their state of mind to. They don't know what it's like to work hard at something, to play hard, and to achieve. They think they've got it made, when they actually are living in a hell on earth. Hell isn't brimstone and fire. Hell isn't pushing boulders up hills over and over. Hell is indolence and ennui. Hell is having nothing to do. Hell is having no activity associated with your name.

I'll tell you something else that will make your life miserable if you let it. It's something we all experience. It's something that creeps up on you while you're paying attention to other matters. It's something that will eat you alive. I'm talking about hate. There is so much hate in the world, you would think it was like air or water—a thing that we can't live without. But we *can* live without it. And we should shun it. It is so destructive, hurtful, and vile. I can't think of a single situation where hate is worth cultivating. Hate is disliking your neighbor just because his religion is different from yours, because he talks funny, because his skin is a different color, because he doesn't agree with your politics, because his hairdo is odd, because he did something to harm you or your family, because he's rude, or because of a thousand other reasons. There's no shortage of excuses for people to hate others. But you have to ask yourself this: Where does hate take you? Does it take you to a place where the situation is made better? The answer is always no. Hate takes you only to a place that is overflowing with even more hate. It is a maelstrom of negative and destructive energy that becomes more difficult for you to climb out of every day that you feed it until finally you are consumed by it. Eventually you will just become a hateful old man who is good for nothing but spewing bile. You will have squandered your gift of life, and you will have no future. And ultimately you will hate yourself. That is the nature of hate.

A much better course of action for you to take is to be kind. You should be kind to your family and be kind to your neighbors. You should be kind to strangers, vagrants, con artists, criminals, enemies, competitors, scoundrels, friends, and even politicians. You can never go wrong by being kind. You may feel foolish at times, but I think you'll discover that your kindness will open doors you never expected to be opened. Kindness can defuse the most volatile situations. It can change the minds of even the most intransigent men and women. It will dissolve the storm clouds above and flood your landscape with sunlight. Just a simple and friendly smile can melt the coldest ice and snow. Just a little kindness shown can take you miles. Stick with it and you'll be leaping over whole continents. Do you think I'm exaggerating? Do you think I'm naive? Just look at those who scoff at kindness and see what becomes of them. And then ask yourself, "Do I really want to be like them?"

A lot of the advice I'm giving you involves living so that you can live with yourself. This is no accident. It took me years to understand that you can't love anyone or anything until you love yourself. I hope you catch onto this truth quicker than I did. For years I abused myself by doing a lot of stupid things, and I paid a price for it. Above all, take care of yourself. Be the best you can be. Try to be the first to smile and the first to laugh. And take good care of the precious life you have so generously been given. Be grateful that you're alive, and show your gratitude by cherishing the gift. Your gratitude will be rewarded in spades, and each day will be another wonderful miracle and another reason for you to say thank you and mean it.

Who do you say thank you to? I guess that is my final and most important bit of advice. You need to believe that someone or something is in charge of the universe. Maybe you believe in God, and that's fine. Maybe you believe in something else. But somehow you must believe that there is a higher power—a moral power, an intelligent power, and, most importantly, a loving power. You must not go through life thinking that we are all just a haphazard life form with two legs, two arms, and a brain living on this planet for no other reason than no reason at all. We are orbiting the sun for an important and meaningful reason, breathing, sweating, thriving, loving, warring, cheating, achieving, fighting, and inventing. Yes, there is a reason for all of it. There is a cause. And the cause is a moral one. You must believe this is true; otherwise, you will be as lost as a traveler without a map in a rainstorm. Turn your wipers on and look for the street signs. And look for the lights. And look for the roads. You will find them all if you look hard enough and pay attention. They will guide you to your destination.

So I have given you my advice for a good life. This letter turned out to be a little longer than I anticipated, but I guess I had a lot to say. It's funny how when you sit to write down your thoughts on a subject, so many ideas come to you. I would never have guessed that I would have had so many things to tell you. And there are likely more I can come up with. If I kept at it, I could probably keep on writing and writing. But when I sat to write this letter, I had no intention of writing an encyclopedia. I just wanted to share some of my thoughts with you. I just wanted to tell you, briefly, what I've learned about life after having lived fifty-one years on this amazing planet. Maybe this will be useful to you. I hope so. At least it will give you some things to think about.

Before I end this letter, there is one final thought I would like to convey. It concerns you accepting help from others. I know you want to be a self-sufficient man, and I know it's often difficult to accept help from others. But honestly, there's nothing wrong with seeking the assistance other people are willing to give you. Don't shove them out of the way. No man is an island. We all live here on this planet together, in one way or the other. There is nothing wrong with acknowledging this. There is no shame in asking for help. I will tell you the truth; without the help of others, I would not be where I am today, and I would not be writing this letter to you. I would not be a good father or a good husband; nor would I be of much use to my friends. You are aware of the trouble I had last year with my sanity, with booze, and with my erratic behavior. So did I solve my problems on my own? No, I didn't. I sought help from a professional, and I followed her advice. Now I take my list of meds religiously, and I avoid things that I know will throw me off course. I aim my arrows toward their targets, and I keep my bow in good working order. Life is now good because I looked beyond myself for help.

I love you, Thomas, and I hope this letter helps you. Even if you disagree with parts of it, you might find that it causes you to ask the right questions. Sometimes that's all one needs for a successful life. My life is not your life, and your life will not be mine. You will find your own way. I am well aware of that, and no matter what you finally do with your life, and no matter how you find your way through it, I'm sure I will be proud.

Love, Dad

I put the above letter in an envelope and handed it to Thomas. I told him to read it when he had time. I also told him no response was necessary. "Just read it and think about what I've written," I said to him. And did he read it? I'm sure he did, but to this day he hasn't brought it up, and we haven't talked about any of it.

LEVITICUS 19:33–34

When aliens reside among you in your land, do not disrespect or mistreat them. They should be treated like your neighbors, like hamburger-eating, flag-waving, Ford-driving, TV sitcom-watching citizens. You must love them as you love yourself and your own family and friends. Remember your ancestors were all immigrants too, demanding hospitality from the Native Americans who lived here before they arrived. I am the Lord, your God. I say this just in case you forgot who you were listening to. What I say goes. Do we understand each other?

EL KÁISER

Do you remember Mateo? He was the Mexican alien who worked for me— the guy who knocked down and busted up the expensive streetlight at my shopping center project in Mission Viejo. He was the guy I fired and then rehired—twice. I don't think I told you that he had a son who was a year older than Thomas. Mateo's son was named Oscar, and Oscar was literally the light of Mateo's life. According to Mateo—and I have no reason to believe he was lying—Oscar earned straight As all through high school. He got a full scholarship to UCLA. I guess the kid was pretty bright, and we got to talking about our two boys one day while eating lunch at one of my jobsites. I didn't usually eat lunch with my workers, but once in a while I would sit down with them to eat and talk. It was good for my employees' morale, and it kept me in touch with what was happening on my jobs. I have always been a firm believer in being more than just the guy with the expensive truck who gives out orders and signs the payroll checks. I didn't want to be *too* close to my workers, but close enough to know what was going on and how they felt about their jobs. Oscar had just finished with his first year of college. Mateo took a bite from his burrito, and then, with a mouth full of beans and rice, he said, "I don't know. I'm glad my boy is in college, but they sure teach some *cosas locas* to the kids in your schools."

"Such as?" I asked.

"Such as the stories they have them read."

"Any story in particular?" I asked, laughing. I knew what *"cosas locas"* meant. It meant "crazy shit."

"He told us last week about what he read. It was the one about the guy who kills his father and sleeps with his mother. And then he scratches his eyes out." Mateo closed his eyes and shook his head. "Crazy," he said.

"Oedipus Rex. It's a classic."

"A classic?"

"Sure," I said.

Mateo shook his head again and said, *"Cosas locas."*

I laughed and said, "I suppose I can see how you would feel that way."

"You know what else they're teaching my boy?"

"What?" I asked.

"They're telling him that God did not make Adam and Eve. That there is no heaven up above us. That we come from apes in the jungle. That Jesus was just a cabinetmaker with some big ideas and a lot of crazy *admiradores.*"

"Colleges can be hard on religions."

"My wife and I raised Oscar to be a good Catholic. Maria is very upset. She doesn't understand, and neither do I."

"You're going to have to keep open minds."

"I don't think God is going to like him believing any of these things. In fact, I'm sure of it."

"Just be patient," I said. I wanted to sound reassuring. "I'm sure Oscar will do what's right in the long run."

"We're hoping."

"Does Oscar have a major?"

"He wants to study business."

"That's a good major. Lots of opportunity."

"That's what Oscar says."

"Encourage him to stick with it. He can do just about anything he wants with a business degree."

"Maybe he'll be rich, no?"

"Maybe," I said.

"Maybe he'll be president of a big company. Maybe he'll be a boss like you?"

"Maybe."

"You make lots of money, right?"

"I make enough."

"You know, I want my boy to be like you. Maybe not working in construction. Maybe working in something else. But making a lot of money."

"There's more to life than making money."

"Sure, sure."

"There are other things."

Mateo took another bite of his burrito and then said, "Can I ask you a question?"

"Shoot," I said.

"How much did you pay for your truck? It's a nice truck, no? I'll bet it cost you a lot of money?"

"It wasn't cheap."

"So how much was it?"

I hesitated. This question made me feel uncomfortable. Then I told Mateo how much I paid for the truck. "I probably spent too much on it," I said.

Mateo whistled and said, "It would take me two years just to buy that truck. It would take two whole years, and that's if I didn't spend money on anything else. No money for gas, rent, *cerveza*, or food. No damn burritos for lunch. Just money for the truck."

"It is a lot," I agreed.

"Would you like to trade your truck for mine?"

"No," I said, laughing.

"No, no, of course not. You make the money, and I do all the work. You're smart. I'm just a stupid worker, but you? You're smart."

"I've made some wise decisions." I didn't really know what else to say.

"Oscar is going to be wise."

"I hope so."

"He's a smart boy. He's not anything like his father. No, he's nothing like me. The boy is going places."

I always hated talking about these sorts of things with my employees. I wasn't at ease with the large gap in our incomes and lifestyles. I can't say it made me feel very guilty; it just made me feel weird. So I did what any "superior" American man in my position would do. I changed the subject. I brought up the World Cup, which I knew all Mexicans loved to talk about. I asked, "So have you been watching the soccer games?"

"Football, you mean?"

"Okay, football."

"We lost."

"Only by one goal."

"A loss is a loss."

"I saw that the goal was scored by Marquez."

"El Káiser. He should've scored three goals. Three goals would've won the game for us."

"There were other players on the team."

"But he's the *hombre*. Mexico was depending on him. We all look up to him, and he let us down."

"Seriously?"

"Un pedazo de mierda."

"That's a little harsh," I said. Mateo had just called him a piece of shit.

"Too much playing around with women. Too much of being the big shot. Not enough football."

"I thought he was happily married."

"Married to that TV whore, Adriana. Big mistake. He was having an affair. That's what my people have been saying. He wasn't focused."

"Some people have a hard time with marriage."

"He's not so great. He's not so great now. Knocked out by Argentina?"

"What did you think of the rest?"

"Didn't watch it."

"None of it?"

"Mexico was out. I had no care after that. I was way too disappointed to watch any more of it."

"Is Oscar a soccer fan?"

"It's football," Mateo said, politely correcting me again.

"Yes, of course, I mean football."

"He can take it or leave it."

"That's surprising."

"His sport is basketball."

"Does he play?"

"He played in high school. I went to some of the games. It was okay. It wasn't football, but he was a good player."

"Is he playing in college?"

"He's too short."

"Aha," I said calmly.

"We tried to get him interested in football when he was young. He just didn't take to it. He's more of an American than he is a Mexican. I guess we shouldn't complain. That is what we wanted. That's why we came to America. I mean, it is and it isn't."

"He's probably too busy with his classes now to waste time on sports anyway."

Mateo scratched his head and said, "Yes, reading about men who sleep with their mothers and kill their fathers."

"Yes," I said, laughing.

"It's a crazy world, no?"

"It can be."

"But who cares?" Mateo said. "So long as the boy is rich. So long as he's rich like you."

I stared to Mateo for a moment. Then I said, "Honestly, I think you believe I have a lot more cash at my disposal than I actually do."

Mateo laughed heartily and said, "Compared to me, you're loaded. Compared to me, you're Carlos Slim Helu."

"Who's he?" I asked.

"He's our Bill Gates. You may be surprised to learn that not all of us Mexicans dig ditches and push wheelbarrows for a living." There was a hint of sarcasm in Mateo's voice. I don't think it was intentional. But I also think he could tell that I noticed it. He took another bite from his burrito and said in a more subservient tone, "Don't worry; I like my job. I work hard for you, and I'm okay."

"I'd like to meet your son someday," I said.

"Yes, that would be a good thing. I would like to meet your son too."

THE ITALIAN PROBLEM

We hear a lot these days about the great Latino immigration into the United States. What we don't hear a lot about is the great migration of Italians a century or so ago. To begin with, there were about three hundred thousand Italian immigrants in the 1880s. Then, in the 1890s, there were about six hundred thousand. In the next decade, there were more than two million, and it is estimated that by 1920 more than four million Italians had come over. Why were they coming? The causes were probably a little different for each family, but in general you could say it was because Italy was a mess. Decades of internal strife had resulted in constant violence, chaos, and abject poverty. The peasants in the rural south of Italy had little hope of living prosperous and fulfilling lives. Further, there were diseases and natural disasters to contend with, and the government was incapable of providing the needed aid. The Italians said, "Enough is enough," and they made a run for it. And they ran to America.

So what did they find? They found themselves exploited, working at lousy jobs, toiling their tails off for low pay in often unhealthy conditions. At the start of the twentieth century, Italian immigrants were among the lowest-paid and worst-treated workers in America. Child labor was common, and children often went to work in factories, in mines, and on farms. Many of them sold newspapers on city streets. It was hardly the life they looked forward to, and to make things worse, they suddenly had to deal with prejudice and hostility from the people who got to America first. The Italians were *not* welcomed with open arms, and anti-immigration feelings abounded. America was also in the grips of an economic depression at the time of the influx, and immigrants were being blamed for taking jobs and lowering wages.

Racist theories made their way into the papers, alleging that the people in this new wave of Italian immigrants were morally and intellectually inferior to the people of Northern Europe. They were depicted as childish and criminal. And the attacks on Italians were not limited to the papers. Many anti-immigrant societies sprang up around the country, and the KKK grew like crazy. Catholic churches were burned and vandalized, and Italians were attacked by mobs. In the 1890s alone, more than 20 Italians were lynched. One of the bloodiest episodes took place in New

Orleans in 1891, where a tenth of the city's population was composed of Italian immigrants. The French Quarter was now known as Little Palermo, and Italians owned and controlled about three thousand businesses in the city. The good people of New Orleans were not happy about this. It was upsetting, to say the least. And the newspapers added fuel to the fire by printing xenophobic stories about Italians and their predisposition to crime. Anti-Italian tensions reached their climax when David C. Hennessy, the New Orleans chief of police, was murdered.

On the rainy night of October 15, 1890, Hennessy was on his way home from the police station. He was headed to the house he shared with his widowed mother. A group of men leaped out from the darkness and opened fire. Hennessy returned the fire, but he was mortally wounded. The dying police chief said to a friend, "They have given it to me and I gave them back the best way I could." The friend asked Hennessy who had attacked him. Hennessy replied, "The Dagoes." Mourners gathered outside the hospital. When Hennessy's body was taken to his home, more grievers came. It was a very big deal, and everyone suddenly wanted revenge on the Italians.

Hennessy's funeral was an enormous affair. Mourners began coming at dawn, and by midmorning thousands were there to pay their respects. The *New York Times* reported on the magnitude of the funeral. It said, "All day long the people crowded into the City Hall to view the body, and it was almost impossible to reach the bier, which had been placed in the same room in which the body of Jefferson Davis once lay in state. The carriage moved through the streets of the city, all of which were so crowded that streetcars and vehicles couldn't move."

Although Hennessy had been unable to identify the men who attacked him, the words that Hennessy had whispered about Dagoes told the mayor of New Orleans all he needed to know. At a city council meeting, the mayor said, "We must teach these people a lesson." The murder was not entirely surprising, given that he had a reputation for being tough, especially on Italian crime. But Hennessy was loved by city reformers, and his death triggered a public outcry. Newspapers called the killing a "declaration of war" and an "Italian assassination." The mayor ordered a dragnet of the city and sent officers into the French Quarter. Over 250

Italian men were taken into custody, and 19 of them were charged with murder.

Over the next four months, the papers reported that these men belonged to a secret society of Italians known as the Mafia. The word "Mafia" began to pop up in newspapers across the nation, reinforcing the stereotype of Italians being associated with organized crime. On February 28, 1891, the verdict of the Hennessy trial read as not guilty for all nineteen men. The city was outraged, and the next day a call to action was printed in the daily paper. John C. Wickliffe, one of the speakers at this city meeting, cried out, "On the spirit of our forefathers; like when we cleared out the carpetbaggers before, we will go to the Parish Prison and clear out these Sicilian Mafia thugs." The crowd then shouted, "Yes! Yes, hang the Dagoes!" Soon over ten thousand people had gathered in front of the old parish prison. Hearing the cries of the crowd, Captain Lemuel Davis, warden of the prison, readied his men.

Out of the crowd came three hundred men with shotguns and other weapons. These men immediately headed to the main entrance and demanded that they be let in. When they were told no, they started beating on the gate with axes, crowbars, and picks. The guard told the Italian prisoners to hide, but the mob quickly found them. The first Italians were immediately shot. The crowd then dragged several more men from the prison and carried them through the streets. They were hanged from the lampposts, and after the lynching had ended, the city declared that order had been restored thanks to the mob. The front page of the *New York Times* the next day read, "Chief Hennessy Avenged."

It was subsequently declared that the mob "embraced several thousand of the first, best, and most law-abiding citizens of the city." So as far as the city was concerned, justice had been served. No further arrests were made, and the dead police chief could rest in peace.

FINE MEN AND WOMEN

"Arizonans should not be judged disdainfully and from a distance by people whose closest contacts with Hispanics are with fine men and women who trim their lawns and put plates in front of them at restaurants, not with illegal immigrants passing through their backyards at 3 AM."

—George Will

"I live in Arizona. I think the Hispanic people are amazing. I think when people talk about illegal immigration, it does them a disservice."

—Charles Barkley

THE NEW COLOSSUS

Give me your tired, your poor, your huddled masses yearning to live free, the viral refuse of your sickened shores. Send all your unskilled and homeless to me, because we need them to man our convenience stores!

MY FAVORITE ITALIAN

His parents were immigrants from Sicily. His dad came from the farming town of Castelvetrano, and his mom from Sciacca. He was born in 1911 in Little Italy, at the Lower East Side section of Manhattan. He grew up speaking Italian but eventually learned English. His father was the prosperous owner of three barber shops in New York, but he also had a gambling problem and soon pissed the family fortune away. Who am I talking about? I am referring, of course, to Joseph Barbera. If you're close to my age, you surely recognize his last name. He is the Barbera of Hanna-Barbera, the creators of all those cartoons you used to enjoy—the creators of the Flintstones, Huckleberry Hound, Yogi Bear, and Top Cat, to name a few. I don't know about you, but my long-ago memories would not be remotely what they now are without a Hanna-Barbera character or two— or three or more. In fact, Hanna-Barbera cartoons *were* my childhood.

Just a few months after Barbera was born, his family moved to Flatbush, Brooklyn, where he was raised. In 1926, his father abandoned the family, and Barbera went to live with his uncle, Jim Calvacca. While in high school, Barbera worked part time as a tailor's delivery boy. He was a hard worker, and he was a tough kid. He excelled in boxing and won a number of titles. But he eventually decided against becoming a professional boxer, and when he graduated from high school, he started working at odd jobs to pay his bills. It was in 1929 that Barbera grew interested in animation after seeing Disney's movie *The Skeleton Dance*. After seeing the film, he began working as a freelance artist, drawing cartoons and successfully selling them to *Redbook*, the *Saturday Evening Post*, and *Collier's*. He also was now taking art classes. He was good. He was soon hired by Fleischer Studios, and then by Van Beuren Studios, and then by TerryTunes. In 1937 he went to work for MGM. This was where he met William Hanna. The rest is history, as they say.

Never mind that I love all his cartoons. I have enormous respect for Barbera as a man. He went from a tailor's delivery boy and boxer with a gambling addict for a father to the founder, owner, and partner of one of the all-time greatest animation studios on earth. His legacy is undeniable. Are you a Hanna-Barbera fan? Did you know that they had a worldwide audience of over three hundred million people in the 1960s and that their works have been translated into twenty-eight languages? They have walked away with no less than seven Academy Awards and eight Emmy awards, including the 1960 prize for *The Huckleberry Hound Show*, the first Emmy ever given to an animated series. They were inducted into the Television Hall of Fame in 1994. In March of 2005, the Academy of Television Arts & Sciences and Warner Bros. Animation dedicated a wall sculpture to them at the Television Academy's Hall of Fame Plaza. Barbera lived to be ninety-five, dying in 2006. Close your eyes and listen, and maybe you'll hear it: "Exit, stage left!" Who could ever forget?

WHAT ARE YOU?

America has become a land of labels. We live and swear by them. So what are you? Are you Italian? No? Maybe you're Mexican. Or maybe your ancestors are from England, France, Africa, Spain, or the Netherlands? Do you have an accent? Are you unique, or are you your father's son? Are you a Native American? Are you a child, a teenager, or an adult?

Are you Protestant, Catholic, Jewish, or a Muslim? Do you wear a towel on your head? Are you a wop, a spic, or a jungle bunny? Are you gay or transsexual? What do you do for a living? Maybe you're blue or white collar, or maybe something in between? Are you a know-it-all doctor, an ambulance-chasing attorney, an infuriating bureaucrat, a gang member, or a car mechanic? Are you a rock 'n' roll front man, a country-and-western crooner, or second violin in the local symphony orchestra? Do you paint? If so, are you a surrealist or an impressionist? Are you blonde, redheaded, or a brunette? Do you have freckles? Do you have moles? Are you mean or nice? Do you play well with others, or are you contentious? Or maybe you're a liberal Democrat, or maybe a Rush Limbaugh Republican?

How do we go about describing you? What is your label? What is your category? How can we decide whether to be your friend or foe if you don't tell us? How can we decide how much money you will make? How can we decide where you should live? How can we decide what kind of clothes you should be wearing? Please tell us so we can organize our prejudices. We want to treat you the way you deserve to be treated.

We like to say that all men are created equal, yet let's be honest; we believe in this about as fervently as we believe there is a Santa Claus who flies around in a sled and climbs down chimneys with a sack of gifts for our children. No, Americans don't believe in equality. Americans believe in labels. You can depend on that. What does the label sewn to your collar say? What about the one sewn to your jeans? What is your waist size? What does the price tag say? What does the sticker on your car window list? What is standard, and what option do you come with? Do you come with seat warmers or custom wheels? Do you get good mileage? Personally, mileage isn't that important to me. But seat warmers? I have to admit I really like having seat warmers.

FLUNKING OUT

Okay, at first I was furious. When I thought of what so many people had gone through to make a life for themselves in this country, it made me feel sick to my stomach. It made me feel guilty. It embarrassed me.

I got the call in the spring of 2007. Thomas was midway through his second semester at Washington State, and he said he had to talk to me. He said it was important. I wasn't sure what to expect, so I listened patiently. "Go ahead," I said. There was a long pause on the phone, and then Thomas continued. While he was talking, I thought to myself, *This is not at all what I expected.*

"I have a big problem," Thomas said.

"What is it?"

"I don't know how to tell you."

"Just tell me."

"I don't want you to be mad at me."

"I promise I won't be mad. I'll just listen, and I'll do what I can to help."

There was another pause. Then Thomas said, "I'm addicted to drugs."

"To drugs?"

"Opiates."

"Jesus, Thomas."

"I told you you'd be mad."

"I'm not mad," I said. "I'm just surprised."

"I need some help."

"Yes, yes, your mom and I will do whatever we can."

"I'm flunking out of school."

"Flunking?"

"I have Fs in all my classes. My counselor called me in and said I was going to be put on academic suspension. Last semester was bad enough, and now …"

"Did you tell him about the drugs?"

"It was a woman."

"Okay, did you tell her?"

"I didn't tell her anything about the drugs. She just thinks I've been goofing off—you know, like a typical dumb freshman"

"I can't believe she didn't ask you about drugs."

"She asked me. I just lied to her."

"Okay."

"I don't know what to do. I've really fucked things up. This is really a mess."

"We can figure something out," I said.

"I want to come home."

"Yes," I said. And he was right. He needed to come home before things got even worse. He needed to be away from the drugs.

"I can straighten myself out at home."

"And then do what?"

"I don't know."

"They probably won't let you back into the school until you prove yourself at a community college."

"No, probably not."

"How bad is your addiction?"

"It's bad, Dad."

And this was when it occurred to me that this problem was probably more than Rhonda and I could handle. Then it was hard for me to believe what I said next. I couldn't believe the words were coming out of my mouth. "We need to check you into a rehab," I said.

There was a pause. Then Thomas asked, "Do you really think that's necessary?"

"I do," I said.

"I don't want to go to rehab. I just wanted to come home and regroup."

"You're in over your head. We're all in over our heads. If this is as bad as you say, we need to get professional help for you."

A million things were going through my mind at this point. I was thinking about the rehabs I went to. I was thinking about the young people who were locked up with me, and how I wondered what was wrong with their parents. What kind of parent raises a kid to become a drug addict or alcoholic? Yet now here I was. I was one of them. I was an alcoholic, and now I was a parent. the parent of a drug addict? Maybe Thomas was just following in my addictive footsteps, a chip off the old block. This wasn't Thomas's fault. It was *my* fault. Wait until Rhonda heard about this! She was going to be furious with me, and she was going to blame me for sure. And I wouldn't blame her if she did. I had passed along my bad genes to her precious son! Her precious Thomas!

"I'm so sorry, Dad," Thomas said.

"No reason to say you're sorry," I said. "We just need to get you clean."

"Yes," Thomas agreed.

"I'm going to come get you."

"When?"

"As soon as I can catch a flight. We'll drive back to California in your car. Pack your car. Be ready to leave when I get there."

"I can drive myself."

"No," I said. "I don't want you driving."

"Okay," Thomas said.

"I'll call you and let you know when to expect me. Just sit tight."

"Okay," Thomas said again.

"And don't take any more drugs."

On that note, we ended our call, and the first thing I did was book a flight to Pullman. I was able to leave early the next morning, and I reserved my one-way ticket. Then I had to tell Rhonda what was going on. I thought she was going to throw a fit, but I was impressed. She was calmer than I expected. In fact, she said she suspected something like this was wrong. So she wasn't surprised, but I could tell that she was worried to death. "I'm glad you're going up to get him," she said. "That makes me feel a lot better."

"While I'm on my way up there, see if you can find a rehab program for Thomas. I want him admitted as soon as possible. Try to find one that specializes in treating kids around Thomas's age."

The next morning, I flew to Washington, and Thomas met me at the airport. I didn't ask him to drive to the airport. I was going to take a cab to his dorm, but he drove. His car was stuffed with all the junk from his dorm room. I looked at my boy. Thomas looked like Thomas to me. He did not look like a drug addict. His hair was combed, and his clothes were clean. I climbed into the driver's seat of his car, and off we went. We would be on the road for hours and would have a lot of time to talk.

So maybe you're asking what had happened? How did my son go from one and a half semesters of college to becoming a drug addict? I was wondering the same thing. It was a lot simpler than you might imagine. What it boiled down to was that he went to college, and a lot of kids were taking drugs. He took them to fit in, and he liked them. And the next thing he knew, he was hooked on them and failing all his classes. It was really no more complicated than that. When we arrived home, Rhonda said she had found a rehab program in Riverside that could take our son right away. We got some sleep that night, and then I took Thomas to the facility first thing in the morning. I signed him in and then wrote a check. Then I left, and as I drove, I cried almost the whole way home. It was awful.

It was so strange. It wasn't that long ago that I had been in rehab, but it was different then; I was the one being locked up—I was the one with the problem. Now I was the one on the outside, hoping and praying that the program would do Thomas some good.

Rhonda and I were on pins and needles the entire time Thomas was in rehab. Each day seemed like a full year. We were allowed to talk to Thomas on the phone each Sunday, but that was it. We really had no idea how he was doing. Then, after three weeks, they held something at the facility they called Family Day. Rhonda and I were asked to come and take part in Thomas's program for a day. I knew what this was like. I had gone through it when I was in rehab. But now I was on the other side of the fence, and it was a completely different experience. This was when you arrived and met the counselors and the other addicts and asked yourself, "Do these strangers really have any idea what they're doing?" You know, I can't begin to tell you how uneasy I suddenly felt. Did anyone tell any of these parents what the odds were that any of their children would actually stay sober? I knew. The odds were horrible, and most of these kids didn't have a chance in hell. Oh, there were lots of encouraging words and hugs and hopeful promises and smiling faces, but the reality was almost absurdly bleak. Yes, I too went to rehab, and I was now sober, but I was one of the lucky ones.

On the way home from Thomas's rehab, I asked Rhonda how she felt. "I feel hopeful," she said. Of course she did. That's how the counselors wanted her to feel. Me? I was hopeful too, but I was also filled with trepidation. During Family Day, one of the exercises we did was to sit on fold-up chairs in front of all the other families with Thomas and list out loud the nice things we felt about each other. One of the things Thomas said that applied to both Rhonda and me was that he thought we were well organized, and I kind of wondered what he meant by this. Did he just mean that we were well organized, or did he mean that he thought we were *too* well organized? Maybe he admired us. Or maybe he thought we were just a couple of middle-aged robots getting up every morning at six, going to work, coming home for dinner, watching a little TV, and going to bed, only to get up at six again the next day and perform the same well-organized routine over again.

Rather than drive straight home from Family Day, I took an exit in Norco. I had no idea where I was taking us. Rhonda asked me what the heck I was doing, and I said, "*Now* we'll see who's organized." Then I drove, and Rhonda just looked out her side window.

No Particular Place

Ridin' along in our automobile,
Me holding on to the steering wheel;
I turned my head to give her a smile,
Her curiosity runnin' wild,
Cruisin' and playin' the radio
With no particular place to go.
Ridin' along in our automobile,
Not sure exactly how we were to feel,
So I told her softly and sincere,
Maybe we're far, and maybe we're near.
She sneezed out loud and blew her nose,
With no particular place to go.
No particular place to go,
Rollin' along through old Norco.
The night was young, but the moon was gone.
The cows were loud, and the smell was strong.
We passed a McDonald's and went on,
The radio playing our favorite songs.
Ridin' along in our calaboose,
Rhonda got her belt unloose.
She leaned over to give me a kiss,
But a big pothole made her miss.
Then she said she was glad to know
We'd no particular place to go.

The Fortune Teller

When you're the parents of a child who's just become addicted to drugs or even alcohol, one of two things can happen. Either the addiction splits the two of you apart or it brings you closer together. It can be awful. Parents might blame each other for the problem, and they can disagree on what needs to be done to deal with the problem. And it isn't like most problems. It's not like you're arguing about which chores your kid should do, or what time his or her curfew is, or whether a C is an acceptable grade in algebra. It is your child's *life* that you're dealing with, and emotions can run high. Feelings and opinions can be formidable, and conversations can be stressful. I've seen drug and alcohol problems divide parents in two. They start blaming each other for the problem, or they can't agree on how to deal with it, or both.

Then there are parents like Rhonda and me. Thomas's problem actually pulled us much closer together. We became a real team. This doesn't make us better than others; it just means we were lucky. We just so happened to agree on things. First, we both agreed that we, as parents, were not the root cause of Thomas's problem with drugs—at least so far as our parenting decisions and efforts were concerned. We both agreed that Thomas's problem was with his DNA and not his environment. You might disagree with this, but that was how Rhonda and I saw it. And it helped that we were on the same page. Second, we agreed on the steps we needed to take to help Thomas get straight. We would let him live in the house with us for a while, but we would require him to get a job or go back to school. We would not allow him to do nothing productive. We would also stay in tune with him and talk to him often. We would keep our finger on his pulse at all times, and we would not make him feel guilty. We would make sure he understood that we saw his problem as the result of the physical constitution he inherited. He was an addict, just as he was a brunette, and just as he had brown eyes. And we would be firm while being understanding. We would not tolerate drugs in his future. Tough love, I think they call it. Rhonda and I agreed on this.

Now for what actually happened. Thomas came home after rehab, but things didn't go quite the way we planned. First there was the job thing. Rhonda and I sat Thomas down and told him we expected him to get a job right away. Thomas said that was fine and dandy, but a week passed, and then a second week passed, and there was no job. On the third week, I asked Thomas if he'd been looking, and he said he had no idea where to look, that he had no marketable skills, and that nothing he qualified for really interested him. Well, I guess I could see his point. I then told him he could work for me. More accurately, he could work for Mateo, performing miscellaneous duties on my jobs. It would work out well. Thomas would be employed, and I'd keep an eye on him. Well, actually Mateo could keep an eye on him, and he would report back to me. Thomas agreed to this idea, and he started work on a Monday morning.

The first thing that went wrong was Thomas sleeping through his alarm. I told him the night before that he had to be at the job by seven. It was a half-hour drive, and he would need a half hour to dress and eat breakfast. I figured he had to get up at six. And yes, he set his alarm for six, as I had asked him to. But instead of getting out of bed when it beeped, he just reached over and turned it off in his sleep. I was in the kitchen downstairs, and at six-thirty, I went up to his bedroom. He was sound asleep, snoring like a hibernating bear.

"Wake up," I said.

Thomas groaned, and he barely opened his eyes. "Wake up for what?" he asked.

"For work," I said.

"Uh, what time is it?"

"It's six thirty. You should be leaving now. You were supposed to get up at six."

"I'm tired."

"You can't be late."

"What time am I supposed to be there?"

"I told you last night. You need to be there at seven."

"At seven?"

"Mateo is expecting you."

"Oh, yeah, Mateo."

"Come on; get out of bed."

"I'm so tired," Thomas said.

"Didn't you set your alarm?"

"I must've turned it off in my sleep."

"Up, up!" I said, clapping my hands. The clapping was supposed to motivate him.

"Why do I have to be there at seven?"

"Because that's when they start. They start at seven, take an hour for lunch, and then stop work at four."

"I can work until five."

"That doesn't work for me."

"Why not?"

"Because," I said.

"I can work until five. That's eight hours."

"Seven to four—that's the deal."

"How about eight until four, and I'll skip lunch? Seven is just too early."

"Come on, Thomas. Don't be difficult."

"You're the one being difficult. Seven is too early. Who gets up at six?"

"Lots of people get up at six. I get up at six."

"But you don't leave at six thirty."

"I don't have to."

"Because it's too early."

"Because that's not when I start my day."

Now Thomas sat up in bed and rubbed his eyes. "This is bullshit," he said.

"You said you wanted to work for me."

"Okay, okay, I'm getting out of bed."

"That's more like it."

"I'm still going to be late."

"Well, not *as* late."

It was infuriating. I tried not to get mad. I probably should've gotten mad, but I didn't. It was, after all, his first day working. *It's a learning process*, I thought to myself. *He'll get the hang of it.*

For the next couple of weeks, Thomas was able to get up for work on his own. Well, usually on his own. Several times I had to get him out of bed. But he wasn't objecting, and once I woke him up, he got himself in gear. I'd say he made it to work by seven about half the time, and the other half between seven-thirty and eight. I told Mateo to treat him like any other employee and to stress to Thomas the importance of arriving at work on time. When payday came, I docked Thomas for the hours he missed, and he didn't seem to care one way or the other. I think that if he had his way, he'd have been working five hours a day. What did he care? He had clothes and a roof over his head at our expense. He had all the food he could eat, also at our expense. He had everything else he needed. So what the heck did he need money for? I would soon find out.

Just five weeks after he was home from rehab, on a Saturday when I was walking past his bedroom door, I smelled the smoke in in the hall. It was coming from his room—the distinctive aroma that I knew so well from my youth. It was marijuana. I knocked on Thomas's door, and he answered right away.

"Hey, Pop," he said, smiling.

"Thomas?" I said. I said it as if it were a question.

"Yes?"

"Are you smoking weed?"

"I am," he said.

"I thought you were supposed to be straight."

"I am straight."

"You are?"

"Of course I am."

"And smoking weed?"

"Weed doesn't count."

This surprised me. "Of course it counts. It's a drug like any other drug."

"A drug?"

"That's exactly why you went to rehab," I said.

"I went to rehab to kick the opiates."

"But weed is also a drug."

"It's a nothing drug."

"A nothing drug? What exactly does that mean?"

"It's like caffeine. It's a nothing drug. Everyone smokes weed. It's harmless."

"That wasn't our deal."

"Did you quit drinking coffee when you gave up booze?"

"No," I said.

"So you still take a drug."

"Coffee is hardly like booze."

"And weed is hardly like opiates."

"I don't know," I said lamely, shaking my head and looking down at my feet.

"Trust me, Pop. It's nothing. It's nothing for you to worry about."

"I wish I saw it that way."

"Relax," Thomas said. Then he stared at me for a moment and finally said, "Did you want something? You knocked on my door."

"Because I smelled the weed."

"So now you know."

"What are you doing in here?"

"I was listening to music."

"You don't plan on going anywhere, do you?"

"No," Thomas said.

"I don't want you driving while you're high." It was dumb, but I had gotten nowhere, and I had to feel like I was putting my foot down about something.

"I'm not going anywhere."

"That's good."

"Was that it?" Thomas wanted to know if we were done talking. I guess he wanted to get back to his weed and his music.

"That was it," I said.

Thomas closed the door. I then went downstairs and found Rhonda gardening in the backyard. She was planting pansies in the flowerbeds. I told her that Thomas was smoking marijuana in his room, and she asked me if I had stopped him. "We can't allow that," she said.

"I asked him," I said.

"What do you mean you asked him?"

"I asked him if he thought it was such a good idea."

"And what did he say?"

"He said we shouldn't worry about it."

"Jesus, Huey."

"He said everyone does it. He said it was a nothing drug."

"What about his rehab?"

"He said he went there to quit taking opiates, and that he wasn't taking them. He said weed was okay. He said it was like drinking coffee."

"And you did what?"

"I told him not to drive."

Rhonda thought about this for a moment. Then she sighed loudly and wiped the perspiration from her forehead with the back of her hand. "What are we going to do?" she asked.

"I don't know," I said.

"I think this is a problem."

"Is it?"

"Don't you think it's a problem?"

"Maybe it isn't," I said. "I mean, it is only marijuana. These days it practically is like drinking coffee. People his age smoke weed all the time."

"Now you're making excuses for him."

"Maybe I am."

"I think we need to be firmer."

"Maybe we do," I said.

But we weren't. Maybe we weren't such good parents after all. We did voice our concerns, but Thomas didn't seem at all worried about it. And eventually he wore us down. We finally agreed that maybe weed wasn't such a big deal. No, it was the opiates that we were really concerned about. The oxycontin and the black tar heroin. Next to them, marijuana seemed rather insignificant.

So now our son was smoking weed in his room regularly. It was not what we envisioned, but we would take what we could get. Then, not long after I hired him to work under Mateo, Thomas quit his job with me. I asked him if Mateo had been treating him well, and he said his quitting had nothing to do with Mateo. He said construction work just wasn't for him—that he wanted to do something else. "I don't like getting dirty," he said. Jesus, he didn't like getting dirty?

Thomas then told me he had found a different job, and I asked him, "Doing what?"

He said he'd found a job working as an assistant for a veterinary clinic in Irvine. He would be responsible for tending to the animals and helping the doctors in this way and that, and I thought to myself, *What a crazy job.* I had no idea he liked animals. But maybe he just liked the idea of animals better than the idea of getting dirty and sweaty with Mateo. Maybe that was it. Maybe he was just picking the better of two evils. I hate to say it, but it hurt my feelings a little that he didn't want to work for me. But I didn't show it. I said it was a good move, and that finding the new job showed he had some initiative. Of course, it also occurred to me that the only reason he was even working was so he'd have money for his weed. But I tried not to think about it that way.

I thought about the letter I wrote to him when he graduated from high school, and now I wondered if he had bothered to read it at all. Or if he read it and thought it was no more than the dumb advice of some guilty dad's last-ditch effort to be a good father. Did he keep the letter? Who knew? I certainly didn't know, and I wasn't going to ask him. Meanwhile, life went on, and Thomas was tending to dogs and cats, smoking weed in his room, and listening to music. His four weeks at rehab and his college days were getting further and further away in our rearview mirrors.

I continued to have a recurring dream during these months. I'd dream that I went to see a fortune teller, and the old woman would reveal a crystal ball on a shiny brass stand and wave her hands over it. She always looked the same. She had long and silvery hair and a brightly colored silk scarf tied loosely around her neck. Her dress was made of purple velvet, and she wore enough costume jewelry to anchor a small ship. She would sit, smiling with her old teeth and looking at me through her stained-glass eyes. I would lean forward and ask her what lay ahead in my future, and she would just cackle and say, "How the hell should I know?"

THIRTY-FIVE BROKEN BONES

He died shortly after Thomas was released from rehab. There was a time when everybody in America knew his name. I don't know if the man was a hero or just an attention-seeking lunatic, but he was definitely an American—red, white, and blue through and through.

His parents named him Robert. Maybe you already know who I'm talking about? He was born in Butte, Montana. His paternal great, great grandfather was from Germany, and his mother was of Irish descent. Robert and his brother were raised in Butte by their paternal grandparents, Ignatius and Emma, and Robert left Butte High School after his sophomore year to work in the copper mines, where he operated a diamond drill for the Anaconda Mining Company. Soon he was promoted to surface work, where he drove a large tractor, but he was fired when he started doing tricks on the tractor and ran into a power line, leaving the town without electricity for hours. Robert then participated in rodeos and skiing competitions for a while, and he eventually joined the army. He was on the army's track team as a pole vaulter. Bored with the army, he returned to Butte and found a place on their semipro hockey team. He also married his first wife, Linda. Then, bored with hockey and looking for a better way to support his family, he tried out hunting and motorcycle racing. Still not satisfied with his income, he decided to try selling insurance. Then he quit that job and opened a motorcycle dealership, where one of his customers taught him trick riding. As they say, the rest is history.

Robert changed his first name to Evel and began his career by jumping over a twenty-foot-long box of venomous rattlesnakes, calling his new show *Evel Knievel and His Motorcycle Daredevils*. Then he began to jump cars, adding more cars to his stunt with each new show. And as the jumps became more difficult, he began to wreck and spend more time recuperating in hospitals, and the public loved it. In 1968 he got national exposure when he was a guest on *The Joey Bishop Show*. Always looking for new ways to get the public's attention, he decided to jump the fountains at Caesar's Palace in Las Vegas. He tried the jump and crashed in a nearly fatal incident, but the attempt to make the jump made him more popular than ever. Then he really got the public stirring when he proposed jumping over the Grand Canyon in Arizona. Of course, there was no way the government would allow this, but it made for some great publicity.

Evel did finally lease some land at the Snake River Canyon in Idaho, and he tried to jump it with a rocket-like cycle, but he failed. In the meantime, he was jumping cars and busses and trucks like a madman, and his fans loved it. They loved his relentless fearlessness. They loved his crash landings. They loved his crazy Elvis-like leather jumpsuits. They loved his enormous ego. They loved all his concussions and broken bones. They say Evel broke thirty-five bones during his career, and he holds the all-time world record for fractured bones at Guinness. Movies were made about him, and books were written. And $125 million worth of Evel Knievel toys were sold to kids. Museums were later opened in his honor, and even a legit rock opera was written about his life. Evel finally died at the age of sixty-nine in Clearwater, Florida, on November 30, 2007.

CRASH LANDING

Here was a great idea. Let's see how many really bad loans our financial institutions can make. Let's see how many cars and busses we can jump. Everything is great while you're high in the star-spangled sky, but the devil is in the landing. Ouch! How many bones did we break this time?

So what am I talking about? They are calling it the Great Recession. It started the same year Evel died and continued on for several miserable years. Unemployment during this time more than doubled. Millions of people lost their homes, and American businesses shut their doors by the thousands. Consumer spending dropped in every category except health care. Real estate values took a nosedive, and many discovered that they now owed a heck of a lot more for their houses than they were worth. There were mass firings and layoffs all over the country, and the household net worth of the average family plummeted. Major institutions we could once depend on ran to the US government for billions in financial bailouts. The country had been beaten senseless and was now on its knees.

PRELUDE

Are you familiar with the story of Bob Citron? They know him well in Orange County, California. He was their balding and bespectacled county treasurer and tax collector between the years of 1973 and 1994. In a county where most voters were Republicans, he was a Democrat, but the voters liked him. He promised what they wanted to hear, and until 1994 he delivered. He kept taxes down while maintaining the county's high spending. How did he do it? He was an investment genius. Through some unorthodox practices, he invested the county money so that he was getting twice the returns of other counties, and the money was pouring in. Who doesn't love a good magician, right? In his last election, he got over 60 percent of the vote. He thought highly of himself and his acumen. He even had citizens writing checks to "Robert 'Bob' Citron" rather than to the tax collector. It was kind of weird, but everyone went along with it. Then along came 1994.

Citron's investment vehicles were all dependent on interest rates staying down. There was no reason to believe that rates would go up. So what happened? The rates went up. All of a sudden, Orange County was hemorrhaging hundreds of millions of dollars. Gulp! The county declared bankruptcy on December 6, 1994, citing paper losses of $1.64 billion. The citizens freaked out, and the story went national. While the county was in bankruptcy, every county program was slashed, and about three thousand public employees lost their jobs. A grand jury investigation found that Mr. Citron should be tried. Facing fourteen years in prison, he pleaded guilty to six felony counts of financial fraud. He spent only a year behind bars—a small price to pay for all the trouble he caused. Maybe the courts were sympathetic. Bob was, after all, a truly patriotic American. And there are no guarantees in life, and no one can predict the future.

THE BRADY BUNCH

The Brady family lived in a nice neighborhood in Albuquerque, New Mexico. Jim, the father, had lived in the city limits of Albuquerque his entire life. He was now forty-three years old. His wife, June, moved to the town when she was five. Her family had relocated west from Maryland thirty-five years ago. Jim and June met in high school, and they married when Jim was twenty-two and when June was nineteen. They now had two kids: a ten-year-old boy named Zach and an eight-year-old girl named Maddy. Life had been good for the Bradys. Jim made a decent living as a backhoe operator, and June worked part-time as a bookkeeper for a civil engineering office. Jim had his own backhoe, which he had purchased with the help of New Mexico State Bank. He still owed money on the piece of equipment, but he'd been making his payments for several years. Someday he would own the backhoe free and clear.

Just last year, the family went to the Hawaiian Islands for a summer vacation. They stayed on Maui in a first-class resort right on the water. It was the family's first exotic vacation. It was certainly the first time they'd spent so much money for a week off. In the past, they had gone on low-cost camping trips in the local Sandia Mountains, doing some hiking and horseback riding, so Hawaii was a very big deal. And why not? Jim was as busy as a bee with his backhoe, and the money was great. He had more work than he could handle, and his customers loved him because he was good at what he did. He was almost always putting in solid twelve-hour days, six days a week, and now he deserved this trip to Hawaii. It was his reward for working so hard. *A 'o ia*, Jim Brady!

The Bradys had the time of their life on the island. It was an expensive vacation, but so what? Thanks to Jim and his trusty backhoe, they could afford it, and they went all out on their trip. They rented a pricey red convertible car, and they ate breakfast, lunch, and dinner at the pricey restaurants. They went on all the pricey excursions, and they relaxed and sipped pricey fruit-and-umbrella drinks at the bars. They got on a bus and attended a pricey local luau. They also bought pricey island clothes at the local pricey clothing stores, and Jim splurged and bought a pair of pricey Churchill cigars. He lit up one of the cigars on the balcony of their hotel room, but the people in the room next door complained, so he had to snuff it out. But no matter. No one was going to ruin the Bradys' vacation. Not this year! No way! They truly had the time of their lives. This would be a vacation none of them would ever forget.

When the Bradys returned home, they turned their attention to their house. It was a fine house, but they knew it could be better. The Coopers down the street had the exact same floor plan, but they had done something with it. They had added a big bonus room for their pool table and a second refrigerator. They had completed the project earlier in the year using money they had extracted from their home equity. The values of the houses in the neighborhood had been soaring like gangbusters, and there was a lot of money sitting idle, just waiting to be spent. "Why not spend it on your house and make the house worth even more than it was before?" Jonathan Cooper said to Jim, and this made sense to Jim. Yes, why not? The logic was flawless. So, two weeks after they returned from Hawaii, Jim hired an architect to draw up plans for the Brady's bonus room.

When the plans were completed several weeks later, Jim took them to the city to get a building permit. Then he went to his bank. That's when he got the bad news. He'd heard some recent rumblings, but they hadn't really registered. But now it was real. The banks were no longer lending money. There were problems. There were some *big* problems. "Sit tight," the banker said. "Some things need to be sorted out."

Like many people, the Great Recession took the Brady family by surprise. It didn't take long for Jim to feel the crunch. His backhoe business slowed down, and then it was as if someone flipped a switch and turned off the lights. Shortly after he'd had the plans done for the bonus room, he found himself without work. The construction projects he relied on for business came to a grinding halt. Fortunately, the family had saved a little money, so they were able to stay afloat and keep the bills paid for the first few months. But then? Well, like so many other families during this time, the Bradys found themselves incapable of keeping up. And the equity in their home quickly evaporated so that within months they owed more on their house than it was even worth.

June was still working during this time, but her part-time salary wasn't near what they needed. It all seemed to happen so fast! One month they were fine and the family had plenty of money. Yes, they had gone to Hawaii. They were even going to build a bonus room. Then the next thing they knew, they had a stack of past-due bills that they were unable to pay. Jim called on everyone he knew, desperately looking for work, but no one needed his services. Almost all the projects were being put on hold. What should he have done? Unless you've been in the same position as Jim and June, you probably don't know the fear, the uncertainty, and the impending doom. There was a big, dark cloud that suddenly grew and grew and blocked out all of the sun and blue sky. There was blackness and bleakness. The horror! It was awful, and there were so many questions. Where were they going to live? How were they going to eat? How would they get around without a car? What kind of work could Jim even find, and what about all the unpaid bills? And what about the kids? What would Jim and June do about them? What were they going to do, period? Jim tried to think, but the blood rushed from his head, and his hands trembled. All at once, he was scared, sick, hopeless, and incapacitated.

Jim's parents had both passed away, so he couldn't look to them for help. June's retired parents were still alive, but they had little money. They were essentially living off their Social Security and a small pension. They certainly didn't have enough to float a loan to Jim and June, even if they wanted to. Then bad went to worse, and June was laid off from her job. The civil engineering firm she worked for was feeling the same economic pinch, and the firm's owner was now having his wife do the bookkeeping. One month after June lost her job, Jim's backhoe was repossessed by the bank, and they were two months behind with their house and car payments. June went to her parents and described the situation they faced.

She sobbed the whole time she talked. It was June's dad, Abe, who came up with the idea. Slowly and deliberately, Abe said, "You're going to be homeless in a month. I don't see any way to stop it. I want you and your family to move in with us. You'll have a roof over your heads. Somehow we'll make it work until you or Jim can find some sort of a job."

It was unthinkable. Moving in with June's parents? "Never in a million years," Jim said to his wife when he heard about the crazy proposal. And he began looking everywhere for a job. He would've done about anything, for any wage. Somehow he would make things work. But there were so few jobs, and the job openings he found were being filled with other, more appropriate, workers. Jim soon saw the writing on the wall. Either they would move in with June's parents or they would be homeless. There was no choice. There was no other way. So they decided to do it. Jim felt so small. He felt small and low like a bug. He felt worthless, powerless, and like an utter failure. But he didn't hide out or try to escape. He bit his lip and joined in with the rest of the family to move all their things into his in-laws' house.

It was ridiculous bringing over so much stuff. They all decided that June's parents would park in the driveway and that the garage would serve as storage. Boxes and furniture were soon stacked to the ceiling. June's parents' house had two spare bedrooms, one that would be for Jim and June, and the other for Zach and Maddy. They would all have to share the hall bathroom. It was miserable at first. Jim grew depressed, and the kids were constantly complaining. June tried to hold the family together, and her parents were great. No doubt they didn't like what was happening, but they never showed their frustration. "Families need to stick together," her dad said. He must've said it a hundred times.

ECCLESIASTES 3

> There is a time for everything,
> And a season for every activity under the heavens:
> A time to laugh and a time to cry,
> A time to know and a time to ask why,
> A time to crap and a time to pee,
> A time to work and a time for TV,

A time to drive and a time to walk,
A time to shut the heck up and a time to talk,
A time to bet and a time to fold,
A time to pretend that you're not getting old,
A time to scratch and a time to itch,
A time to act like you know which is which,
A time to wear plaid and a time to wear stripes,
A time to fall for the media's hype,
A time to listen and a time to look,
A time to tell others that you read lots of books,
A time to be near and a time to be far,
A time to buy that luxury car,
A time to add a room to your home,
And, of course, time to learn you won't make it alone.
Hello in-laws, thanks for letting us stay
Until this Great Recession goes away.
Praise the Lord, and pass the Hamburger Helper;
I haven't had anything to eat all day.

PATIENCE

It wasn't so bad living with June's parents. There are some things you can say about Americans. I mean, there are lots of snide comments you can make about them, and a lot of criticisms of them are justified. Americans can be argumentative, materialistic, arrogant, selfish, greedy, shallow, litigious, competitive, and sometimes downright mean. But when push comes to shove, we get along. We stick together. We are on the same team as you, and we enjoy each other's company.

Have you ever seen a movie titled *The Defiant Ones*? It's a great little film that came out in 1958 starring Tony Curtis and Sidney Poitier. The two men are convicts, and they escape from a southern chain gang when the bus transporting them and some other inmates crashes in a rainstorm. Curtis's character, John "Joker" Jackson, hates blacks, while Poitier's character, Noah Cullen, hates whites. The men are chained together, and when they make a run for it, they are forced to cooperate with each other to survive. Captured at one point by a lynch-happy mob, the men are rescued by Big Sam, played by Lon Chaney Jr., himself a former convict. Lon is wonderful in the role. He's one of my all-time favorite character actors. By the way, no one could've played Lennie Small any better in *Of Mice and Men*. Did you see that one? It was amazing.

Anyway, the men finally come upon a lonely widow, played by Cara Williams, who falls for Joker and offers to help him. She has a car, and she suggests that he drive with her and her son north to safety. They know the law will be looking for two men, not a man, woman, and child. She then steers Cullen toward a shortcut through the swamps so he can find a nearby train on his own and hop aboard, taking it to freedom. Joker agrees to the plan, but after Cullen leaves, the racist widow tells him that Cullen will never survive the shortcut—that it goes into a swamp filled with horrible pitfalls and deadly pockets of quicksand. Furious, Joker abandons the woman and runs off to find Cullen. It turns out that Joker has given up his chance for freedom to save his friend Cullen, and after finding Cullen, the two men run together, making it through the swamp. They attempt to catch the train, but they are unable to board it together. They stay together and are eventually captured by the sheriff. Where there once was hatred, there is now love and friendship between the two men, despite their failed escape attempt. So what do we learn? We learn that Americans, even lowly convicts, stick together in the face of adversity. I love how this story ends, and I love the message.

The script for the movie is credited to Harold Jacob Smith and Nathan E. Douglas. Nathan was a man named Nedrick Young, a blacklisted writer whom producer Stanley Kramer hired knowing he was using an alias. Both the script and the photography eventually won Academy Awards. And by the way, also in the film was the former Little Rascal Carl "Alfalfa" Switzer, making his last appearance in a movie. If you blinked, you missed him, but it's an interesting bit of trivia if you're a movie fan, as I am.

But enough about the movies, and back to the Brady family. I said it wasn't so bad with everyone living together at June's parents' home, and it wasn't. It was a little strange at first, with everyone getting used to the new situation. And it wasn't easy for Jim, since he had never really gotten along too well with June's father, Abe. It's not like he hadn't tried, but Abe never really liked Jim. He believed his daughter could've found someone better than a backhoe operator to spend the rest of her life with. He never came right out and said it to Jim's face, but everyone knew he'd wished his daughter had married someone with more potential for financial stability. And now here Jim was, without any work, living in his small house, unemployed and incapable of supporting his family.

But an interesting thing happened. After having lived with each other for six months, Abe began to like Jim more. He could see firsthand how hard Jim was trying to find work so he could support June and the kids. He never gave up and threw in the towel. Finally Jim landed a menial job as a cashier at a nearby gas station. It was a lousy little job, and the pay was poor. But it was something, and something was sure better than nothing at all. Jim could now contribute to the family's living expenses.

Jim's father-in-law could have shaken his head and said, "Jesus, is that really the best you can do?" But he never said anything like that. Instead he told Jim that he respected him. He told him he was proud. He told Jim not to worry, that recessions never last forever, and that the job at the gas station was only temporary. Then he did something he had never done before. He invited Jim to come fishing with him for catfish at Isleta Lakes. It was his favorite spot to fish. Jim told him he didn't know much about fishing. "I'll teach you all you need to know," Abe said, and they drove off to the lakes on Jim's day off. It was a warm day, and the lakes had just been stocked. The two men sat quietly with their lines in the water. They had caught nothing. It had been about an hour in the sun when Jim finally spoke up.

"Do you ever catch anything here?"

"Oh, yeah."

"The fish don't seem to be biting."

"Have some patience, son."

"That's the story of my life lately."

June's dad smiled. Then he said, "Patience is a good thing to have."

"I suppose it is."

"That's the problem with America today. Everyone is so blasted impatient. No one is willing to wait for anything. We all want everything now, now, now."

"I guess that's true."

"Of course it's true. Why do you think we're in this recession? What do you think caused this whole mess?"

"What caused it?" Jim asked.

"Impatience. Everybody in this country wanted everything right away. That's not the way the world works. They were all putting the cart before the horse. No one was willing to wait. Mark my words. Waiting is the price you have to pay for not wanting to wait."

Jim thought about this. "What exactly does that mean?" he asked.

"It means that if people were more patient, there wouldn't be recessions. People need to be patient. But that's not how Americans operate. It never has been, and probably never will be.

Jim reeled in his fishless line, and changing the subject, he said, "Do you think we're going to catch anything?"

"Patience."

"Ah, yes, patience again."

"If they don't bite today, they will tomorrow."

Jim cast his line again, and he said, "About what you were saying. I still don't exactly get how our impatience causes recessions."

"Ah, I thought you would ask."

"And?"

"What was the cause of this recession? It was the result of house loans going bad. Thousands of them, all at once. And why did they go south? It was for two reasons. First, you had a whole group of people who were impatient, not wanting to wait until they could afford a house before buying one. They didn't want to wait. They wanted their houses right now, whether they made enough money or not. Second, you had some large financial institutions who wanted to make loans and sell securities before they were ready to be sold. They wouldn't wait for quality or prudence. They wanted to sell the investments, pronto. Above all, they were impatient. And yes, they were greedy too, just like the people taking out the home loans. If all these idiots had just been patient and waited until the time was right, then this fiasco would never have happened, and they wouldn't now all be waiting for this sick economy to rebound. But by refusing to wait, now they are stuck waiting, miserably, waiting for the mess they created to sort itself out. Patience, Jim. It's like they say. Patience is a virtue. But patience has always been in short supply in this country."

Jim thought for a moment and then said, "That does make sense."

"Of course it makes sense. I said it."

They both laughed, and Jim changed the subject again and said, "Are you sure they just stocked this lake?"

"Have you heard anything I just said?"

"Patience, right?"

"Yes," the father-in-law said. "Have another beer." They had brought a cooler with a six-pack of Budweiser beer and some ham and cheese sandwiches, and Jim reached in and pulled out a cold bottle. He twisted off the top and took a sip.

"It's actually kind of nice here," Jim said.

"You mean peaceful?"

"Yes, it's peaceful."

"You should do this on your own."

"I don't have a fishing pole."

"You can always borrow mine."

"Thanks," Jim said. "Maybe I'll bring Zach and Maddy here."

"It would be good for them."

"I think Zach might like it. I'm not sure about Maddy."

"It would be good for both of them."

"You're probably right."

Abe was lost in thought for a moment, and then he said, "I don't think I ever told you this, but I think you're a good father."

"You do?"

"You have two fine children."

"Thanks," Jim said.

"And you've been a good husband to June. I like the way you treat her. And it was nice of you to take your family to Hawaii. None of us have ever been there before. We all always wanted to go but never got around to it."

"It was fun."

"I'm sure it was."

"Funny, but it now seems like centuries ago."

"You know, I'm actually glad for this recession. It's been as annoying as hell, but I got to know you. You're no longer a stranger. Funny how things work out, isn't it?"

"It is," Jim said, and he reeled in his fishless line for the umpteenth time.

"Can you grab me another beer?"

"Sure," Jim said.

"Hand me one of those sandwiches too," Abe said, looking at his watch. "It's noon, and I'm getting a little hungry. It's time to eat."

THE LAYERS OF NACRE

It's interesting how pearls are made. Do you remember learning about this in school? Oysters make pearls. They produce them as a defensive response to foreign objects. The process begins when a foreign body—such as a grain of sand, a parasite, or some other unwanted organic material—makes its way into the oyster's shell and comes in contact with the mantle. The mantle is the layer that protects the oyster's internal organs, and when the oyster's mantle sees the invading body as a threat, it deposits a protective substance called nacre. Over time, the oyster will apply more and more layers of nacre to the foreign body, forming a pearl. Contrary to what a lot of people think, there's never been any shortage of pearls in America. They may not be cheap, but they are all over the place. You just have to know where to look for them.

HENRY

The recession lasted a couple years before the economy got back on its feet. It was encouraging having our lives come back to normal. Well, at least it was as normal as could be expected. I was building actual buildings again, and this was great news. It had been two years since I was building anything you could call substantial.

So how exactly did June and I make ends meet during the lean years? That's a good question, and I'm going to answer it for you. We did better than a lot of people, in part because of some good old-fashioned nepotism, and in part because of my own American ingenuity.

During the recession, Rhonda didn't lose her job. Her dad, being her employer, made sure of that. It was true that he laid people off at his agency owing to the lack of work, but he didn't lay off his daughter. Rhonda kept her job at full salary, and she was making decent money. For Rhonda it was as if there were no recession at all.

My business, on the other hand, went right into the toilet. Hardly anyone was building anything, and the projects that were being built were being bid on by every desperate contractor in town. It wasn't worth the effort to submit bids, so I had to look elsewhere for work. And I found it. It turned out people who found themselves in trouble were turning their houses over to the banks in record numbers. The banks, bless their stingy hearts, had no desire to be in the business of owning homes, so they wanted to sell them off as quickly as possible. But work had to be done first. Many of the homes they were taking back in foreclosures were in bad shape and needed to be fixed up a bit before they could be put on the market. And that's where I came in. I began calling the banks, one by one, and I palmed my company off as a restoration specialist. I promised low prices and quick completion of the work, and I was hired. I had Mateo and four of his Mexican buddies working full-time, six days a week. The money we were being paid wasn't near what it had been when we were building new buildings, but it was a heck of a lot better than nothing. This money, combined with the money that Rhonda was making, kept us afloat.

One of the many homes we worked on was a two-story disaster in the town of Lake Forest. I say it was a disaster because that's exactly what it was. When I first visited the property, it was hard to believe. The family who had lived in the house must've just dropped everything and made a run for it. I have no idea why. I'm guessing they took only what they could fit into a few suitcases, leaving the rest of their possessions for the bank. But what they left behind was worthless. There was a lot of miscellaneous junk, including threadbare furniture, dingy drapes, filthy throw rugs, and closets that were stuffed with clothes, games, linens, toys, videocassettes, books, binders, boxed photos, cleaning supplies, old tools, and some holiday decorations. In the kitchen, there was a pile of dirty dishes, pots, and pans in the sink, and strewn all over in the bathrooms were old razors, empty deodorant cans, Q-Tips, cotton balls, and old soap bars. The kitchen and the bathrooms smelled something awful. In fact, the whole house smelled bad. I don't think the house had been cleaned for months.

In addition to the all crap, there were cracked mirrors, broken windows, holes in the walls, doors off their hinges, and missing cabinet doors. The outside of the house wasn't much better than the interior. The yards were overgrown and full of weeds, and several rain gutters were hanging from the eaves. And there was more. I could go on and on listing the work we had to do in order to make this dump look halfway presentable to buyers. It was weird but also good. I mean, it was weird that people would leave their house in such disarray, but it was also good because it gave my guys plenty of work to do. And plenty of work to do meant lots of money in my pocket.

While I was doing this renovation work, I always made it a point to check on my jobs at least once a day, to be sure Mateo and his men were doing what they were supposed to be doing, and to answer their questions. And, of course, I constantly needed to give Mateo cash to buy materials. I remember the first day I came out to this house. Mateo and his men were working indoors, and I arrived in the front room. Right away I noticed something through the glass patio door. There was a dog. He was a German Shepherd, and he was standing there looking into the house as though he wanted in. I called Mateo over to the patio door, and I asked, "What's the deal with the dog?"

"I don't know," Mateo said. "He's been here all morning."

"People shouldn't let their dogs run loose."

"No," Mateo said.

"Do you know who he belongs to?"

"No idea."

"Have you tried chasing him away?"

Mateo shrugged and said, "He's not bothering us. We just leave him alone."

"Well," I said, "so long as he isn't bothering you."

"He's fine," Mateo said. Then he took me to the kitchen to ask me a few questions.

I remember the next day. I was standing in the front room again, and there was the dog, looking in at me through the glass patio door. This time I opened the door and shooed the dog away. He whimpered at first and then ran around the corner of the house and into the side yard. Mateo showed up. "How's he getting into the yard?" I asked.

"There's a hole in the fence," Mateo said.

"You ought to fix it."

"It's on the list," Mateo said. "But we're working on the inside first." He took me into the downstairs bathroom to ask me a question. It turned out that they had tried to clean the toilet bowl but the black stains would not clean off. "A new toilet?" Mateo asked.

"Let me ask the bank."

"This toilet is *no bueno.*"

"I agree," I said. "But don't replace it until I get the bank to sign a change order."

The next day, I arrived at the job and gave Mateo the go-ahead to replace the old toilet. I walked through the kitchen. It still smelled like hell, but Mateo and his men were making progress. "*Mucho basura,*" Mateo said.

"Yes," I agreed.

"We're going to need another Dumpster."

"Go ahead and order one."

"That dog is still here," Mateo said.

"He is?" I asked.

"Same place."

I walked to the front room, and sure enough, the German Shepherd was curled up outside the patio door. He was asleep, making himself at home. "I wish I knew whose dog this was," I said. "I'd tell them to keep him on their property."

"He's not a bad dog."

"How do you know?"

"He's just hungry. We've been feeding him."

"Don't you know any better than to feed a strange dog?" I said. "He's going to keep coming back forever. Next time he shows up, chase him away."

"But he's hungry."

I opened the patio door, and the sound startled the dog. He jumped up and stepped backward, growling. "Shoo!" I said, and I waved my arms at him. At first, he didn't budge. Then I lunged toward him, and he scampered away, running around the corner of the house and into the side yard. "Keep him out of here," I said to Mateo.

"Sure, boss."

"And stop feeding him."

The next day when I showed up at the house, I went straight to the kitchen. It was getting better, and the smell was going away. Mateo told me he needed another couple hundred dollars for supplies, and I gave him the cash. Then I walked over to the front room, and I looked out the patio door. Sure enough, there was that goddamn dog, curled up on the stoop and sleeping. "Mateo!" I called out.

Mateo came from the kitchen. "Yes?" he said.

"I thought I told you to get rid of the dog."

"Get rid of him how? He keeps coming back. We chase him away, and he keeps coming back."

"Have you been feeding him?"

"No, no food."

"Honest?"

"Yes, honest."

"Does he have a tag?"

"I think so," Mateo said.

"Did you check it?"

"No, he won't let us get near to him."

"Maybe he'll come to me," I said. "Get me a piece of some food." Mateo went to the kitchen where he kept an open bag of *chicharrónes* to snack on. He came back and handed me one of the crispy snacks. I opened the patio door very slowly, and the dog stood up. He began to back away from me, trying to figure out what I was up to. I then got down on my knees and offered the dog something to eat. I reached out, and he walked up to me. What a dumb dog! I reached out with my other hand and grabbed his collar, and he didn't resist. He just sat there looking at me with his sad eyes. This needy old dog was really starting to bother me a lot. "Let's see what we have here," I said, looking at his tag. "It says his name is Henry, and there's a phone number." I told Mateo to grab his cell phone, and I read off the phone number to him. Mateo called the number on his phone, and I then grabbed the phone from his hand and listened. Of course, I should've known. The number was disconnected, and there was no forwarding number to call.

"He belongs to the house," Mateo said.

"What do you mean he belongs to the house?"

"I'll show you." Mateo walked to the kitchen. He came back with a dog dish, and on the side of the ceramic dish it said "Henry."

"Shit," I said.

"Same name, no?"

That's when I realized what had happened. The idiots who lived in the house had left their dog behind. I had heard about people doing this because they couldn't take their dogs with them. And now I was stuck with their dog. "You want a dog?" I asked Mateo.

Mateo laughed and said, "No need a dog."

"I guess I'll take him to the animal shelter."

"Poor dog," Mateo said.

"Yes, poor dog."

I led Henry into my truck, holding him by his collar, and I had him sit on the backseat. He was very trusting. I think he thought I was his friend. I then got the address for the animal shelter from my cell phone, and off the two of us went. Henry looked out the window at the passing scenery while I drove. I could see him in my rearview mirror. It was sort of sad in a way, and I felt for him. He didn't have the slightest idea of where we were going.

When we arrived at the shelter, I told Henry to wait for me. I wanted to check the place out first. Don't ask me why, because I honestly didn't know. I rolled all the windows open a crack to be sure Henry had air, and I locked the doors. I then went into the place. The very first thing I noticed was all the barking dogs. I had never been to an animal shelter before, so rather than step up to the front counter, I walked through the outside aisles. There were rows of chain-link cages containing the stray dogs. Some of them were barking, and some were just cowering silently in the corners. Each of them had a food dish and a water bowl. Some cages had feces on the concrete floors, and the place smelled horrible, like urine and dog shit. And I thought all the barking was going to drive me crazy. It was heartbreaking, all these homeless caged dogs without families to care for them.

And that's when it hit me. It hit me like a ton of bricks, and it tugged at my heart. I suddenly felt awful. How could I drop Henry off at a place like this—this noisy and disgusting hellhole for animals that no one loved? Honestly, I felt lower than I'd ever felt in my life. I felt like a lout. No, no, I couldn't do it!

"Can I help you, sir?" a young man said to me.

"A lot of dogs," I said stupidly.

"Yes sir. Did you see one that you liked?"

"No, no," I said. "I have a dog."

"Oh," the young man said.

"I've got to go."

"Let me know if I can help."

"Will do," I said thoughtlessly, and then I got the heck out of there. I went back to my truck in the parking lot and climbed into the driver's seat.

Thirty minutes later, I was home, and I found Rhonda in the kitchen. I stepped in, and I said, "Close your eyes. I have a surprise for you."

"A surprise?"

"I've brought home a new member to our family."

"A what?"

"His name is Henry. You're going to like him."

"What on earth are you even talking about?" Rhonda asked. She was laughing.

"Just keep your eyes closed until I tell you to open them. I'll be right back. Stay right where you are. I'll just be a minute."

"Okay, if you insist."

Then I went to the truck and retrieved Henry. His tail was wagging. Such a dumb dog. I don't think he even knew how lucky he was.

1 CORINTHIANS 13:11

When I was a snot-nosed child, I spoke like a child, I thought like a child, and I reasoned like a child. When I became a man, I sold off my toys and grew the hell up.

GROWING UP

The Great Recession changed me. Or maybe I was just due for the change and it happened to come coincidentally around the same time the Great Recession came and went. I don't know for sure, but I did change. I was not the same man I once was. I was no longer interested in junk. By "junk" I mean all those things that money can buy that you buy for no other reason than the sake of owning them. I no longer cared what others thought. I was no longer competing with everyone or trying to prove how clever I was. Did I drive a new Mercedes, a new Cadillac, or a brand-new Lexus?

Did I still have that Rolex watch on my wrist? Did I take my family to the Caribbean during the summer, or skiing in Aspen during the winter? Did our front yard look like the gardens of Versailles year-round? What exactly was my net worth? How many bankers did I have in my back pocket? What was my credit score? Where did I get my hair cut? Enough was enough! There had to be more to life than this! I knew it, and I had always known it. But it was always a struggle. It was a battle between what I knew was right and what I was busy doing. I was speeding down the freeway. So which exit was I going to take? What would the sign say?

The sign would say family. I used to think it was all so funny. I used to laugh at John-Boy, Grandpa, Cindy, Jim-Bob, Emily, and the rest of them all living under the same insipid farmhouse roof. But they were Americans. Their blood pumped red, white, and purple-blue. They were what made this country great—the American family. Why had it taken me so long to see the truth? Where had I been all these years? I'd been at car dealerships, jewelry stores, shopping malls, and real estate offices. I tried at times, but I had to be honest. I had to come to terms with what I was: just another shallow character on a TV sitcom, just another art critic, just another rock 'n' roll fan, just another picky restaurant patron, just another building contractor cutting down trees and laying out parking lots, just another guilty father with a handful of hypocritical advice for his loving son, just another guy with an expensive haircut, just another credit-card-armed chain-grocery-store customer with his shopping cart filled to the brim. So ring up all my purchases and tell me how happy I am now that this awful Great Recession is finally over. *No, no, no, not now*, I thought. *This time it is going to be different.*

THE ANSWER

"The only rock I know that stays steady, the only institution I know that works, is the family."

—Lee Iacocca

FAMILY MAN

I began with Rhonda. Can you think of a better place to start? She was my soul mate. She was the person I had chosen to live my entire life with. She was my lover and the mother of my child. It wasn't until I had decided to turn over this new leaf that I discovered just how different Rhonda and I were. I'm not saying it was a bad thing. But it was a thing. Take the news media in this country as one example. Rhonda was a huge fan of the news. She would've agreed with P. T. Barnum when he said that, "He who is without a newspaper is cut off from his species." But as far as I was concerned, nothing could've been further from the truth. The news media in this country was about as far from our species as Alpha Centauri was from the porch swing in my backyard. You'll learn next to nothing from newspapers or TV news shows. Do you really want to get in touch with your species? Get off your fat rear end and venture out into the world. Interact with people. Live, for real. Attempt to get a few things done, knock on some doors, and say hi to some neighbors. You'll be surprised to learn that the world is really a far better place to live than you've been led to believe. You have been duped by the talking heads and the byline writers! But my wife? Despite my attempts to convince Rhonda otherwise, she remained a fervent news addict. And she was so annoying. She knew I was deliberately ignoring the news, so she'd bring me up to date on all the sordid and grisly details of every idiotic story that editors saw fit to broadcast. "Did you hear about that horrible guy who strangled his wife?" she'd say to me over breakfast, or, "Can you believe what those terrorists are still doing? The world isn't a safe place anymore. What in the world is going wrong here with this planet?" And I thought to myself, *This is my wife. This is the woman I love!*

Listen; I don't believe that people have to be the same in order to get along with each other. That's not what I'm saying. What I am saying is that while I was trying my best to see the world a little differently, Rhonda wasn't changing at all. And it wasn't just about the news that was being spoon-fed to us. The news was just the tip of the oatmeal-for-breakfast iceberg. Rhonda worshipped junk. I think I already told you what junk was. It was Rhonda's new BMW, the ultimate driving machine. It was the Rolex watch I wore; Rolex was the proud sponsor of the US Open. It was everything they sold at Nordstrom's and Macy's, and it was the glossy discount coupons that came in the mail for Bed Bath and Beyond. It was the hand sanitizers, and Glade air fresheners, and miracle wrinkle creams, and Botox shots, and the yoga classes, and self-improvement books, and juicers, and the latest in nonstick pans, and limited-edition lithographs, and cell phone ringtones, and autographed photos of famous athletes, tattoos and all, and exotic fruits and vegetables, and 3-D movies, and the electric can opener, and musical birthday cards, and all-inclusive island vacation resorts. You've got to have it. Yes, you've got to have it all!

In large part, I blame Rhonda's upbringing, and I blame her dad. The man thrived on and constantly extolled the many virtues of his advertising business. It was running through his veins and arteries, and he passed the genes on to his daughter. Never mind what you're selling, just sell, sell, and sell. Keep the big junk-ball rolling forward. Keep the all-American public hungry, interested, and obsessed, no matter what the cost. As the recession receded, I tried to talk to Rhonda about this on several occasions, but I had no luck bringing her over to my way of thinking. I had no luck at all. She pointed out—rightly, maybe—that advertising was the heart and soul of the American economy, that it was the fuel that made the pistons move up and down. And she said I was naive if I believed otherwise. Maybe she was right, but I still wanted to think there was a lot more to life than selling shiny new-and-improved products. At least this was the assumption I was now operating on. Think of turning over a new leaf. Think of pushing away all those silly childish things, if only for a second.

There are some other interesting things about my wife that are worth noting. These are things that I didn't discover until after we were married. They are nothing worth getting divorced over, but they should be mentioned. First there was Rhonda's affinity for chores. I don't mean *her* chores. As far as she was concerned, she had her chore end of the bargain completely under control. I'm talking about my end, meaning the burned-out lightbulbs, the leaky faucets, the running toilets, the squeaky door hinges, the malfunctioning clothes washer, the swollen and stuck windows, the jammed trash compactor, the torn screens, the loose towel bars, the roof leaks, the cracks in the floor tiles, the dripping shower head, the clogged bathtub drains, the sunburnt peeling paint, the leaf-congested rain gutters, the hedges and shrubs that needed trimming, and the broken lawn sprinklers. I had no idea what I was in for when I said, "I do." None of these tasks were mentioned in our wedding vows. Shortly after I built our house, Rhonda had me install a big whiteboard in the pantry on which she could scribble my chores and keep me on the ball. I love Rhonda, but—and this is God's truth—I hated that fucking white board.

Here's another interesting thing about Rhonda. She claims to hate shopping. I didn't understand what kind of game she was playing with me, but "hate" is hardly the word I would use. My wife has never met a store she didn't like. And I mean any kind of store. Wind her up and send her in, and she's sure to find something that we need—something we can't possibly do without. She spends money on some of the stupidest things, and then she always tells me what a great bargain they were. "They were on sale!" "They were twenty percent off!" "Two for the price of one!" "It was a clearance sale!" You name the pitch, and she'll fall for it. And this is funny, isn't it? This is an intelligent woman who was in the advertising business herself, and she falls for the same ludicrous nonsense that she targeted at everyone else. I've never been able to figure this out, and I've never understood what she means when she brags about being frugal. Even today she brags about it, all the time.

Okay, it sounds like I'm picking on my wife. But I'm not saying anything that isn't 100 percent true. I'm just trying to be honest about the person I married. I'm not glossing over anything. Rhonda is who she is, and she will tell you so. She isn't shy about it. She will also tell you that she knows and cares nothing about the arts, one of my passions. Years ago, I used to feel she said this just to get under my skin, but I now don't think that was the reason for it. She was just being honest. She didn't know a Dali from a Miro, or a Picasso from a Degas, or a Manet from a Klee. Seriously, she didn't have a clue, and it didn't embarrass her one bit. She couldn't tell Mozart from Handel, or Miles Davis from Benny Goodman, or Black Sabbath from Metallica. Her favorite music group was the good old Supremes. She listened to them over and over, the same old songs, and she never grew tired of them. And as far as reading went, she never read any Homer, Dostoevsky, or Hemingway, or any other notable authors for that matter. She's read only a couple books I know of. One was a fantasy about a talking cat, and the other was about the racehorse Seabiscuit. I read the Seabiscuit book so we'd have something to talk about, but I passed on the talking cat.

Okay, maybe you're thinking that we had a love for sports in common. I liked watching sports, and yes, it would've been nice to watch them with Rhonda now and again. But no, no, she didn't like sports at all. And I liked watching old movies, but Rhonda couldn't stand them. My favorites were the old black-and-whites, but Rhonda especially didn't care for anything that wasn't in color. Me? I could spend an entire day watching old movies. But Rhonda, not even fifteen minutes. So what did she do in her spare time? She had a horse, and that's what she did with her time. She was crazy about riding that horse. She kept the horse at a barn nearby and rode him whenever she had the chance. No movies for her. No artworks, music, or books. Just horses and horseback riding, over and over. I went riding with her one time, and I swore I'd never do it again. I'd never been in so much discomfort in all my life. It was torture. I felt as if I'd been clobbered about the groin and buttocks by some thug with a heavy telephone pole. It took several hours before I was able to walk normally again.

But enough about the love of my life. Let's move on to my son, my flesh and blood, my amazing progeny, the young man who will carry on in life with my last name. When Rhonda gave birth to Thomas, it was one of the happiest days of my life; there are no words that can describe the joy, the pride, and the deep, deep love I felt. To create a human life is the most remarkable thing a couple can ever do. To hold that child in your arms for the first time, to watch him breastfeed, to hear him cry, to look into his eyes—nothing compares to it! You name him, and you take him home, and you love and care for him, and you change his diapers, and the next thing you know, like magic, you have a walking, talking young man in your house. Thomas, my only son. Thomas Baker, the boy who then flunked out of college and had to go to a rehab for twenty-eight days. But no matter. The boy is on the mend. Now he works for a local veterinarian, looking after their animals, filling food dishes and water bowls, in charge of cleaning out cat litter boxes and taking the pets for walks, holding them down for their shots and treatments. "Whose son is that?" the people in the waiting area ask. He's *my* son—all 180 pounds of him.

Listen, I love my son. Don't ever think that I don't love him. I am proud of him, and I would do anything for him. But that doesn't mean

I have to lie about him, so let's call a spade a spade. The boy is headed nowhere. He has set his sights on nothing, and if he's not careful, that's exactly what he's going to get out of life. And it concerns me. You want to know what I see when I look at Thomas? I mean, for his future? I see what Thoreau called a life of "quiet desperation." I can think of no curse worse for a young man. I mean, just think of all the possibilities life out holds out to our kids. The world is vast, and the opportunities are endless. It's like having an entire galaxy at one's fingertips! All you have to do is open your eyes and heart to life. Dare to dream! Take a handful of chances! Pick a road! Yet what is Thomas doing in this, the prime of his life? He is recovering from an opiate addiction and working nine-to-five at a little veterinary clinic, tending to other people's pets. He told me himself that each day while at work he can't wait to leave and come home. And what does he do at home? Nine times out of ten, he sits back in his beanbag chair in his room, smokes his weed, and plays video games until his thumbs are sore. He jumps from city to city, and from planet to planet, without really going anywhere at all. It's all pretend, and he may as well be back with his old friends, back with his black tar heroin.

I had a conversation recently with Rhonda regarding Thomas, and I asked her, "What do you think Thomas is going to do with his life?"

"I don't know," she said.

"Aren't you concerned?"

"Of course I'm concerned."

"He's headed nowhere."

"He's still just a kid."

"When I was his age, I was headed somewhere. I wasn't sure where I was going, but I knew I was going somewhere."

"He's not you."

"That's for sure."

"You need to let him find his way at his own pace."

"Find his way where?"

"He'll have to decide."

"I don't think he's even thinking about it."

"All kids his age think about it. They just don't all like talking about it."

"Do you really believe that?"

"I do," Rhonda said.

"You know what I think? I think this whole drug addiction problem sent our son backward by miles. We should never have sent him away to college in Washington. It was a huge mistake. He wasn't ready for it. We should've had him live in the house with us and go to college somewhere local so we could keep an eye on him and guide him in the right direction. Now he's been permanently damaged."

"He's not permanently damaged."

"Then what is he?"

"He's healing."

"Healing?"

"Yes," Rhonda said.

"Healing by tending to animals for minimum wage? Healing by playing video games and smoking weed?"

"Yes," Rhonda said.

"I don't see it."

"Everyone is entitled to their own private history. You're entitled to yours, and Thomas is entitled to his. You need to be more patient."

POOR ARE THEY

"How poor are they that have not patience! What wound did ever heal but by degrees?"

—William Shakespeare

SORRY TO OFFEND YOU

Okay, I've covered my wife and son. But what about my parents? What was the deal with them? Well, my father had been completely out of my life since the day I decided to stop talking to him. You know, right after he dumped my mom. I had no idea what he had been doing since, or how he was getting along. I had put the old lout out of my mind, and for the time being I was keeping it that way. Although I had heard one thing.

According to Bob, my brother, Dad moved to San Jose to be closer to his new wife's family. But that's all I knew.

On the other hand, I knew a lot of things about Mom. Dear one-of-a-kind Mom. First, let me tell you what I *thought* she'd be like at this age. We all have our own expectations, right? There's nothing wrong with expectations. I had always pictured Mom living out her seventies as the perfect twenty-first-century grandma. I never pictured her with thin blue hair, red rouged cheeks, or reeking of old woman perfume. Instead I imagined her as being fit as a fiddle, nicely dressed, and always pleasant. She wouldn't be a befuddled and annoying stereotypical old person with a cane; rather, she'd be fun to be with. She'd be hip to our modern times, but she'd also do all those traditional and wonderful things that grandmas do. She'd bake chocolate chip cookies for us when we came to visit, and she'd make up pitchers of real lemonade using the lemons she had picked from the tree in her backyard. She'd have plenty of candy in her cut glass candy dishes, and she'd never complain about her health. She'd tell us all her interesting stories about her childhood—stories none of us had heard before. She wouldn't be repetitive. She'd talk to Thomas and describe what life was like in America way back when she was his age. And she'd tell Thomas about her own parents: her hard-drinking father and overworked mom. It would be so good for Thomas to hear all of this. He needed to hear what my mom had to say. It was important. The more a boy knew about his grandparents, the better. But keep in mind that the Mom I'm describing is the Mom of my imagination. The Mom I am describing and the seventy-year-old Mom I actually got were not the same people.

So who did I actually get? What was my mom like? She was more like a wild and unruly pimple-faced teenager than a sweet and kind old woman. Half of the time, I didn't know whether to laugh or be angry with her. She could be infuriating. Maybe I didn't have a right to be angry, but I sometimes felt I was being gypped out of the mom I deserved. I think it all started with the divorce. That's what got the ball rolling. It started with that silly Mustang she bought right after they signed the divorce papers. God, how she loved that stupid car, speeding all over town as if she was always in a hurry, radio blaring and windows rolled down. Mom and her hot rod Mustang!

And all her boyfriends! I could hardly keep track of them all. There was Larry, the retired attorney; Jock, the retired insurance agent; Clayton, the retired police lieutenant; Jeff, the retired grocery store manager; and Albert, the retired blackjack dealer from Vegas who moved to Orange County to get out of the heat. There was also a gravelly voiced flat-nosed thug named Rudy Gray who Mom said used to do odd jobs for a Mafia crime family in New Jersey. Rudy made me a little nervous, but Mom liked him. In fact, she liked all of her boyfriends. None of them seemed to care much that she wasn't loyal to any one man. There seemed to be enough of my mom for all of them.

Here is something interesting to know about Mom's habits in her seventies. She never drank alcohol. I mean not *ever*. Her dad was an alcoholic, and I think she believed that drinking was hereditary. I think she believed that if she drank, she would become like her father. She loved him, but for sure she didn't want to be anything like him. When I had my own problems with drinking, I think it only reinforced this notion. In fact, I think my mom blamed her father for my alcoholism. She told me so when I was recovering. "You got this awful affliction from my father," she said.

But besides drinking, Mom did just about everything else you wouldn't want a grandma to do. She cussed up a storm like a truck driver on steroids. Seriously, you've never heard such a foul mouth on an elderly woman. Thomas got such a kick out of it, and it made him laugh. It embarrassed me, although I admit there were times when I also laughed. But it wasn't just the cussing. Mom also took up smoking. All her life she had never been a smoker, but when she turned seventy, she bought a pack of menthol cigarettes, and she now smoked like a chimney, always with a cigarette poking out from her lips, always with smoke swirling out of her nostrils. I told her how bad for her health smoking was, and she just laughed and said, "I'm seventy fucking years old, what in the hell should I be worried about? I'll be in the city morgue from old age before I ever die from cancer."

Maybe the weirdest thing Mom did, however, was to take up playing cards. I don't mean bridge, like other women her age. I'm talking about poker. Every Wednesday, Albert the blackjack dealer would hold a poker game at his house, and he would invite all his beer-drinking gambling buddies over. They would play poker until dawn. It was low stakes, mind you, but it was for money. Mom wouldn't miss a game, and she'd place her bets with all the men like an old pro. Sometimes she'd lose money, and sometimes she'd win. She was just one of the guys, except that she drank Coke rather than beer. And they'd treat her like one of them. They'd tell dirty jokes while they played, with Mom right there with them. She told me some of the jokes they told each other. I remember one of them. I told her not to tell the joke to Thomas, and she laughed and called me a prude. Imagine how I felt with my own mom calling me a prude.

The joke she told me was about this smart-aleck schoolboy named Matthew. The boy was sitting in the back of the class, looking out the window and obviously not paying attention. The teacher called on him and said, "Say that there are three ducks sitting on a fence, and you shoot one with a shotgun; how many are left?" Matthew thought for a moment and then said, "That's an easy one. There are none left."

The teacher said no and told Matthew that there were two ducks left on the fence, but Matthew argued that the noise from the shotgun scared the other two away, leaving none. "There are two," the teacher insisted, at first a little annoyed. Then she smiled at the boy and said, "But I like the way you're thinking."

Matthew smiled and then said, "Now I've got a question for you."

"Okay," the teacher said, crossing her arms. Matthew then said, "Three women are walking out of an ice-cream parlor. One is biting her ice-cream cone, one is licking hers, and the third is sucking her cone. Which of the three is married?"

The teacher blushed and said, "Uh, well, I guess the one who is sucking."

Matthew replied, "Nope, it's the one with the wedding ring on her finger. But hey, I like the way you're thinking."

Sorry if I offended you. I've heard worse jokes, but yes, this joke is in bad taste. I'm just trying to give you an idea of what life was like with my poker-playing seventy-year-old mother. When she told me this joke, I'll bet my face turned as red as a McIntosh apple. It wasn't the joke that embarrassed me; it was the fact that Mom was telling me the joke. I knew she noticed my reaction, and I also knew she got a kick out of it. That was my mom.

Mom would drive my brother, Bob, out of his mind. He would tell me, "We need to do something about her," and I would reply, "Like what?"

He never had an answer. I'm pretty sure Mom's behavior was even more disturbing to Bob than it was to me. At this point of his life, he was trying so hard to be a righteous man. Motivated by the strong morals of his third wife, Margaret, he wanted to be the sort of father his daughters could look up to. He wanted to be a role model. The last thing he wanted was to be associated with a mother who drove a Mustang, had a harem of boyfriends, and told jokes about oral sex.

You know, I never could quite get a handle on my brother. We weren't that far apart in age, but we were never very close. We tried to be best friends, but it just didn't happen. Sure, we talked a lot, we were always friendly with each other, and helped each other out when the opportunities arose, but there was always a distance. Our reactions to our mom is an example of this. It was true that Mom could embarrass me, and I often wished she were less rambunctious and more reserved. But she could also make me laugh, and honestly, I was happy that she was happy. But Bob, on the other hand, didn't find anything amusing at all about our mom's behavior. If we had lived back in the nineteenth century, I think he would've had her committed. The older my mom got, the wilder and looser she became. And the older Bob got, the tighter his underwear knotted up. Looking back, I'm glad I went through my drinking problem when we were younger. If I'd gone through it more recently, Bob would've dropped me from his life like a hot potato. He wouldn't have been able to handle the debauchery. These days, he had no patience. He had turned into the kind of guy who would throw you a lifeline and then turn his back, pretending not to know who you were.

STRANGE WORLD

Well it's such a strange world that I'm living in;
She was my woman, and she was my wife.
What is this thing called life?
Such a strange pair that we have become,
Living with this thing that we call our son.
Should I just turn and run?
Please shut down my car.
Don't let me go too far.

Lock all the doors and hide the key.
Roll down the garage door.
Will they all say that I lost the war?
It's such a strange time that we're passing through;
My mom was fine until she up and grew
Into a you-know-who.
My brother is lost at sea
But knows exactly what he wants to be.
So when will I be free?

TO THE FLAG

I should tell you that Bob had a friend named Mike Harper. Mike had a twenty-six-year-old son named Aubrey. I didn't know Mike from Adam, but I came to know Aubrey well because the kid had a drinking problem. He was in a bad way, so Bob introduced us to each other, hoping I could help him get sober. It turned out Aubrey had been going to AA meetings, but the meetings weren't doing him any good. Despite all the problems his drinking had caused, he couldn't kick the obsession. In fact, since going to the meetings, his drinking was worse than ever. Mike and Bob were talking about Aubrey when Bob said, "You know, my brother was able to quit drinking without AA, so maybe he can help your boy. We should get them together and see what happens." Three weeks later, Aubrey Harper was in our front room. Rhonda and Thomas went to see a movie that night so Aubrey and I could be alone. He was sitting in one of our chairs, and I was seated on the sofa with Henry curled up on the floor at my feet. Henry was listening to us talk. He was pretending to be asleep, but I knew he was listening. Dogs are clever that way.

"So my brother tells me you have a drinking problem," I said.

"You could say that," Aubrey replied.

"Tell me a little about it. I mean, just briefly. I don't need every sordid detail."

"Well, I guess it started in high school. I used to drink a lot in high school."

"During class?"

"No, never during class. I drank after school and during the weekends. Usually with my friends at first."

"At first?"

"During my senior year I began to drink alone."

"Was it interfering with your life?"

"Not really. I enjoyed it. I looked forward to it, and it made me feel good."

"That's how it usually starts. I loved drinking when I was a teenager. Did it all the time. In fact, it was my favorite pastime."

"Yes," Aubrey said, smiling, as if we were now on the same page.

"When did it first become a problem for you? When did you notice that it was interfering with your life?"

"It was during my first year of college. That's when it started to cause problems."

"What happened to you? Did you drink during class? Did you go to class drunk?"

"Sometimes."

"And then?"

"I started skipping classes."

"So that you could drink?"

"No, mostly because of the hangovers."

"Ah, yes," I said.

"It was weird. I was getting along with all my friends. I mean, I was getting along great with everybody. People seemed to like me when I drank, and I liked them. But school? I was ignoring my schoolwork and skipping classes. It all seemed so boring, sitting there and listening to the professors go on and on. When I was in high school, I got all As and Bs. But now I was getting Cs and Ds. I even got a few Fs. I felt bad about it. I felt bad about wasting all my parents' money. I mean, I cared, and yet I didn't. I really just wanted to be happy, and drinking made me happy."

"Did you meet many girls?"

"Yeah, a ton of girls."

"Did you go to a lot of parties?"

"All the time. There was always a party to go to, every night of the week. I didn't usually get back to my room until early in the morning, so I'd sleep off my hangovers in bed, and I missed a lot of my classes."

"Go on," I said.

"Then I learned something about hangovers that I wish I'd never learned. You can get rid of them by drinking again. So I'd keep a spare bottle of vodka in my dorm room. I'd drink the vodka to get rid of my hangovers. Yes, I'd be drunk again, but I'd feel much better."

"Did your parents know about your drinking?"

"They didn't have a clue."

"Did they ask you about your grades?"

"They never asked to see them. They just assumed I was doing okay."

"Did you graduate?"

"Barely."

"And then?"

"I got my first job. I worked for a guy I met on Craigslist who was doing computer maintenance for small companies. I was to be his right-hand man. He figured I knew what I was doing because I had a college degree in computer science. He had no idea what a screwup I was. If he'd asked to see my grades, he would've known. But he never asked."

"And how did your job go?"

"Actually, it went pretty well at first. I was excited about having a job, and I worked hard at it. I was working between ten and twelve hours a day. My boss was very happy with me, and he paid me well. I was out of college, so there weren't all those parties to distract me. In fact, I no longer even had a social life. After work I just watched TV and drank, and that was about it. I behaved myself for about a year before I began to drink during work hours. I'd chew spearmint gum and eat a ton of mints so my boss wouldn't smell the booze on my breath. At first I'd just drink a little— enough to get a little buzz. Then I'd have to drink more to maintain the buzz. Then I'd drink more to make the buzz feel stronger. The next thing I knew, I was struggling to pretend to be sober while I worked. Sometimes I'd make stupid mistakes. And sometimes I could hear my words slurring when I tried to explain what I was doing to customers. A couple times I had some trouble keeping my balance. I was getting pretty drunk. I was growing more and more fearful I would be found out, and eventually I was. Now aware of my strange behavior, my boss took me to McDonald's for lunch. While we were eating our burgers and fries, he said, 'I have to ask you a question, Aubrey. I need you to be honest with me. Do you have a drinking problem?' Jesus, I froze like a marble statue. Then I shuddered. What should I say? What would he do?"

"What did you say?"

"I lied."

"Of course, you did," I said, smiling.

"Then he asked me to hand him my backpack. I knew I was screwed."

"Because your booze was in your backpack?"

"Yes," Aubrey said.

"Did you hand him the backpack?"

"I did, and he looked inside. He pulled out my half-empty bottle of vodka and set it on the table. He said, 'You need to get help. But for now, you're no longer working for me. I hope you understand.' I nodded like an idiot. We finished our hamburgers and fries, and then he drove me to my apartment. He didn't want me to drive my car, since he knew that I'd been drinking. He didn't say a word during the drive. When we got to my apartment, he said good-bye and shook my hand. Then he said, 'If you apply for another job, you shouldn't use me as a reference. I'll have to tell the truth. It wouldn't be right for me to lie.'"

"And you said?"

"I said okay. I said I understood."

"And did you understand?"

"No. I thought he was being a dick."

"And that was it?"

"Yes, I was screwed. I had no job. I had no reference. And I was addicted to the booze. I knew I was addicted, and I had no idea how I was going to make a living."

"Did you go to your parents?"

"Hell, no. My dad would've freaked out. My mom would've cried. I didn't want to upset them. The last thing I wanted was for them to discover my problem."

"So what did you do?"

"I got good and drunk."

"Ha," I laughed.

"And I got good and drunk the next day, and the day after that. I went on a real bender. I stayed in my apartment and watched TV and drank vodka until I nearly ran out of money. That's when I should've sought help, but no, I wasn't thinking straight. I knew I was going to have to get my hands on some money. I needed a job, but doing what? Who the heck would want me? Then, on one of my vodka runs, I noticed a Help Wanted sign in the window of a liquor store, and I asked the guy running the cash register about it. It turned out that the guy I had asked was the owner and that his regular clerk had just quit without warning. I told the guy I happened to be looking for a job, and he asked me if I had any experience. I lied and told him I was a college student who was earning his way through school and that the job would be perfect for me. I said, 'Please, sir, I would be perfect for this job. I don't have any experience, but I'm smart, loyal, and good with people. And I could really use the work. I almost have enough saved up for my final semester.' He said, 'I was actually looking for a person with experience, but it would be nice to have a kid like you take the job who wasn't an idiot. You can't believe the morons I have to deal with at this place. Maybe a college student would be perfect. It might be a breath of fresh air.'"

"So he gave you the job?"

"He did," Aubrey said. "And he told me I could start right away. The pay was bottom-of-the-barrel, but I figured I'd have access to all the free booze I could drink. It was great. And I discovered that not only could I take a bottle of vodka a day for free, but I could also lie about the sales and pocket some extra cash. I found myself stealing a couple hundred dollars a day. It was perfect. What an easy job. I could drink all day and night, and I wasn't hurting anyone. I was just a guy doing his job."

"But you were stealing."

"I guess I was."

"The guy gave you a job, and you paid him back by stealing his money and his booze?"

"He had plenty of money."

"How do you know that?"

"The guy drove a brand-new Lincoln."

"So that gave you a right to steal from him?"

"I'm just saying that I wasn't really hurting him. I was getting what I deserved in wages, and he was getting what he wanted, someone to mind his store. At least, that's how I saw it at the time."

"Go on," I said.

"Well, the guy was smarter than I figured. He caught on to me after a couple of months, and he began watching his inventory more closely. Then one night, after I had closed and locked the place up, I was met by a couple cops and the store owner in the parking lot. I had a couple bottles of stolen vodka hidden in my backpack and about three hundred dollars in cash stuffed in my jeans pocket. The cops found everything and arrested me, and they put me in the back of their police car. They drove me all the way to Orange County Jail, where I was fingerprinted, booked and told I could make a phone call."

"And you called your dad?"

"Actually, I called a friend of mine."

"And he bailed you out?"

"Not exactly."

"What happened?"

"My friend wasn't able to post bail. He didn't have any money, so he called my dad. Dad bailed me out and took me to his house. And that's when the whole thing unraveled. After listening to me talk for an hour, it was obvious to my dad that I had a serious drinking problem, and he called his attorney the next day. He then insisted that I go to AA meetings. One per day, he said. It was the attorney who suggested AA. Dad didn't know anything about alcoholism, but his attorney did. It turned out the attorney's sister was an alcoholic, so Dad figured the guy knew what he was talking about. So there you have it. The whole thing blew up in my face, and now I was in AA, trying to believe in surrender and a higher power so I could reclaim my life."

"Did you do any jail time?"

"No, not really. Dad met with the liquor store owner and got him to drop all the charges. It cost my dad a few thousand dollars."

"But you still haven't been able to quit drinking?"

"No. AA is a joke."

"A lot of people find that it works."

"It doesn't work for me. If anything, it just makes me want to drink more."

"I see," I said, and I thought about this. I thought that maybe I could help since I didn't like AA either. "You can quit drinking," I said. "I haven't touched any booze for years, and I don't go to AA meetings."

"That sounds good to me," Aubrey said.

"But it will take a lot of effort on your part. It will take a commitment. And you'll have to be honest. You'll have to be honest with me and to yourself. You've got to stop all the lying. Are you ready for that?"

"I'm ready for that."

"Are you?" I gave Aubrey a serious look. I wanted him to know that I meant what I said.

"I am ready."

Aubrey's eyes were welling with tears, and it looked to me as if he was going to cry. Yes, the kid was sincere. He wanted his sobriety, and by God, I would help him earn it. I felt good about myself. It was a great feeling to know that I could help a young man in trouble.

For the next several months, I met with Aubrey twice a week, and we talked. There were no twelve steps. There was no God or higher power. I explained to Aubrey that he was responsible for his life and that, despite what they taught in AA, his sobriety would be up to him. It was a matter of personal responsibility. It had nothing to do with turning his life over to supernatural beings. "You, you, you," I said. "It's all up to you. You have no control when it comes to drinking alcohol, but that's only true when you're drinking. When you're sober, you're no longer under its spell. When you're sober, you are in charge. You're able to do the right thing. Take that first drink, and you're out of control. But if you don't take that first drink, then you will be the master of your life. It's all about not taking the first drink." We talked and talked, and I repeated my mantra over and over. Aubrey seemed to understand what I was trying to say. I felt after several weeks that we had made a lot of progress. I was tough on the kid at times. I told him it was time for him to grow the hell up and stop acting like a baby. I told him not to blame alcoholism for his problems. *It* was his problem. "It's all up to you," I said. I told him to rely on himself.

We had some great talks. I believed I had gotten through to Aubrey. I talked to Rhonda about it, and I told her how much I enjoyed working with Aubrey. Then, late one night, I got a call from him. He had been drinking. He rambled on about how he was never going to make it, and then he told me something that was very upsetting. He said he'd been drinking before all of the meetings we'd had. He said it was all a lie—that he never had stopped drinking at all. "I've been dishonest with you," he said. "I'm not cut out for this, and I'm never going to get sober. I'm a liar. I'm a no good, two-faced, rotten, dyed-in-the-wool liar."

At first I was angry. No one likes being lied to. Then I thought about it, and I recalled my own behavior when I tried to quit drinking. I was really no different. I was a dyed-in-the-wool liar too. In fact, I was a liar's liar, chairman and chief executive officer of the old eighty-six-proof liar's club. And why not? I was an American, and wasn't lying the American way? Wasn't I just doing my patriotic duty?

Seriously, this country is filled to the brim with liars: talentless people lying about their talents, people lying on their job applications, citizens lying on tax returns, people lying to their spouses about their romantic longings, parents lying to their kids about their made-up childhoods, children lying to parents about everything under the sun, senators lying to congressmen, governors lying to their voters, presidents lying to the general public about their wars, generals lying to their soldiers, Hollywood writers and actors lying to their moviegoing audiences, businesses lying to their clients and customers, and priests lying to their congregations about who is loved by God and who isn't. Jesus, does anyone in this country ever tell the truth? And now Aubrey had been lying to me. "Don't be so hard on yourself," I said. "You're going to get through this."

When I was a kid, my father told me the story about the little boy who cried wolf. That story was supposed to keep me honest, and it would've worked if lying were that childishly simple. But lying isn't simple at all. In fact, it can be very complicated. "I now pledge allegiance to the flag of the United States of America, and to the large and small lies for which it stands." That's what we all should be saying—drunk, hungover, or sober.

THE TRUTH

"With Clinton, there's no question that I would have made fun of his out-and-out lying. But he's also a good friend."

—Chevy Chase

SEA MONKEYS

Praise the Lord, and pass the lies! How old are you? Do you remember Sea Monkeys?

I read a lot of comic books when I was a kid, and in every one of them you could find a Sea Monkeys ad printed alongside the ads for X-Ray Specs and Charles Atlas books. Sea Monkeys were friendly little families of happy creatures inviting you to invite them into your home. I remember as a child how truly amazing they seemed. Could it be true? Could a kid really buy underwater monkeys for pets? Well, of course it was true! The advertisement said so, and ads didn't lie. And the ad strategy worked like a charm. Kids from all over the country sent away for their very own pet monkeys. Harold von Braunhut, the man who "invented" Sea Monkeys and labelled them with their catchy and irresistible name bragged that he bought 3.2 million pages of comic book ads each year, and he said that the ads "worked beautifully."

Lying to kids? What a way for a grown man to get rich and famous. So what were Sea Monkeys? What were all the wide-eyed kids getting for their money? They were getting fish food—tiny brine shrimp that looked nothing at all like the drawings in the ad. They came packaged dry, and all you had to do was add water to bring them to life. They were interesting, in that regard, but they were still a lie. They were not monkeys, and they did not have smiles on their faces. The mommy monkeys did not wear lipstick, and they did not have arms and legs or colored ribbons in their hair. And they were tiny. You know, I never did order any Sea Monkeys for myself. I would've, but my dad told me they were just a scam and wouldn't give me money for them. I doubted him, and for years I resented his suspicions. I suppose I now owe Dad an apology.

Of course, Harold von Braunhut isn't the only avaricious adult in our country who has zeroed in on gullible kids. It's been attempted time and time again by many. It's an American tradition. So I'm not saying the monkeys are unusual. Sea Monkeys just happen to be my favorite. "So eager to please, they can even be trained!" Believe it or not, that's what the ads said.

LOCK IN A SOCK

Here are stories about a couple of Americans. There's a good chance you won't like what I have to say about them, but try to keep an open mind. I'm going to be talking about two rats. Do you know what I mean by rats? I mean men who came out and told the truth—men who came out and informed the authorities of bad or illegal actions. I think there's a lot to learn from the way these sorts of men are treated in our society. It says a great deal about how we as a nation view the truth, and about our very curious relationship with it.

The first American I'd like to talk about is a man named James Joseph "Whitey" Bulger Jr. Maybe you already know a few things about him. He was an organized crime boss who led the Winter Hill gang in the Winter Hill neighborhood of Somerville, Massachusetts. Federal prosecutors indicted him for nineteen murders, but this was just the tip of the iceberg. This awful man lived a long and illustrious life of crime. Seriously, this guy was hard-core. I'm not sure of the exact year, but Bulger eventually became an informant for the FBI. He started telling authorities the truth about what he knew about other criminals. He wasn't just being a nice guy. He was truthful for selfish reasons, but he was still a rat. Long story short, this crime-boss-turned-rat couldn't get along with the FBI or with his own criminal buddies, so he wound up running away and hiding in California. He successfully lived in Santa Monica, in a secret apartment with his girlfriend. He was able to live his senior days unmolested for sixteen years until he was finally tracked down.

Bulger was arrested, tried, and tossed in prison at the age of eighty-nine. He was finally moved into the United States Penitentiary in Hazelton, West Virginia, on October 29, 2018. At 8:20 a.m. the next day, Bulger was found murdered in his prison cell. He was in a wheelchair and had been beaten to death by a group of inmates armed with a sock-wrapped padlock. His eyes had been nearly gouged out, and his tongue had been badly mutilated. Employees at this prison had warned Congress earlier that the prison was dangerous and understaffed. Maybe that's why Bulger was sent there. A notorious hitman named Fotios "Freddy" Geas was the primary suspect in the murder, and he has never disputed his role in it.

Geas was quoted as saying that he "hated rats." He stuffed a lock in a sock, and it was so much for the rat Bulger. The government got its death sentence for Bulger after all. Glad to hear that Bulger did not die of natural causes, the son of one of Bulger's murder victims was quoted as saying to reporters, "I can only hope his death was slow and painful." Needless to say, not many tears were shed for Bulger.

In 1986, another rat surfaced in the news media, and this rat's name was Oliver Laurence North. Ollie was also a killer, but in a much different way. He was a military man who cut his teeth killing Vietnamese. How many Vietnamese did he kill? I have no way of knowing. But he took part in a war that killed over a million. Was it a righteous war? I'll let you decide. Dwight Eisenhower admitted early on in the conflict that 80 percent of the Vietnamese people wanted communism. Well, that wouldn't do. The United States decided that the people of Vietnam had no right to choose their own form of government if it didn't coincide with our agenda. So we slaughtered a million of their citizens as they tried to defend their God-given right to self-govern. We dropped more bombs on them than we dropped in all of World War II. We showered them with fire and napalm. We turned their little country into a nightmarish hellhole of death and destruction.

Now, this is just my opinion, but what we did in Vietnam was far worse than anything Mr. Bulger did. Yes, Bulger was a crook and a murderer, but what he did during his lifetime didn't even hold a candle to the Vietnam War. He was, as they like to say, small potatoes.

Anyway, Ollie had a chest full of medals to prove his valor and loyalty to the United States. So why was Ollie a rat? He was a rat, wasn't he? In exchange for immunity, he told Congress all about the Iran–Contra deal. It's interesting to note that he wouldn't tell them truth without the immunity, being as he was such an "honorable" man. But like Bulger, he too looked out for himself and acted in his own best interest. And who could blame him for that?

If you don't recall what happened, I'll describe the story in a nutshell. The United States sold some weapons to Iran to get a group of hostages freed. Then, in direct violation of the law, profits from the arms sale were to be sent to the Contras in Nicaragua. That was the long and short of it. It opened a hornet's nest as to who told whom to do what, and who knew about the plan, and how such a cockamamie and illegal scheme could be carried out under Ronald Reagan's watch.

All said and done, Ollie survived the fiasco. Rather than be put in prison for breaking the law, he flourished. No lock in a sock for Ollie. No eyes gouged out or tongue sliced up. Join in with the effort to kill a million Vietnamese, and you're suddenly not a gangster. You're a red, white, and blue hero in the eyes of America.

You should know that Ollie moved on with his life. Never mind the one million people killed in Vietnam. It was now just water under the bridge. There would be no more orders rolling down to Ollie. He finally left the military and wrote several best-selling books, hosted his own radio show, and appeared on TV. He even did a stint as the president of the NRA. All said and done, he's lived a pretty darn good life—for a rat. And compared to the rat Whitey Bulger, he came out smelling like a rose.

LIAR, LIAR

Liar, liar, pants on fire,
Your nose is longer than a telephone wire.
Ask me, baby, why I am so blue;
A lie for me, and a lie for you.
Our honesty is an oddity,
And the truth is a commodity.
All those comics and their Sea Monkeys,
Lying about the Vietnamese.
We buy and sell truth like silver and gold;
It's always fun and never gets old.
Liar, liar, pants on fire,
Jump out of the pan and into the fryer.
My daddy taught me to tell no lies
While dressed in his favorite disguise.
The truth will set you free, Mom said,
But we're doomed until the day we're dead.
I can't make heads or tails of us,
All crowded into this crazy bus.
The road sign ahead, what does it spell?

One more mile to the gates of Hell.
Liar, liar, pants on fire,
All this talk about truth is making me tired.

THE COSTA CONCORDIA

The year 2012 was big for me. It was the year I decided to stop building.
I'd simply had enough of the construction business—enough to last
me a lifetime. I'd had enough of working my tail off to tame unruly
subcontractors, careless employees, annoying suppliers, and nitpicking city
and county inspectors. It just wasn't fun anymore. I was waking up every
morning wishing that I were someone else, and that's never a good sign.
So I wound things down and finished my last job. I then drove to a big art
supply store in Santa Ana. That is what I always wanted to be—an artist!
Ever since high school, I had wanted to do this. I think Rhonda thought
I was out of my mind. Surely she thought I was now retiring, and in the
back of her mind she was thinking that fifty-seven was way too early. I
tried to explain that I wasn't actually retiring yet but was just changing
professions, and this kept her appeased for a while. So long as she believed
I still had a profession, I think she figured it was all right. True, it was not
what she wanted for me, but she was nice enough to put up with my dream
and go along with my new plans—for a while, anyway.

I don't paint, but I do like to draw. So I bought a ton of drawing paper,
pencils, pastels, and ink pens. I bought a drawing table that I assembled in
my home office, and I got a light for it that swung around on an adjustable
arm. Then I found a small radio so I could listen to background music and
talk shows while I worked. It was so weird to be drawing again. I hadn't
drawn anything since my college days, and I felt odd at first, as though I'd
stepped into someone else's life. But gradually I began to feel comfortable.
At first I dipped my toe in the water by sketching miscellaneous objects,
seeing what I could and couldn't do. I'd draw things that I found in the
house, or scenes from pictures I found in books and magazines, or this
and that from family photographs. Then I decided to get serious and draw
an actual piece. Do you know what I mean by this? This piece would be
a finished product. It would be an actual work of art—an artwork that

was worthy of being framed and hung on a wall. Something with a title. Something with a purpose and a message.

Just a month earlier, the *Costa Concordia* hit a huge rock in the Mediterranean and overturned. Do you recall this mess? The *Concordia* was an Italian cruise ship, and I remember Rhonda saying, "That's why you'll never get me on a cruise ship, ever. No way in hell." As if all those poor Italians didn't already have enough strikes against them, three hundred passengers were rescued, and around thirty others died. The captain, who had caused the incident, made a run for it. He got the hell off the ship as soon as he could, leaving the crew and passengers to fend for themselves. I laughed when I heard this. I also heard the ship went off course and hit the rock because this captain steered it too close to land in an effort to wave to his friends on shore. Oops! The captain was later found guilty of manslaughter, and he was sentenced to sixteen years in prison. All said and done, the fiasco cost the cruise line $2 billion. This was what I wanted to draw—the capsized cruise ship lying still on its side, halfway filled with seawater, the biggest human-caused disaster of the year.

When Rhonda found out what I was drawing, she tried to be polite, but I knew what she was thinking. She was wondering who on earth would want to buy my drawing of a stupid cruise ship capsized at sea? Who would want *that* sort of thing hanging on their living room wall? This wasn't Rhonda's fault. Maybe I had misled her. I had earlier explained to her that drawing was going to be my new profession, so it was my fault for calling it a profession. I think she figured I was going to be producing art that people would want to buy and hang on their walls. I never had this in mind, but I can see how she got the idea in her head. The truth is that I only wanted to draw things that interested me. Was I being selfish? Maybe I was, but that's exactly what artists are, right? That's what real artists are. I mean, that is, unless they're just trying to sell their drawings and paintings for money, in which case they shouldn't be called artists, but businessmen. Real artists don't give a flying fig how many of their works they can sell to the public or whose walls they're on. Real art is much deeper than that.

Anyway, the *Concordia* drawing was just the beginning of my foray into art. The next drawing I did was of a recent horrible car accident, copied from a front-page photograph in our daily newspaper. The story was that some girl stole her dad's car and flew off the freeway at over a hundred miles per hour, smashing into a tree. It was grisly and upsetting.

"Why on earth would you draw a car wreck?" Rhonda asked me. She was polite but also perturbed. "No one is going to want to buy a drawing of a car wreck. No one is going to want to hang *that* on their wall. Why don't you draw a vase of colorful flowers, or a rural landscape, or a still life, or some wild animals? People like drawings of animals."

I had to set her straight. It was not fair to lead her on like this. So I told her I wasn't drawing with any plan of selling my work to anyone—especially people who loved rural landscapes or wild animals—but that I was drawing for myself, that I wanted to be an *artist*. "Maybe it's not a profession at all," I said. "It's art, and I want to be an artist."

You should've seen the look on her face. Her expression said, "I should never have let you retire."

THAT RAT RACE

I ain't gonna run in that rat race no more.
No I ain't gonna run in that rat race no more.
Well, I wake up in the morning
And I jump out of my bed,
Brush my teeth until they hurt,
Run my comb across my head,
Spill my juice and drop my pancakes on the kitchen floor.
I ain't gonna run in that rat race no more.
I ain't gonna run in that rat race no more.
No, I ain't gonna run in that rat race no more.
Well, there's coffee on my shirt,
And syrup on my cuff.
Rhonda shoves me off to work and says,
"Let me know when you've had enough."
Then she smiles at me and slams the kitchen door.
I ain't gonna run in that rat race no more.
I ain't gonna run in that rat race no more.
No, I ain't gonna run in that rat race no more.
Well, I start up my truck,

And the cell phone plays a song.
It's one of my workers
Saying everything is wrong.
They can't tell the ceilings from the floors.
Ah, I ain't gonna run in that rat race no more.
I ain't gonna run in that rat race no more.
No, I ain't gonna run in that rat race no more.
The banker says we're short.
The inspector says we're wrong.
The owner says we're late.
The architect says we're gone.
I shout out loud, "I can't take this anymore."
I ain't gonna run in that rat race no more.
I ain't gonna run in that rat race no more.
No, I ain't gonna run in that rat race no more.
Well, I tried my best;
It was fun for a while,
But it's time for a change
When you can't find your smile.
Gonna draw and draw until my fingers are blue and sore.
I ain't gonna run in that rat race no more.

THE PICTURE OF RUDY GRAY

Four months into my career as an artist, Rhonda couldn't take it anymore. I think seeing me fritter my life away at my drawing table while she worked was too much for her to bear. And there were things that needed to be done. They were important things, and necessary things. We were at our kitchen table and eating dinner one night when Rhonda brought the subject up. She acted as though her great idea had just crossed her mind. She said, "Now that you're retired, you should have time to tend to some things around the house."

"Things around the house?" I asked.

"You know, things."

"What kinds of things?"

She probably already had a list written up, but she acted as if she was just winging it. "Oh, I don't know. Like painting the house, for example. How long has it been since the house was painted?"

"Inside or out?"

"Either."

"A while, I guess."

"A fresh coat of paint would do wonders."

"It probably would," I said. I didn't want to agree with her, but she was right. The house hadn't been painted since I'd built it twenty years ago.

"Then you agree with me?" Rhonda asked.

"Some fresh paint would look good," I said.

"I've been thinking of changing the colors."

"You have?"

"It would be nice to have a change."

"What colors were you thinking of?"

"I don't know."

"I could call one of my painters. They would be able to help you with colors, and I know a few of them who do very good residential work."

"You want to hire them?"

"Yes," I said.

"Can we afford that?"

"Afford it?"

"We're living on my salary now. We could easily afford to hire a painter if you were still working, but you're not making any money, Huey. What you *do* have is time. You have plenty of spare time on your hands."

"*Spare* time?"

"You know, time not working."

Clearly Rhonda still didn't get it. She still thought of me as being retired, needing to find something to do. "I'm very busy with my art," I said.

"The house isn't going to paint itself," Rhonda said, ignoring my comment.

"No, it isn't," I agreed.

"Well then?"

And that's how it started. The next thing I knew, I was at the paint store buying paint, brushes, rollers, tarps, masking tape, caulk, spackle, and sandpaper. I was a painter. I went to work on the house, starting on the inside. The first room I did was the front room. Then I did the halls. Then I did the family room. You should know that I didn't exactly put my art plans on hold. Not entirely. The deal I worked out with Rhonda was a fair one. I would draw in the mornings, and then I would paint the house in the afternoons. I was still being allowed to draw, and Rhonda was getting the house painted. And best of all for Rhonda, I was making myself useful. And since I was making myself useful, Rhonda no longer cared about what I was drawing. I could draw a blind rat eating a pepperoni pizza on a sailboat at Lake Elsinore for all she cared. It didn't matter whether or not I was able to sell a single drawing. It didn't matter that no one cared about my artwork other than me, because it was now just a time-killing hobby. And me? I was drawing. I was now as happy as a pig in you-know-what.

It's funny. I did try to share my drawings with Rhonda. I knew she loved me, but honestly, I think she hated my drawings. She didn't understand them, and she didn't like them. But that was fine.

I'll tell you who did like my drawings. It was my mother. She thought they were extraordinary. Of course, I was her son, and that was probably why she liked them so much. But I still liked hearing her compliments. Everyone likes to hear people tell him he's doing a great job, and everyone likes to hear people tell him he has talent. After a while, Mom came up with an idea. I don't ordinarily like to draw things suggested by other people, but Mom's idea intrigued me. She wanted me to draw a pencil portrait of one of her boyfriends, but not just any boyfriend; she wanted me to draw Rudy Gray. Rudy? Of all her boyfriends, the one who once did odd jobs for those guys in the Mafia?

My first inclination was to say no to her, but then I thought about it. Rudy did have a very interesting face. It was rough looking, yet kind. It was stupid, yet surprisingly intelligent. Rudy could be scary, yet I could also see what my mom liked about him. In his own strange way, he was charming and real, and I wondered if I could capture these qualities on paper. It would be a challenge for sure, so I told my mom yes, I would draw Rudy.

Three days later, I went to his house with paper and pencil, and I had Rudy sit and pose for me. And then I went to work. I felt as if I were in an episode of *The Sopranos*.

The first thing I discovered about Rudy was that he loved to talk. Seriously, he talked the entire time I was at his house. He talked about his wife who had died in a car accident five years before. He talked about his two kids and how successful they were. One was a medical doctor, and the other was a trial attorney. Unlike their father, both of them were on the up-and-up. Neither of them seemed to mind that their educations had been funded with money earned through organized crime. It was important to Rudy that his kids not live the same sort of life he did. Then—and this surprised me—Rudy told me about some of the things he had done to earn money. I didn't want to hear about them, thinking I would then know more than I should, but Rudy kept talking and talking.

Rudy told me about a Mafia guy he worked for named Sal who was owed fifty grand from a man named Blake Zimbalist. Blake was a landscaper who had a penchant for playing poker, and Sal put on several of the games he played in. Sal held one game to which Blake was invited, and it didn't take long for Blake to run out of money. Sal loaned Blake money to stay in the game, and Blake continued to play. Rudy said, "The idiot lost the entire loan in a half hour, and finally he went home. The next day, Sal called on him to make good on the loan, and Blake said he'd have the money the next day. Well, the next day came and went, and the money was not there. Then a week came and went, and still no money. Then a month came and went, and Sal gave me a call. He asked me to collect the money. I was now to get fifty-five thousand—five for me, and fifty for Sal. He wanted the cash right away. He said he didn't want any more promises. He wanted his money now."

"So did you get it?" I asked.

"I went to see Blake, and he blabbered the same bullshit he had been giving Sal: that he had no cash, that he'd lost it all recently playing poker. He said he'd been trying to earn it by working but that business was slow and his customers weren't paying on time. He said, 'I've got one guy who owes me sixty thousand, but I can't get the fucker to write me a check. He keeps complaining about cash flow problems. He keeps saying the problem is only temporary, but that until the problem is fixed, he can't pay me.'"

"So what did you do?" I asked.

"I got the name of the guy who owed Blake money."

"And you went to see him?"

"I did. The guy's name was Chad. Chad was an architect. As best as I could tell, he had a good reputation and a decent-sized business. I went to see him in his fancy office in Long Beach. The prick made me wait for a half hour before seeing me. Finally I sat down with him and was able to politely explain the situation. I tried to be civil. You see, I didn't consider myself to be a thug. I was a businessman. I was just there to collect a receivable. I said to Chad, 'You owe some money to a landscaper friend of mine. As I understand it, you now owe him about sixty grand. I think you know who I'm talking about. He owes another friend of mine approximately the same amount of money from a poker game, and the debt is now seriously past due. I was hired to collect the debt.' Chad got a funny look on his face and said, 'So you're a bill collector?' I said, 'You could say that.' Then we stared at each other. I gave Chad a look that could kill a fucking elephant. I think he understood that it was in his best interest to pay."

"So did he pay?" I asked.

"No, he told me he was short on cash. He said he barely made his last payroll. He said, 'I loaned sixty-four grand to my brother last month, and he hasn't paid me back yet. It was probably a big mistake, loaning him that much money. But he said he needed it. And he said he'd be able to pay me back soon.'"

"Let me guess," I said. "You went to see the architect's brother?"

"I did."

"So what was his story?"

"The guy was a banker."

"A banker?"

"He was a hotshot banker who was living a little too high on the hog. He had gotten himself way overextended, and he was scrambling. He was behind on all of his bills. When I went to see him, I guess his brother had called to warn him about me. I got to the bank, and he let me into his office and closed the door. 'I don't want anyone here to hear this,' he said. 'But I'm in way over my head. I've been trying to sell some of my stuff to raise the cash. Honestly, I've been doing my best. I can get the money I owe my brother soon. I just sold one of my cars, but the buyer hasn't paid me the cash yet. As soon as he writes me a check, I can pay you. I'm sure the guy is good for it. He's a friend of a friend. I don't think he'd try to screw me.' I stared at him and said, 'I need this guy to pay now.' Then the banker said, 'I'm sure he will when you explain who you are.'"

"So you went to see the car buyer?" I asked.

"I went to see him."

"And?"

"It was another fucking sob story."

"What was his problem?"

"It turned out that this guy was a stockbroker. He'd tried to cash in some stocks in order to get the money for the car, but when he checked the stock prices, he saw they had taken a surprise nosedive. The stocks were only worth a fraction of what he owed the banker for the car, so he was waiting until the stock prices went back up again. It was crazy. All I wanted was for some dumbbell landscaper to pay his poker debt, and now I was with a stockbroker, talking about the value of his stocks. I wasn't born yesterday. I knew stocks went up and down in value—usually because they were being manipulated by the people with the most shares. It's a racket, you know. It always has been. So I decided to move on from the stockbroker and get to the heart of the matter. I asked the stockbroker for the name of the company he owned stock in. I found the company's website on the internet, and I went straight to their corporate offices. I tried to meet with the CEO, but the secretary said I needed to have an appointment. 'How's this for an appointment,' I said, and I showed her the gun in my shoulder holster. Her eyes got big, and then she buzzed her boss and told him there was a 'man with a gun' demanding to see him. The guy came out and said to me, 'We don't want any trouble.' I said, 'I'm not here to cause trouble, but I do need to see you.' I removed the gun from its holster, and I set it down on the secretary's desk. 'No gun, no trouble,' I said, holding up my hands. The CEO said, Okay, come in.' I followed him into his office."

"And?"

"The guy was a typical CEO prick."

"In what way?"

"I told him the situation, and he acted like he had no idea what I was talking about. He said, 'We don't control the stock market. No one manipulated the stock prices.'"

"Maybe no one did," I said.

"Well, maybe they didn't, and maybe they did. But I had reached the end of the line. It was getting late in the day, and I just wanted Sal's money. Finally I had reached a guy who did have some cash. So the question was, could I intimidate him? I said, 'Listen; unless you write me a check for fifty-five grand, this is going to get real fucking ugly, and I don't think that's what you want. You can either pay me, and I'll go away; or you can cause a lot of trouble and get yourself into a very sticky situation not just with me but also with the people I work for. And the people I work for aren't near as nice as me. You're a smart man, or you wouldn't be CEO of this big company. So it's up to you. Yes or no?'"

"And what did he say?" I asked. I had stopped drawing, and I was staring at Rudy.

"What do you think he said?"

"I don't know."

"What would you have done?"

"I would probably have paid you. I mean, if I had the money to do it."

"Oh, he had plenty."

"Then, yes, I would've paid you."

"Well, he didn't."

"So then what did you do?"

"I left."

"That was it?"

"Not exactly. Waiting outside of the guy's office were two uniformed cops. The secretary had called them while I was in her boss's office. They had my gun, and they handcuffed me and arrested me for assaulting the secretary. They took me downtown and booked me, and I called Sal from the jail. He came right away and posted my bail, and while he drove me back to my car, I told him what had happened. He smiled and said that I did a great job, but that it was probably best that I stay away from the cocky CEO for now. 'I'll get someone else on it,' he said, and that's exactly what he did. He sent two guys named Vinnie and Abe. I heard they broke four of the jerk's fingers before he finally wrote the check. Sometimes it pays to be stubborn, and sometimes it doesn't. I don't think that idiot realized who he was dealing with. That was a shame. Maybe I should've made myself a little clearer."

"So that was it?" I asked. "What about the charges against you?"

"Sal's attorney got the charges dropped."

"Well, that was good."

"Yes, that was good."

I resumed my drawing. Then I said to Rudy, "That was quite a story."

"It was, wasn't it?" Rudy laughed heartily and said, "Now you just have to decide if I was telling you the truth or just pulling your leg."

It took me four half-days to complete Rudy's portrait. I was very happy with it when it was done, and so was Rudy. In fact, he loved it. He wanted to keep it, and he asked me how much money I wanted for it. It was the first time anyone had ever asked to purchase one of my drawings, and it took me by surprise. What was it worth? I really had no idea. A couple hundred bucks, maybe. I laughed to myself when I thought about how much that Jackson Pollock painting had sold for. Two hundred million for some paint splatters on a canvas. "Listen, just take it," I said to Rudy. "I'm just glad that you like it. I want you to have it."

"Seriously?" Rudy said.

"Yes," I said.

"I should pay you something."

"No, I really don't want anything. If you like it, it's yours."

My mom told me later that Rudy hung the portrait in the front room of his house, where everyone could see it. She said he was very proud of it. She said he'd never had anyone do his portrait before. "But your kid's a queer duck," he said to her. "He should've charged me something. He shouldn't be working for free. Only a sucker works for free." I laughed when Mom told me this. It was exactly the sort of thing a guy like Rudy would say. But I was getting a little wiser with age, and I honestly didn't want Rudy's money. It wasn't because Rudy was a former criminal. I was just learning that there are wages in life that are more valuable than cash.

BURIED IN FOREST LAWN

Two and a half million Americans die in this country each year. What becomes of them? Since we are largely a Christian culture, most people think they're going to heaven. A few know they're going to hell. So where am I going? I'm not a very religious person, so I'm not a large believer in heaven or hell. But I would like to think we go somewhere pleasant after we die. It'd be nice to live where all the women are pretty and all the men are handsome, where there is no pollution, where there are no politicians, attorneys, or news reporters, where you can eat and drink anything you want without gaining weight, where you like all you neighbors, and where everything for sale is at a price you can afford. And it would also be nice to be reunited with any long-lost loved ones who died before you. I'd like to see my grandpa again. Not my mom's father, but my father's father. I haven't told you anything about him. He was quite a character.

It was my grandpa who taught me how to play chess. He taught me how all the pieces moved and gave me some tips on strategies. Every time we visited him, he would get out his chessboard and challenge me to a game. I'll bet I played him a hundred times, and I never won once. Now that I look back, I think it was kind of strange that he never let me win. I sometimes played chess with Thomas when he was young, and I always lost now and again to build his confidence. At the end of each game, my grandpa would say, "Nice try, boy, but it's going to be a cold day in hell before you ever beat me." Grandpa died when I was twelve and was buried in the grassy slopes of Forest Lawn Cemetery in Los Angeles, where they labeled his grave with a plain bronze marker.

SATISFACTION GUARANTEED

Welcome to Acme Markers, the number-one manufacturer of markers in all of Southern California. All our markers are made in the USA. We use the finest materials and employ the nation's most capable and conscientious craftsmen and artists. If you place your order today, we guarantee you'll receive your shipment in less than thirty days. We firmly stand behind every marker we sell. If you are not 100 percent satisfied with your marker, we will refund your money, no questions asked. We've been serving the general public for over eighty years, and we are one of the most respected names in the marker business. Call our 800 number today to receive your free color catalog. In the meantime, check out these current limited-time-only offerings:

All Slant Markers at 10 Percent Off

Do you want the look of an upright marker without having to pay the high price? Our slant markers sit in an upright position and have the same look and feel. Our slant markers all have a polished face with pitched rock edges. We offer all different sizes and many irresistible designs. These markers are as long-lasting and durable as any marker on the market.

All Bevel Markers at 20 Percent Off

The bevel markers are much like our flat markers. They lie flat on the earth and have a slanted face that gives an upright look. Like our slant markers, our bevel markers have a polished face and rock pitched edges. We offer a wide variety of sizes and designs. Durable and long-lasting, these economic markers will mark the resting place of your deceased loved one for centuries to come.

Our Best Buy—All Flat Markers at 25 Percent Off

Flat markers are our most economical product. Not everyone is Bill Gates, right? If you're on a budget, flat markers may be exactly what you're looking for. Flat markers lie flat on the ground, and like our other markers, they come in a wide variety of sizes and colors. Paying a little less does not mean lower quality. These fine stone markers will beautifully mark the resting place of your loved one for years and years.

Woof, Woof, Meow—Two for the Price of One

Memorialize your beloved pets. Our Pet Memorial Markers are eight inches tall by sixteen inches wide by three inches thick. We have a wide selection of design options and colors you can choose from. Save money now and buy your pet markers in advance. This two-for-one offer will not last long!

Bronze Markers Sold at Cost

All of our bronze memorials are sand cast and poured with a memorial quality statuary bronze alloy containing a minimum copper content of 87 percent. We ordered too much bronze, and we need to cut our inventory right away, so our mistake is your gain! For a limited time only, we are selling these beautiful markers at cost. Call our offices today for precise quotes based upon your specifications.

Overwhelmed? Not sure of exactly what you want? Come visit our conveniently located showroom and let one of our friendly sales associates find the best product for you. Our sales staff has over sixty combined years of experience in the business. Yes, we do know what we're doing! Our showroom opens at nine and closes at seven. We are located between the Taco Bell and Suds Laundromat in the Hacienda Shopping Center in downtown Burbank, and there's always plenty of free parking. There is also free coffee and donuts for all our visitors who arrive between the hours of nine and eleven!

THE SAVAGES

Before the advent of the savages, the native people flourished in North America. There was no such thing as a single organized Native American religion that was anything like the white man's Christianity. There were no written sets of rules, beliefs, or spiritual teachings among the many tribes. Instead all these rules, beliefs, and teachings were passed down orally from one generation to the next. Each tribe has its own. There was one common aspect among nearly all tribes, however, and that was the idea that the spirit of a person lives on after the person dies. Some tribes believed that they could talk to the human spirits, and that the spirits could travel to and from the afterlife to visit the living.

Belief in reincarnation was also a popular notion among many tribes. Like the ancient Egyptians, many of these Native American death rituals were focused on giving the spirit things it would need to arrive safe and flourish in the afterlife. Many tribes would leave food, jewelry, tools, and weapons for the spirit. Some tribes would sacrifice slaves and horses in honor of the person who died. Often the death of a child would have its own rituals. In the Ojibwa and Chippewa tribes, a small doll would be made from the child's hair, and the mother would carry it around on her person while she was mourning. Other rituals included painting the cadaver's face red for good luck, or washing the body with a good luck yucca solution before burial. Sometimes feathers were tied around the corpse's head as a form of prayer. Other common rituals, such as smoking a special ceremonial pipe were incorporated into funeral rituals. Some tribes were fearful of the dead. They would burn the home and possessions of the person who had just died so that his or her spirit could not return. And others, such as the Navajo, would refuse to use the name of the dead person for at least a year after the person's death, in the belief that doing so would call back an angry spirit from the afterlife.

That's how things were before the European savages arrived with their crucifixes, Bibles, coffins, rifles, smallpox, and steepled churches. Ashes to ashes, dust to dust. If you were good and behaved yourself, you got to go to heaven. But if you acted like an ass, you would spend an eternity in the scalding hot caves of hell. Did you know there were approximately seven million people living in America before Columbus arrived? Maybe even more.

So Long, Mom

Mom died on April 27, 2014. Her death came as a total surprise to all of us. No one could believe it. She was doing so well, and she had no health problems. She was speeding in her Mustang when she accidentally ran a red light. I say it was accidental because I can't imagine her having done this on purpose. She was broadsided in the middle of the intersection by a gigantic Kenworth semi-truck and trailer. The truck driver barely had time to put his foot on the brakes, and the cops told us Mom died instantly. It took them hours to scrape her remains out of the severely crushed car. I never did see what was left of the corpse. I didn't want that gruesome visual to be my last memory of her.

Mom's wishes were that she be cremated, and she wanted her ashes spread in her backyard garden. We did cremate her, but we did not spread her ashes. Bob wanted to keep her ashes in an urn, and I figured this was fine. Bob now keeps the urn in his home office on the shelves behind his desk along with a picture of our family from happier times. I always thought it was curious how sentimental Bob was about Mom's ashes, being that she drove him crazy. Obviously he loved her a lot more than he let on. It was Bob who arranged for a big memorial service to be held two weeks after the accident. He leased a large room at the Hilton in Irvine and invited everyone. Then he asked me to write a nice eulogy. He said I was better with words than he was, and he was right. So I didn't argue with him. I went diligently to work on the eulogy. I set my drawing endeavors aside, and I wrote while Henry kept me company. Henry was curled up on the floor in his dog bed, watching me. His sad brown eyes said it all.

The eulogy, which I was to read aloud to everyone at the memorial, went as follows:

My mom is gone. I can't believe I'm uttering those words. We all have to go sometime. That's what they like to say, but somehow I thought Mom would be with us forever. Maybe it was because of her indomitable spirit. She was never a quitter, never one to tip her king, never one to throw in the towel. She just kept on moving forward no matter what. It wasn't her nature to be crippled by frustration, anger, resentments, or sorrow. I never once saw Mom give up at the plate, no matter what pitches were thrown at her, and self-pity and self-doubt were never in her lexicon. In my book, she was a competitor and a winner right up until the tragic day that she died.

She was also my mother. My brother and I probably saw a side to her that none of you had the opportunity to see. We were bathed in her love right up until the day God took her away. There has been no better mother on earth. There has been no kinder, sweeter, more well-intentioned, more loving, more caring, more nurturing, or more teaching woman on this planet, ever. Was she perfect? No, of course not. But there was nobody better. I wouldn't trade the years I spent with my mom for anything. Everything good about me can be traced back to her. Every good decision, every act of kindness, and every bit of compassion that has salted my life can be attributed to this wonderful woman.

I think we forget a lot of things as we're growing up. We take so much for granted. I know I certainly did. But who made my childhood so special? Who made sure there were hot pancakes, maple syrup, and butter on the kitchen table every morning for breakfast? Who bought the orange juice and milk? Who packed my peanut butter and jelly sandwich sack lunches for school? Who always made sure my underwear was clean? Who drove me to the store for my new clothes and shoes when I needed them? Who always had money in her purse? Who bought me chunks of white chocolate at the mall candy store? Who took me to see the doctor when I didn't feel so good, and who swung by the pharmacy to pick up my medications? Who drove my friends and me out to the beach on those hot summer Saturdays? I can remember Mom at the beach. She was so young then. Her skin was warm and tan, and the yellow sunlight danced in her auburn hair like liquid gold. She always brought along a radio to the beach and listened to rock 'n' roll while she watched us play in the water. My mom was pretty cool. Dad never came to the beach. It was always my mom.

There are a lot of stories I could tell you about my mom. One story comes to mind right now. I remember that when I was around ten years old, I was into making models of cars. It was a big thing back then. We'd buy the Revell model kits from the local hobby store and put them together with rubber cement glue. We'd paint them, stick decals on them, and display them up on our shelves. I must have had ten or fifteen of them in my room. There was one car I hated. I don't remember the make of the car, but I remember that I did a lousy job on it. It was one of my first attempts at model making, and you could see the gobs of dried rubber cement glue and poorly aligned pieces. There were dirty fingerprints in the paint, and the decals were crooked. It looked like a five-year-old had put it together. Anyway, I decided to destroy this model, and how would I destroy it? I would burn it!

My dad had a barbecue in the backyard. He had enough charcoal briquettes and lighter fluid to cook an entire side of beef. The idea came to me. Surely dad wouldn't miss a little lighter fluid and a few briquets. I filled the barbecue with briquettes and soaked them with the lighter fluid. I lit the fire and got the briquettes good and hot, and then I placed my crappy model on the grill. I was going to cook the thing until it was nothing but ashes. At first the model began to smoke, and then the plastic began to melt. The smoke was as thick as molasses, and it smelled like burning tires. I squirted more lighter fluid on the model until it burst into red and yellow flames. Now I was getting somewhere! "Burn, burn, burn," I said, and I added more lighter fluid. It was great! The model was consumed with fire.

After five or ten minutes, there wasn't much left of the model to burn, but I noticed something. The model had not turned to ashes like I expected. Instead there was now a big, molten plastic mess on my dad's barbecue grill. My dad's prize grill! Mom suddenly came out of the house, and she asked what I was doing. I told her I had burned up one of my models, and she saw the mess I had made on Dad's grill. "I'll clean it off," I said, being a stupid kid and not realizing there was no way to clean the melted plastic off the metal grill. "Your dad is going to lose his mind," Mom said. "You've ruined his barbecue grill!" And that's when it hit me. I was going to be in big trouble, and this would mean being whipped with Dad's belt. I was going to feel the wrath of my angry dad with his leather belt on my pink and tender backside. Mom then said, "Don't you worry, Huey. We'll take care of this. Your dad will never have to know."

So what did Mom do? Well, Dad's birthday was coming up that weekend, and my mom went out and bought Dad a new barbecue. We took the ruined barbecue to the dump and hid the new barbecue in the side yard. Dad never did notice that the old barbecue was missing, because Mom made sure he didn't go into the backyard. On his birthday morning, we put the new barbecue where the old one once stood, and Mom put a big red bow on it. Later, when we were opening presents, Mom told my dad to go outside and look. "Why?" Dad asked, and Mom laughed. "Just look," she said, and Dad went out the patio door to investigate.

There was the new barbecue with the bow on it, and my dad grinned from ear to ear. He liked it! He didn't just like it; he was crazy about it! "It's wonderful," he said. "That old barbecue had seen better days."

Mom said, "You can say that again," and when Dad wasn't looking at her, she gave me a wink. I stood there and smiled nervously. We never did tell my dad what had happened to his favorite old barbecue. It was our secret, just between Mom and me. I loved my mom. That's what my mom was like.

I'm truly going to miss her. I'm sure all of us are going to miss my mom. What are we going to do without all of her unwavering loyalty to those she loved, without her contagious smile, without her perpetual hope? No matter what challenges came her way in life, she never lost faith in the goodness of life. For my mom, life was always worth living, no matter how difficult it became. My mom turned a ruined barbecue into a new birthday present. She turned an ugly divorce into a sporty new Mustang. She turned lemons into lemonade. I learned so much from her. I learned, but you know what? I don't think I ever thanked her. And she never demanded that of me. I think she always knew that I loved her. I think she knew all of us loved her, because she always had faith that life was the way it was meant to be. No, she never climbed Mount Everest, became a US senator, ran a billion-dollar business, invented a life-saving medical device, won any gold medals in the Olympics, painted a great masterpiece, or composed a great symphony. But she was wonderful. And what better compliment can you pay a person? I loved her, and I will miss her.

When I was done delivering the eulogy to the guests at the memorial, I had a feeling I'd said the right words. I was happy with what I'd written.

I mean, I probably could've said a lot more about Mom, but maybe I'd said just enough. I think everyone got the message. She was a wonderful woman.

BURIED IN MASSACHUSETTS

"I hope it is true that a man can die and yet not only live in others but give them life, and not only life, but that great consciousness of life."

—Jack Kerouac

THE WEDDING

One year after Mom passed away, Thomas got married. He married a girl he met at the veterinary clinic. She had brought her cat in to be spayed, and they struck up a conversation while Thomas was taking in the pet. Her name was Elaine, and she worked for the county public works office as an administrative assistant. She was two years younger than our son, and about three inches shorter. Rhonda and I liked her a lot. She was a blue-eyed blonde, as cute as a petunia. Three weeks after they met, they were sweethearts, and two months after that, Thomas came to me. He told me that he now wanted to be an actual veterinarian, and he wanted to know if we would foot the bill for him to go back to college. I said yes, of course, and the next thing we knew, our son was a student again. He was a student with a serious girlfriend.

Thomas wanted to go to UC Davis, where they had an excellent veterinary program. He wasn't able to get in because his grades were so bad at Washington State. So he signed up for classes at our community college to prove he was now serious about doing well in school. The plan was to get impressive grades at the community college and then transfer to UC Davis after he had a successful year of college under his belt. It was while Thomas was enrolled that he and Elaine announced their engagement. The wedding was to be held in the summer of 2015. The day came, and the minister from Elaine's family's church pronounced the couple husband

and wife. The wedding was up in Beverly Hills, where Elaine's mom and dad lived. They then held the reception at the Viceroy L'Ermitage, also up in Beverly Hills. The wedding and reception were quite fancy. I'm sure the events cost Elaine's parents a fortune.

Elaine's parents seemed like decent people. Her dad, Jack, was a residential real estate broker in Beverly Hills, and her mom, Cindy, was a nurse at Cedars Sinai. You wonder when your kids get married just what the in-laws will be like. Will they accept your child? Will they accept your family? Will they be poor, middle class, or rich? Will they be jerks? Will they wish their kid had chosen someone else? Well, they certainly weren't poor, and never once did Jack or Cindy make Rhonda and me feel as though we weren't good enough for them. They welcomed Thomas into their family despite his floundering when he first met their daughter. I don't know whether they knew anything about Thomas's drug problem at Washington State or not. If they did, they never said anything about it. I didn't ask Thomas whether they knew. I figured it was none of my business. So long as they liked him, that was all that mattered.

You should've seen Thomas at the reception! He was dressed in a tuxedo, and he was all smiles. He conducted himself like a champ, talking to everyone. I was so proud of him. The boy was finally growing up, behaving like a young adult. Then came the time. I mean *the* time—the moment of truth. A young man wearing a red bow tie and holding a microphone in his hand was making rounds at the tables, and the guests were toasting the newly married couple. The toasts were nice. They were the usual sort of stuff. Some of them were funny, and some were pregnant with advice and words of dime store wisdom. I was the last to speak, and I had come well prepared. I had been working hard on my toast for the past several days, and I had it written down on a sheet of paper that was folded and stuffed in my jacket pocket. The man handed me the microphone and said, "Last but not least, we now have the groom's father. I assume you have some encouraging words for the bride and groom?"

"I do," I said. The man handed me the microphone, and I stood up to make my toast. The room was suddenly so quiet one could have heard a mouse sneeze. The toast I had prepared on paper went as follows:

Thomas and Elaine. You are now husband and wife. You are now a team. You are as one. And you have made promises to each other, and I know you take these promises seriously, as you should. Rhonda and I were married over forty years ago. We, too, made promises, and we have travelled the road. For the most part, it has been a wonderful journey, but like any married couple on the face of the earth, we had to face certain challenges. These were challenges that made us wiser, and facing these challenges made our marriage that much stronger. Now I'd like to share with the two of you some of what we've learned.

First and foremost, there is love. There is your love for each other. Love is what brought you together, and it may seem to you now that your love will never die. But let me tell you something I've learned about love. It is not just a word or a feeling. It is a living thing. You must work to keep it alive. You must feed it, water it, care for it, and nourish it. You must devote a serious chunk of your time to keeping it strong and healthy. Ignore it, or take it for granted, and you will be disappointed. Think of it as a rare and fragile plant in your garden that must be tended to morning, noon, and night. You can watch it grow, and you can watch its flowers bloom. You can revel in its glory each and every day, but never make the mistake of believing that it will continue to thrive without your diligent guardianship.

As you begin your journey as husband and wife, you're likely to hear others advising you both to be honest at all times, especially with each other. They will tell you that a marriage cannot survive secrets. But is this true? Must you really tell each other everything? Let me now tell you what I've learned. All of us deserve some privacy, to a degree. Marriage is not about relinquishing all personal privacy. Yes, marriage is about sharing, but not sharing everything under the sun. Each of us has a right to his or her secrets, so don't be angry if you don't get to know the truth about every square inch of your partner. Allow for a teaspoon of mystery and a pinch of the unknown, and give your partner his or her own space to breathe and be a human being. Believe me when I say that a little mystery is a very good thing, and that respect for your partner's privacy is essential. Respect for each other's privacy can be the sole difference between a marriage that flourishes and one that winds up overexposed, burnt by the harsh light of day, and eventually destroyed.

I'll tell you another thing that people who advise you will often have wrong. They say that arguing is essential for a healthy marriage. They say, "Get it out in the open and argue about it." The truth is that arguing is exactly what you two don't need. Arguing is not talking, and you should be talking, not arguing. Arguing always involves two people taking sides, maintaining positions, protecting territories, and, worst of all, trying to be right rather than trying to seek real resolutions. Why do people always have to be right? Why do they want so badly to win? There should be no winners or losers in a marriage. There should be only an us, not a me-versus-you. You should talk. That is the key to a happy marriage. Talk and talk. Don't try to be the one who's right. Try to understand what you're each talking about. You both have the same goal in mind, right? You want to get along. You want to be happy and content together. You want to live as a team, not as adversaries.

I have another piece of advice. Do not expect your partner to be a mind reader. I can't tell you how many marriages have suffered because of this—because of one partner expecting the other to read his or her mind. I don't know why couples do this, but they do it all the time. It isn't fair. Tell your partner exactly what you expect and desire. Tell your partner clearly what will make you happy. And be honest about it. There's nothing wrong with making your desires transparent. I can't even begin to tell you how many couples I've seen who play this mind-reading game over and over, and it almost always ends with disappointment. And slowly but surely, disappointment can destroy a marriage. It eats away at it. It pulls the pleasure right out from under you.

Finally, as you both travel your paths of life, travel as a team. You are going to be facing the world together. You must learn to depend on each other, and you have to be totally faithful to each other. This doesn't mean you can't have friends and interests, but you will primarily owe your lives to each other. *You* decided to get married, so learn to live with your decision. Above all, know that your partner will unconditionally trust you. Your partner will always give you the benefit of the doubt, believing all you say. Your partner will risk all for you, and your partner will walk on hot coals for you. Your partner will even die for you. Do not underestimate the headiness of your partner's commitment. And don't take it for granted. You must honor your wedding vows above all else. If you are truly loyal, not only will your union last a lifetime, but you are likely to experience a wonderful and rewarding life that others who are less fortunate can only dream of. Live with love, loyalty, and integrity, and then consider yourself one of the lucky ones!

Well, that's what I wrote. That was the toast I had in my pocket. But I didn't pull out the paper. I did not read it. I decided it was too long-winded and maybe a little too serious for this joyous occasion. Everyone was having so much fun. So rather than read my toast, I said, "Here's to Elaine and Thomas. Rhonda and I wish you both all the happiness in the world. Now you're a married couple. You are certifiably certified. They say that Groucho Marx once said that, 'Marriage is a wonderful institution, but who wants to live in an institution?' Well, I guess that's what I wanted. And guess what? I wouldn't change a thing. Now you have also joined the club. God bless both of you. Keep your noses clean, and be happy."

It was stupid, right? What a dumb toast. I sat down and handed the microphone back to the man with the red bow tie, and he then carried the microphone up to Thomas, who was seated and facing all of us, beside his bride. "Any last words?" the man asked as Thomas grabbed the microphone. "As a matter of fact, I do have something I'd like to read to you," Thomas said. "It was written by a man much older and much wiser than me. It was written several years ago by my father." Thomas then removed a sheet of paper from his jacket pocket and unfolded it. It was the letter I wrote to him when he graduated from high school. *Well, I'll be damned*, I thought. The passage he read was the following:

> Maybe you believe in God, and that's fine. Maybe you believe in something else. But somehow you must believe that there is a higher power—a moral power, an intelligent power, and, most importantly, a loving power. You must not go through life thinking that we are all just a haphazard life form with two legs, two arms, and a brain living on this planet for no other reason than no reason at all. We are orbiting the sun for an important and meaningful reason, breathing, sweating, thriving, loving, warring, cheating, achieving, fighting, and inventing. Yes, there is a reason for all of it. There is a cause. And the cause is a moral one.

When he was done reading, he folded the letter and stuffed it into his pocket. Then he said, "My dad wrote that to me when I graduated from high school. Beautiful, isn't it?" There was a pause while people politely nodded their heads. Then Thomas said, "Now that we've got that out of the way … let's party!" He raised his champagne glass toward the guests, and everyone cheered. The band started up, and couples hurried out to the dance floor. Rhonda put her hand on mine, and she said, "That was nice."

"It was," I said.

"I forgot about your letter."

"I'm surprised he still has it."

"Of course he has it. I feel like dancing. Do you want to dance?"

"Why not."

COME ON BABY

Come on, baby; let's do the twist.
Come on, baby; let's do the twist.
Put down your champagne glass,
and go like this.
Yeah, twist, baby, baby, twist;
ooh yeah, just like this.
Blow a little kiss,
and do the twist.
Thomas is married,
And Elaine's his bride.
Kids were squirming;
The women all cried.
We're gonna twisty, twisty, twisty
Till we tear the joint down.
Come on and twist, yeah, baby, twist.
Ooh, yeah, just like this.
I'm gonna dance now,
and do the twist, yeah.
Yeah, give me a life of marital bliss.
Give me a life of marital bliss.
Everyone's getting married;
They're all doing the twist.
Come on and twist, yeah, baby, twist.
Ooh yeah, just like this.
Come on; blow a kiss
and do the twist.
Just say, "I do,"
And twist on now, twist.

AN ACT OF KINDNESS

Rhonda and I got home from the wedding reception at about eight at
night. We changed clothes and watched a little TV. And we talked a little.
It was a strange feeling knowing that Thomas was now married. It was a

milestone in our lives—a sign that we were getting older. It was nice, in a way, but it was also sort of depressing. No one wants to get older.

We went to bed at eleven and soon fell asleep. And then, suddenly, the phone rang. "What time is it?" Rhonda asked. I looked at the nightstand clock.

"It's almost twelve thirty," I said.

"Who would be calling at twelve thirty?"

"I have no idea."

"Well, answer it," Rhonda said. Her eyes were still closed. She just wanted to sleep.

I picked up the phone and answered. "Hello?" I said.

"Mr. Baker?" a voice said.

"Who is this?" I asked.

"I'm sorry to call so late."

"Who *is* this?"

"It's Neil."

"Neil who?"

"Neil Sanborn. You know, Thomas's friend."

"Oh, Neil. What can I do for you?"

"Can you give me a ride?"

"A ride?"

"I'm kind of stuck in a situation."

"What happened?"

"I got arrested."

"Arrested?" I said. This got my attention. Why would he have been arrested? "What'd you do?"

"It's kind of a long story."

"Why do you need a ride?"

"I have no way of getting to my apartment. They're about to release me, but I don't have any wheels. I have no way of getting home."

"Where's your car?"

"It's at the apartment. I got a ride to the wedding from friends."

"And where are you now?"

"I'm in Huntington Beach. They're letting me use their phone."

"Who is *they?*"

"The police."

"What'd you do?"

"It's a long story. I don't mind telling you what happened, but can you give me a ride?"

"Jesus, Neil. Did you try calling your dad?"

"He'd kill me if he knew where I was."

"What about your friends?"

"No one is answering their phones. Please, Mr. Baker. Can you help me? They're now telling me to get off the phone."

"You're at the Huntington Beach police station?"

"Yeah," Neil said.

"It'll take me an hour."

"Thanks, Mr. Baker. Thanks so much. I really appreciate it. I knew you'd come through. I've got to go now. I'll be standing in front of the station. I'm still wearing my tuxedo. You can't miss me."

Then Neil hung up—or the cops hung up the phone for him. I set down the receiver, and Rhonda rolled over and opened her eyes. "Seriously?" she said.

"I can't just leave him there."

"I guess not."

"Do you want to come?"

"You've got to be kidding."

I climbed out of bed and got dressed. I didn't even bother to comb my hair. I looked up the location of the police station on the internet and wrote it down. I then went outside to my truck and backed out of the driveway. I drove through the dark streets, listening to the radio. When I arrived at the police station, Neil was standing out front as promised. He was still wearing his wedding tuxedo. He was one of Thomas's ushers. God knows what he was doing in Huntington Beach. One of the lapels on his tuxedo was badly torn, and one of the side pockets was ripped off completely. "Christ, kid, you're a mess," I said as Neil climbed into my truck.

"I am," Neil said.

"Are you going to tell me what happened?"

"Do you know where my apartment is?"

"I have no idea," I said. Neil explained how to get there, and again I asked him what happened.

"We had kind of a wild night."

"I can see that."

"Man, I've got a splitting headache. Do you have any aspirin or anything?"

"No," I said, laughing. Then I looked closer at Neil. He had a black eye and a swollen lip. "Jesus, did you get in a fight?"

"Sort of."

"With whom?"

"Well, that's the strangest thing," Neil said. "I don't even know."

"What do you mean you don't know?"

"It's kind of a blur."

"Did you black out?"

"No, I didn't black out. But it's kind of a blur. We were having fun, and then it wasn't such fun."

"Who's we?"

"Me, Jeff, and Arthur."

"Where were you guys?"

"We were at a bar downtown in Huntington. We were sitting at a table, and everything was going fine. We were reminiscing, talking about old times. Then Jeff noticed these three girls at the bar. They were drinking and talking, minding their own business, but Jeff got it in his head that one of the girls was looking at him—you know, coming on to him."

"Was she?"

"I didn't notice it. But Jeff was dead sure of it. He was pretty drunk, so he could have been imagining the whole thing. I mean, I hadn't seen the girl look our way at all. Anyway, he stood up and walked over to the girls, and he tapped one of them on her back. He said something to her, but I couldn't hear what he said. It was very noisy inside the bar, and there were a lot of people talking and laughing. After Jeff spoke, the girl just shook her head and turned away from him, and he tapped on her shoulder again, harder. When she turned to look at Jeff, she appeared perturbed."

"Perturbed?"

"You know, like he was bugging her."

"Okay," I said.

"Then Jeff said something to her that really pissed her off, because she grabbed her drink and splashed it in his face. As Jeff was wiping the drink from his face, this huge guy with a big black beard appeared from nowhere.

The guy must've weighed three hundred pounds. It turned out he was a bouncer, but we didn't know it then. The guy grabbed Jeff by his arm, and he jerked him away from the girls. And that's when it all went down."

"When what went down?" I asked.

"The fight."

"Ah, the fight."

"Jeff threw a punch at the bearded guy, but he missed by a mile. Then he threw another punch, and this time he landed his fist in the guy's jaw. It barely fazed the guy, and he grabbed Jeff by his throat. With his free hand, he punched Jeff in the stomach, and Jeff bent over, coughing. That's when Arthur stood up from the table. I said, "Don't get involved," but he ignored me. He ran over to the bearded guy and he slugged him in the back of the head. The girls were now screaming, and one of the guys at the bar got involved. He went after Arthur while Jeff stood up from the floor with his fists clenched. Then another guy at the bar got involved, and this is where it gets murky. The next thing I knew, there were six or seven guys all throwing punches and grabbing each other, Arthur and Jeff included. And the girls were cursing at Jeff and Arthur. I heard someone in the place yell, "He's one of them!" He was looking right at me. I was still sitting at the table. They must've seen that we were all wearing the same tuxedos, and they decided to go after me too. And before I even knew what was happening, I was a part of the fight. Sure, I threw a few punches, but I was just trying to protect myself. Then out of nowhere came the cops."

"Who called them?"

"I don't know."

"How did they get there so fast?"

"I have no idea."

"Go on," I said.

"The cops broke up the fight, and they took the bearded guy aside and talked to him. They talked for a few minutes. They didn't bother to ask Arthur, Jeff, or me any questions at all. Then they handcuffed the three of us and hauled us out of the bar like common criminals. Jeff was throwing a fit, cussing at the cops and complaining about the guy with the beard. Arthur was beat up pretty bad, so he wasn't saying much."

"And you?"

"I was trying to tell the cops that I wasn't involved in the fight. 'You're with them, right?' one of the cops asked. 'Are they your friends?' I nodded, and he said, 'That's enough for me.'"

"But you didn't do anything."

"That's what I tried to tell them."

"So they brought you to the station?"

"They put us in a holding cell."

"So where are Jeff and Arthur now?"

"They're still at the station, still in the cell."

"Why'd they let you go?"

"The guy with the beard came to the station to file his complaint, and he told the cops I had nothing to do with the fight. The cop in charge said he was going to charge me with being drunk and disorderly, but he never got around to doing anything. Then he left. I think his shift was over. The cop who took his place told me I could use the phone to call someone to pick me up, and that's when I called you."

"And you didn't call your dad?"

"He would've killed me."

"But you were innocent, right?"

"My dad thinks I'm an idiot. He'd tell me that I shouldn't have been there in the first place. I know exactly what he'd say. He'd say, "What the fuck is wrong with you? Do you have shit for brains?""

"You're sure he'd say that?"

"He says it to me all the time."

"I see," I said.

"But you're cool, Mr. Baker."

"I am?"

"All Thomas's friends know that you're cool. You're not going to tell my dad anything about this, right?"

"I don't even know your dad."

"That's good, right?"

We arrived at Neil's apartment, and I pulled my truck up to the curb. He opened the door and stepped to the sidewalk. I said, "Take care of yourself, kid."

"Thanks, Mr. Baker. I really appreciate this."

"I know you do."

Neil thought for a moment, and then he said, "I was glad to see Thomas get married."

"So was I," I said.

"It was a nice wedding."

"Yes, it was."

"Thanks again. I guess I owe you."

"You owe everyone," I said.

THE RIPPLE

"Remember there's no such thing as a small act of kindness. Every act creates a ripple with no logical end."

—Scott Adams

THE INJECTION

The year is 2018, and I am sixty-three. I sat down six months ago to write the book you are reading now. I guess I am at that age where I am beginning to look back at my life to wonder what it all means. It means so much, doesn't it? Take all the life experiences, all the relationships, all the events, my ideas and thoughts, and all the conclusions I've reached; they form sort of a tapestry. They are me. They are one man's life, colorful and drab, pleasant and unsettling, happy and morose, grim and hopeful, painful and euphoric—yarn, thread, rope, and a little ribbon, all woven in and intertwined with each other. It's not as if my life is over, but I am now getting a clearer picture of what the whole tapestry is about. And I've noticed something about myself. I am pleased with what I see. Yes, I am pleased with all of it: the good, bad, and the ugly. I see all events depending on each other, giving each other meaning. And I can say honestly that I wouldn't trade my unique tapestry for anyone else's. I am happy with who I am, content with my regrets, and proud of my accomplishments.

A few things have happened recently that I ought to tell you about. First, Henry passed away last year. It was rough. He was my first dog, and

I was surprised at how much his death affected me. We had to put him to sleep. He had cancer in his stomach, and there was nothing the vet could do. When Mom left us, it was painful, but when it was Henry's time to go, it was almost unbearable. All I could think of were the good times we had together, and I thought of the day I rescued him. The poor, dumb animal. He had no idea how close he came to being left at the animal shelter. He didn't have a clue. And then he became one of our family, living with us, eating his meals, sleeping in his dog beds, getting his belly scratched, and playing fetch in the backyard with the dog toys Rhonda bought for him. He was my best buddy. He went everywhere with me. He loved going with me in my truck, checking construction jobs while I was still in the building business, and going on my daily errands. He got to know Mateo and the boys, and he got to know my customers.

He loved it when I stopped at the McDonald's drive-through windows. He always knew I'd order a couple hamburgers just for him—plain, with nothing on them, just meat and bread. He would gobble them down like nothing, but to him they were everything. His bushy tail would wag like crazy. I think McDonald's was his favorite place in the world. He'd eat the meat first, and then the buns. And then it was as if it came to an end overnight. I was holding his warm, trusting body in my arms as the vet injected him. As I held him tight, he breathed his last breath. That was that—one deadly needle into his fur. No more fetch. No more burgers in the truck. No more wagging tail. My wonderful friend was gone forever.

AMEN

"The world would be a nicer place if everyone had the ability to love as unconditionally as a dog."

—M. K. Clinton

AN AMERICAN STORY

Also, I recently put an end to the years of father–son silence. I have been conversing with my dad again. I have mixed feelings about this, but I think it was the right thing to do. It's so curious, isn't it? It's amazing how long we can hold on to our resentments. Yes, he did some lousy things when I was younger, but you know what? Life goes on, and it's not like I'm perfect. No, I'm far from it. I wasn't one to be throwing stones.

You know, I can't really take credit for talking to my dad again. The credit should go to Bob and all the times he prodded me to put an end to the estrangement. "He's really not such a bad guy," he would say. "He's getting old, and he's going to be ninety soon. You're running out of time, Huey." Well, my first inclination was always to say, "Let the time run out. What the hell do I care." But I changed. I noticed the change coming a couple years ago. I learned that sixty-plus years of living on earth changes one's perspective—in my case from being hard and obstinate to being kinder and more forgiving. It's probably the most important lesson I've learned in all my life. I wish I'd learned this earlier.

You should know that I've done a heck of a lot of drawings over the past several years. I also met an art dealer in Laguna Beach who liked what I'd been doing. This art dealer's name was Harold Parsons. I was introduced to Harold at a dinner party at a friend's house. Harold came to the party with a date, but he wasn't married. Harold was in his late forties, and while he wasn't an artist, he was obsessed with art. He owned a little art gallery in Laguna where he featured all the artists he had supposedly discovered. We got to chatting about art while we were eating, and Rhonda brought up my drawings. "You really ought to see what Huey's been doing," she said.

"I'd like to see," Harold said.

"He's got a whole office filled with drawings."

"Do you?" Harold said to me.

"I have quite a few," I said.

"Tell me about them."

"What do you want to know?" I hated talking about my art. What was I supposed to say?

"What do you draw?"

"Stuff," I said stupidly.

"Pencil? Ink? Charcoal?"

"A little of everything," I said.

"Sounds interesting."

"He's quite good," Rhonda said. It was weird to hear her say this, since she never showed an interest in them. But that was Rhonda.

"Have you had any showings?" Harold asked me.

"No, no, no," I said, laughing. "I just do it for myself. You know, as a hobby."

"I'd be interested in seeing what you've done."

"You could come over," Rhonda said.

"Any objections?" Harold asked me.

I stared at Rhonda, and then I looked at Harold. I said, "I guess that would be okay."

Two weeks later, Harold came to our house. Rhonda made a pot of coffee for him, and I showed him into my study. Harold looked at my drawing table and said, "So this is where it all happens?"

"Yes," I said.

"Do you mind if I look through these?" he asked. He was referring to the many drawings I had strewn around the room in stacks. I felt terribly uncomfortable. And I was embarrassed. I wasn't used to having people look at my drawings, but I told Harold to go ahead and look. "Very interesting," he said as he began going through the drawings. "Interesting subject matter and technique. Yes, I like them."

"Like I told you, it's a hobby."

Rhonda brought in Harold's coffee, and he set the cup on my drawing table. He didn't seem interested in the coffee. He was still focused on my drawings. "I feel like I'm getting to know you," Harold said.

"You are?"

"These are very personal, aren't they?"

"I guess some of them are."

Finally, Harold was done looking, and he picked up his cup of coffee. "What would you say to me showing some of these at my gallery?"

"At your gallery?"

"How would that make you feel?"

"I don't know," I said. And I honestly didn't know. I'd never really thought about anything like this.

"He'd love it," Rhonda said.

"I would?"

"Of course you would."

"I'd love to display your work. Of course, we would have to get the pieces framed. Not all of them, mind you. I mean just those we decide to show. I'd pay up front for the framing. I'd just be asking for a cut of your sales."

"My sales?"

"Are you interested?"

"He's interested," Rhonda said.

The next thing I knew, Harold was walking away with a stack of my drawings to take to his framer. He took the ones that he thought his clients would like. The show was held four months later, and Harold invited everyone he knew to the opening. The event would start at six o'clock, and they would be serving hors d'oeuvres and wine. I didn't have to do anything. All I had to do was dress nice, comb my hair, and show up. It was going to be interesting to see how people reacted to something that had once been so private. I thought it might be nice. But it might also be a disaster. I had no way of knowing.

Harold told me that we had to have a name for the show, and he asked me what I thought we should call it. I thought about it and then told him we should call it *An American Story*. He stared at me for a moment, and then he smiled. "Perfect!" he exclaimed. "I can't think of a better name." I wasn't sure whether he really liked the name or whether he was trying to be nice. But we went with it.

Well, when the opening night came, I showed up with Rhonda. I had told Bob about it, but I wasn't sure if he'd come. There were a lot of people there whom I didn't know, and all of them were standing around and looking at my drawings, drinking wine. Christ, I was nervous, and I suddenly wished that I had never agreed to do this. What if someone asked me about a drawing? What was I going to say? Honestly, I think a lot less thought went into them than Harold realized. Such a phony! That's what I was. I suddenly took Rhonda aside and said, "I really want to get the hell out of here."

Rhonda smiled and said, "No, not yet."

"I don't know what I'm going to say to these people."

"Just say anything you want."

"I feel like such a fake."

Rhonda put her finger over my lips. "Don't sell yourself short, Huey."

Then I saw Bob and his wife enter through the front doors. They were dressed nicely and laughing. And they weren't alone. Jesus, of all the dirty tricks! They had come with my father! He had flown down from San Jose just to see the show. True, I'd been talking to him over the phone recently, but we hadn't seen each other in person. And there he now was. He looked so old. He looked like an old man. He was my dad, the guy who used to whip me with his belt, the same man who used to intimidate the living hell out of me. I couldn't get over how fragile he was. When they approached Rhonda and me, Bob said, "Someone special has come to see your show." My dad smiled and reached for a handshake.

"I had no idea you were coming," I said, clasping his bony hand gently.

"Wanted to see," Dad said.

"Help yourself."

"This is so impressive."

"It wasn't really my idea," I said.

They then began walking through the exhibit, looking at my drawings. They were taking their time, looking carefully and enthusiastically at each drawing.

"You're the artist?" a woman asked me. She appeared from nowhere.

"I am," I said. I looked at her. She appeared to be in her fifties. She had braided gray hair and big hoop earrings. She looked like a woman who was into Tarot cards and owned a lot of cats.

"Impressive," she said.

"Thanks," I replied.

"I especially like your drawing of the German shepherd."

"That's Henry," I said.

"Henry?"

"That was his name."

"Was he your dog?"

"He was," I said.

"You must've loved him."

"I did."

"I've always wanted a dog. But I have cats. I don't think they'd get along."

Cats. What did I tell you?

Harold then interrupted us. "You just sold the Hershey bar drawing," he said. He was referring to a drawing I did of a Hershey bar, the brown paper wrapper peeled back and a bite taken from it.

"No kidding?" I said.

"The buyers want to meet you."

"Okay," I said.

For the next thirty minutes, the guests came up to me and asked me about the drawings. It wasn't as bad as I thought it would be. The people were nice. They weren't grilling me or asking difficult questions. They just seemed pleased to meet me. Then Bob and Dad came up to me, and I looked at my elderly elf of a father. He was smiling, and he said, "Wonderful show, son."

"Thanks," I said.

"Very revealing. Like reading someone's diary. I feel as though I now know so much more about you."

"You do?"

"Oh, yes. I'm glad I came."

Two weeks later, Dad had his heart attack. I flew up to San Jose to visit him, and he died while I was there. One minute he was looking at my drawings, and the next minute he was on his way to his afterlife. He probably went to heaven, but no doubt not until God gave him a good verbal thrashing for depriving me of my Stingray bicycle and for falling out of love with my mom. I don't think you have to be a saint to go to heaven. You just have to have made a reasonable attempt to be a good person. And I think my dad did that.

HERE

"Within the soul of America is freedom of mind and spirit in man. Here alone are the open windows through which pours the sunlight of the human spirit. Here alone is human dignity not a dream but an accomplishment.

Perhaps it is not perfect, but it is more full in realization here than any other place in the world."

—Herbert Hoover

A LOT OF BEER

There are almost four million square miles of land in America, divided unevenly into fifty different states. There are four million miles of paved and dirt roads, and three hundred twenty million people who travel those roads. Americans own seventy-eight million dogs and eighty-five million cats. They consume about six billion gallons of beer every year and eat almost two billion pounds of potato chips. By any measure, this is a very big country. Me? I am one man. I have a wife and a son, and I once owned a dog. I will probably go to the animal shelter for another dog. Between the three of us, we own three automobiles, about five wristwatches, two basketballs, about thirty pairs of shoes, and a lot of clothes.

I am what I do. I am what I know about, and I am what I experience. I'm so much, and yet so little—one man, a speck on the map. There is so much to my life, yet as I have tried to describe it to you, I feel I have barely scratched the surface of its vastness. And how does this make me feel? If you were to ask me what I am now thinking, I'd tell you—despite my thinning hair, aching back, and yellowing toenails—that my life is just beginning.

So what did you think of this book? Did you find it to be intriguing and thought-provoking? Or maybe frustrating? Or how about confusing? Or maybe you just thought it was stupid. I'll tell you what my intention was. I wanted to write a story that unfolds as life comes—not as a perfect linear experience, but as a steady montage of ideas, experiences, recollections, songs, stories, feelings, beliefs, and ideas. It's not something that makes sense at first glance. We have to work to make sense of it. We have to think. We have to add up the many numbers, conjugate the verbs, and dot the i's and cross the t's. We have to be on our toes.

I am an American. I'm not used to having to work for my entertainment. Are you an American? I'll ask again: What did you think of this book?

Did you find it thought-provoking or compelling? Did it make you wonder about your own life? Was it valuable to you? Or did you just think it was a gigantic waste of time? Those are the pertinent questions. I've been having that dream again—the one about the fortune teller. Remember her? She was the one with the silvery hair and purple velvet dress. In my latest dreams, I pose these new questions, and she waves her hand over her crystal ball and says, "How in the hell should I know?"

Then I realize in my dream that I paid her only twenty bucks. You get what you pay for. I wake up from the strange dream, and Rhonda is sound asleep. There's no reason to wake her up, so I look toward the window. It's still dark outside. I close my eyes and return to the night.

In a few hours, the sun will rise and the birds will sing. I'll make a pot of coffee, and Rhonda will turn on the kitchen TV to the morning news. Somewhere in this country, a mother will nurse her newborn baby, a signal will change from red to green, a dog will eat its breakfast, a door to a business will be unlocked, and a man, somewhere, will be looking around his house, saying, "Where the heck did I put my keys?"

CPSIA information can be obtained
at www.ICGtesting.com
Printed in the USA
BVHW030434290820
587580BV00002B/269